MW01258522

EVIL WAYS

BOBBY NASH

BEN BOOKS

EVIL WAYS

First BEN Books Edition
2012

EVIL WAYS

ISBN: 1480253456
ISBN-13: 978-1480253452

Printed in the USA

Publisher's Note:

Published by BEN Books, PO Box 626, Bethlehem, GA 30620

http://BEN-Books.blogspot.com

BOBBY NASH
Dedicated to Harriette Austin for her years of unwavering
support, staunch advice, and friendship. This one's for you, H!

EVIL WAYS

"FBI! Do! Not! Move!"

Tensing beneath the loose tan coveralls, Jeff Davies knew his time was up. Slowly, oh so very slowly, he straightened to his full five feet eleven inches, arms cautiously rising. He knew the drill. He kept his hands open so the man behind him with the gun would see that he was unarmed.

Jeff Davies hated guns. Never touched the damned things. No good had ever come from them. His younger brother had died at age twelve because an angry, unpopular kid decided he'd had enough and carried his policeman father's service revolver to school one morning. Young Pete Davies was murdered because some thirteen-year-old would-be-assassin was too nervous to shoot straight.

"Interlock your fingers behind your head."

Jeff did as he was told. Not that he needed much instruction. This was not his first time on the wrong end of the law. Doubtless, it would not be his last. He knew the drill all too well.

"Take two steps back."

Of course, Jeff complied with the lawman's instructions. He moved slowly, careful not to give the agent any just cause to pull the trigger. In his mind a voice screamed, *No sudden moves. No sudden moves.*

No.

Sudden.

Moves.

"Get on your knees and cross your legs at the ankle."

"S…sure," Jeff stuttered.

He couldn't believe how nervous he was. He wasn't sure which was worse: having a Federal Agent behind him with a gun pointed at his head or staring at the timer slowly counting down to zero on the bomb in front of him.

Regardless, Jeff Davies was having a bad day, but he felt confident that the cause was worth it. He believed in the righteousness of his actions. He believed in the cause. By taking his time now, keeping the unsuspecting agent occupied, the others could get away. It was a sacrifice he was willing to make for his friends.

Someone grabbed his arms, jerked them roughly behind his back and Jeff felt the cool familiar metal of handcuffs against his skin and heard the audible clicks of the locks as if they moved in slow motion.

"Make sure you read him his rights," the agent said. Jeff had yet to catch a glimpse of the man who caught him. "Then evacuate this area," he heard him say as he was forced to his feet.

"Yes sir, Agent Palmer. You heard the man, people," another agent yelled to his cohorts as they pulled Jeff Davies around and rushed him away from the bomb he had planted. He knew there was no time for the bomb squad to arrive. There was nothing the FBI could do. The Treasury Building was about to become one very large pile of rubble.

The last thing Davies saw before being whisked away was the timer reach two minutes.

Counting down.

"What do you think, Harold?"

FBI Special Agent Harold Palmer stood next to his friend, Special Agent in Charge of the Joint Terrorism Task Force Carter Reidling. Harold and Carter had been friends for a long time, partners even longer. Harold was still getting used to Carter being in charge.

"I think we should be anywhere but here," Harold deadpanned.

"Funny."

"I think you should get out of here, Carter."

"We've got a minute."

Harold pointed to the timer with red numbers counting down. "Fifty-two seconds, actually," Harold said as he knelt down in front of the bomb. "I don't think either of us can run that fast any more."

"Can you diffuse it?"

"Diffuse it?" Harold snorted. "Hell, I shouldn't even touch it. There's enough C-4 here to level the building, the parking lot, and about a mile stretch of the highway in either direction."

"Okay. That's bad," Carter said quietly.

As usual, his odd knack for witty dialogue at the wrong moment was in typical form. Harold assumed his friend had seen one too many action movies and was scarred for life by them. Maybe he could arrest Jerry Bruckheimer for corrupting his friend's common sense.

"Bad is an understatement," Harold said as he prodded the explosive trigger, pulling it free of the block of the explosive silly putty. "C-4's out."

"Okay."

"Gimme a second, Carter." Harold said. He used a small pair of needle nose pliers to get inside the small device, careful not to disturb the twin vials of liquid inside. "If these two liquids mix, *KA-BOOM*."

Carter flinched slightly, tried to cover it and hoped his friend had not seen the slip in his action hero composure.

"Timer's reset. We're back to three minutes," Harold announced.

"Remind me to give you a raise," Carter said after letting out the breath he'd been holding. This was not their first run in with explosives so Carter was taking it seriously. Well, as seriously as Carter took anything.

"Let's not get ahead of ourselves, boss," Harold said, standing up slowly. He lifted the explosive device gently, careful not to rattle any of the overly sensitive parts bombs usually had. "There's still enough explosive in this to do some damage. Maybe take out a floor or twelve."

"What do you need?"

"Bomb squad would be nice."

"But you'll settle for…?"

"Clear me a route out of the building for starters. I think I remember seeing something useful out there," Harold said as he walked briskly down the corridor. "And we--"

The two liquids started mixing.

"--better hurry!"

Harold, running now, bolted through the open double doors at the building's rear. Two agents were holding them open for him.

He shouted to them as he passed. "Take cover!"

Now what? Come on, Palmer. Think. Think.

Then he saw it. Right where he remembered.

Bingo!

The garbage truck was sitting at the end of the cul-de-sac at the building's rear. The driver had parked it and was standing with the gaping onlookers who were being kept out of the way by Washington D.C.'s finest.

Harold tossed the bomb in the back and pushed the button to compact the garbage.

"Get these people…"

"*Back!*" was the word Harold was going to say, but was replaced by the loud explosion inside the two-ton garbage truck. The blast lifted the truck ever so slightly, sending it toppling over onto its side, which only added to the noise as the truck's side impacted the concrete.

Harold lay on the ground nearby, face down, arms over his head.

Somewhere close by, someone screamed his name. Probably Carter, but who could tell with all those damned bells and whistles going off all around him. Everything was kind of fuzzy, like he was inside a barrel stuffed with cotton gauze. For a second he couldn't remember where he was.

Then Carter was there, shaking him. Asking him something, but it was so hard to understand. "Did it work?" Harold asked. At least that's what he thought he said. "Truck work?"

"Yes," his friend nodded. Harold wasn't positive, but he could've sworn Carter called him a luck son of a fish. Later he'd realize he just heard it wrong.

An hour later after being thoroughly worked over by EMS, Harold and Carter stood beside the ambulance parked next to the overturned garbage truck. "I can't believe that worked," Carter said as the paramedic finished his work up on Agent Palmer, but he doubted Harold was paying much attention to anything except staring at the overturned wreck.

"Is he going to be okay?" Carter asked the medic.

The paramedic, a woman named Sanchez, shrugged. "He suffered a mild concussion which is not surprising considering the size of and his proximity to the explosion." Carter's face must have betrayed his concern. "Don't worry, sir. It's not as serious as it sounds. The ringing in his ears will fade in a few days. After that, he should have a physician check him over to make sure there's no permanent damage to his hearing, but he should make a full recovery."

"Thank you," Carter said as he pulled a business card from his badge wallet and handed it over to the medic. "Make sure a copy of the report is forwarded to my office, please."

"Not a problem, Agent… Reidling," Sanchez said, reading the name off the card. "Does he need a ride home?"

"That's okay," Carter waved her off. "I'll make sure he gets there. Thanks again."

Walking over to the truck, Carter stepped up next to his friend. "I can't believe that worked," he said again.

This time Harold heard him. "Yeah. I was surprised too," he commented.

Carter gently slapped his friend on the arm. "You know what I think?"

"I shudder to guess."

"I think someone has seen one too many action movies."

"Oh, ha, ha. Very funny."

"I'm also thinking," Carter said as they turned and left the garbage truck behind, "maybe you need a nice little vacation."

"You'll get no argument from me."

"That," Carter deadpanned, "would be a pleasant surprise."

EVIL WAYS

BOBBY NASH

EVIL WAYS

1.

It was late.

It was dark.

It was cold.

It was wet.

At the moment, those four facts comprised her entire universe.

It was probably somewhere around midnight, she assumed, but really had no way of knowing for certain. She had *lost* her watch hours ago. Time had no meaning for her since her terrifying ordeal began earlier this evening after she got off work.

But that was earlier.

All that mattered now was freedom.

The disheveled young woman ran frantically through the woods. Equally as tired as she was scared, it was nothing short of amazing that she could even stand, l et alone run barefoot through the forest. Someone was chasing her, she knew. She could not see or hear anyone following, but she knew.

She knew.

Knew *he* was there.

Too scared to stop and catch her breath, she ran faster still. Fear propelling her ever onward, deeper and deeper into the enveloping shroud of darkness brought on by the thick foliage and trees that seemed to reach up and blot out the moon and its precious light.

It was exceedingly difficult to see the narrow path through the trees in the inky darkness. She knew there was a hiking trail here somewhere. But where? The path, if it could be called that, was not easily traversed and the endless singing of crickets and other insects that called these woods home only served to add to her confusion. The ground, damp from the evening's earlier rainstorm, further hindered her movements. She wasted precious energy in an effort to keep her footing.

Suffice it to say this was not as easy as one might guess. Several times she fell to the mud covered ground several times. Each time she wanted nothing more than to just lay there and sleep. But, as

EVIL WAYS

much as she wished it so, that was not an option.

Failing to notice a large, twisting root protruding from the ground ahead of her, the woman tripped, lost her balance, and fell once more.

And she fell hard.

After laying there for a scant few seconds that felt to her like an eternity, she forced herself onward. Despite the pain, she got to her feet. Then, after checking over her shoulder for what felt like the thousandth time, she began running again. Faster and faster. The only thought percolating inside her brain was that she had to get away.

Get! Away!

She did not know exactly how long she had been running by that point. All she knew for certain was the fear. She was afraid for her very life. Her thoughts raced uncontrolled through her mind. Her imagination exploded with possible scenarios.

All worst case, naturally.

She could hear his footsteps as he moved easily through the woods as if the forest itself were metamorphosing to get out of his way. Or so she imagined. It was impossible, of course. She could barely hear enough to register her own footsteps over the thumping in her chest as her heart threatened to leap free of its bodily restraints.

She mentally tried to calm herself, but after all this time on the run, she was cold and tired, panting uncontrollably and nearly out of breath. Struggling to force away all of those feelings of dread, she pushed ever onward. Ignoring the pain from the various cuts and lacerations that dotted her arms and legs, pushing back the pain in her leg muscles even as the thick black mud began to mix with her blood, stinging as it did so.

The constant din caused by nature as it sought to close in on her like an invisible fist gloved in darkness.

Still, she ran.

What other option was there?

Fighting back might have been a possibility at first, but he had already shown her once how powerful he was. As the bruises all across her milky brown arms reminded her. She had no desire for a second lesson.

Freedom can't be far away, she told herself. Not that she really believed it, but she repeated the mantra nonetheless. She had to believe. She needed to keep hope alive or else all would be lost.

She would be lost.

And that was unacceptable.

Abruptly, she slowed to a halt as a new pang of fear grabbed her swiftly by the heart. A large darkness lay before her. It very nearly swallowed her whole. She knelt at the edge of the darkness, peering into its inky blackness.

There was nothing there.

The ravine.

The ravine meant that she had been running in the direction of the lake. That way did not lead to safety. She had been running in circles. Not away like she had hoped.

She cursed her inability to discern her exact location in the seemingly endless forest. She had lived in this town when she had been a small child, had hiked these paths as a teenager, had her first kiss out by the lake. She still worked at the club in town at least three or four times a week.

This should not have be this hard.

She stared at the complete, waiting blackness of the ravine. If only she had heard the water over the beating of her heart and over her deep gulps for precious air.

"Which way do I go now?" she whispered, barely able to let the words escape from her swollen lips lest *he* would hear them and find her.

If she had not stopped when she had, her flight would have ended suddenly. And prematurely. Frantic, she began to look for a sign that would tell her how long, how deep, or how wide the drop off was. All she knew at that moment was that it probably led to the lake. The only problem was which direction led to the lake. Left or right? She had no idea which way to run. There was nothing to help her in the darkness. She had no other choice but to turn back and hope beyond all hope that her pursuer had given up the chase.

She should have been so lucky.

Unsure how, she knew that he had found her at last.

Turning slowly, she peered into the darkness behind her and he was there As she knew in her heart he would be.

As he always was.

The dark man.

His very presence chilled her to the bone. She had no clue who he was or why he was doing this. In fact, most of the night was a complete blur to her. It took every ounce of will power to hold onto her identity. *Rebecca,* she thought over and over. *Must never forget myself or he wins.*

The man Rebecca thought of as *The Dark Man* simply stood before her, unmoving. His muscular frame blotted out what little of the pale moonlight had filtered through the trees. He was tall, dressed all in black with a dark jacket that had a hood on it. The hood hung low across his back. A black ski mask served to hide his features.

All save his eyes.

Those dead eyes where nothing remotely akin to love or compassion could possibly reside. He looked down at her as she tried to once again get to her feet. She stood carefully, her back to the deep waiting ravine. She could feel his unseen, haunting eyes burn into her very soul, but as she tried to scream out in pain, in desperation, the voice refused to come to her.

Her scream died instantly in her throat.

Instincts immediately kicked in and she made a bold leap toward the creature standing before her. *It's either him or the ravine,* she thought as she attacked her tormentor. She hoped to push him over the edge into the ravine. She hoped that would kill him.

Even if she had to go over with him.

Fear and pain were now replaced by rage.

Undiluted rage, fueled by her hatred. Fueled by her fear. Fueled by her desire to live, or at least to take this bastard to hell with her. He grabbed her long curly black hair and effortlessly swung her already beaten body away from him. Springing quickly to her feet, Rebecca renewed her attack feverishly, unrestrained rage boiling out of every pore.

He easily blocked her less than graceful attacks. She was fighting out of primal fear, while he had cunning, training, and calm reserve on his side. He continued to remain calm even as she pressed her clumsy attack and his silence only served to infuriate the woman and drive her on harder and harder. The dark man almost appeared pleasured by the female's ferocity.

Almost.

The woman whose name had been Rebecca tore and clawed at her oppressor, but his skills were incredible. Far outweighing anything her battered body could muster. *He's done this before,* she knew. That thought terrified her more than anything that had happened to her up to that point.

Almost as a reflex, the dark man easily blocked each of the young woman's attacks until he became bored with her.

"You're no longer any fun," he said just above a whisper, grabbing her by the hair with his right hand while the left hand found a secure hold on her right arm.

"Why are you doing this, you bastard?" Rebecca screamed, continued fighting.

An admirable trait. The dark man admired that about his prey. He liked her *spunk.*

Finally tiring of her inept assault, he ended it quickly with a back handed blow, his right hand to her jaw. A wet snap filled the chill night air and the woman fell silently to the ground. Her fighting spirit laid low at last. Amazingly, she clung to life, not that it would matter. Her life span could now be measured in minutes.

"I win," he whispered.

The hunter claimed his prize.

As usual.

His smile was prideful as he glided in silently to hover over the unmoving body of the young woman whose name he had not cared to learn. As he knelt down to prepare the body, the dark man took a moment to reflect on the events of this evening. The girl had shown great spirit in the face of adversity. He could respect that, but his duty was as clear. As it had always been.

As it would be in the eventful days to follow.

They would be arriving soon.

He ran a gloved finger along the line of her face, tracing the contour of her broken flesh. A bruise had formed where he had struck her. It marred an otherwise beautiful soft brown face. It was a shame really, that he had been forced to kill her. But he could not alter the plan. Not this late in the game. Though he regretted the death of one who fought so valiantly, she would serve a special purpose in the plan.

Her death, while indeed tragic, would bring glory to that which he so valiantly served.

Oh yes. Her death was simply one more step in the plan.

One more sacrifice.

One more inconvenient life taken before her time.

One step closer to the goal.

A single blot on a statistics chart. To think of her as anything else would have been unseemly. It would make him less than he was. To him, a fate worse than death.

The time is coming soon, he reflected silently as he had done a hundred times before, *It won't be long now. Soon, the others will arrive. They will be drawn like flies into the web. The invitations have been delivered. They will be coming soon.* The dark man could hardly contain his excitement.

"It won't be long now!" he screamed proudly to the heavens. A roll of thunder echoed his ravings. The rain would be returning soon to wash away all evidence of his encounter with the woman at his feet.

In the inky darkness of the early morning, standing over the body of his victim, the mysterious dealer of death did the unexpected. He laughed. He laughed loudly and for many long moments his voice could be heard above all the natural sounds of the forest.

He laughed and he could hear the dark forces of hell laughing with him.

Then, adding a silent farewell to the woman who fought so valiantly, he gently hefted her unconscious body in his powerful arms. A soft moan escaped her parched lips. It was the name of her lover.

A familiar name.

Her final thoughts were of him. Probably wondering where he was. Why he had not saved her. His name rolled easily off her broken lips. It was the last sound Rebecca would ever utter as the darkness claimed her.

And the dark man's laughter filled the night.

2.

Harold Palmer was enjoying himself.

The long stretch of highway called out to anyone with the courage to get out there and follow it, wherever it may lead. As the song proclaimed, "*I could go east. I could go west. It was all up to me to decide.*" With Bob Seger and the Silver Bullet Band belting out classic tunes on his portable CD player, Harold Palmer set himself up to take the challenge the road offered him. This was his first vacation in three years and his wife had insisted that he, *now how had she phrased it*, "Get the hell out of the house and relax."

Sound advice.

That wife of his was not only beautiful, but she had a wonderfully brilliant brain resting on those exquisite shoulders. Why she stayed with him was a matter he had never wanted to explore, but he knew that he was damned lucky to have her.

And so, here he was on the open road. He had picked up the motorcycle from the impound lot before leaving Washington D.C. for his vacation. The impound supervisor had loaned it out to him reluctantly, but stressed deeply that it had better be returned in one piece. He had, of course, agreed to be responsible.

Yeah right. Like there was ever any doubt.

Harold Palmer was one of the most responsible men around all year long. He gave his all to everything; his wife, his three-year-old daughter, and his job. These things were all important to him,; that was never questioned. Nor was his loyalty. One always knew where they stood with Harold Palmer. But when would there be time for him? His wife, Beverly, had asked that question of him two days earlier.

Not surprisingly, he had no good answer.

As usual, she had already put much thought into the matter before hand. She had suggested, demanded really, that he take this trip. He had wanted to get out to this part of the country for more than a few years, but one thing or another had always found a way to creep in and disrupt his plans. Usually that interruption was work related.

Not this time.

EVIL WAYS

He had accrued many hours of vacation time at the Bureau and after a wonderful talk with Beverly he took Carter up on his offer and put in for two weeks off. Carter happily approved his friend's vacation request, over the objection of Assistant Deputy Director Mills. Mills had an open case he wanted Agent Palmer's help with. Carter told Director Mills point blank that it could wait two weeks. Reluctantly, Mills relented, but he was none to happy about it.

Funny thing about working for the government: they offer time off, but they don't seem overly thrilled when you want to use it. Luckily, the FBI had more than enough field operatives to handle any major catastrophe that might pop up during his absence. Carter took great delight in reminding him that they had managed to do just fine before he signed on and he was pretty sure that the Bureau would still be there when he got back. *It's not as if the FBI's schedule revolves around Harold Palmer after all,* Carter had said with his usual wit.

Harold knew that he was an important part, but he also knew that he was just one of many agents. And, like the others, he had become fully aware of the hard-boiled fact that he was replaceable.

Everyone could be replaced.

Harold had resisted his wife's advice at first, wanting to spend his vacation with her and their daughter. He planned to go to the zoo, the park, take a day trip, just the three of them. "Quality time," he had told her, but bitter experience has proven that arguing with Beverly was pointless, especially if her mind was already made up. She had already decided what was going to happen. She knew that he needed the time away and she also knew he wouldn't volunteer to take the trip without her and Lucy. Now that he had almost reached the end of his journey, he couldn't be happier about the decision.

Just a few minutes earlier, at his last bathroom break, he had called home from a pay phone because he couldn't find a signal for his cell phone. *Now that's what I call rural.* He told Beverly how right she had been. She was right, of course, and she knew it as well as he did. *But it never hurts to say it.* Luckily, she hadn't felt the need to rub his nose in that fact. There would be plenty of time for that after he returned home next week. He had spent five minutes talking to her and Lucy, his young daughter. Truthfully, he missed them both terribly, but this trip had to be taken. Too much time had passed since last he had seen Ray, at least two years. And that was not the best of times. For either of them.

This visit was imperative. *If not now, when?* Time was pressing down on them all. He could not -would not- allow any more time to come between them.

In truth, Beverly understood all too well the importance of family. She was, after all, the youngest of eight children. She had three older brothers and four older sisters and yet somehow managed to find the time to keep in touch with each and every one of them. With them scattered across the country, that was no easy task. Still, she found a way to manage. Harold only had one sibling, his baby brother, and they had only spoken a handful of times in the past two years. All Beverly wanted was for her husband and his brother to be as close again as they had been when they were children.

Of course both of them were exactly alike. Both were strong, stubborn, opinionated men. If any initiative were to be taken, Beverly would have to take it upon herself to set the wheels in motion, which is exactly what she had done.

Back on the road, the miles zoomed past. In the median, grass, flowers, and weeds of various varieties blurred past, a sea of greens, reds, whites, and yellows. The autumn chill had begun a little sooner than most had expected. Harold found himself shivering, partly from the cold, partly from excitement.

The long stretch of country highway was all but deserted at this time of the day, the morning rush over by at least an hour. The occasional car would come into view every so often and he made mental note of how nearly every driver raised their hand in a friendly wave.

"They don't do that much back home in D.C.," he muttered to himself as his breath fogged up his facemask. Stifling a small laugh, Harold continued onward, his final destination ahead.

Out of habit he took in every detail of the landscape. The trees were turning and all the earth colors bloomed into majestic focus along the edge of the highway. Yellow, brown, and orange leaves danced around on the chilled breeze, moving in time to a silent melody only they were privy to.

Harold took it all in.

It was not as though he had never seen trees changing with the seasons. Quite the opposite, in fact. His family had grown up in a small town only slightly larger than the one he was speeding toward. He, his mother, dad, and younger brother had all seen nature's beautiful dance on more than a few occasions.

Mom would pack a large lunch and the whole family would load up in the old family car and drive for hours just so they could catch a fleeting glimpse of nature's beauty as the leaves changed colors before the winter chill set in. Mom's eyes would light up and she was happy. Her happiness was always contagious. The Palmer family would have the best times on those weekend excursions.

But, as in all things, the child grew up and became a man, and the man stopped noticing the little things as the hustle and bustle of everyday life began to close in on him. He had forgotten how beautiful all of this could be. It had a peaceful, calming effect on him. Almost tranquil. Serene.

Perhaps too much so.

"Whoa!"

Instantly, Harold's attention snapped back to reality as a large deer leaped across the road in his path. Harold instinctively swerved the motorcycle to avoid it. Somehow, he managed to stay upright and after a few seconds was back on course as though nothing had happened. He had allowed the vivid colors to momentarily distract his attention from the road. Probably not his best move.

"Good ol' reflexes," he muttered between chattering teeth.

Those good old reflexes had saved his life on more than one occasion since childhood. He and his brother had always wanted adventure, they craved it, but their parents were pretty savvy. They always seemed to be one step ahead of the boys, especially Dad. He always told them that he knew the boy's every plan, every excuse, every scheme, mainly because he had done the very same things when he had been their age. This, of course, made the boys redouble their efforts to pull one over on dear old Dad. And after many tries they actually succeeded.

Much to the boy's regret.

The old rock quarry near their home had been labeled off limits to the Palmer children and both knew it. Dad drilled it into their brains. That made it that much more inviting. They had sneaked in through a tear in the fence. It was a wonderful adventure. The caves became an alien landscape and the boys became space rangers. Harold pretended that he was Buck Rogers while his younger brother opted to play his hero from TV, Captain Kirk of the Starship Enterprise. As imaginary aliens swarmed all around them the valiant heroes fought back bravely. Battling to the point of exhaustion the space rangers were victorious over their enemies.

Then there was a cave in.

The two boys were trapped underneath tons of rock for thirteen and a half hours before they were discovered. Dumb luck had saved them, and Dad's eyes bored holes through the boys after the doctors checked them over and said that they were fine, save for a few minor cuts, a broken arm for Harold, and mild dehydration. Dad never said a word; he just stared at them. That image still followed Harold to this day. Every time he had a close call, he could feel his father's presence, watching. He welcomed that presence at times. He knew Dad was watching over him. At least he hoped as much.

Dad had many opportunities to watch over his eldest son at his job. As an FBI field agent, Harold often found himself in dangerous situations. Being shot at, attacked, explosions, you name it, he had probably seen it in his time with the Bureau.

Harold was tired.

The past two years had become a blur as one case bleed into another. He could hardly distinguish between them anymore. The bomb at the Treasury Building was just one more in a long line of close calls over the last few years. He didn't even tell Beverly about the worst of them anymore. She had enough to worry about without adding to it. Pulling double duty between the Violent Crimes Task Force and the Joint Terrorism Task Force certainly kept him busy.

Not only did his body need the rest, but his mind as well.

For his own peace of mind, Harold had to get away from it all. Even if for a few weeks. Then he could return to work with a fresh perspective and renewed vigor. That was one of the main reasons this trip was so important. With the hectic pace of his life, Harold Palmer needed peace, quiet, and a little relaxation more than anything else right now.

And Sommersville, Georgia was just the place to get it.

Speaking of the devil. Harold noticed a green mileage sign off to the right of the highway. "Sommersville. Fifty miles," he whistled softly. His long journey was almost at an end. He should be there by mid morning, maybe sooner if he hurried. *"No,"* he thought to himself, remembering his earlier run in with the deer. *Better not push it. Last thing I need is a speeding ticket.* He laughed at that thought. *Or worse.*

He turned up the volume on his CD player as That Old Time Rock 'n Roll began to play and as the beat got louder, the bike went faster, thoughts of traffic violations pushed aside.

"Oh well," he mused, allowing a casual laugh. "I'm a rebel. Gotta take a few chances I suppose."

With that Harold Palmer sped off toward Sommersville.

3.

The remainder of the ride into Sommersville was as uneventful as Harold expected.

He still looked at the sights, taking in the natural beauty, only now he was being more conscious of the road as well. The North Georgia Mountains had a reputation for being at their best around this time of year. Harold now knew this to be true and wished his trip would take him farther into the North Georgia Mountains. *Maybe on the way home.*

Beverly and Lucy would love to see the beautiful vibrant colors. The thought of his precious family caused a small ache in his gut. He wished they had come with him, but he had already been down that route. Once that wife of his set her mind to something, Harold's only recourse was to relent and surrender to the inevitable because there was a better chance of snow falling in hell than changing her mind. Beverly was quite the formidable negotiator. *Dictator.*

No sense crying over it this late in the game.

It was hovering around 10:30 am when he finally reached the small town of Sommersville. A large, freshly painted wooden sign greeted him at the city limits. It read simply: **Welcome to Sommersville, Georgia** in large wooden letters. Then followed the standard city limit signs about the Chamber of Commerce, the Mason, the local football team; the Panthers, and the population of 7,120.

Small town USA, Harold thought. *Be it ever so humble.*

Below all of the usual information, the sign ended in what Harold was beginning to realize was the same friendly manner indicative of the town: **Have a nice day.**

Nice town. Seems friendly enough.

Harold couldn't help but brandish a slight smile at the imagery of a peaceful little town where everyone was happy and where everybody knew everyone else. *No privacy, that's for sure.* He pushed the thought away as he turned his borrowed motorcycle onto the town's main street.

Cruising along with the small cluster of traffic, there were maybe fifteen or twenty cars on the road, he marveled at the architecture of the rustic buildings. Banners adorned the street as the town worked to prepare for its annual Autumn Festival.

Sounds like a good time, Harold thought to himself, wondering what exactly happened at an Autumn Festival. He watched as several volunteers set up booths and arranged a large assortment of banners and signs. The banners and signs featured a myriad assortment of messages and displays ranging from **WELCOME HOME** to **HAPPY HOLIDAYS** and everything in between. Some of the large cloth banners that adorned the local museum, which Harold noted was smaller than the supermarket where he and Beverly shopped, featured pictures of various colors and designs from the abstract to the surreal. All in all, the Autumn Festival looked like one hell of a bash. It seemed to Harold that everyone in the cozy little town would come out for the festival

"It's probably the biggest thing this place sees in a year," he mused. "Wow! The town sure looks nice." A sharp whistle emphasized his point.

Ray had said in a recent letter that the town had just finished a major refurbishing job, which probably explained the freshly painted sign he passed a couple miles back. It looked amazing, but Harold almost wished to have been able to see it before the restoration, just to get a before and after image in his mind. Too bad. Just one more thing to regret later. As if life hadn't already handed him an armful of those. Surely Ray would have a photo of the town before the restoration.

At a whopping speed of thirty-five miles per hour, Harold eased the motorcycle into the closest service station for a gas fill up. Harold paid for his gas and a soft drink, an indulgence he had learned to live without most of the time, but this was a vacation, after all. What better time to splurge? He asked the lady behind the register for directions to his final destination.

"The newspaper?" The pleasant woman whose nametag said that her name was Amelia said with a giggle in her voice. "Yes sir. If you go down Main Street for another two miles, past the courthouse, the paper's building is on the right. You can't miss it." Her smile was sincere.

Harold returned her smile as best he was able and thanked her for her help. He then headed for the door and without consciously thinking about it told her to have a nice day.

Maybe the niceness is starting to rub off on me. Harold winced at the prospect of trying to have manners while simultaneously trying to wrestle down a suspect. Manners and the FBI might not always fit together very well. However, it never hurt to try, or so he suspected. "I can do that much I suppose," he announced to no one in particular.

Finishing off his soda with big gulps, he once again donned his borrowed black helmet. Harold started up his motorcycle and headed off toward the newspaper building.

It only took a few minutes to find the place. Right where Amelia had said it would be. "Can't miss it," he repeated. Then, after finding a place to park, Harold Palmer headed for the appropriate building.

He could not get over the feeling that the town of Sommersville looked as if it had been scooped right out of a Norman Rockwell painting. It had a homey feeling to it. Harold could imagine himself being happy in a place like this. He could let his daughter grow up free here.

The citizens that were walking about didn't seem to have a care in the world, but Harold also knew from bitter experience that appearances could often times be deceiving.

And more often than not they were.

Taking the four steps up to the entrance two at a time, Harold rubbed his fingers across the red letters professionally emblazoned on the glass door.

THE SOMMERSVILLE GAZETTE

He looked at it for a long moment, beaming with pride before deciding to go on in. He pulled open the door and stepped inside the cool interior of the Sommersville Gazette's main- not to mention only- office. The small room was friendly and inviting, a lot like the rest of the town. The blinds on the windows were rolled open and what little there was of the early morning sunlight spilled warmly into the reception area. Several small flowerpots were arranged around the room in a careful manner, probably by the receptionist. Ray had never been one to spend any amount of time on decorating. Harold doubted Ray ever gave such trivial things as decor a second thought.

Harold walked from the door to the main desk across brown carpet that almost matched the color of the wall paneling. The receptionist greeted him with a sincere smile and a polite demeanor. *Is everyone in this town happy?* Harold asked himself.

To her, he simply said, "Hi."

"Hello," she replied casually. "Can I help you, sir?"

He continued to smile at her, then promptly Harold reached into his jacket pocket, pulling out his wallet, he flashed her his Federal Bureau of Investigations credentials. "FBI, ma'am." He put forth his best professional attitude. "Your boss in?"

"Y-yes sir," she stammered, obviously caught off guard by his appearance. *FBI agents are supposed to be dressed more professionally as a general rule. In a suit and tie, not jeans, T-shirt, and leather jacket.* Not that she had ever met an FBI agent in person before, only having seen them on TV and in the movies. This guy sure didn't dress like those X-Files agents she had seen on the tube. She tried to compose herself, failing miserably. Harold almost felt bad for her. "But he--he's busy," she finished.

"Right."

"I can page him if..."

Without waiting for her to finish, Harold Palmer made a beeline for the nearest office door, behind which lay the sole reason for his trip. He opened the door without so much as a knock. Quickly, the FBI agent took stock of the room. Near the outer wall sat a large wooden desk piled high with papers, folders, photos, and the like. His target was sitting behind the desk talking to someone on the telephone. A large gray light table sat against the opposite wall with nearly as much clutter as the desk. The walls had the same dull brown paneling as the outer office, but there was no carpet in the office, only hardwood floors. *Probably spent the entire decoration budget, if there was such a thing, on the reception area.* Several chairs were spread across the office in a haphazard fashion with only a few around the large conference table in the center of the room. The room had the look and smell of what he expected from a small press newspaper editor's office, although he had never actually stepped foot in one until that moment.

"You can't just..." the receptionist's voice trailed off behind him as he stepped across the threshold and into the editor's office.

Surprised, the man in the office gaped in utter astonishment, suddenly aware of Harold's presence. His eyes went wide, and he prematurely ended his phone conversation. "Uh, let me call you back, Jen. Yeah. Bye." Hanging up the receiver, the newspaperman started to stand without taking his eyes from the new arrival.

Taking a moment, he straightened his shirt and loosened tie, then slowly the editor approached the invader. "FBI, huh?" His voice was flat and restrained. His footsteps echoed off of the hardwood floors.

"Yeah." Harold watched as the man slowly approached. "Wanna make something of it?"

The other man stopped and pondered the question before responding with a smile. "Oh yeah." He paused. "Yes, I most certainly do."

"Bring it on."

The two men moved dangerously close until only mere inches

separated them. Harold looked down at the shorter man. Harold was only a few inches taller, but he made sure the younger man noticed. At the threshold of the office, the receptionist watched in abject horror as the two men began to square off against one another.

"Franklin, I..." she started, but a curt stare from her boss was cause enough to make her to stay out of it. She complied with her bosses wishes, albeit reluctantly, and backed up against the far wall.

Then with startling speed the FBI agent moved in for the kill. The receptionist expected the worst, but suddenly the FBI agent did the last thing she would have ever expected. The two men embraced one another in a large bear hug. A small squeal of excitement echoed from one of the men, but she could not tell from which one. When they finally parted they were both smiling and laughing. The receptionist was, to say the very least, understandably confused. Harold placed his hands on the younger man's shoulders.

"Damn, Ray. It's been too long," he said to the younger man.

"Yeah, Bro. Yeah it has."

"Excuse me?"

Both men turned toward the receptionist's voice. "Oh, Lisa," stammered her boss almost as if he had completely forgotten that she had been standing there. "I'm sorry. Lisa, this is Harold Palmer." He paused for dramatic effect before continuing. "Special Agent Harold Palmer of the FBI." He introduced his guest to the startled receptionist.

"Hi." Lisa tried to sound calm and professional, failing miserably. "Harold is my brother," her boss said, trying to clarify things.

"Oh," said Lisa, obviously still somewhat confused. "A --uh-- pleasure to meet you, Mr. Palmer. I think."

Harold turned toward her, still smiling. "Sorry to have shaken you up, ma'am, but I just couldn't resist pulling something like this on Ray. You understand?"

She nodded. "Yes. I think I understand." She hesitated, rolling around a thought in her brain. "Ray?" she finally asked.

Her boss piped in an explanation before Harold could utter a sound. "My brother here is the only person in the free world to ever call me by my middle name and live. Franklin Ray Palmer."

"You know," Harold chimed in, "like the comic book character The Atom."

"Oh," the receptionist was starting to feel awkward in the midst of this little family reunion. "I'll just be..." Erratically she pointed toward the location of her desk in a *that-a-way* motion. "I-I'll just be out here at my-- uh-- desk."

"Thank you, Lisa," Franklin Palmer said as she disappeared around the corner. He then turned to regard his brother as if for the first time. "Damn, Harry, you sure do know how to make an entrance."

Harold gave his younger brother a wink. "I learned from the master."

"Yeah?"

"Yeah. Damn, Ray, it's good to see you."

The two men regarded one another for another moment. It had been nearly two years since they had last seen one another, and that had not been a happy time for either of them. It was at their father's funeral. At the time, the two brothers promised to get together more often, but their busy lives always found some small way to interrupt every plan they had made. But now that they were standing face to face both men realized at long last just how much they had each missed the other. Sure, they occasionally spoke over the phone, but to be here in person said far more than any mere words could.

"So, Harry," Franklin began as he returned to the chair behind his desk and a mountain of papers. "How long you planning on staying?" He motioned for his brother to take a chair. Harold complied.

"I don't know," Harold said. "I've got two weeks of vacation. So, I figured I'd stay for at least a week." He eyed his brother for any hint of a negative reaction. None was forthcoming. "Or," Harold continued. "Until I get on your nerves and you give me the boot."

"Well, it's been good seeing you again then. Bye."

Harry was momentarily struck speechless. Dumbfounded, he stared at his brother, waiting for the punch line that he assumed was coming. He was not disappointed. It followed shortly. "Just kidding. Don't tell me that working for the FBI has taken away all of your sense of humor, such as it is. I can't have my only brother being a stiff now can I?"

"Let's hope not. Stiff in my line of work doesn't necessarily mean no sense of humor."

"Yeah. Makes a strange sort of sense. Well, Harry, where are your things?"

"Out on the bike. I didn't bring much." Harold motioned toward the front of the building to where he had parked his borrowed transportation.

"A bike? You?" Franklin laughed out loud.

"Yes. You sound surprised." Harold looked at him in askance.

Franklin shook off a laugh. "Just a little. You never were one for *real* adventure as I recall. You were always the big Boy Scout. I'm the one who stayed in trouble most of the time, if you recall."

"Things change," Harold answered.

"Apparently so," said Franklin, motioning toward Harold's leather jacket. He grabbed his own jacket from the back of his desk chair and headed toward the door behind Harold. "You on a motorcycle. This I've got to see." Smiling at a memory, Harold followed his brother out of the office and past the receptionist. She forced a smile, apparently still befuddled over the earlier scene between the two siblings.
Franklin absently remembered to tell her that he was leaving. "I'll be back later, Lisa. Hold down the fort. Okay?" He was already out the door before she could answer.

"Yes, sir."

"Bye, Lisa," Harold added as he followed Franklin out into the morning sunlight. "It was very nice to meet you." There had finally been a break in the gray clouds, allowing a small sliver of sunshine to poke its way through.

As the door started to close, Harold heard the receptionist tell him goodbye. "A pleasure, Mr. Palmer," she said.

He wasn't sure whether she actually meant it or not, but he let it go all the same. Tossing a wave at her, Harold Palmer walked out into the morning sun.

4.

Tom Myers was not a morning person.

He lived for sleeping in. It was one of his many vices. He had often commented that he wasn't truly conscious until a full pot of coffee had made its way into his gullet. Unfortunately for Mr. Myers his job often involved his early arrival at the station. As sheriff of Sommersville and the rest of the surrounding county, which consisted mostly of farmland and woods, it was his job, his duty really, to brief his deputies on their daily activities. He helped them prepare for any event, and in a quiet town like Sommersville such a thing was generally easy. There weren't usually any major crimes, or many minor ones for that matter, in this sleepy little town. There were the occasional little nit-picky things like kids egging houses, the rare fight, a few traffic violations here and there; and, of course, the weekly domestic dispute involving the Macaveys. They tended to get into it at least once a week. Tom or one of his deputies was almost constantly out at their farm. It had been his experience that the majority of the people in this town tended to exceed the speed limit, teenagers especially. But, Sheriff Myers was a lenient man and everyone knew that. He was young once and he knew that most of the kids in town were good kids.

Most of the time.

This particular morning had started off anything but ordinary.

His wife had decided to pick this morning to have yet another argument about their finances. Sure, money had been tight for the past few months, but the town had invested a large portion of their time, effort, and money into this year's Autumn Festival. The town council was inviting investors from the surrounding areas and several from out of state, hoping to sell any of them on relocating their businesses to the outskirts of Sommersville, or at the very least getting them interested in opening new plants and businesses here. It would be a boon to the town to have new resources start pouring in. New businesses meant new jobs. New jobs meant more money for the town. More jobs meant more people moving in. Add all that up and the town could begin to build onward and upward. Then, and only then, would Tom Myers be getting a raise. He knew that. He understood it. Granted, he didn't much like it, but he understood it nonetheless. Why was it so hard for Mildred to get it through her thick skull?

That was a question he had asked himself on more than one occasion. Even though he had spent much time thinking about it, Tom had yet to discover the answer to that little enigma, and he highly doubted that enlightenment would come to him today, if ever.

He regretted that he left the house without settling things, but it seemed that of late he couldn't win an argument with Mildred. Generally, that was because she was always right. He guzzled the last of his morning coffee that Mildred had made for him. Unsatisfied by the warmth from the downed coffee, he tapped on the heater in an effort to knock off the morning chill.

Having already taken his morning drive around the town, Tom was heading back to the office. The morning tour of Sommersville had become a sort of ritual for the sheriff. Every morning he would leave the station after briefing his deputies and drive through the center of town, then turn out toward the Johnson farm on Route 20. He usually stopped to catch up on the local gossip from Mr. and Mrs. Johnson.

For two old people that never seemed to leave their home, the Johnson's seemed to know everything about everyone. In truth, Tom had come to enjoy the elderly couple's company, and h ad even invited them over for dinner a few times. They were a sweet couple and they always had a kind word for Tom. Plus, they always asked after Mildred and Mrs. Johnson made one terrific cup of coffee. The Johnson's had practically adopted Tom and his wife. Tom supposed that there were worse things that could happen to a middle aged man. Besides, the gossip that they heard and told was generally correct nine times out of ten.

A scary thought, when one thought about it. *Funny*, the sheriff thought to himself. *I've done this for nearly twenty years and I don't even know the Johnson's first names.*

Not surprising, really If Tom Myers was one thing, it was polite.

Myers always respected his fellow man. Called everyone outside of his close, personal friends by Mister or Missus. His parents raised him fairly well and he would hate to waste all of the time and effort that they had put into teaching him those manners. Besides, being a public official meant he had certain obligations to the people he served. One of those obligations was respect as far as Tom Myers was concerned.

After bidding a farewell to the Johnson's, Sheriff Myers continued on his way, driving out past Winding Creek and crossing the old covered bridge. The old bridge had been a favorite hide out for local kids when they decided to skip school. Tom had spent many a day out here himself when he had been a youngster. Knowing how it had been for him and his friends, he tried not to hassle the kids too much, but he had to be more responsible now than he had in the old days. After a time, the kids just found a new place to hide.

Problem solved. Well, somewhat solved.

Every morning the sheriff followed the same path, the same cycle, and every morning he found himself at Lake Greene and the old fort, Fort Greene, that overlooked it, standing guard. He passed by the place every day. He claimed that it was to preserve a sense of history, but it was really just a thin excuse to get away from his responsibilities in town.

The old fort was a Civil War left over. At least three battles were fought on this very location. The state turned it into a landmark about thirty years earlier. People were no longer allowed inside the decrepit structure. A fence had been erected around the Fort to keep sightseers at a safe distance about three years back after a tourist fell through one of the rotten floorboards. Luckily the man survived, but the Historical Society could not take chances by allowing people inside any longer. The state of the old landmark had fallen into disrepair over the years and the State Historical Society reportedly had not had the time, the manpower, or the funds to do anything about it. One day, they promised, Fort Greene would be restored. Sheriff Myers hoped it wasn't already too late. The old building didn't have too many years left to it.

With over half of his morning evaporated like the fog, the sheriff wearily headed back to the office and the mountain of paperwork that would undoubtedly be waiting for him as usual. "Ahh, it's good to be me," he said sarcastically as he turned his beat up brown Chevrolet truck out onto the main road that lead into town.

As usual, his little trip around town proved to be uneventful. He sagged in his seat with minor disappointment. Tom Myers craved adventure. He always had, although he would never admit to anyone his dream of being like Sean Connery or Harrison Ford, a man of action and intrigue.

"No one could understand how frustrating it was to be a cop in a sleepy town like this," he had said on many different occasions. Even when a big case fell in his lap, Tom just could not make anything happen. There had been two deaths in Sommersville during the last four months and he had yet to find a single helpful clue. "Some sheriff." He was talking to no one of course. The sheriff had trouble expressing himself to others, so he often spilt his guts to his truck.

It may sound strange, but it beats therapy.

He laughed at the thought.

Tom was known to throw himself into his hobbies as well. To everything he did, Tom Myers gave one hundred and ten percent. Talking about his troubles and thoughts helped him to sort out his thoughts from the jumble that he often found them in.

His ruminations finished for the day, Sheriff Myers turned up the volume on his radio. There were only two options in Sommersville. There was a local rock 'n roll station and the local country station. It really wasn't much of a choice since the same man, Mr. Clarence Donat, owned both. Often times both stations would have the same disc jockey on at the same time since they were run out of the same building.

This morning Myers opted for some good ol rock 'n roll to help pep him up for the rest of his day that lay ahead. Ironically enough, the station was playing one of his favorites Tom Petty tunes.

As Tom Petty and the Heartbreakers were "Running Down A Dream," Tom Myers sighed, knowing that his dreams had passed him by.

Along with his life.

He let out another sigh as he passed the city limit sign.

WELCOME TO SOMMERSVILLE.

"Be it ever so humble."

5.

It had been a long morning for Harold Palmer.

A few dozen *"harry palm(er)"* jokes at his expense later, he hopped on his borrowed transportation and followed his brother to his home just outside of town.

It took them all of ten minutes to get there and Harold was starting to feel the tug of hunger on him by the time he arrived. "Should've grabbed a bagel at that gas station," he chided himself. "Guess I can grab something at Ray's. He's bound to have something to eat. Or there's always the old standbys." Harold patted his jacket pocket to confirm that his little goodies were still where he had left them. "Be prepared," he whispered, repeating the Boy Scout motto he had learned as a child.

Franklin Palmer turned his teal green Blazer onto a small back road and then immediately took a left turn off into a combination dirt and gravel driveway. The heavy rains from the day before had turned his driveway into a slick, muddy path.

Harold cautiously followed on his motorcycle. Carefully trying to keep it upright, he pulled to a stop just beside Franklin's house. It was an old house, probably been on this location for fifty or sixty years, Harold assumed. The architecture was nothing like what Harold would have expected from his brother's home. *It suits Ray,* he decided. The yard was also impressive It was huge, nothing like the small quarter acre lawn he had back in Virginia. He allowed himself a minute to just lose himself in the swirling golden orange leaves blowing in the mid morning breeze. A dog ran wild through the yard, only to disappear into the dense woods alongside his brother's property. Harold gave passing thought to whom the pet might belong to. He filed the question away as something to ask about later.

"Nice place," Harold told his brother.

"Thanks, Harry," Franklin agreed, obviously very proud of his home.

While climbing the six steps to a large screened in front porch he fished around in his pants pocket for his house keys. The grey house, Harold immediately noticed, was in dire need of a paint job. Still, all in all, it was a nice place. Very homey. Just like everything else in this town. He followed Franklin onto the screened porch as his brother unlocked the deadbolt. Franklin opened the door and invited his guest inside with a theatrical wave of his arm and his best impression of Igor. "After you, brother."

"Thanks, Ray."

The inside looked a lot like Harold would have imagined. Mostly empty. The walls on the inside looked as if they had been painted recently and the carpet still had that "new carpet smell" to it. Very few decorations adorned the walls. A few of his favorite newspapers had been framed and placed awkwardly around the living room, but that comprised the extent of the home's decorations. One framed piece contained the paper, which boasted Franklin Palmer's first byline. Another was a front-page article declaring the end of World War II. Against the far wall he could see a framed paper announcing the death of Elvis Presley that had not yet made its way to the wall. A recent acquisition no doubt. Another frame sported the article that announced Franklin's purchase of the local newspaper two years earlier and his claims to honor the community. It even had a bad photo of the erstwhile publisher with a bad haircut and a dopey grin on his face.

"Now that's the little brother I remember," Harold said, pointing at the grainy newsprint image.

Franklin had moved off toward a back bedroom while Harold took a look around. A bookshelf containing a large library of books and novels on various subjects ranging from science fiction to horror to the classics ran the length of one wall. Franklin Palmer had obviously been keeping up with his reading. Harold scanned the shelves, trying to see if his younger brother still had the same interests as he used to. Close, but his tastes had drifted more to the darker side of human nature. Books on the occult, a faded copy of The Anarchist's Bible, U.F.O.'s, witches and werewolves, vampires, Salem Witch Trials, and the like. Franklin had definitely become quite the horror freak Harold always suspected he would. He remembered back when his younger brother sought out any and every thing he could relating to vampires while watching every disgustingly graphic horror movie he could lay his grubby little hands on.

"Nice place," Harold reiterated.

"It's not much, but it's my home away from work," Franklin said as he reentered the living room, "It's a bit of a fixer-upper, but I spend so much time at the paper that I haven't had a lot of time to put into decorating. Mostly I just sleep here." He thought about it then added, "Sometimes." He made a motion toward the walls with his hand. "I did manage to get a couple of coats of paint on some of these walls a few weeks back, but other than that it's- well, truth to tell, it's been rather hectic. What with the murder and all."

"That's cool I gue--Waitaminute? Murders? Here?"

"No. Not murders. Murder. One. Singular. No "*s*" on the end of it. But yeah a murder," Franklin answered as he grabbed a few drinks from the refrigerator. "These things happen in more than just your major metropolitan cities, you know."

"I stand chastised," Harold grinned. "Please, continue."

Franklin rubbed a hand through his playfully unkempt hair. "Local police found a body about two weeks ago. It was found just outside of the city limits. The county sheriff thinks that the deceased may have been from the nearby college, but they still don't have any clues to substantiate anything. No witnesses. No clues. No suspects. No nothing. I guess killing has no jurisdiction does it?" He handed a can of soft drink to Harold, who took the drink and popped the top. Good and cold. Just the way he liked it.

"No, I'm afraid it doesn't," he answered his brother's question.

"I'd offer food, but the cupboards are bare, as usual. Sorry." Ray motioned toward the kitchen behind him as if that would explain everything.

"Not a problem," Harold answered, pulling a candy bar from his jacket pocket. "I've got it covered." He gave his younger brother a smile and a wink. "Be prepared. Remember?"

"Right. Still the Boy Scout I see," Franklin observed as he moved some old piles of newspapers aside to make a space for his brother on the couch. Harold sat and watched with some small measure of amusement as Franklin searched for a place to sit for himself. Giving up, he opted for moving a stack of magazines from the coffee table and sitting on the edge. "About the killing?"

"I'd really rather not discuss it, Harry. It was very brutal and very disturbing. I'm only now getting to where I can sleep at night without seeing it in my dreams."

"Sorry. I didn't mean to dig it up."

"Not a big deal. How could you know?"

"Still," Harold said, staring at the floor. "I know what it's like. I don't like to think of you going through it. I'll not mention it again. Promise."

"Okay," he agreed, changing the subject. "So, how's Beverly and the runt? Why didn't they come along?"

"Beverly is doing great, Ray," Harold beamed from talking about his family, almost glowing. It made him seem less tired when he spoke of his family. Franklin was envious. He had only felt that way about one woman in his entire life. Too bad it hadn't worked out as he had hoped. Harold pulled out a photo of him and his family. He handed it to Franklin as a gift. "Lucy is doing great. She's a handful, but we manage. Beverly thought that you and I needed some time together and didn't want to interrupt our... *bonding*." He raised his fingers in mock quotation marks. Franklin stifled a grin with a small effort. "I always did like that wife of yours. Good head on her shoulders, smart, and pretty. How did she ever end up with a loser like you anyway?"

"Dumb luck."

"Yours or hers?" Franklin asked halfheartedly.

Harold smiled. "Mine, of course."

"Figures," Franklin added offhandedly.

The two brothers laughed then and it is as if the years that had passed between them dissolved away into nothing. *Harold and Franklin together again. Dad would have been so very proud.*

After a moment of insane laughter, reality managed to intrude on their reunion. Franklin pointed toward the back bedroom. "You can stay here as long as you like. I have a room made up back there. It's a little cramped, but you should be okay."

"Thanks, Ray." A silence passed between them. "And Ray, I'm very happy to be here." Harold lifted his canned soda in a toast. Ray copied the maneuver, tapping the cans together gently.

"I missed you too, bro." A moment of silence passed between them. "Come on. I'll show you to your room." Franklin attempted his best imitation of an uptight hotel bellboy. Harold followed, his luggage in hand. "Must be the real bellboy's day off," he said.

The room was just as Harold had expected. Messy. It seemed almost as if the disorganization from the living room had spilled over into this small, spare bedroom. A small bed sat off to one corner. "It's not much, but it beats the couch," Ray said.

"It'll be fine." Harold flashed his brother another smile. "Believe me, the Bureau has put me up in places a lot worse."

"Thanks, Harry, I feel much better now."

"How's room service in this place?"

"I don't know. You like bologna? I'm sure the grocery store will have a pack or two."

"Oh," Harold feigned a pain in the heart. "It's just like being back home."

"Don't push it, bub."

"Right." He tossed his bags upon the only clear spot on his small bed and proceeded to move the small piles of papers to the floor.

As Harold rearranged the papers for optimum room, Franklin noted how tired his brother looked and said as much.

Harold did not disagree with the assessment. "I've just been working too hard lately," he said. "It's been just one case after another. And each one seems to get worse and worse."

"Yeah. I saw a story about that bit at the Treasury Building on CNN. That looked pretty intense."

"You don't know the half of it."

"Tell me."

Tapping his right ear gently, Harold sighed. "It was bad. Bomb nearly went off inside the building. Still got a little ringing in this ear."

"Permanent?"

"Nah. Doc said it should clear up in a week or two. It will be almost as good as new. I'll probably have problems as I get older or if another bomb goes off in my face."

"Sounds like a real close call." Franklin took a sip. "So you came here?"

"I just had to get away before I exploded or something." Harold regarded Franklin. "You ever feel like that, Ray?"

"On occasion," he replied. "I had big dreams when I came here, but it seems like I just can't catch a break. I don't make enough money to hire a staff, with the exception of Lisa, so I end up doing most of the work myself. Sure I have a few freelancers help out every once in a while, but mostly it's just me."

"That's rough." Harold took a sip of his drink, stared at a spot on the floor. *Nothing like uncomfortable silences.* Finally, he spoke. "But you're managing, right?"

Franklin shrugged. "Yeah. I am. Sometimes I wonder if it is worth it though. There are definitely less stressful ways to make a living."

Harold started to say something, but was interrupted by the telephone ringing in the other room. Franklin politely excused himself and left his brother alone in the guestroom while he answered the phone. Leaving Harold all alone with the task at hand. "Just like when we were kids," he whispered to himself. "Good to know that some things never change."

By the time Franklin returned to the back room, Harold had managed to clear off the bed and had started to unpack his clothes and things. Franklin was still listening to the voice on the other end of the cordless phone. "Are you sure?" he asked into the phone. Harold could tell from Franklin's tone, it was not good news.

"Are you absolutely sure about this, Lisa?" he asked again. He scribbled furiously on a notepad he kept in his pocket while his assistant passed along the information. "Yes, yes. I know." Another long pause as he scribbled out more nearly illegible notes. "I'm on my way. Let them know I'll be there shortly. Thanks. Bye."

"Trouble, Ray?" Harold asked mostly out of concern and partially out of curiosity.

"There's been a murder. Police found a body. I've got to go."

"Need some company?"

"As my big brother or as an FBI agent?"

Harold let out a *harumph* as he pulled a gun and holster from the bottom of his luggage. "Is there a difference?" he asked as he began checking his gun.

"Guess not." Franklin watched intently as Harold strapped on the shoulder holster. "You want to put on a suit too. You know, so you'll look more agent-man like? I know you guys have an image to uphold."

"I'm on vacation, Ray. No suit."

"But you'll take your gun on vacation?" Franklin asked, not bothering to hide the innuendo behind his words. Franklin had never really cared much for guns. Harold knew it made his brother uncomfortable, but long years of experience, not to mention the Boy Scouts, had taught him to always be prepared.

For anything.

"Never leave home without it." He threw his brother a wink. "After you."

"Now I know why Beverly sent you away for a vacation." He prodded his brother with a strong slap across the back of his shoulder.

Harold responded with a wink. "Har-de-freakin'-har!" he said. "Come on, will you! You did say you were in a hurry, didn't you?"

"Yes sir." He saluted.

As the two men head toward the Blazer at a moderate jog, Franklin eyed his brother, admiring the take-charge attitude. He remembered how much he had disliked that about Harry when they were kids. Harold reached the Blazer first and was strapped in and ready by the time

Franklin arrived with his gear.

Within seconds, the two men were speeding down Miller's Trail Road toward their destination.

"By the way," Harold said to Franklin. "Have I told you yet how happy I am to be here?"

"Yes," Franklin answered. "And boy, am I glad you are."

6.

The town of Sommersville was abuzz with anticipation.

Not to mention all of the usual last minute headaches that came along with preparing the entire town for the Autumn Festival. All of the businesses along Main Street had pitched in to get Sommersville ready for the annual gala event.. They had pulled out all of the stops. Men, women, and children of all sizes and ages had come out to do their part. The community had pulled itself together and had become closer as they all worked toward a common goal. *And it does look nice,* Sheriff Tom Myers noted.

Myers watched with amazement as the town's folk worked feverishly to finish up decorating the storefronts along Main Street. His mind drifted off to the plans he and his deputies had been making for decorating the police station. The deaths (*murders?*) over the last few months had caused them to put such trivial concerns like decorating on the back burner for the time being.

Nothing could scare off potential investors like a serial killer.

But was this really the work of a serial killer? Or were they simply unrelated incidents that did not fit together? Possibly, or maybe it only appeared on the surface as if they did. How many people must die for a murderer to become a serial killer?

Tom still wasn't convinced that the two deaths were the work of the same person. He could not be sure, but he refused to rule out the possibility that there was a maniac running loose in his town with malicious intent.

All Tom Myers knew with certainty was that two people were dead. That was all that was important. Hopefully, they were the first and last victims of a hypothetical serial killer. If only Tom or one of his men could find some clues, a suspect, or just something to go on. Unfortunately, there had been none. Things were not looking well for a quick resolution to the investigation.

And that was exactly the problem.

He and his people had been unable to make an arrest. There were no clues. No motives. No suspects. Then, without warning, the killing stopped. As suddenly as it had begun, it was over. The supposed killer (there never was any real proof to one individual committing the crimes) had apparently moved on, leaving the good people of Sommersville behind for good.

Or so Tom hoped.

Sheriff Myers was glad too. He had not relished the fact that the killer could have been someone from this town. Not this town. Everyone around these parts knew everyone else. Most he was on a first name basis with. Things like this were not supposed to happen in a peaceful place like Sommersville.

But it had happened and no matter how hard he had tried, Tom Myers could never forget the bodies. Their faces contorted into agonizing positions. Their frail bodies broken beyond all hope of repair. That was the only similarity between the two deaths. If one person had committed those horrible crimes, then he or she was an animal. No normal person could ever conceive of something like that, much less carry out the deed.

The thought of that memory brought forth a violent lurching in his stomach as the sheriff turned onto South Lumpkin Street, his office less than a mile away. As he pulled his old brown workhorse of a pick-up into the parking lot, he noticed three of his deputies running out of the side door.

"Sheriff!" one of the men yelled to him.

"What's the matter, Dooley?" he asked as he pulled the truck to a stop in front of the police station.

Benjamin Dooley was Tom's second in command. A real *go getter* in Tom's eyes. He had no doubt that Ben Dooley would be sheriff one day if he really wanted it. However, Tom had learned from past experience that Ben had no real desire to be the boss. It took some doing on Tom's part to get the man to accept the senior man position. Tom had come close to begging before Ben had finally accepted.

"Oh, Sheriff," Deputy Benjamin Dooley's face began to sink. "There's been another one."

"Another?..." Tom Myers started to ask, but the meaning behind Ben Dooley's words cut through his heart like a knife. "Damn."

"We're getting everything together now." Dooley said as he turned toward the other officers as they loaded up their own vehicles.

"Okay, Dooley," the sheriff said. He was in charge and had to be decisive. He informed the deputy, "I'll head on out to the crime scene. You supervise these guys and get your tails out there as quick as you can. Got it?"

"Yeah, Boss."

"Where was this one found?"

"Lake Greene." Dooley eyed his sheriff cautiously. Tom Myers was not usually quick to make a decision. The suddenness of the sheriff's orders took Deputy Dooley momentarily aback.

"Lake Greene?" Sheriff Myers echoed his deputies words.. "I was just out there. I drove past the Old Fort not ten or fifteen minutes ago. Where is the body?"

"By the inlet. Cross the walk bridge to the little island in the lake. Jackson is there already. He called it in."

"Thanks, Dooley. Let's get going." Myers started to pull off to the crime scene, but stopped suddenly, calling out to Dooley one more time. "And Dooley."

"Yeah?"

"Let's keep this as quiet as possible. For now." The sheriff knew that Dooley would understand. They all vividly remembered the panic that had gripped the town when the last victim's body had been found. It had not been a pretty sight. Neither Benjamin Dooley nor Tom Myers ever wanted to live through that kind of hell again.

It looked as though that choice had been taken out of their hands.

"Right," Deputy Benjamin Dooley answered. "Quiet."

"We don't need a scare now do we, Dooley?"

"No sir, Boss. We wouldn't want that would we?"

"No," Tom whispered. "No we wouldn't."

7.

It took nearly ten minutes for Tom Myers to get back over towards Lake Greene.

Upon his arrival the first thing Tom noticed was the old dirt road where the deputy's call had originated. He glanced around for any sign of Christopher Jackson, his deputy. He could find no trace of the man, save for where his all- terrain four wheel drive monster of a truck had barreled down the mud encrusted, pot hole filled dirt path which ran along the edge of Lake Greene. A small piece of yellow police line tape fluttered lazily in the breeze from a short stick that had been forcibly driven into the ground, f rom the look of it, probably by the rock lying next to it.

No doubt about it, this was the place. Reluctant to destroy his only mode of transportation, Sheriff Myers sighed, then after a few agonizing seconds of extreme decision making, carefully made his way down the bumpy path to the crime scene. The road was nearly as rough as he remembered from the last time he had come to the lake to go fishing. The rain from the past few nights had not done much to help the already poor condition of the small dirt road.

In actually it was little more than a narrow path, barely a road at all. It was used often enough as anyone could tell judging by the condition of it. Eventually, the County Forestry Commission had installed a chain over the entrance of the road to keep the people out, *"for safety reasons"* they said in a press release that was run in the local newspaper.

Suffice it to say that had not worked very well.

No, not very well at all.

The road was nearly impassable, the tires slamming into deep ruts at odd intervals, tossing the truck from side to side.

"Just what in the hell was Jackson doing out here in the first place?" the sheriff cursed loudly, slamming his fist down hard on the worn console of his police issue vehicle. Tom was keenly aware of how close to the edge of Lake Greene the small road was. He doubted it would take much for a vehicle to slide off into the lake. Another couple of bumps and finally Tom Myers had reached relatively flat ground. He glanced feverishly around for his deputy. His search was quickly rewarded when he caught sight of a red handkerchief being waved by a familiar figure a short distance away, near the far edge of the lake. Deputy Christopher Jackson Jr. waved down his boss and Tom automatically changed course to intercept.

Parking just off the cuff of the far end of Lake Greene, Sheriff Myers donned his brown hat, cautiously moving toward his deputy across the wet, muddy, and uneven surface. Deputy Jackson was standing there waiting for him with his hands stiffly planted on his hips. "The man has no patience," Sheriff Myers mumbled angrily to himself. "None whatsoever."

"Tom." The deputy addressed the sheriff as the older man crossed over to the crime scene. Totally ignoring titles, as is his usual custom, Christopher Jackson motioned for his boss to follow him into the woods. Myers nodded and the two men began trudging their way across the unsure, almost non-existent pathway. "This way, Tom," the young deputy said.

As he clambered along behind Deputy Jackson, Tom Myers noticed how peaceful the woods seemed at the early hour. He wondered why he had never paid attention to that fact before. The water from the previous night's rain had caused a certain sparkle to settle on the vibrant colors of the changing fall leaves. Finding any real clues in this mess would not be an easy task. Both men were aware of this, but they were required to go through the motions. The job demanded it of them.

After a few long moments of silent hiking, the two men found themselves approaching Potter's Ravine. Potter's Ravine was a tributary that ran off into the far end of Lake Greene. As a kid, Tom Myers and his friends spent many a summer's day playing in the Potter's Ravine. It was a place of wonder and discovery. They didn't know it then, but it was also very deadly. One of his childhood friends, name of Willy Jenkins had once slipped while trying to climb the edge of the Ravine. It was a terrible ordeal as the EMS and some of the locals worked to get little Willy out safely.

Willy now owned a video rental store in Sommersville. He managed to get on with his life, even though he lost the use of his legs that August morning those many years ago.

Tom made a point to stop in to see Willy every once in a while. They never talked about *it*. Although neither man would mention it, they both knew why Tom Myers made his visits. Both men knew full well that Tom felt responsible for what had happened to his friend. One of them could not forgive, while the other could not forget. Tom had been the one that dared Willy to climb the ledge that day. Willy hadn't wanted to do it, but Tom would not let it go. For as long as he lived, Tom Myers would never let himself forget that it was his fault.

Even though Willy and the Lord had found it in their hearts to forgive him, Tom could never forgive himself.

"Over here, Tom." Deputy Jackson's words snapped Tom Myers back to the present as they reached the small area near Potter's Ravine, which marked their final destination. The small white bridge across the lake stood out against the dark backdrop of the woods. The bridge and the area just on the opposite side of it had been cordoned off with the same police tape Deputy Jackson had used to mark the turn off. The tape was emblazoned with the words **POLICE LINE--DO NOT CROSS** on them. A black tarp had been placed over the body in the roped off area. The sheriff knew what to expect under the tarp. He had seen it before. He knew what horrors he would find, but it did not make it any easier to look. This was the part of the job that he hated most of all. Luckily, in a small town like Sommersville there were not many opportunities to handle those types of cases.

Dreading his duty, but not shirking from it, the sheriff quickly crossed the small foot bridge until he stood before the black tarp. Ducking under the roped off area Tom slowly, silently lifted up one edge of the cool black tarp. A small stench struck at him from beneath the covering. Tom felt his throat constrict. Suddenly, his senses were alerted to everything around him. He could feel the light dew on his fingers as he glanced at the body underneath. He could hear the insects with precise clarity. He could see every curve on the victim's face. It was a sight that would haunt Tom Myer's dreams for the next several nights. Maybe more. With effort he fought down the bile rising in his throat.

"My God!" he managed to get those words out before the bile reached his mouth. With no other recourse available, Tom made a run for a nearby tree and deposited everything he had eaten since last night violently onto the ground. He coughed once, then twice. It did not help.

"W-who could do such a thing?" he asked his deputy, not expecting an answer.

Not knowing what answer to give, Christopher Jackson simply shook his head. Truly, this was a sick thing to have happen to anyone. They have all seen it every evening on the six o'clock news and it bothered them, but they had learned to accept that things like that happened in the larger cities like Atlanta. It became a harder pill to swallow when it hit so close to home.

Too close to home in the sheriff's case. His house sat about five miles south of the far end of Lake Greene through the forest. Much too close. It could easily have been Mildred or any of his neighbors that live out close to the lake.

Something like this should not have happened. Not here. Not ever. Not in Sommersville.

"You okay Tom?" Deputy Jackson asked. He handed the sheriff a canned soda from his coat pocket. Obviously, he was saving it for later, but Tom easily accepted the offered can, popped the top, and downed half of it in one quick gulp. He could still taste the bile, but the drink helped a little, even though it was more warm than cool. The sheriff let out a long breath before nodding toward his Deputy.

"Thanks." He took another gulp of the warm soda, held it in his mouth, hoping to keep the sweet taste in his mouth. He swallowed, but the awful taste still lingered. "Do we have an ID on her yet?" He asked.

"Not yet." The deputy turned away from his boss. He knelt beside the broken body and neatly tucked the black tarp back into place, careful not to disturb any evidence. "She was just like this when I found her." He sighed heavily. Tom could hear the hurt in Jackson's voice Tom understood as well.

"You all right, Chris?" he asked. Jackson was not normally open with his feelings, but Tom could swear the younger man was on the verge of tears. It was so unlike the usually unflappable deputy.

"I'll be fine, Sheriff," the deputy answered uneasily. It was a half-truth at best. Myers noticed the use of his title instead of his first name which was a surprise coming from Chris Jackson. Tom decided not to press the subject. Truth be told, this was a little out of both their league.

The sheriff watched his deputy stare at the black tarp, almost as if he could stare through it at the broken body lying underneath. Chris Jackson's face was flushed. At that moment something clicked in Tom Myers mind. His deputy knew this young woman. He couldn't prove it, but Tom Myers was sure of it.

"Chris," he started to ask when the first of the squad cars rolled across the broken landscape into the Lake Greene area, red and blue strobe lights painting the crime scene.

Tom let the question drop, but both he and Chris Jackson knew that this was not the last either of them would speak of this incident.

"Sheriff?"

"Over here, fellas." Tom took a step back as his forensics squad moved into the crime scene, crossing the bridge one by one. He supervised their efforts from a respectable distance as the professionals did their jobs. Tom knew they were aware of their duties. The last thing they needed was someone watching over their shoulders, commenting on every slight move they made.

Sheriff Myers felt content merely to observe. He watched their progress with rapt attention to every detail the forensics team unearthed. Mentally, he filed each nuance for further investigation later. The image of the victim was not one that Tom thought he would ever forget.

The forensics team continued with their task even after the sheriff moved away from them. He dug around the pockets of his dirty brown jacket. Searching. "Dammit," Tom muttered as he made his way toward his truck. Reaching his ride, Tom Myers opened the passenger door and leaned inside. He began rooting through the clutter on the floor, the seat, and the console. Tom Myers was many things, but he had never been accused of being the neatest individual, as his wife could attest. Opening the glove box he finally found that which he sought.

Jackpot.

He pulled out the half empty pack of cigarettes. He had hidden them there from Mildred on the day he promised to give them up. "Just in case," he had told himself. "Just in case." Today was the day for *just in case*. Plus, the smell would cover the scent of the victim. Tom could still smell it lingering around him.

He started to root around again.

"Just my luck," he muttered to no one. "No freakin' lighter." He stood, stretching out the large knot in his back when he noticed one of his deputies indulging in the same bad habit that he himself so desperately wanted to. "Hey, Janetti!" he yelled to the deputy, startling him out of his reverie.

"Sir?" Theodore Janetti answered. The man had just enough of a hint of nervousness in his voice to allow Tom Myers to feel that he still had a little bit of power left at his command after all.

The sheriff stared directly at the man, his facial expression unwavering. "Bum a light?" he asked. Janetti nodded nervously and let out a sigh of relief at the same time. Pulling his lighter from a jacket pocket, Theodore Janetti tossed it gingerly through the air toward his boss.

It was a good catch by Tom Myers. He grabbed the lighter, cupped his hands, and used his thumb to flick the switch. The small blue flame ignited on the second try, and after a couple of quick puffs, the cigarette began to burn. Tom inhaled deeply, holding the smoke in a second before finally allowing the first puff to blow from his lips.

"God I've missed this," he said as he tossed the lighter back across the small distance to Deputy Janetti, who easily caught it and replaced it in his left pocket. Tom nodded, "Thanks, Janetti." He took a long drag off of the cigarette and the stress of the day began to roll out of him along with the smoke. It was all an illusion he understood, but at that moment he really couldn't care less.

The sound of a car horn caught his attention. A green Blazer bounced across the ruts in the path leading to the lakeside. Immediately, Tom Myers knew who had come to pay a visit and he did not like it.

Not one damned bit.

"Ah, shit," Myers mumbled. "Just what I need."

8.

"Damn. Just what I need," Myers said, dropping ashes onto the wet ground.

The water dissolved the ashes into gray mush around his shoes. Tom moved over to the front of his truck and leaned back lazily against the grill, his elbows propped on the hood behind him. There he stood and waited for the new arrival, a scowl firmly etched on his worn face.

The teal Blazer slowed to a halt near Myers. The driver was all too familiar to him, but the passenger appeared to Tom as if he had been holding on for dear life. After killing the engine, Franklin Palmer, local reporter and all around pain in the ass, stepped out of the Blazer and immediately made a beeline toward Sheriff Myers.

Palmer was well equipped. He had a camera, a notepad, and a pen out and ready. Previous experience told Tom that there was probably a micro cassette recorder in one of the reporter's pockets. The reporter, and Tom used the word loosely, was dressed in slacks and a nice shirt, but no tie. Tom remembered that Mr. Palmer had once mentioned how much he detested ties so he would only wear them at the office, funerals, or weddings (which Franklin, ever the eternal bachelor, laughingly referred to as a *stand-up funeral*).

A faded Atlanta Braves baseball cap and a Nascar jacket comprised the remainder of the younger man's attire. The reporter looked as laid back as they come, but once the man started working, there was no stopping him. And Heaven help anyone foolish enough to try and get in his way. If only more of Tom's deputies could be half as professional as Franklin Palmer.

Tom blew out a large plume of smoke before letting the cigarette fall to the ground where it sizzled upon impact. With his left boot he twisted the butt into the soft mud, burying it.

Seeing Franklin Palmer at a crime scene was not really a surprise for the sheriff. The surprise was in the fact that it has taken the man this long to find out about the crime and to make his way out to the scene. *Probably a mole in the department*, Myers suspected.

The reporter was very good at his job. The Sheriff respected that. He definitely understood it well enough.

"Thought you quit?" the reporter greeted him.

Myers ignored the comment. "Franklin," he started as the man moved over to stand beside him. "You are aware this is a cordoned off crime scene don't you?" He pointed back to the entrance that the man had driven over on his drive up. "That's what those little yellow tags that say 'police line do not cross' mean. You can read can't you, Palmer?"

The reporter simply smiled, regarding the sheriff with a toothy grin. "Nice to see you too, Tom."

The passenger finally stepped out of Palmer's Blazer and slowly walked over to where the sheriff and reporter were conversing. The newcomer silently took up position just behind Franklin Palmer. The stranger was dressed far more casually than the reporter, wearing jeans and a T-shirt with a fairly expensive black leather jacket. Tom noticed the bulge underneath the man's coat near his left arm. *Gun?* He wondered. *Or something else?* Best to keep an eye on the stranger.

Franklin held up a finger, motioning in the same direction that Tom had, toward the stream of yellow police tape. "Keep out? So that's what that means," he said sarcastically. "You know, I always had trouble with my reading. That's why I became a reporter. I don't have to use big words like 'cross.'" He tossed a sly wink at the sheriff, who tried to stifle a smile, but failed. Obviously this was some game the two men played. Harold had seen it before, had even played the role himself a time or two.

"So what's up, Tom?" Franklin asked as he stepped effortlessly into full professional mode, the snappy banter coming to an abrupt end.

"Dead girl in the woods." The answer was so simple and straightforward, almost clinical.

"Another one." Franklin feared he already knew the answer to that pronouncement.

"Afraid so." The sheriff's tone dropped an octave.

"Local girl?" Palmer asked.

"I don't think so," the sheriff answered.

The passenger spoke up at last. "How do you figure that, sheriff," he asked.

Tom Myers opened his mouth to answer then stopped. He pointed a large finger at the stranger. "And who exactly are you, Mister...?" he asked, fishing for a name.

The stranger reached slowly into his pocket and seconds later produced a wallet with an ID card inside. Holding the card up to the sheriff so he could make out all of the pertinent details the new arrival introduced himself. "Agent Harold Palmer. FBI." A brief pause. "A pleasure sheriff..."

"Myers," Tom answered.

"A pleasure to meet you, Sheriff Myers." Harold said.

"FBI?" Tom almost stumbled over the word as if he had never spoken it. "Who called you guys in?" Harold started to answer, but before he could open his mouth the answer dawned on the Sheriff. "Wait a minute! Palmer?" Tom crooked a thumb toward Franklin. "You related to this clown?" he asked Harold.

The FBI agent nodded. "'Fraid so. That clown's my baby brother."

Tom nodded in familiar understanding. "Ahhh," he said after a second.

Franklin did not get the joke. "Ahhh what?" He looked eagerly from one man to the other. The two men were sharing a joke at his expense and he didn't much care for it. "What's so damned funny?"

"Never mind, Ray," Harold said after a second. "I'll explain later, *little brother*." Then he tapped his younger brother on the head as if he were a prized pet.

Understanding suddenly dawned. Franklin got the joke. "That's not very funny," he said.

"Oh yes it is," Tom said. "Come on. I'll show you what we have. Follow me."

Slowly, the two brothers filed in after the sheriff of Sommersville into a scene that none of them would forget.

# # #

The two brothers followed Sheriff Myers across the moist landscape surrounding Lake Greene. Harold looked around quizzically, taking in every detail. "Nice place," he commented as they strode along. Tom simply grunted an agreement. He knew that this place of beauty, and the home of so many fond memories, would never be the same. He would never be able to look upon the crisp waters without thinking of the horrible sights that he had seen this day.

Nope, he thought. *Never again.*

"How much further, Tom?"

"Just over that rise and across the old foot bridge, Palmer," the sheriff pointed at something off to the left, away from the lake. "Careful. It's kinda slippery."

EVIL WAYS

As Franklin moved ahead, Myers got to know the vacationing FBI agent a little better. "So, what do you do for the Bureau?"

"Oh, I get around," Harold quipped modestly. "Currently, I bounce back and forth between a couple of task force teams."

"Which ones?"

"I'm on the Anti-Terrorist Unit and Violent Crimes."

Myers whistled. "Pretty tough work, I would assume."

"It has its moments," Harold said. "Before the terrorist attacks back in 2001, I spent very little time working the JTTF, the Joint Terrorism Task Force. These days, things are hopping. This is my first vacation in quite awhile."

"And this is how you choose to spend it?"

"Well, I came to see my brother so where he goes…" Harold gestured toward the younger Palmer on the other side of the foot bridge.

"Speaking of which," Myers interjected. "I guess we'd better get over there and see what's what. You, uh, are welcome to join us, of course. I'm open to anything you might have see or suspect."

"Thanks, Sheriff."

"Tom, please."

"And I'm Harold."

Before long the two of them joined the reporter at the crime scene. They were staring at the body, still concealed underneath the tarp. Several local police officers milled about as well as paramedics and a forensics team. Harold had witnessed similar sights many times over the eleven years he had put in with the Bureau. It was not a welcomed sight, but he had learned how to deal with it over time.

"Condition of the body?" Franklin asked, beginning his interview.

The sheriff lifted one corner of the black tarp, allowing the reporter to get a good look. Harold found, to his surprise, that he was impressed by his brother's reaction. Or lack thereof. The man was behaving like a professional. A far cry from the way baby brother Ray had acted in his youth. *Who'd a thunk it?* Harold mused.

Franklin leaned down, placing one knee in the wet mud around the body. He looked very closely at the position of the body, mentally noting placement of limbs, smells, sights, everything. He jotted down the detailed notes containing distinct information, filling his notebook with useful facts for use later on.

Franklin held his own like a trooper until he finished writing down his notes. At that point he looked like a man that was very nearly ready to toss his cookies. Harold Palmer had seen the look many times over, especially in rookie agents.

He placed a reassuring hand on his brother's shoulder. "You okay, Ray?" Harold asked.

"No," answered his younger brother. "Not all right. Not all right at all."

9.

Harold Palmer had worked over one hundred homicides in his career with the FBI.

He had seen things that would cause even the strongest of people to turn to jelly. Some sights chilled him to the very core of his being. Others merely made him nauseous. The grizzly scene at Lake Greene fell somewhere in the middle.

"Near as I can determine, the victim was beaten and tortured for at least three hours. Maybe as many as five. She was apparently raped, unless the attack happened after consensual sex," Harold offered as he and Sheriff Myers looked over the scene.

"No real way of knowing for sure," Myers added."

"She put up a strong fight from the look of things. Her body is covered with lacerations, some of which could only have come from rocks and tree bark. She ran through the woods before the end," Harold pointed to the dense foliage around Lake Greene. "But that was after she had been tortured, I'd bet."

Harold Palmer and Sheriff Myers moved away from the crime scene to allow the forensics team the room that they needed to conduct a thorough investigation. Franklin Palmer was allowed access and he chose to remain behind to take notes and observe. To his credit, he tried to stay an adequate distance out of the team's way.

"The way I see it, she escaped from whoever did this," Harold told Sheriff Myers. "Are there any houses or buildings within running or walking distance from here? Anyplace she could have been held for any length of time?"

Tom Myers pointed out across the lake at a large clump of trees. "I live a few miles on the opposite side of those trees. There are a few houses that run along that same street as mine. There is quite a bit of space between all of the houses."

"Space?"

"Pastures and fields. A horse farm. A couple of cow pastures." The sheriff pointed in a different direction toward where each would lie. "The rest are just houses and woods. We are pretty far out in the sticks here in Sommersville, Mr. Palmer." The sheriff motioned to the surrounding woodlands all about them. "See?" he said as if it made all the difference.

Harold scratched at his chin, not necessarily convinced. "How about on this side of the lake?"

"Nothing."

"Why not?" asked the confused FBI agent. "What's so special about this side of Lake Greene?" He motioned with his hands at the expanse of wooded area around where they stood.

Tom Myers made a sweeping gesture with his right hand out in an arc toward the woods. "This is part of a national park. The state owns and operates in this area." He paused a moment before adding, "No houses."

Tom stopped a moment to think. "However, there are a few utility sheds where the park service keeps their equipment locked up, but they are on the far side of the park. Nowhere near us. Sorry."

Harold let out a deep breath. "Damn. I was hoping we could track her path before the moment of her death, but the rain has made that virtually impossible."

"I know," Tom agreed. "I've had my men do a sweep of the woods, but whatever tracks might have been made has been washed away with the morning's rain. That puts the murder at sometime after midnight as best I can tell."

"I'd have to agree," Harold answered.

"So do I."

Deputy Chris Jackson walked up next to the two men. "We're ready to move her out now, Sheriff." A beat passed between the two officers. Then two. "We'll start wrapping this up as soon as forensics is finished."

"Okay," the sheriff said, his eyes transfixed on his deputy. "Why don't you head on home for awhile, Chris. Let Dooley and Janetti handle the wrap up. Get some rest and we'll talk later."

Deputy Jackson protested. "If it is all the same to you, Tom, I'd rather stay and finish this." He stood stock still waiting for his next order, his eyes never connecting with those of the sheriff.

"It is all the same to me, Chris." Tom made a motion with his thumb, pointing over his shoulder, motioning toward the deputy's car. "Go home. Dooley can finish up."

"But..."

"Chris. Go. Home. I'll stop by after we've finished up here." The sheriff's tone was steady and unwavering. It was plain to see that the deputy wanted to argue his point further, but thought better of it and surrendered to the older man's authority.

"Alright," he agreed, albeit reluctantly. "Call me if you need me, Tom." He turned to regard Harold. "Nice to meet you Mr. Palmer."

Harold nodded at the deputy then gave his offered hand a firm shake. Then, Christopher Jackson turned on his heel and headed off toward his police car. He was not happy about this latest turn of events. Eventually, Deputy Jackson was driving away from Lake Greene. Bound for his apartment in Sommersville.

"He going to be alright?" Harold asked, trying not to pry too deeply.

Tom watched as his deputy turned onto the main highway. The car disappeared from sight as soon as the traffic allowed him to turn safely. "I hope so. He's the one that found the body this morning. He's pretty shook up about it. I thought it best if he put a little distance between himself and this crime scene."

"He almost seems to be taking this personally," Harold noted to the sheriff.

The sheriff did not answer. He just stared after his deputy. Too far out of sight now to see. Gone.

"Harry?" The voice calling his name belonged to Franklin Palmer.

Harold turned away from the sheriff and watched as his younger brother approached. Behind him, the body of the woman was being taken away to the coroner's office and an autopsy. "You find something, Ray?"

"Nothing the forensic boys didn't already find." The younger Palmer said, moving into position between his brother and Tom Myers. "How do you want to play this one, Tom?"

"How long can you keep this out of the papers, Franklin? I'd like to find out who this girl is… was… before we make it common knowledge. I want to find her family first."

"Okay," Franklin agreed. "It's not too late to get it in the Sunday edition, but I'll put this off until the Wednesday edition. By then, I have to print something or people will think we're covering something up."

"Which we are, by the way."

A moment passed between them.

"Thanks, Palmer. I owe you one." Tom said, stumbled over the unpleasant words. Apparently the two men had a love/hate relationship that Harold was having trouble pinning down. "Hopefully we can catch this guy before anyone else gets hurt."

"Ray?"

Franklin held up a finger to stop Harold's next question. "And I will of course be kept up to date on everything you find until then won't I, Tom?"

Tom Myers physically seemed to droop. "Of course. Come by in the morning and I'll let you have a look at the coroner's notes. Deal?"

"Deal." Franklin smiled. He was insufferably proud of himself, which only seemed to irritate the sheriff further.

Myers turned around, ready to leave when he stopped. The sheriff turned back toward the reporter. "By the way," he said, pointing a finger toward Harold. "Why does he keep calling you Ray?"

Harold let a small chuckle escape. Franklin winced. "Nickname of sorts," Franklin started.

"It's his middle name," Harold said straight out, amused that his brother made a big deal out of such a small insignificant thing. "He really hates it."

"Really?" Tom Myers cracked a wicked grin.

"Now wait just a minute," Franklin interjected, but his protests were completely ignored by the two older men. He suddenly felt very outnumbered.

"I started calling him that when we were just kids," Harold continued, ignoring the glare boring into him from his brother's eyes. "I guess it kind of stuck." Harold reached out a hand to the sheriff, who shook it warmly. "It was nice to have met you, Sheriff," Harold Palmer said.

"You too Mr. Palmer." Tom began to leave. "I'll see you tomorrow, *Ray*," he called back over his shoulder, making sure to enunciate the name.

Harold chuckled under his breath.

Franklin felt his teeth grind together.

"Nice guy," Harold said.

Franklin said nothing. He just stood in silence, fuming.

10.

The sky burned a crimson red as twilight encroached.

All around the small community of Sommersville, GA lights came on as automatic systems kicked in and shop owners prepared themselves for the evening business rush. The town sprung to life as the school kids hit the streets. This was their time. The streets of Sommersville belonged to them after the sun retreated beyond the horizon.

All along Main Street banners were in place for the Autumn Festival. It was the one big celebration that this town threw every year. People from all around flocked to the city as streets were cordoned off and vendors and craft makers set up their respective booths. It was an event for the whole family. A day when everyone forgot all of the normal day to day problems and took time to enjoy the splendor of their beautiful city and meet and greet with one another. It was a time of reunions and introductions. Friends, family, neighbors, loved ones, and even the most bitter of enemies were brought together as one community for one day each year.

It was a festive time.

Dr. Billy Connelly pulled his new Ford Mustang onto Main Street. The town was just as he had remembered it. Nothing much changed in Sommersville. Billy had lived here. He had grown up in this place. He had gone to school here. Had his first date here. Had his first party here. His first kiss, first sexual experience, first… everything. Well, almost his first everything. He'd had his whole life molded here.

Sommersville was a good place to be a kid.

After High School however, Billy knew that he had to move on.

College beckoned and he enrolled at the nearby University of Georgia in Athens as his mother had wanted. She had been so proud of him. While attending UGA, he discovered that he had a penchant for medicine. That was the start of a long and arduous road for William Connelly. Medical School followed College, which led to a residency in an emergency room in Miami, Florida.

For four long years he had toiled in the ER, working feverishly while continuing his education. Long days and low pay were the norm, but the experiences he learned in that short period of time would stay with him for the rest of his days. He wouldn't want to relive them, but he wouldn't trade the experience for anything in the world.

Just a little over a year ago, he was offered a chance to join a private practice in Miami. A very well known and respected practice at that. It was the chance of a lifetime and he jumped at it. His years of training and dedication were paying off at last.

Then the letter came

He immediately felt his gut tighten when he received the plain white envelope a month ago. It was from someone in his old hometown of Sommersville. The return address had a familiar name on it, Leo Brand. It took Billy about three seconds to place where he knew it from after he opened the letter. Leo had been a person that Billy had vaguely known growing up. Leo was class president his senior year of high school. A letter from the former class president could only mean one thing.

SOMMERSVILLE HIGH CLASS OF 2002 10 YEAR ANNIVERSARY.

A lump caught in his throat.

He looked at it many times over the weeks following its arrival. *Had it really been ten years? Time truly does fly by, doesn't it? Ten years. Where did they go?* He had even considered not going, but there were people Billy had wanted to see again after all the years. That was when he stumbled upon an idea to make the drudgery of a high school reunion more bearable. He would get the old gang back together a little early and they could spend some quality time together. A chance to catch up on one another's lives.

Pulling into town was like driving into the past. All of the old memories began to bubble back to the surface. "It's like I never left," he whispered to himself. "Like I've been here forever."

Billy Connelly bid a fond farewell to Sommersville about eight years earlier. The day of his mother's funeral in fact. He had come home to visit from College, but he had been too late to say his final goodbyes. After her funeral, Billy left Sommersville with a promise never again to return. "Never again," he had said repeatedly. And at the time he had meant it, every word.

However, never turned out to not be such a long time. Time healed all wounds.

Or so the cliché said.

While time did heal all wounds, Billy wasn't quite there yet.

At least time had served to lessen the sting of those wounds.

Plus, he hadn't seen many of those people in ten years. It would be good to get together and catch up on the good old days.

The traffic signal flashed from red to green and he moved on with the other four vehicles in his lane, his being the newest of them. *Probably cost more than any two of them combined,* he assumed and the thought made him feel good.

He drove on through the town that had once been his home. Passing the bank building where he opened his first checking account. He saw the old Mom & Pop grocery store where he had gotten his first job. *Out with the old, in with the new.* It was still there, sort of. The building remained, only now it housed a DVD and video rental shop instead of a grocery store. He noticed the fire station across from the video store. That hadn't been there the last time he visited home.

Home.

Funny for a man that had been away for so long to think of it in those terms, but the past oftentimes had an ability to grab hold of a person in ways that they could not even begin to understand. It grabbed on tight, refusing to let go no matter how hard a person tried to fight it.

He spared a quick glance down a side street toward Doc McNalley's office. Billy made a mental note to stop in and see how his old friend had been faring. The doctor had been a great motivator for a young Billy Connelly when he had finally decided that medical school was the way to go for him.

Gotta stop in and pay my respects tomorrow, Billy told himself. *So much to do and no time to do it in. Same old story.*

Passing the courthouse, the newspaper office, and restaurant row, Billy caught a glimpse of a hotel off to his right. "That's new too," he whispered. "The place is actually growing. Who would've thought?" He suppressed a laugh.

He had considered staying at his mother's old house, but he just couldn't work up the courage to do so. Too many memories surrounded that old place. Those memories were waiting for him and he could not, would not, dare to face them now. He made a promise to himself to stop by on this trip.

Besides, he decided. *The place is probably falling apart. No one has lived there for years.*

He couldn't say why he never sold the place. After all, there had been many offers to buy it. Good offers, too. Some more generous than others. Somehow, it had just not seemed right. That was his *Mom's house.* He could not bring himself to sell it. Not even when he had been struggling to make ends meet during medical school. Maybe the time had come at last to put the ghosts to rest and let go of the past. *Maybe.*

Gunning the engine on his finely tuned feat of American engineering, he pulled his new car into the hotel parking lot, and found a space near the far wall away from the usual traffic. The last thing he wanted was to risk banging up his new toy.

He looked to the sky. "Looks like rain," he muttered. Quickly, he got out and started walking toward the entrance at a brisk pace, taking only a brief second to turn on his car alarm with a shrill *beep*. It had become a habit for him to do so, but here in Sommersville it almost seemed ridiculous. *What kind of crime happened in Sommersville, Georgia after all?*

"Hi." The young desk clerk announced as she greeted him with a smile when he stepped up to the main desk. "May I help you sir?" She asked in a liltingly sweet voice.

"I'm Doctor William Connelly," he told her, trying to be as professional as possible. The desk clerk did not look overly impressed. He could not blame her really. He wouldn't have been impressed with him at her age either. "I believe I have a reservation," he said.

Dr. Connelly watched as she began tapping away at the computer keyboard. He couldn't help but notice how cute the teenager was, but he tried to push those thoughts away. She quickly typed in his name on the reservation computer. "Yes sir, Dr. Connelly. You are in room 312." The young brunette pointed off to her left. Billy turned to follow her gesture. "Elevators are right over there, sir. And here is your key, sir." She handed him a flat piece of plastic akin to a credit card. "Just slide it in the door and it will automatically unlock for you."

"Thank you," he said as he retrieved the offered key card, not bothering to mention that this was not the first hotel he had ever been a guest of.

"Room service is available until ten p.m. If you need anything, just call the front desk. Do you need someone to collect your luggage for you, sir?" She asked, still smiling and flashing her pearly white teeth.

"Thank you very much," he said with a polite nod of his own. "I'm in the Mustang out near the wall." He tossed her the keys. "Make sure I get those back okay?"

"Yes, sir," she said. "Enjoy your stay, Dr. Connelly." She smiled again. Very polite. He didn't think that people, especially kids still knew how to be that polite. He blushed when he realized how old that stray thought made him feel. Not so very long ago he had been her age. When had he become… gasp… *an adult?*

He jotted down a mental note to leave her a nice tip and perhaps a good comment about her with the hotel's manager. *Professionalism should always be rewarded,* his mother had always said. She could be very profound when she wanted to be.

"I hope so," he answered, knowing that there was absolutely no way that she could know why he was here, but she could probably hazard a guess. He spied a few familiar faces in the lobby, but no one that he knew really well back in his high school days. He tossed a casual wave at a few of the more familiar faces as he passed by on his way to the elevators. He had only a small handful of friends back then. It made keeping in touch easier. At least in theory.

They had not kept up on their promises of keeping in touch with one another very well. There was always something that managed to get in the way. Work, school, families, careers, and… other things tended to occupy ones time. Billy knew this from first hand experience. There was always just one more thing to do before…

"It will be good to see the old gang again," he thought. He had made several phone calls over the past few days, planning, preparing, and making sure that everything would be perfect for this weekend. The whole gang would be at the reunion. A few of them had even said that they could get into town early and spend a little time together. Just like the old days.

The elevator opened seconds after he depressed the **'up'** button. He stepped inside, pressing the appropriate floor. Feeling the subtle vibrations of the elevator car told him that it was moving steadily up the shaft toward its final destination on the third floor.

A loud *PING* announced his arrival as the door slid open and he stepped out into the hallway. "Three twelve," he mumbled, looking for his room. "Ahh," he said, finding the correct spot. Swiping his key card, Dr. Connelly opened the door to his room and stepped inside carrying his one small bag.

Dropping down on the large, bed Billy Connelly took in a deep, cleansing breath. It had been such a long trip. It would have been a lot quicker if only he had flown, but the good doctor was not too keen on flying. "My mother once told me that only two things fall out of the sky," he had told his assistant when she had suggested that he fly out as opposed to driving. "Bird shit and fools. I'm neither." They had shared a laugh at that one. Reluctantly, he canceled his flight plans and he drove up from Miami to the sleepy little town of Sommersville.

A straight eighteen hours of driving had taken its toll and the young physician was soon fast asleep. The sound of the falling rain had undoubtedly had a hand in putting him under so quickly. The rhythm of the rainwater tapping on the windows had always had that affect on him. *Good, I could use the rest.* Unfortunately, the bellhop's knock at the door ended his brief rest a mere ten minutes later. "Timing was everything," he groused as he crossed the darkened room.

After collecting his belongings and making sure to retrieve his car keys, Billy tipped the young man generously. Then, Dr. Connelly allowed himself to drift off to dreamland once again. There would be plenty of time to unpack, do a little sightseeing, and talk about old times in the morning.

After all, he had all weekend.

All the time in the world.

11.

All Harold Palmer wanted to do was spend some quality time with his brother.

Was that so wrong? He wondered. *Obviously so.*

Not wanting to spend the evening alone at Ray's home in the country, Harold volunteered to accompany the intrepid reporter back to his office to catch up on the day's work. Plus, he was kind of curious as to what his brother did for a living, so he happily followed. Later, he realized how much work his sibling actually put in and he was impressed despite himself. There were reports to be filed, copy to typed, proofed, and corrected.

After that, Franklin spent time editing stories submitted by his freelancers, he called them "copy," to fit the space allotted.

When the copy was all typed and proofed, Ray sifted through small stacks of photos to find the shot that most vividly portrayed the essence of the article he was working on. He scanned in the picture, cropped and pasted it in place on the computer. He had mentioned to Harold several times during the course of the evening that before he could afford the computer he had been forced to do the process by hand. A process that took far longer. Harold wondered how anyone could stand it. "A little tedious, isn't it?" he asked.

"A bit, but you get used to it," Franklin said as he printed out a hard copy to proof. "Luckily, I found a job I love. I guess I can finally understand you a little better."

"How so?"

"Well, I always wondered why you loved your job so much. It's almost as if the danger of it never fazes you. I could never understand that."

"And now?"

"I have a little better idea. I mean, I can't really compare our jobs too closely, but I think we both love what we do."

"Yeah. I do love my job, Ray. But you're wrong about one thing."

"Oh?"

"I am constantly aware of the dangerous nature of my job," Harold said, suddenly interested in looking at the cracks in the floor. "I've never told her, but my biggest fear is that one day Carter, or someone else from the Bureau will knock on my door one day and have to tell Beverly that her husband is dead. Or try to explain to Lucy that her Daddy is never coming back. That's what keeps me awake at night, Ray."

"And I was just worried about bullets hurtling by your head in the middle of a dark alley."

Harold laughed.

"So," he said, changing the subject while stretching out the kink in his back. "Explain to me what you're doing here."

Franklin launched into a lengthy explanation of page layout, ad sales, and a lot of other technical terms Harold would be hard pressed to remember come morning. Still, as routine as his baby brother's job seemed he was impressed, maybe even a little envious.

Franklin was doing what he wanted with his life. Sure, things weren't easy. The good things seldom were, but Harold could see a gleam in his brother's eye when he worked. No matter how much Franklin complained about the amount of work he had or the money problems he dealt with, he wouldn't give up his dream.

Harold just sat quietly out of the way and let his brother do his thing. Eventually, the elder Palmer dozed off into peaceful sleep on a small couch in the office.

It would be shortly after midnight before Franklin would wake him to return home.

By the time he woke, it had begun to rain.

12.

"Come in."

Tom Myers slowly opened the door to Deputy Chris Jackson's tiny apartment.

Making sure to shake off the rainwater from his brown uniform jacket beforehand, he stepped inside. The door, to Tom's surprise, was unlocked. Inside, the place looked very much like what a bachelor's place should look like. Empty pizza boxes were stacked on the small round table in the kitchenette. A pile of dishes threatened to fall off of the counter top into the sink and the floor. Three, maybe four days worth of dishes waited to be cleaned and put away. Clothes were strewn about the place, haphazardly. A trashcan was overturned, its contents scattered across the kitchen. His oak bookcase sat empty, the contents of which having been slung from one end of the room to the other.

Chris Jackson had thrown one hell of a tantrum.

Chris was sitting, slumping actually, in a comfortable looking reclining chair in the middle of the living room, situated in front of a small coffee table and a television set which was not on. The deputy was still wearing his muddy uniform. The shirt had been unbuttoned to reveal his white T-shirt beneath. It hardly resembled anything remotely like a police officer's uniform. He had a beer in his hand. A six pack sitting in a bucket of ice next to his chair with five other bottles lying scattered about the living room around him. This was not the Chris Jackson that Tom Myers had come to know during the last eight years. That Chris Jackson had been neat and tidy. He would never have allowed his living area to become this cluttered, this unlivable.

"Chris?" Tom stepped slowly into the apartment and closed the door gently behind him. Not that Chris would have heard it even had he slammed it. Over in a corner the CD player was belting out old blues tunes. Clarence Carter blared loudly. Very loud.

"Your neighbors are complaining about the noise," the sheriff said comically, hoping to ease the young man's tension. "You'd hate for them to have to call the cops, wouldn't you?" Chris just tossed an uninterested look in his direction as if he had just noticed the man in his apartment, then he took another large swig of beer.

Setting his jaw, Tom took a step past his deputy, moving over to the CD player. With the tap of a button, the small room fell quickly into a deep silence, the only audible sound was that of the light rain hitting the roof of the apartment complex.

"Chris?"

"I really needed that," the younger man said, wavering. "It helps drown out everything else. I need that right now, y'know?" His lower lip was trembling, Tom noticed.

"I can sympathize, Chris," Tom said as he moved close to his deputy. "Believe me. I can sympathize." Chris did not answer. He simply stared off into nothing. "Are you okay?" This time Tom asked with a touch more force.

"No."

An honest answer.

Tom knelt down on the floor to Chris Jackson's left. He let his hands fall on the arm rest of the recliner. "The landlord told me that you had him hold onto your gun. You weren't planning on doing anything rash were you?" Chris downed another swallow of his beer, finishing it off.

"I hadn't planned on it," Chris answered, straining for every word. "Just a precaution." He paused, examining the bottle of beer in his hand. "You never know."

"Good thinking, pal." Tom sucked in a lung full of air. It smelled rancid, a mix of beer and leftover food at least three days old. Something was terribly wrong with the picture. Dead wrong. Tom stared into the face of his comrade in arms. Hating himself for broaching a painful subject, Tom had to ask. From the look in Chris Jackson's eye, he understood what was about to happen. He simply nodded in his bosses' general direction.

"I couldn't help but notice something earlier." Tom said at last, searching for the right words. "You knew that girl we found today, didn't you?"

"Yes." A single tear began to flow down the right side of Chris' ebony face. Tom could tell that was not the first tear to leave his deputy's eyes since he left the crime scene.

"I need to know, Chris." Tom searched for something in his friend's face, clarity perhaps. Maybe for a sign. Tom, himself had only a vague idea of what he was looking for.

Answers. I need answers.

EVIL WAYS

"Sit down, Tom," Chris said, pointing toward his couch across the room from the recliner. It was covered with old magazines and a small pile of clothing. No room to sit. Tom politely declined the offered seat. He did, however, take a seat on the edge of the nearby coffee table. Right in front of Deputy Jackson where they could look at one another. Eye to eye. Face to face. Man to man. Friend to friend.

Chris simply reached for another beer. "Mind if I have one of those?" Tom asked, reaching out with his right hand. "I think I'm going to need it."

Chris handed his boss a beer. It was good and cold. Just the way Tom liked them, although it had been some time since his last one. Mildred had asked him to quit and he had agreed to try. He twisted the top off then took a large gulp. It felt good going down. He looked at Chris Jackson. "Well?" he asked.

Chris downed a small swallow of his beer. He leaned forward in his chair and stared at his boss, almost staring through him as if he were not even in the room. "I did know that girl," he said at last. "She told me her name was Rebecca Thompson, but I don't know if that is her real name or not. Part of me had hoped that it was." Tom leaned back slowly, giving the man a little space. Space to sort out the details of his time with the victim.

"Why wouldn't she tell you her real name?"

Chris did not acknowledge the question. He simply continued with his story. "I met her out at Thunderbird's a few weeks ago." Another tear welled up in the corner of his eye. "I watched her dance and the world around me melted away. She was the be all and end all of my universe. I stood there and watched her, transfixed by her beauty as she swayed and moved to the music. The music seemed to pulse through her. My God, Tom, I think I was in love with this woman." A heartbeat passed, then another. "Well, at the very least, I was in lust."

"What happened, Chris?" Tom downed the remainder of his beer and gently placed the bottle on the coffee table beside him. "What next?"

Chris Jackson's eyes were glazed over, deep in cherished memory. "What happened next?" he repeated Tom's question. "What happened next was the hottest night of sex I have ever had in my entire life. That girl could have walked out of that bar with anyone in the room, but she left with me. Me! We came back here and she stayed the night and the next day. I meant to thank you for scheduling me that Sunday off, but I never did get around to it. Sorry."

"That's all right. I'm glad it worked out for you. Go on."

"I went back and watched her dance five more times since that night. And every time we ended up here. She said that she had never met anyone like me. She told me that I made her feel special." Another tear escaped from his eyes. "She made me feel alive. More alive than I have in a long time."

Tom let out a breath. "Why didn't you tell me this earlier, Chris? I could've helped. Or at least been there for you." Tom hesitated for a brief second. "I mean, you are my friend, man. You know I'll help if I can."

"I know. Thanks." He took another drink from the bottle. "I appreciate that."

Tom stared at his deputy. "Do you know anything that might affect the investigation? Anything at all? Even if it doesn't seem all that important."

Chris sniffled, then wiped his nose with his shirtsleeve. Shaking his head, the deputy uttered a nearly incomprehensible sound.

"No."

"Okay, Chris. Okay. I'm going to request that you take some time off and get your head on straight. All right? And by *request*, I mean *a direct order*."

Tom hoped the younger man got the message, but deep down he knew that he wouldn't. If it had been Mildred, Tom wouldn't have backed down either. How could he expect Chris Jackson do any less?

"Tom," Chris said. "I've got to see this thing through. She des...I owe it to her memory to find out who did this. Don't take me off of this, Tom. Please." The younger man was literally begging for Tom's approval. "Please," he repeated.

Tom set his jaw. "Okay, but I don't want you doing anything stupid. I'll keep you in the loop, but not as an active participant in the investigation. You are a bit to close to this." Tom took a deep breath. Chris simply stared at him in silence. "Chris, this is very serious. Don't turn into Bruce Willis or John Wayne and I'll keep you in on this. Understood?"

Chris nodded. He understood.

"Now, listen to me," Tom said. "If I see that you are having problems with this then I will personally pull you off of the schedule for a slight vacation. I don't want to, but I will. If that doesn't work, then I'll lock your ass in the jail until we get things settled. I want you to understand that very well, Chris. I have to know that I am getting through to you. Understood?"

"Understood."

"Good." Tom stood and moved off toward the door. "Get yourself cleaned up. I want you in my office at eight a.m. tomorrow morning. Now get some rest, you look like hell."

"I feel like it, too."

Tom opened the door and stepped out into the hallway.

Before the door closed, Tom could hear Chris say, "Thank you." Tom decided not to answer. He closed the door quietly behind him. Once he was alone in the hallway the sheriff allowed himself a second to let out a heavy sigh.

He turned and looked at the door to Chris Jackson's apartment, hoping that he had not just made a huge mistake. "You're welcome," he said to the man on the opposite side of the door.

Inside, Chris Jackson could not hear the sheriff's parting comment. All he could hear was the rapid beating of his lonely, broken heart.

Slowly, Sheriff Tom Myers made his way down the short flight of stairs from the second floor to the main foyer of Chris Jackson's apartment building. The landlord stepped out of his apartment near the bottom of the stairwell as Tom approached. The man had heard the footsteps echoing down the stairwell. Tom saw him and walked over to explain that things were under control.

"How is he?" the landlord asked. He seemed genuinely concerned for his tenant.

Tom forced a smile he did not feel. "I think he'll be fine. He just had a very traumatic day. After he gets some rest I'm sure he'll be back to normal."

"Thank God," the landlord said. "I was beginning to worry about him."

"So was I. Thank you for calling me when you did."

"No problem, Sheriff. What shall I do with this?" the landlord asked, pulling out the deputy's service revolver and handing it toward Tom, butt first.

Tom accepted the gun from him. "I'll take it. In the morning when he gets ready to leave tell him I have it at the office. He can get it after he starts his shift."

"Oh, yeah," the landlord said. He reached into his pocket and pulled out a handful of bullets. "I unloaded it when he gave it to me. Here are the bullets." The landlord poured the bullets into Tom's outstretched hand.

Tom thanked the man again and bid him a good night.

"Yes sir, Sheriff. I'll give Deputy Jackson your message." The landlord waved as Tom walked out of the foyer. Tom adjusted his hat before venturing once again into the rain. "Good night, Sheriff," the landlord called. "Give Mildred my best."

Tom waved back as he climbed into his pick up truck. "Will do. G'night."

Above, Deputy Chris Jackson watched as the sheriff drove his pickup out into the rain. The man was probably on his way home. The rain was starting to fall harder and harder as Chris stared out the window into the cold chill of the night.

He was still staring long after Tom Myers was out of sight.

13.

The rain finally stopped.

With the first rays of sunlight, Sommersville, Georgia began to pull itself out from under the gloominess of a week of constant rain. Tom Myers had overslept, which usually signified the beginning of the inevitable *shitty day* domino effect that would no doubt spiral downhill for the rest of the day.

Still, the sheriff of Sommersville wearily climbed, more appropriately, rolled out of bed and groped in the darkness until he found himself in the master bathroom. A quick shower and a shave later, not necessarily in that order, and Tom Myers was nearly ready to face the day. He could smell the sweet aroma coming from the kitchen as he dressed, which prompted him to speed things along. Twenty years of marriage and his wife, Mildred, still found the energy to get up every morning to make him a feast of a meal to start his day off right.

He offered her a smile as he entered the small kitchen area. First pouring himself a cup of coffee, then Tom poured one for her as well. He kissed her gently on the back of the neck as he placed her steaming cup of coffee on the counter next to her.

"'Morning Dear," he said. "Sleep well?"

"Um-Hmmm." Her grunt of an answer informed him that the conversation of last evening had only recessed and was ready to reconvene.

Uh oh.

"Tom," she started, turning to face him.

He stopped her short by holding up his hands in front of her. A peace offering of sorts. *A truce.* "Honey. I know that I, we, both of us, said a few things last night that we might regret. I'm sorry." He tried to force a smile from her, but failed. "How about this. I'll seriously think about what we talked about. I will. I promise. I'll even make a few calls and find out some information. Then we'll talk about it." He looked at her face. It was unreadable. *Is she thinking it over?* "Honey?" he questioned.

"Okay Tom," she answered at last. "We'll talk about it later. I know

you have a busy day ahead of you. I won't press the matter. For now."
She moved from the stove to the kitchen table with Tom's breakfast,
carefully placing it in front of him. "Eat," she said, a small smile
creeping onto her face.

Tom picked up his fork and tore into the breakfast. "It's delicious," he
tried to say between bites. She nodded at his unintelligible mumble. He
hoped that meant she understood what he had just said. After all these
years together, he seemed satisfied that she could understand his
mumbled sounds as if he had spoken clearly.

Quickly finishing off the last of the breakfast and a second cup of
hot coffee, Tom grabbed his uniform jacket and thermos, which he was
sure held a few extra cups of Mildred's phenomenal coffee. *The woman
should market the stuff.* As he passed Mildred on the way to the door, he
stopped to give her the standard kiss goodbye on the cheek as he did
every morning. He pulled back and looked at the woman before him as if
had never really looked at her before. *The love of my life,* he thought. He
kissed her again, more passionately this time. The office would have to
wait just a few minutes longer for his arrival.

"I love you honey," he said to her and meant it. She knew it. They
had been married too long for her not to know how Tom felt about her,
even if he sometimes had trouble saying it. Or showing it.

"I love you too, Tom." Mildred pulled herself away from her
husband's embrace, using the back of her hand to wipe her mouth.
"Even if you are a stubborn pain in the ass."

"I thought you liked my stubborn streak?"

"Only when it works for me, not against me."

Tom smiled.

"Don't you have to go to work?" Mildred asked, giving him a big
smile. His heart ignited at the sight of it.

"Screw 'em," he said half jokingly. "Maybe I can take the day off.
Hell, why not the whole week. We can lounge around here for a day or
two. Maybe take a trip. What do you say, honey?"

Her face fell again. "You know we can't do that. We have
responsibilities. Besides, our problems will still be here waiting on us
when we get back. You know that as well as I do. We'd only be putting
off the inevitable."

"I know honey," Tom stammered. "But there has to be another way.
There has to be." He searched her eyes for understanding. It just was not
there for him this time. Tom let out a heavy sigh. "I've got to go to
work," he said, his voice near to cracking. "I've really got to go."

EVIL WAYS

And then he was gone.

Duty calls.

After pulling out of his driveway, Tom began his daily trek into Sommersville. For some unknown reason he decided to pass up on the usual visit to the Johnson farm. He simply waved as he passed by. The elderly couple returned the wave and kept right on with their morning chore. They were already out in their large yard, busily working in Mrs. Johnson's flower garden. Tom could imagine himself and Mildred doing things like that after they retire. Unless of course, Mildred got her way in the little argument they had been having for the past few weeks. He decided to make an effort to stop by and talk with the Johnson's on his way home in the evening.

Right now the sheriff had other thoughts to occupy him. Those thoughts were mostly of Mildred, of course. She could be mean as a hornet one second and the most loving woman in the world the next. How could she, a woman that professed to love him, want him to give up his family's land? She had to know how important it was for him to hold onto the one thing that his father had managed to own in his all too short life. The man had worked himself to death to provide a place for his family, something the Myers family could call their own. A legacy that Tom Myers simply could not imagine living without. He could foresee no reason, any reason at all, to ever sell the land.

Still, he had told Mildred that he would think about it. And he could not lie to her. It was just that he could never bring himself to even try. That was one of the promises he had made to himself when he married her twenty years earlier. To love, honor, cherish, and not to lie to. That about summed it all up.

The Myers property spanned twenty-two acres of some of the prettiest green fields that Tom had ever seen in his entire life. Not to mention the small lake in the center of the property fed by a small stream. Over the years Tom had drowned many a worm out there. He never caught much, but just being out there was calming in a way that he could not readily explain. It was almost as if his father's spirit lived on in the lake, as ridiculous as that might sound.

How could he think of getting rid of that? It was impossible. He had hoped to one day have a child of his own that could roam free on that land as he had done during his formative years. An heir to pass the hallowed land to. He hoped for it still, no matter what the doctor's had said about their chances. Tom Myers was a man who believed in miracles even though he could not always see them.

But he knew they happened. They had to.

It all stemmed from his faith and belief in the Almighty. Miracles came along with God and he had been known to work in mysterious ways. Mildred served as his anchor to that faith. If not for her, Tom realized, he would probably never have seen the inside of a church, much less become a Christian and church member.

Tom had doubts that his marriage could have lasted twenty years without that faith. Certainly, he never would have given up his drinking without the help of Mildred and his new "family" from the church. They had camped out at his home during the worst of the withdrawal pains. They had prayed for (and with) him, helped him, cared for him, and they had loved him. Eventually, the struggle was won. Tom was able to crawl out of the bottle and get his life flowing in the right direction. Sobriety had made him a better man, a better husband, and a better sheriff. Tom fully believed God had smiled down on him.

Who would've thought it, Tom had said on numerous occasions.

A younger Tom would have laughed out loud if someone had told him how his life would turn out. He would have laughed long and hard at that one. But, there he was. There was no denying that the biggest miracle of Tom's life was at this moment washing up his breakfast dishes. *The love of my life.*

The Johnson's returned his wave as he passed by. Doubtless, they would assume that he was just too busy to stop, which was true enough. Preparations for the Autumn Festival and the accommodations for the Sommersville High School's Class of '02 ten year reunion would normally be more than enough to keep Tom and his staff busy for the next week. The discovery of the murdered young woman yesterday had only complicated things.

Ironically enough, Tom passed Lake Greene as thoughts of the young woman, Rebecca, flashed across the recesses of his brain like lightning. Without conscious thought, Tom Myers turned and looked toward the spot where Deputy Chris Jackson had found the body. Although he could not see the exact spot from the highway, he knew it is there.

He stopped in mid thought. A sensation flashing before his mind's eye.

Something's not right here.

Hitting the brakes hard, Myers pulled his police truck off of the main stretch of highway onto the grassy embankment, kicking up dirt and grass as the vehicle slid to a stop on the wet grass. Careful of oncoming traffic, he threw the truck in reverse and quickly backed up to the entrance of Lake Greene. The entrance path was still blocked off by the yellow police line tape. After a long struggle and repeated phone calls, Tom had been able to get the local office of the Forestry Commission to put up a thick chain across the expanse of the path, effectively closing it off to vehicles. People did not need to be traipsing around in the woods. Not with a killer around.

Stopping the truck next to the thick iron chain, Tom killed the ignition. He stepped out of the vehicle without closing the door and leaned against the side of it, his gaze transfixed on the spot that he still could not see through the thick foliage. Nonetheless, he knew it was there.

Two minutes passed.

Then five.

Finally, a full ten minutes had elapsed. Tom was staring at the area as if he could see through the hills and trees, across the little bridge that reached over the lake's boundary, and into the area where the girl had been found. Something, a feeling perhaps, Tom wasn't sure which, but whatever it was, it called to him. A twinge in his gut that told him that there was something, an important piece of the puzzle that was right in front of him. All he had to do was reach out and grab it.

"What is it?" he said between gritted teeth. His fist smashed down on the roof of his truck, leaving a small dent. "What is..."

Tom Myers' voice died out in his throat. The answer jumped up and shouted, *here I am!* Tom stared at nothing, lost in shocked disbelief. It was an answer that could only lead to more and more questions. Questions Tom Myers desperately needed answers to.

"Son of a Bitch," Tom snarled a moment later. "How blind am I?"

Tom hastily got back inside of his pickup, fired up the ignition, and quickly pulled out onto the main stretch of road and headed toward town. Toward the office. He had a meeting to attend.

A meeting that had just became much more important to him.

"How did you know she was there, Chris?" Tom said, speeding up, the answer to that particular question calling him to the station.

"How the hell did you know that girl was there?"

14.

"We're here."

The taxi pulled to a stop outside the front door of the Marriott Hotel, just off of Restaurant Row in downtown Sommersville.

It had traveled a long way on this trip. The distance between the Atlanta International Airport and the tiny little town of Sommersville stretched roughly sixty-eight or sixty-nine miles. The trip took a minimum of about an hour and a half with Atlanta's hectic rush hour traffic.

The battered old yellow Sedan looked like it had been the only survivor in a war and its color scheme clashed with the stark newness of the hotel. The driver jumped out, enthusiastically opening the door for his passenger. The driver apparently loved what he did and that did not go unnoticed by his passenger.

Once the young man was safely deposited at the entrance, the driver grabbed two very expensive bags from the trunk and moved them over to the hotel's bellhop at the entrance. "There you go, sir. Safe and sound as promised." The cabby held out a hand to his fare. "That'll be forty eight dollars and sixty three cents please, sir." He stopped, his fare apparently lost in thoughts and memory. "Mr. Phillips?" he prodded.

"Huh, oh, sorry. Forty-eight sixty-three? No problem." The man pulled out his wallet and retrieved two crisp, clean bills, a fifty and a ten. "Here you go, sir. It was a marvelous trip. Go enjoy breakfast on me." The man handed the cabby the fare plus a modest tip. All that and a big smile. The cabby tipped his tattered hat to the man before moving back to his car, smiling all the way.

"Have a real nice time at your reunion, Mr. Phillips," he said before getting into his cab. He tossed off a wave as he pulled his old, yellow jalopy out onto Main Street once again. The man watched the cab driver go, tossing a casual wave back.

"That breakfast offer good for everyone?"

The man turned at the familiar voice, slightly startled that he had not heard the person speaking to him approach. He stared intently at the well-dressed gentleman before him. Recognition was instantaneous.

"Well, I'll be damned." His words brimmed with joy. "They'll let anybody sleep in this place won't they?" His hands immediately went to his hip in a sign of annoyance and snide arrogance.

"They let you in didn't they?"

The two old friends, Billy Connelly and Charles Phillips laughed as they moved to embrace one another. It was a long embrace of two old friends that had not kept in touch as much as they might have liked. Now, face to face at last, the years just seemed to melt away. What had felt like forever now seemed to only have been the blink of an eye. In each of their minds they were kids again.

"My God, Billy. It sure is good to see you." Charles Phillips said. He meant it too. These two had been nearly inseparable as children. They had been the best of friends. The only thing that kept them apart now was the three thousand or so miles between Florida and California.

"Charlie," Billy pulled back to look at his friend. He held him by the shoulders. "You look great. Those earthquakes must really agree with you."

The two men stood in the parking lot talking for what seemed like only a moment before another cab honked the horn and startled the two of them from their reverie. They realized that they were blocking the entrance and they move off toward the lobby together. Billy Connelly hefted one of the bags and escorted his friend to the main desk.

"This place nice?" Charles asked.

Billy winked. "I had no complaints," he answered.

"Then I guess it'll have to do, huh?" Now it was Charles' turn to smirk. "I know how finicky you high priced doctors can be."

"Only the best will do."

"But of course."

"Let's get you checked in and then we can go get that breakfast," Dr. Connelly said. "If you're paying, then I'm feeling a might bit peckish."

"Funny. I see you still haven't had that sense of humor transplant."

"Ha. Ha."

The desk clerk pretended not to eavesdrop on the two as he typed in Charles Phillips' information into the hotel's computer. It was not polite to listen in on a guest's conversation because one never knew what one might hear. It was a strict hotel policy, but it was not an easy rule to follow. "Enjoy your stay, sir," the desk clerk said as he passed Mr. Phillips a key card for his room.

"Room 313." Charles read his room number aloud.

"Really. Hey, we're neighbors. I'm in 312." Billy played it up.

Charles decided to play along. He let his shoulders slump. "And they say you can never go home again. Sheesh!" He looked to the young man behind the desk. "Just like old times." He let out a half laugh.

The desk clerk returned the smile, although he did not fully grasp why the comment was funny. *Just humor the guests so they'll leave a nice tip.*

The two old friends laughed all the way across the lobby to the elevators as the desk clerk watched. "Just like old times," he repeated Charles' sentiment. "Those must have been good times."

15.

The Kettle was a little greasy spoon diner that had been a prominent fixture in the town of Sommersville for as long as anyone could remember.

Or cared to remember for that matter.

The food was moderately good, the coffee drinkable. The place had an old home feel, a rustic charm that made everyone feel welcome. And that fit with the overall ambiance of Sommersville, Georgia very well. The prices were reasonably affordable and the service came with a smile. Plus, if you wanted to know anything about the comings and goings in Sommersville, then the best place to be was The Kettle.

The diner had been nicknamed by local reporter, Franklin Palmer as the "small town information superhighway." There always seemed to be someone on hand that could tell anything about anybody. Ninety nine percent of what was said would undoubtedly be pure gossip, plain and simple, but occasionally that one percent of reliable information often found a way to sneak through. Sometimes when you least expected it.

You just had to know which information was good and which less so. Luckily, the younger Palmer brother had learned how to weed out the good from the bad, the gossip from the facts. Most of the time.

The door opened with a chime as a small bell above the door cheerfully announced a new customer. The waitress, her nametag identified her as Amy, a fairly attractive twenty-nine year old smiled and welcomed each and every guest to The Kettle. This time was no different.

"Hello Franklin," she announced as Franklin Palmer and his brother Harold stepped into the overly warm eatery. The smell of kerosene from a portable floor heater assaulted Harold's nose. The fumes were a little bit strong but he kept that to himself.

The waitress did not seem to notice Harold's discomfort as she escorted them to a booth along the far wall, near the back of the restaurant. "Your usual table?" she asked. Franklin simply nodded before tossing off casual greetings to people Harold could only assume were regulars as well. "Here you go, Franklin," Amy said as she pointed at a booth. Franklin Palmer had been sitting in the same booth for the two years since he had been in town, since moving in to take over the local paper. Although the question was pointless, it had become something of a ritual between the two. He would become worried if she didn't ask.

Harold watched the exchange without comment, fascinated to see this side of his brother's life.

No sense in messing with tradition, Franklin mused as he lead Harold to his usual booth and the two men slid into it across from one another.

"Nice place," Harold said. "Come here often? Going out on a limb, I'm guessing you're a regular here."

"Nice piece of detective work, Agent Palmer. Now I see why the Bureau holds you in such high regard."

Franklin started to say more when Amy walked up next to the booth. "Coffee?"

"Absolutely," Harold intoned. "Two of them, please."

Franklin laughed. "A coffee and the usual for me. My brother here will have a coffee and..." He let his words trail off, waiting on his brother to complete his breakfast order. Even as Harold examined the small menu card he could feel the eyes of both Amy and his brother on him.

What the hell, I'm a rebel remember? he thought. "I'll have the same please." He handed the small menu back to Amy and she swiveled on her heel and was gone. Harry leaned in close to Franklin. "Ray, what the hell did I just order?"

Franklin smiled. "Trust me, you'll love it." Harold just looked worried. "Trust me," Franklin repeated, which only made Harold more concerned.

"The last time you said those words to me I was grounded for over a month. You do remember that don't you, Ray?"

"Of course I do. You won't let me forget it." Franklin tapped the side of his own head. "It is firmly ingrained right here. You know, for posterity's sake."

"Then I feel for posterity." Harold joked.

Franklin laughed again. "So do I, pal. So do I."

"Here you guys go." Amy quickly returned with a coffee for each of them. She also placed a full pot on a round wicker heat mat next to Franklin. "I thought you might like a refill," she said to Harold. "Or three."

"Thanks."

"Don't mention it. So you're Franklin's brother, huh?" She eyed Harold as if trying to look for the family resemblance.

"Surprised?" Harold asked her.

"A little. I don't recall Franklin ever mentioning that he had a brother." Amy let her gaze swing back and forth from Harold to Franklin. "You've been holding out on us, Mr. Palmer." She wagged a finger in his general direction. "Shame, shame."

Franklin held up his hands in mock surrender. "Sorry," he said. "It just never came up. Sorry." Both Amy and Harold watched as he attempted to squirm his way out of the situation. "Really."

Harold leaned in close to Franklin across the table. His eyes went wide. "You never mentioned me? Are you," he swallowed a deep breath, appearing wounded, "ashamed of me? Me? Your only brother? I'm crushed!"

"Oh brother," Franklin groaned.

"Exactly," Harold exclaimed. "Oh brother. That's me. Good boy." Harold patted his younger brother on the top of his head like he would an obedient pet. Franklin groaned at the prospect. Amy stifled a laugh.

Amy, still smiling, headed back to work as two other customers entered the small restaurant. They too were announced by the little bell's ring. Harold leaned back in triumph, watching as Franklin dropped his head in his hands.

"Harry? When did you say you were leaving?"

"Ten minutes after I drive you crazy." Harold could tell that Ray was trying unsuccessfully to hide a smile. He eagerly awaited the comeback. Ray always had a comeback.

"Why did you bother to unpack?"

Ray always had a comeback.

Amy escorted the new arrivals two booths down from Harold and Franklin. The two men were laughing and talking without a care in the world. Harold turned and watched as they found a seat. *Probably in town for the reunion,* he guessed, as they did not go through the routine of talking to every other patron in the place like his brother had. When the noise level dropped back down to normal level, he regarded Franklin again. "So, Ray," he started, his voice a little quieter now. "What is your take on the young woman the cops found? Anything new?"

"No." Franklin physically seemed to shrink under the question. It was a topic that had been weighing heavily on his heart. "That type of thing isn't suppose to happen in a place like Sommersville." He looked up at Harold. "Not here."

"I know how you feel, Ray. Believe me, I've seen my fair share of this over the last few years. And no matter where I go, where the job takes me, someone always says that very same thing. 'I can't believe it happened here.' They don't want to acknowledge the fact that evil, for lack of a better word, doesn't follow state or city boundaries. It's everywhere." Harry thumped his chest with a balled up fist. "It's all in here. We have to decide whether or not to allow things like this to happen or not. Some people find that they like the evil side of life a little better. It is easier to accept those primal urges. The hard ones to accept are the responsible ones because you have to work at them. Not everyone can do that." He paused as if reviewing an unpleasant memory. "Some just don't want to," he finally added.

Franklin finished off his first cup of coffee as Harold polished off his second. "Yeah, well I still have trouble thinking of things like that happening here in this sleepy little town I've come to call home. You see the evil and the chaos every day of your life. That's your job and you have learned to handle it."

"More or less," Harold interjected.

"You've probably become accustomed to it, Harry. You expect to see it because you know that it is there. I have to believe that people are basically good. Otherwise I'll lose my faith in mankind all together and without that I'm no good to anyone. Not my readers, my friends, you, or myself. I can't live like that. I have to believe in something better."

"Makes sense," Harold said as he poured his brother another cup of coffee before refilling his own cup. "And just so you know, I only handle it because I have to. It's the training. Beverly can tell you about all of the nights I've literally cried myself to sleep. Especially early in my career. Not to mention the nightmares. It is not something that you can ever get used to. Truth to tell, I'm not so sure I would ever want to. If I become desensitized to it, then I'm no better than the person who committed the crime. Does that make sense to you, Ray?"

"I think so. Feeling is what makes you... I don't know..." He thought it over, searching for the right word. "...different. You know that you could never do something that horrendous. Something like that?"

"Exactly, Ray. If it doesn't affect me anymore, then how can I become emboldened to find the person or persons responsible? I cannot allow myself that luxury. It takes a lot of courage and fear combined that allows me to do my job and to do it well. It also takes me knowing that I have Beverly and Lucy to come home to every night. They, and even you, are my anchor to reality and even to my sanity. Without that, without each of you, I would have gone insane years ago."

Harold looked as though he wanted to say something further, but he stopped, holding it in. He didn't want to burden Franklin with the hell he faced in his life on a regular basis. So, he decided to change the subject.

Franklin noticed the change in his brother's demeanor. Before he could comment however, Amy returned with a large serving tray that carried their breakfast plates. She gingerly began sitting the plates in front of the two men. Two eggs with the yolks still runny, four strips of nearly burnt bacon, two hand made buttermilk biscuits, and grits with cheese on top. She placed butter, grape and strawberry jelly, and eating utensils, a fork, knife, and spoon beside the plates. Finally, Amy put two small glasses of orange juice next to each of them. Salt, pepper, and extra napkins were already on the table.

"Anything else I can get for you boys?" Amy asked.

Harold waved a dismissive hand. "Not for me. Thanks."

"Franklin?"

"I'm good, Amy. Thank you."

"My pleasure," Amy said with a smile. "If you need anything, just holler."

"No problem," Harold said as the waitress turned around and headed off to another set of customers in a booth by the window.

Franklin Palmer regarded his food. "Looks good," he said.

"Yes it does," Harold noted as he salted his eggs. "Question. I noticed that you do have an oven in your house. Do you ever actually eat at home?"

Franklin shook his head as he chewed on a piece of bacon. "Not usually. I like to think of this as my kitchen. Besides, you know how much I dislike doing dishes. This way I don't have to clean anything." He took a bite of his biscuit. "Ah, progress."

"Cute."

"I thought so, Harry."

Harold smiled at Franklin as he buttered his biscuit. "I'm not surprised at all."

Franklin let his tone turn serious again. "I-I never realized," he stammered, suddenly nervous about discussing his brother's career choice. "About your job I mean." He sampled another bite. "I mean I did, but I didn't at the same time. I'm sorry that you have to go through that. Really sorry."

"Hehn!" Harold gurgled a sound. "It's a dirty job, but..." he began.

"Somebody's gotta do it," the two of them finished the sentence in unison.

"Wow! Stereo." Harold let out a laugh.

"I'm glad you told me all of that," Franklin said as he sipped his coffee.

"How else can I make you feel sorry for me?" Harold tossed his younger brother a wink. "Besides, I can see that this is starting to affect you." He paused. "I heard you in the bathroom vomiting last night. Since you didn't seem to be sick, I can only assume that it is a case of the nerves."

"Nerves?" Franklin half giggled. "Yeah, I guess it is at that." He took another drink of his coffee. "I've never had to deal with death like that before. When I was a reporter in Atlanta, I often dealt with the story of how people died, with car crashes, with drive by shootings, and gang fights. To me it was just another story. I covered the facts after the evidence had been cleared away. I wrote about death and killings without ever having to be a part of it. They were just names and places on a piece of paper. Very rarely did I think of them as real people, living breathing people with families, friends, loved ones. I never realized as I was doing it, but I was, hell we all were glamorizing the violence without getting across the important things."

"The important things?"

"Yeah, Harry. The important things. We passed the information along and since we didn't think of these people as real, then the public didn't get the feeling of the loss as it really occurred. We were not just casual observers. We were part of the problem, Harry." Emotions began to churn deep within Franklin Ray Palmer.

"We were a big part of the damned problem."

Tom Myers' office was not spacious by any stretch of the word. The well-worn office was roughly the size of his bedroom at home. Maybe smaller.

His cheap metal desk sat along the far wall away from the door. He had positioned it so that he had full view of the door and anyone that walked through it. His back was against a large double window overlooking the old bank across the street, allowing the sunlight to shine in on him as he attempted his daily paperwork. Trouble was, there had been very little in the way of sunshine of late. Today, a small sliver of sunlight had somehow managed to peek its way out from behind a blanket of thick gray clouds.

Three sets of grey file cabinets lined the wall off to the sheriff's left. Three small chairs were situated off to the right of the desk so that Tom could sit comfortably and still manage to stare down anyone that came to be sitting in those chairs. The only thing about the office that he wished he could change was the color. The room had been repainted the year before as part of the city's restoration project. The restoration committee had researched the original aspects of Sommersville and discovered details about his office. They decided to return the entire building to the way it had been all those years ago when it was first constructed.

Normally, Tom wouldn't have minded the city spending a little cash on the place. It had sorely needed it. Unfortunately, the painters were instructed to paint the entire station in an off white color. It resembled a yellow or tan more than a white color, especially under the heavy fluorescent track lighting. Tom hated it immediately. He tried to reason with the city commissioners about the colors, but his request for a change fell on deaf ears. Like it or not, Tom was stuck with it.

And he did not like it very much. He hated it then. He hated it just as much today.

But he had learned to tolerate it as the color slowly wore down his resistance, not that he could have done much about it. Tom had placed a few prized photos around the room to mask the tone of the paint. It had helped a little. Very little. A picture of Mildred, several pieces from the history archives showing earlier incarnations of the Sheriff's Office during Sommersville's history, and three framed movie posters from his study at home.

The movie posters were a personal privilege. They were his hobby and maybe a little more. They proved an escape from the everyday. Albeit a temporary one. He could only afford one hobby so Tom decided to make a hobby out of his love for movies. He loved movies indiscriminately, all movies and all genres were of great interest to him. Of course he had his favorites and three of them adorned the office wall where he could keep an eye on them. If nothing else they made for fascinating conversation pieces.

They also made the place feel like it belonged specifically to Tom Myers. A personal touch so to speak. He looked them over from his desk as he often did when he felt pressure. The 1975 hit JAWS was his favorite poster and it was the closest to his desk. That movie had changed his life. Okay, not really, but it made him feel good about himself to say it. For a short time after accepting the position of sheriff, Tom had tried to picture himself much like Chief Martin Brody. Luckily for Tom, however, that Sommersville was nowhere near the water. And he bore absolutely no resemblance to Roy Scheider either, but it was still a good image.

The other posters were also of favorites like the first ALIEN movie and RAIDERS OF THE LOST ARK. He occasionally changed them out to breathe new life into the room. His latest find was a good copy of the poster for the movie CASABLANCA. Truly a prized possession. A good find which would someday soon find a place of honor in Tom Myer's private office. At the moment it was hanging in his living room at home.

There was a knock at the office door. He had been expecting this, dreading it.

"It's open," he called out.

The door opened slowly and Chris Jackson gingerly stepped into the small office, closing the door behind him. "'Morning Chief," he said softly. Last nights drinking binge seemed to have left the poor boy in a bit of a slump.

Too bad, Tom decided, feeling only a little pity because he had been there himself once. He pointed toward one of the three chairs. "Sit." It was not a request so Chris took the offered seat without comment. "You and I need to have a little chat, Chris." Tom's tone was more forceful than he had meant it to be, but Chris needed to be reminded of a few things. Like who was actually in charge around here. And Tom was going to make sure that what he had to say got through to his deputy.

"Yes sir," Chris said as he slumped down into the chair.

"I have a few questions that I just can't seem to find answers for. I was hoping you could help me out. Kind of," a brief pause. "Fill in the blanks so to speak," he said. "Chris, I know that you and the victim were..."

"Rebecca."

"Beg your pardon?"

"Her name was Rebecca, sir."

"Sorry. I won't beat around the bush with you, Chris. I'm sorry to be this blunt, but I have to have some answers. Look, I know that you and... Rebecca were very close and I know that makes this just that much harder on you, but I have to know. How did you know where to find the body? How did you know she was there, Chris? How?"

"Sir," Chris leaned forward, every muscle tightening to intensity. "I want to find out who did this as much as you. I do, really. But things are... complicated."

"They always are."

"But in this case..."

"Chris! Answer the fucking question. How. Did. You. Know?"

"I- I received a phone call early yesterday morning. The caller wouldn't tell me his name, said he was a friend, then he gave me a message that he said was from Rebecca. The person on the phone told me to head out to Lake Greene and Rebecca would meet me there. How was I to know?" A single tear started to trickle down Chris Jackson's left cheek.

"You said it was a man on the other end of the phone?"

"Well, I -uh, well I think so. It was muffled, hard to make out, almost like listening from inside of a tunnel. And I could hear commotion in the background so I assumed it came from Thunderbirds and didn't give it a second thought."

"Why didn't you just tell me this sooner?"

"I tried, Tom, but you sent me home. Then, last night I was so trashed that I only vaguely remember you stopped by. I'm ashamed of that. I've never let the alcohol do that to me before. I have no excuse for my behavior."

Tom stood and walked around to the front of the desk. He grabbed a chair and slid it over next to Chris so that they were face to face much as they had been in Chris' apartment the night before. "I want you to listen to me, Chris," Tom urged. "Hear what I tell you and you hear it good. I believe you. I do."

Chris breathed a loud sigh.

"But get this straight," Tom continued. "I will not let you within a country mile of this investigation. As of ten minutes ago you are officially on vacation. Don't worry about the pay. I've taken care of it."

"But Tom, Sheriff, you can't do this! I need…"

Tom lifted a finger, silencing his deputy. "I already have, Chris. Don't make this any more difficult than it already is. I'll keep you informed and I can promise that we will get whoever is responsible for this murder, but you have to promise me that you won't get in our way."

Chris stared at him in stunned silence. This was not the type of thing Deputy Jackson expected to hear from Tom Myers. The sheriff was usually more easy going.

"Chris, believe me when I tell you that this is for your own good. Take the vacation. You have a reunion coming up in a couple of days. Take some time and visit with some of your friends. Didn't you say that a few of them would be coming into town early? Hook up with them and talk about old times, have a few beers, shoot some pool, whatever. Just put this out of your mind. Let me deal with it. Alright?"

Chris Jackson nodded his reluctant agreement.

"I've made a few calls and we are trying to find a next of kin for the vic... for Rebecca. Can you help with that?"

"No. I don't know any of her family. Things were very… casual with us."

"Okay, Chris. It's okay. Look, get on out of here. I'll give you a call when I get something. I promise."

"Thanks sheriff... Tom. I appreciate what you think you're trying to do for me."

"I'm trying to keep you from self-destructing, Chris. One day I hope you'll thank me for it."

"Don't count on it."

"I'm not. Go home. Get some rest. I *will* call you later."

Chris stood stiffly. He went toward the office door in silence. Then he said, "My gun?

"Pardon?"

"My gun. Where is it?"

Tom tapped the top of his desk with a finger as if his deputy could see the gun lying in the desk drawer. "I've got it. Your landlord was a little nervous with it in his possession. He gave it to me. Don't worry. It's safe."

"Can I have it back? I feel a little naked without it." Chris seemed to liven at the analogy, but he could not completely hide his pain.

Tom pursed his lips, sucking in a lung full of damp air. He had been playing this moment over and over in his mind, curious as to how Chris would react to his decision. His head shook negative. "Nope. I'll give it back after you've had time to cool off. Now get out of here. Some of us have work to do."

"Good bye, sheriff." Deputy Jackson's dry parting line left Tom with a dreaded feeling knotting up in his stomach. Their relationship might never be the same after this investigation.

"Behave yourself," Tom said as the door closed behind the retreating deputy.

And then, Tom was alone with his thoughts and worries. Tom worried about his deputy and friend. "Please don't do anything stupid," he said to the empty room.

Then the silence took over and it would be a long while before Tom Myers moved from that spot. When he finally moved, he turned to stare at the first of his three movie posters.

"Well, Martin," he said to the JAWS poster. "How'd I do?

17.

WELCOME TO SOMMERSVILLE.

Barbara Fram was fixated on the large sign as she passed it. It had been nearly ten years since she had left the sleepy little community where she had grown up. Ten years sounded like such a long time, yet it felt just like yesterday.

Young Barbara Fram had left shortly after graduating from high school. She had wanted to do something with her life. Things had become complicated in her young life. Complications she did not want to deal with at the time. Things had changed. Her life had come to the proverbial crossroad and she found herself wanting more, wanting to do more. She had changed. At the time she really wasn't sure what it was that she wanted to do, but she had been fairly certain that she couldn't do it in Sommersville. So she packed her belongings, said her good-byes to her family and friends, and then she had a nice long talk with Billy, her boyfriend at the time. He didn't understand her position, not that she had expected him to. The boy could be a little thick at times. That was part of his charm. He didn't like it and he very loudly, very publicly let her know how he felt, but in the end it was her choice. Not his. She had felt that the town had labeled her as simply being 'Billy Connelly's girl friend, Barbara Fram.' She often heard it phrased in that fashion. Like it was one word. Like she could not exist without Billy Connelly.

Barbara Fram decided to prove them all wrong.

So she left it all behind. She left her boyfriend, her close friends, her family, and her hometown, destined to move on and do *something* with her life. It was the start of a long and often arduous odyssey. A road that had taken her places that she had never thought she would ever see. She considered herself lucky. She had found her dream. Not everyone was so lucky.

Ten years later she found herself returning to the hometown she had run from with the feeling that she had just started to find the thing that she wanted to do with her life. She hoped that this wasn't considered taking a step backwards.

One step forward, two steps back. The phrase kept rolling through her mind like thunder.

After traveling around for a few years, Barbara found herself in New York, auditioning for a play. It was strictly on a whim. She did not get the part she tried out for, but the director thought she had a real talent and gave her a part in the play anyway.

The lead part

Barbara flourished on stage and drew rave reviews from critics and fans alike. She spent six years on and off Broadway in play after play after play. She was starting to realize her dream. Hollywood was the next logical step. She was already on the right track. Her first television movie aired three weeks earlier and the next one would be out in time for the November sweeps. She had to give up being the lead, but Barbara really did not mind it much. She only saw television as another step in her career. Maybe she could make it into the movies eventually.

At least that was her dream.

Nothing much had changed in Sommersville. Barbara had kept in touch with her best friend since grade school, Lisa Kimmer. Lisa had been Barbara's rock during those critical stages of life when nothing seemed to go just right. She was the one that Barbara shared her biggest secret with all those long years ago. A secret that they shared with only one other.

Lisa was married to Joe Woodall and they seemed happy together. Joe had been a hotshot jock back during high school and college, but that all changed after he went into the Air Force. Joe learned a lot about life and he settled into his in Sommersville with his bride. It was one of Barbara's biggest regrets that she missed the wedding.

Joe had a great job and a great family and he took great care of both. They had two adorable children. Barbara couldn't wait to see the little rugrats again. It had been at least two years since Joe and Lisa had flown out to New York to catch one of Barbara's plays on Broadway. Sometimes Barbara envied Lisa her life. Other times she wondered if she could ever settle down like those two and live happily ever after. It was a daunting thought and it sent a slight shudder through Barbara Fram. A shudder that she couldn't determine to be a good sign or not.

Lisa Woodall had volunteered to pick Barbara up from the airport when the old gang had decided to get together a little early and have a private reunion on their own. It had been arranged at Billy Connelly's request and Lisa had not been sure that Barbara would show up. She and Billy had not parted on the best of terms, but that had been ten years ago, ancient history by now. Hopefully they had both matured and put the past behind them where it belonged. Lisa had known that it would be hard, but the reunion had its high points as well and she was overjoyed when Barbara had agreed to come.

Out of the small group that used to hang out in the old days only Lisa Woodall and Chris Jackson had stayed and made their homes in Sommersville. There had been eight of them in the old gang. Barbara, Lisa, Billy Connelly, Chris Jackson, Charles Phillips, Jake Page, Ted Hollis, and Wilson Hartford. They had been inseparable back in the day.

"The good old days."

"What?"

Barbara hadn't realized that she had spoken aloud. "Uh, nothing," she said to Lisa who was driving them into Sommersville. "Just thinking out loud. A lot of old memories here, y'know?"

"Yeah," Lisa Woodall agreed. "I'm really glad you decided to come."

Barbara smiled. "I wouldn't have missed this for the world."

"I'm just glad you're here."

"Me too," Barbara said, turning once again toward the window and taking in sights she had not seen in years. "So when is this big shindig of ours supposed to happen?"

"Tomorrow evening I think. Billy, that's Dr. Connelly now, anyway, Dr. Billy has supposedly taken care of all of the details. He probably had his secretary take care of it. The rest of the gang should be getting into town sometime tonight or tomorrow." Lisa turned her car off of Main Street onto a side road that lead to her home. "I can't wait to see everyone again. The last time hadn't been this festive," she said quietly as her memories filtered back three months past. Painful memories of burying an old friend.

"Tell me about it," Barbara quipped. "Tell me about it."

Three months back the old gang, with the exception of Billy Connelly, had met for the funeral of another friend. Wilson Hartford had been one of their best friends for years and he had been as eager as the others to have everyone together again at the reunion after all of these years. Unfortunately, his life was cut short by a hit and run driver while he was vacationing in Colorado. Reports stated that the car came out of nowhere and slammed Wilson into a wall. Death was instantaneous. The Denver police were never able to find any suspects nor were they able to make any arrests. It all happened so fast. So senseless.

They had all flown in from their separate lives to pay their respects to a fallen friend. Dr. Connelly had been unable to get away from work, but he had made a phone call in to Wilson's widow and he had also sent flowers and money to help the family. He had been there in spirit if not in person.

That was three months ago.

A sad time.

Things would be much more festive this time around, she hoped, although Wilson would still be sorely missed. It had been after the funeral that they had come up with the plan to get together a few days before the reunion and spend some time together. They had planned things out while on the phone with Billy in Miami. The circle of friends had been apart for too long and they made a promise that they should all keep in touch more often. The death of their friend had a profound effect on each of them. They needed one another more than ever.

The weekend would be a much needed time of peace and relaxation for each of them. And Barbara Fram was determined to make the most of it.

"Here we are." Lisa put the station wagon into park and turned off the ignition. Barbara looked at the cozy little brick house where her friend lived. Her perfect little house and her perfect little life. There were times that Barbara envied her friend. Barbara opened the door and stepped out onto the driveway. She whistled as she took in the beautiful yard. Lisa had obviously put in many hours of work on it and it showed. Barbara leaned over to get a better look at some of the flowers growing all around. She glanced around the yard.

"What are you doing?" Lisa finally asked.

"Hmmm," answered Barbara. "Oh. I'm looking for the white picket fence."

"Funny," Lisa sneered. "That's around back."

The two friends laughed all the way to the door of Lisa's home. They were still laughing an hour later.

Sadly, the laughter would not last.

Well, well, well, what have we here?

From the wooded area across the street from the property owned by Joe and Lisa Woodall, *he* watched.

The little starlet had returned. This excited him more than he had expected. For a short time, he had thought she would not come. Surely, all those Hollywood spotlights had erased the memories of her old life.

Apparently I was wrong, the killer thought. Any other time he would be angry with himself for making any such transgression.

Errors were not tolerated.

Failure was punishable.

He had failed once before and it cost him dearly. He would not fail again.

Yet, he could not help but smile as he watched the happy women talk and laugh as they walked to the house. Not for the first time, the killer imagined how easy it would be to take care of them both right then and there. Imagine the fear as Joe and the kids returned home to find Mommy and Auntie Fram lying on the kitchen floor, their throats slit ear to ear: their blood splattered across everything.

For a fleeting moment he was tempted, sorely tempted, but for everything there is a time and place.

And, fortunately for the two blissfully unaware bitches across the street, this was neither the time nor the place.

But soon, oh so very soon, the time would come.

Steadying the tremor of excitement in his hands, the killer focused the binoculars on the window, watching Soccer Mommy Lisa show Miss Bright Lights, Big City around her little suburban ranch with the brick front and stucco siding.

As he watched them hugging, laughing, talking, touching hands to shoulders, he could feel the familiar tingling sensation grow. He was aroused. Soon, oh soon. He tried to control it, knowing that his body was not in control of him, the mind was. Mind over matter. He could control it.

Control.

EVIL WAYS

It.

Control... it!

But the thought of those two writhing around passionately, sweat puckering their naked flesh was more than he could bear. An old fantasy, to be sure, but one he had often had over the years. In his mind's eye he saw himself lying on a king sized bed. At the foot of the bed stood teenaged Barbara Fram and Lisa Kimmer, dressed only in sheen silky wraps, which fell to the floor in front of him. As if they were kittens moving to a bowl of the sweetest milk ever tasted, they climbed on the bed and moved toward him, their hips seductively swaying. With a gleam in their eyes and a smile on their lips, the girls moved forward and...

And he could no longer control himself. With his targets only feet away, the killer closed his eyes, gave in to his lustful urges, and pleasured himself right there in the woods.

He would offer penance later.

19.

"Sheriff?"

"Yes?" Tom Myers answered. The voice came across his intercom from the office's desk clerk. He waited until after her message filtered across the pager on his phone. He forgot to tap the button as usual, and then remembering that she could not hear him unless he pushed it, he tried again. "Yes."

"Mr. Palmer and his guest are here to see you."

"Great," Tom said silently. He gently tapped the call button again. "Send them in please and hold all of my calls for a while could you."

"No problem, Chief," the desk clerk answered.

A knock at his office door alerted Tom to Franklin Palmer's presence. "It's open," he said loudly enough to be heard. The young reporter opened the office door, taking a step inside. As Tom had suspected Harold Palmer was standing behind his younger brother. Without preamble, Tom motioned for them both to come in and take a seat. They did so.

For a brief moment, Tom continued writing on a piece of paper in an open folder on his desk. The two brothers waited as patiently as possible, but Harold seemed to be getting a little restless. As a FBI agent Harold Palmer was used to having the full attention of whomever he was addressing. The waiting did not come easy for him. Franklin handled the situation better. As a reporter he was often kept waiting by potential and scheduled interviewees. It goes with the territory. Harold and Franklin shared a look as both began to wonder if the other was out of patience yet.

Tom finished his notes, closed the folder, then chucked it into his *out box*. He turned to regard the brother's Palmer. "Gentlemen," he said as he leaned back easily in his cushioned chair, a subtle reminder that his chair was far more comfortable than the ones they occupied.

Harold nodded a greeting to the sheriff. "Sheriff Myers."

The sheriff addressed the two men in turn, "Good morning, Mr. Palmer. Franklin."

"Tom," Franklin acknowledged the sheriff. "I just wanted to stop by and get an update on our mystery victim. What can you tell me?" The reporter pulled out his pocket notebook and an ink pen. He flipped open to an empty page.

"I have a partial ID on the victim, but I cannot confirm it until we run it down, find the family. She was a UGA student and we believe her name was Rebecca, but as I said, we haven't been able to confirm that yet." Tom leaned on his desk, his elbows propping him up. "One of my Deputies thought that he might have recognized her."

"Recognized her? From where?" Franklin wrote down a few scribbled notes in his little notebook. "Is she a local girl?"

"No. Again, we don't think so. She may have been a dancer out at Thunderbirds. I've got a few of my deputies going over there when they open this afternoon. Hopefully someone there can confirm her identity and we can try and contact her family. At best, all we have now is a name that may or may not be her real name. For all we know, Rebecca is just a stage name she uses when she dances." Tom tried to stretch, his back feeling sore and knotted. "That's all I have. Sorry I don't have anything concrete for you, Palmer."

"No problem," Franklin answered. "I'll see what I can dig up from our directory files and see if we can find anything on a Rebecca. Even if she doesn't live in Sommersville, she works just outside of town. She has to have a name on something here. Maybe she shops here. I'll get to work on it as soon as I can."

"I appreciate the help, Franklin," Tom said. He turned to address Harold. "I'm sorry that we seem to be encroaching on your vacation. Your brother tells me that the two of you were hoping to spend some time together. I'm sorry."

"It's not your fault, Sheriff," Harold said. "Besides, I'm still spending time with Ray here. Granted, I would rather be fishing, but I guess beggars can't be choosers can they?" Harold chuckled at the cliche. "Don't fret over it, Sheriff. I'm glad to help out in any way that I can. I may be on vacation, but I'm still a human being and things like this really get me right here." Harold tapped his chest just above his heart.

"I appreciate it all the same," Tom Myers said. "And please, call me Tom."

"Right. I will. Thanks, Tom." Harold stood, ready to leave. Ray and the sheriff also got to their feet. Myers moved around his desk to show both men out. He noticed Harold admiring his movie poster collection on the wall. "Now this I like," the FBI agent declared.

"Thanks," Tom enthused. "It's a hobby of mine. I collect old posters and some of the newer ones, but mostly the classics that I like. It keeps me busy and it beats the hell out of therapy. The job can be very stressful. This helps me to relax. Besides, I've found that it beats getting tanked and forgetting everything I did for the last twenty-four hours. You know what I mean?"

"I can see your point. I may have to look into this. The wife keeps telling me I need to get a hobby. Thanks." Harold reached out a hand to Tom and the man shook it with a firm grip. Tom held open the office door and Harold stepped out.

Franklin also shook the sheriff's hand as he exited. "I'll get back to you if I find anything on our victim," he told Tom. Myers nodded. Quietly he said to the reporter, "Thanks. I would love to put an end to this before the festival. Just let me know what you find."

"I will. Later, Tom."

Tom Myers watched as Franklin Palmer crossed the modest lobby area and exited through the double glass doors at the front of the station house. The sheriff turned on his heel and started back into his office when the desk clerk stopped him. "You still want me to hold your calls for a while, boss?"

"Yes, please." Tom Myers looked tired. The desk clerk was obviously trying to help out. "And see if you can find me some aspirin. I have one hell of a headache."

"Yes, sir," the desk clerk said.

Tom Myers moved back into his office, closing the door. Slumping in his chair, Tom dropped his head onto the desk. "It's going to be a long day," he mumbled aloud to no one in particular.

20.

Franklin Palmer stepped out into the morning sunlight, allowing the door to the Sommersville Police department to close behind him.

He had not gotten much out of Sheriff Myers, but that was to be expected this early in the game. Still, Tom had managed to spotlight a few details that Franklin definitely wanted to follow up on. First and foremost was the victim's name. Rebecca. He would pass that less than glamorous job onto his secretary, Lisa, while he checked out the Thunderbird connection.

"What's Thunderbirds?" Harold asked as Franklin got into the Blazer. Apparently they were both on the same wavelength.

"Thunderbirds is a bar just outside of the city limits. Alcohol, occasional live band, and food on one side."

"On one side?"

"Yeah. Thunderbirds is actually two bars in one. The one side is for anyone old enough to drink and wants to hang out with their amigos and shoot some pool or play darts, whatever. The other side has "adult entertainment" as they call it. That's where Tom thinks our victim might have worked."

"A tit bar," Harold said, amused. "I thought this was the middle of the Bible Belt?" he questioned. "That's the last thing I would have expected."

"Oh it is, Harry. The city council wouldn't let them set up shop in the city limits. They told the owners that they could have either nude dancing or alcohol, but not both. The owners decided to move their establishment outside of the city limits. That way they can still get the Sommersville business and they can also get the college action as well. Most of their dancers are college girls. I hear they make good money."

"You don't say?" Harold's snide comment fell on deaf ears. "You know, I have been in one or two of those in my day."

"What, my brother the Boy Scout in a strip club? Will wonders never cease."

"Hey, I had my moments, but they were before Bev."

Franklin smiled.

"And if you whisper one word to her I will come back down here and kick your ass."

"You never could kick my ass."

"I've been practicing."

"So," Franklin asked his guest, changing the subject. "What do you feel like doing this evening, brother dear? Any sights that might interest you? We have a National Park, but of course you've already seen that haven't you? We have a nice downtown strip, but you passed that on the way in. We have a new Burger King in town if that interests you." Franklin inhaled a deep breath. "So, Harry. What'll it be?"

Harold rubbed his chin, feeling the stubble growing there. "I don't know, Ray. You got any place in this town where a man on vacation can get a decent beer?" He tried to hold back the grin on his face. Despite the seriousness of the situation, he was actually enjoying himself.

"Well now that you mention it, we do." Franklin smacked his older brother on the shoulder. "See?" he said. "Even after all these years, we still think just alike."

"Well, now I'm really depressed, Ray." Harold squeezed the back of his neck to release the tension building there. "I may need two beers."

"Really?" Franklin acted as though he had been stabbed through the heart.

"Maybe more," Harold tossed his brother a quick wink. "Maybe more."

21.

"You can pull over right here."

The plain looking car carrying Jake Page came to a stop just outside of his mother's house. The driver got out quickly and grabbed the young man's belongings, moving them to the tiny front porch of the small brick house. The driver knocked once, then twice before the lady of the house appeared at the door. The sight of a man she did not know gave her a moment's pause.

"May I help you?" she asked the man curiously.

The driver smiled at her. "I believe I have something here that belongs to you, ma'am."

"What would that be?" she asked nervously as she noticed the bags at his feet. She did not recognize them. These bags did not belong to her and she told him as much.

"Hi, Mom."

The voice hit her like a physical blow. She knew that lilting voice. She knew it very well. Her son had returned home.

"Jake!" Her excitement bubbled over and she ran out the door, past the stranger standing there, and into the waiting embrace of her only son. "Jake," she shouted again as tears streamed down her face.

"Hi, Mom. How have you been?" His voice was wavering just as hers had. "I've missed you," he said after a second. He noticed the driver watching them, but trying not to stare. Jake released his hug, pulling out his wallet to pay the driver. He handed over the appropriate amount plus a sizeable tip. After thanking the driver and sending him on his way, Jake Page grabbed his bags and followed his mother into her house.

The house Jake grew up in. Home.

She led him through the old house to where his old bedroom had been all those years ago. All of his old things were long gone. Where his bed had once been was now home for a nice pool table. *This had to have been something that Dad wanted,* he suspected. "I like it," he told her. "Where's Dad?"

"Your father is still at work, Hon," she answered. I've made up the extra bed in the spare room for you. It's not much, but its home."

"Mom, I can stay in town at one of the hotels if you don't have the room." Even as he said the words, Jake knew what her response would be.

She laughed in that way that only Mom could. "It is no bother at all, Son. Now get your things put in there and then you can tell me everything that has been going on since you last came home." She sat on the couch. Jake simply nodded and put his bags in the spare room. He knew better than to try and argue with her. She could be quite stubborn when she wanted to be.

"Thanks Mom," he said after returning to the living room.

"Welcome home, Jake," she said as her one and only son took a seat next to her and commenced telling her the exciting things that have happened in his life recently.

Jake had decided to go to the nearby University of Georgia after high school. This enabled him to stay at home and help his parents out. His Dad had been very ill and for a short while it did not look as though he would survive the summer of 1997. Then a miracle happened and Mr. Page's inoperable cancer went into remission and his condition improved. The doctors were speechless and could offer no logical scientific reason for the turn around in Mr. Page's condition. Jake and his Mother had been so very happy to have him back. Mrs. Page had prayed for a miracle and God had answered her.

Relieved, Jake once again turned his attention to his first love. Music. Jake and a few of his buddies from school had formed a small band when they were in middle school, but that all ended when they graduated from high school and went their separate ways. Once he made it to college, Jake met a few new friends that shared his passion for music and performing so he joined with them to play local concerts and the like. They were a fairly popular attraction on the local Athens music scene.

Eventually that ended as well, but Jake had tasted his dream and threw himself fully into it. He arranged to have a demo recorded and he submitted it to every recording label he could find from the smallest to the largest.

No one seemed interested in the least.

Then, after two years a record label decided to take a chance on this unknown commodity and Jake Page recorded his first album, which had been titled "My Hometown." He didn't expect much to come from it. The most he and his manager could hope for would be enough regular airtime to let the public get to know Jake's name so that his second album would have higher sales.

Things didn't exactly happen the way they had hoped.

Jake's first single, "Flashback," flew to the top of the billboard charts. People everywhere were singing and playing his song. You could not turn on a radio or a music video channel without hearing *Flashback*. It was a joyous feeling and Jake Page knew that he was finally on his way.

On his way to the top.

Unfortunately, the public fell in love with only one of the songs off of his first album. The critics were harsh, far worse than he could ever have expected anyone to be. He endured relentless name calling, Jake Page bashing, and all of the magazine articles that referred to him as just another pretty boy one hit wonder that couldn't make the cut. Heartbroken, but eager to succeed, Jake started working on a second album. He swore to himself, and his manager, that the critics would eat their words one day. Finally, the album was completed and the first single released for general airplay. This time the critics praised his efforts and the first single was already becoming widely accepted by fans and radio stations alike.

With the general release of his second CD two weeks away, Jake Page simply wanted to forget all about the pressures of the music business, see some old friends, and spend some quality time with them and with his folks. With his busy and often demanding schedule it was often hard to get back home. Just getting a chance to make a phone call to his Mom and Dad was proving next to impossible of late. This weekend would make up for that.

Besides, here in Sommersville he could be a regular person, not just Jake Page the Rock 'N Roll star. Here he hoped he could be a regular person again.

Knowing he would be surrounded by friends all weekend was a nice little bonus. They were not swayed by the trappings of show business. Even Barbara had gotten her acting career started. If anyone could understand what it was like to be in the public eye, it was her. These people were his friends. They would still treat him the same way they always had. With them he was just one of the guys. This weekend promised to be one to remember.

Just one of the guys.

His mother listened intently as Jake poured out the details of the past few months. She hung on every word, every story with genuine interest. He told her about all of the towns he had visited and all of the interesting people he had met. It had been a thrill ride for him and his enthusiasm burst forth with every spoken word. He spoke of new friends made and of the old friends that he has been waiting to see during this reunion. He told her of the woman he had become involved with, the woman with whom he had fallen in love. They talked of things that were important to him and she listened genuinely, taking in every detail as if it were a delicacy to be savored.

He was her son and she was proud of him and of the accomplishments he had made. Yes, she was very proud of her little boy. Very proud indeed.

22.

Thunderbirds Bar and Lounge was located just outside the city limits of Sommersville. Originally the owners had intended to set up shop in the sleepy little town, but the determined city commissioners fought tooth and nail to keep it out. It was a hard fought battle and in the end the city won.

They would allow the bar to set up within the city limits if, and only if, they refused to sell alcohol while providing adult entertainment or vice versa. The owners of the bar reasoned that they couldn't make enough to successfully run their establishment under those guidelines so it was announced that there would be no nude dancing club in Sommersville.

The town council rejoiced. They had won the battle.

Just not the war.

Determined to make their business venture work, the future owners of what would come to known as Thunderbirds made a deal to buy a small plot of land just outside of the city limits and set up their business there. The Sommersville city council was unable to touch them and the county was more than happy to take tax money from such a lucrative business as a nightclub and bar. The people of Sommersville could still hang out at a bar close to their homes and the city had to live with the fact of all of that extra tax money they were losing. The owners of Thunderbirds laughed themselves all the way to the bank.

The men flocked to the place in droves.

Two years later, the owners decided to restructure their format and soon began construction for Thunderbirds II. Now there were two bars, adjacent to one another. One offered adult entertainment while the other is simply a bar and lounge with drinks, dancing, and the occasional live band. Now everyone in town had a place to go to get away from it all, if only for a little while.

Again, the owners laughed all the way to the bank.

Rumor had it that there were plans in development for a full sized pool hall to be placed on the adjacent property. This would benefit the community's teenagers by giving them a place to hang out. The rumor was that the pool hall would be a no alcohol zone. If they wanted a drink, and were old enough, they could walk a few dozen feet to Thunderbirds. Or they could not drink. Their choice. As usual, there were complaints, but most people had accepted the fact that Thunderbirds was here and that it wasn't going anywhere.

As usual for a Friday night, the place was packed. Cars from all over the county and even the next county over filled the parking lot full to capacity. Eventually, patrons of the bar started parking along the side of the road and walking to their final destination. Harold counted a minimum of twenty vehicles from all over the surrounding area. He felt safe in assuming that there would be even more here before the night was over.

Pulling to a stop just outside of the parking lot, Franklin Palmer whistled softly at the amount of people here tonight. "Man, this place is packed tonight," he said as he put his Blazer into park and shut off the ignition.

"Wonder what the special occasion is?" Harold asked from the passenger seat. "Looks like they are rolling out the red carpet for somebody," he noticed. "Any big celebs in town?"

Franklin looked at his brother and shrugged. "They must have heard you were coming," he said jokingly.

"My reputation precedes me."

"One of the folks in town for the reunion is Jake Page. I heard that he and a few of his friends are planning a little get together. Maybe it's here tonight."

Harold snorted, "Ray Palmer. A reporter with endless sources. HA! Where'd you hear about this little get together, the gossip fence?"

"Funny," Franklin said as he stepped out of his Blazer onto the moist grass. The rain had stopped, but its presence still lingered. "I'll have you know that my sources are usually reliable," Franklin boasted.

"Usually?"

Franklin had that annoyed look on his face. His tone soon matched it. "Like the FBI never comes across, shall we say, less than reliable information."

"Well…"

"Come on. Let's get inside. We don't want to miss the show."

"Whoopee," Harold sounded less than enthused. "We don't want to miss this."

Franklin gave Harold a little nudge. "Come on. There is nothing to be afraid of. I'm sure it'll be perfectly safe for you in there."

A second passed silently.

"Be a man, you wuss."

"I know it'll be okay," Harold agreed, skeptically. "But I got married just so I wouldn't have to go into places like this anymore. I don't like the crowds. It's noisy. It smells. I don't drink. And you know how I get edgy when I'm in large groups. I feel like people are staring at me."

"Trust me," Franklin said with a grin. "Nobody will be looking at you."

"Right. I suppose not. Alright, let's get this over with," Harold agreed with a resigned sigh. *Beverly is going to kill me if she ever finds out about this. Or maybe she'll kill Ray. Yeah. Kill Ray. I guess I could live with that.*

Together, they trudged across the gravel parking lot, sidestepping water-filled holes as best they were able, only to fall into line behind the other patrons ready for a night out on the town. They all came to this place with one sole purpose, to have a good time. They wanted to put the troubles of their workweek behind them and let their hair down for a few hours before returning to their normal, everyday lives and routines. This was their time.

And Thunderbirds was the only game around.

"Which side do you want to hit first?" Franklin asked as they approached the rustic building. "The bar or the strip club?" He pointed toward the two separate entrances. Each was packed with people waiting to get in.

"I really don't care, Ray. Let's just get this over with."

Franklin Palmer sighed. "What a wimp," he muttered under his breath.

"I heard that."

"Of course you did, Harry."

"Sheesh. I get no respect."

"Why should things be any different from when we were kids?" Franklin tapped at his own forehead. *Memory like a rock.* It was a private joke between them.

"It's going to be a long night."

"Thunderbirds?"

Barbara Fram said the name in a tone that told her friend, Lisa Woodall that their meeting place was not exactly what she had expected. Barbara had been expecting a nice get together at someone's home or at a restaurant. She wanted a chance to talk to her old friends and share the experiences that they had lived. How could they do all of that in a noisy public place like a bar?

"Thunderbirds?!?" Barbara repeated.

"Hey, I don't make the rules, here," Lisa intoned. "Billy called and said for us to meet him and the others at Thunderbirds around seven or seven thirty. He said to be there, so we'll be there. Okay, Fram?" Lisa pouted a little foe the benefit of her oldest friend. "Okay?"

"Okay, Lisa. Okay. Let me grab my jacket."

"Good," Lisa gave her friend an overly friendly smile and a wink. "Tonight ...we party."

"I can hardly wait."

Lisa wasn't completely convinced by Barbara's excitement.

Barbara did not allow her friend the chance to start in on her. "Just shut up, get in the car, and let's go."

"Now you're talking, Fram. Now you're talking."

# # #

Dr. William Connelly and Charles Phillips walked briskly across the parking lot of the Marriott hotel toward Billy's shiny sports car. Billy had preferred to drive them both in than to waste time on a cab as Charles had suggested. Racing the motor, Billy Connelly gunned the engine and pulled out onto Main Street. Turning left at the traffic signal, Billy headed out toward the city limit sign and their final stop.

Thunderbirds.

"Why Thunderbirds?" Charles asked. "Won't that be a little bit crowded?"

"I hope so. I thought that it would be best if we all got together and had a good deal of fun before we started getting nostalgic and blubbery over old memories. And I'm sure we'll discuss Wilson at some point. I just want everyone to have a good time before we get on with the rest."

"I guess I can see where that might be a good idea," Charles admitted. "Have you heard from everyone?"

"Yes," Billy answered. "I talked with Lisa on the phone earlier. Fram is staying with her. Jake called from his Mother's place to let me know that he was in town. I left a message with Chris' answering machine. I guess he's still working. I'm sure he will be able to stop in after he gets off. Ted called and said that he had a late deposition to give in Atlanta and should be in town by eight or so. And we're here so I guess everyone made it in."

"Yeah," Charles said, his somber tone betraying his thoughts.

"Hey," Billy allowed his playful demeanor to fall away. "I miss Wilson too. He meant a lot to me." He placed a reassuring hand on his friend's shoulder. "It'll be okay," Billy told him.

"I know. It just won't be the same without him," Charles added quietly.

"I know what you mean," Billy agreed as he drove his car on toward their destination on the outskirts of town.

Jake Page kissed his mother on the cheek and shook his father's hand. "I'll stop in later. It will probably be tomorrow morning before I get in. I have no idea what those guys have planned. You remember how we used to be when we all got together. If I can't make it in tonight I'll give you a call."

"No problem, Son," his dad said with a smile. "Have a good time and say hello to the guys for me."

Jake walked out of the house he grew up in and stepped into the waiting cab. As the cab pulled off, Jake waved to his parents and they return it and smile.

"Where to?" the cab driver asked.

"Thunderbirds, please."

"Yes, sir," the driver said. "Going out for a night on the town?"

"Something like that," Jake answered.

"You don't sound too thrilled about it," the cab driver inquired. "I can take you somewhere else if you want." It wasn't really a question.

"Thanks," Jake replied. "But I made a promise. I guess I'm just a little anxious about seeing the old gang again. I just wish they hadn't decided to have our little reunion in such a public place, if you know what I mean."

"Oh, I understand, Mr. Page." The driver said. Jake noticed the man smiling at him in the rear view mirror.

Jake was momentarily taken aback. "I hadn't realized you recognized me."

"Oh, yes. It's a pleasure to have you in my cab. By the way, I loved your album. When's the next one coming out?"

"Soon. In two months if all goes as planned," Jake put on his best professional smile. "I hope," he added under his breath.

"I can't wait," the man driving said. "Now, you just sit back and relax and I'll have you there in no time."

"Thanks."

"It's my pleasure, Mr. Page," the driver beamed.

Jake put his hands up in front of himself. "Please, it's Jake. Just Jake."

"Jake it is then," agreed the driver. "Jake," he muttered again, not completely believing how down to earth the rock star was, although Jake might argue that part about being a star if he had heard it.

The rest of the ride was spent in silence.

#

"Tom?"

"Hiya Mildred. I just wanted to let you know that I'll be a little late getting home tonight, Honey. I've got to head out with some of the others and check on some things about that... uh, about a case we're working on." Tom hit his head with the ball of his fist. He tried so very hard to spare his wife from the perils and pitfalls of his job. A daunting task, but the last thing Tom Myers wanted was for Mildred to know the kinds of evil ...for lack of a better word... that was out there in the world. Add in the fact that Tom and Mildred lived relatively close -too close in Tom's own humble opinion- to the crime scene and it was easy to understand the sheriff's apprehension at leaving his wife alone in the house. Especially late at night.

"Oh," Mildred answered. "Is this about that dead girl?"

"Huh, oh, uh, yeah. How did you know about that?" he asked nervously, hoping that word had not gotten out through the grapevine about the girl found at Lake Greene.

Mildred's laughter filtered through from the other end of the phone. "You talk in your sleep, dummy. Remember?"

"Heh. I guess I never could put anything past you, Honey." He dropped his voice to a whisper. "I'll try to get home as soon as I'm able," he promised her.

"I know you will. I'll leave your supper in the microwave. Just in case you're hungry when you get in." A silence invaded their conversation. Neither of them uttered a sound, but to listen to the others breathing. Finally, Mildred broke the awkward silence. "Just be careful," she said.

"Always."

"I love you, Tom," Mildred said. He could hear her voice crack as it always did when he had a difficult and potentially dangerous case. Lucky for them both, dangerous cases did not happen often around Sommersville.

EVIL WAYS

He cradled the phone closely to his ear. "And I love you too," he whispered to her. "I'll talk to you soon. Make sure you lock up all of the doors. Okay?"

"I can handle it, Tom. This is not the first night I've spent at home alone since we've been married. Stop worrying about me and get out there and do your job."

"Yes Ma'am," Tom felt himself nearly snap to attention. "And for the record," he finished. "I will never stop worrying about you. Good night, Honey."

"Good night, Tom. I love you."

"Love you too," Tom said before hanging up the phone on his desk. He allowed himself a moment to stare at the photo of Mildred sitting on his desk. He looked at it and for a long moment, Tom Myers realized how much this woman had come to mean to him over the years. He believed that, quite possibly, he loved her more now than the day they first met. If such a thing were possible. He also understood that maybe he had come to take her for granted all of these years of marriage. Maybe he had, but no longer. Tom Myers knew what he had to do. It was a duty he had dreaded since the arguments about it began a few weeks ago.

For his wife, the woman he would die for, he decided to sell his family's property. He just hoped that his family would understand. He hoped that his parents would look down from heaven and not frown over his actions.

Tom Myers just could not bear to think that the spirits of his parents were disappointed in him. No, he could not bear that at all.

Tom reached over and tapped the call button on the phone on his desk. "Dooley," he called.

Deputy Benjamin Dooley instantly popped his balding head around the office door. "You called, Boss," he asked.

"Yeah, Ben. Get yourself changed into regular clothes."

"Tom?" Ben wore a puzzled expression on his face. "What's up?"

"Just get changed. We're going club hopping tonight."

23.

The inside of Thunderbirds was exactly as Harold Palmer had expected it to be.

Loud.

Very loud in fact. Between the hundred or so people crowded into the adult entertainment side, not to mention the dancers, the bar's employees, and the like, the noise level was incredibly higher than Harold could tolerate. And who knew how many more people were jammed into the other bar next door. He tensed as the realization set in that before the night was over there would probably be even more people trying to crowd their way into the place. His head started pounding loudly about five seconds after he and Ray had stepped through the door. He inhaled deeply, but instantly realized how bad a mistake that was. The smell of cigarettes, alcohol, and sweat all mixed together form a unique scent that Harold found to be quite nauseating.

"You alright?"

Harold did not respond to Ray's question. Partially because he could barely hear it, but also because answering the question seemed relatively pointless at the moment.

"Hey, Harry," Franklin Palmer shouted in his ear. Concern was evident on his face if not in his voice. "You alright?"

"Do I look alright?"

"Touchy," Franklin backed away. "Wake up on the wrong side of the Bureau this morning, Brother?"

Harold started to say something, but stopped himself. *This is no time to start reliving our childhood years,* he decided. Holding up a finger, Harold stopped his brother's annoying gaze. "Let's just get what we came for and get the hell out of here. Is that alright with you?"

"Sure thing, Harry. No problem."

That's more like it.

"No problem at all."

Thinking he had won the battle, Harold beamed with victorious pride until he was stopped dead in his tracks when his younger brother turned around and walked off without another word straight to the bar.

EVIL WAYS

He took the first available seat he could find. Pulling out a bill, he waved it in front of the nearest dancer, who immediately shimmied her way over to him.

Harold Palmer put a hand to his face, trying to hide his embarrassment. *This weekend is going to kill me,* he winced. *Yep. I'm a walking dead man.* Taking in another deep, nauseating breath of stale air, Harold Palmer walked over and pulled up a seat next to his younger brother. Not that Franklin had any clue that he was there as his eyes were securely affixed to the lovely dancer in front of him. She danced, moving to the rhythm of the music as it drowned out all other noises in the place. Not an easy feat considering the noise level of the place. All that Franklin could hear was the beating of his heart as his pulse rate sped up. He put a hand to his heart just to confirm that his it was still beating. It was, albeit faster than normal. He whistled at the dancer, although Harold doubted very seriously that she could even hear him over the din around them. However, she smiled seductively at Ray all the same.

"Will you grow up," Harold scolded him, his impatience threatening to boil over.

Franklin turned away from the beautiful dancer and looked deep into his brother's eyes. "Look, Harry. I'm not a kid anymore. Stop treating me like one and let me enjoy myself." Franklin gave him that *trust me* look. "Besides, I'm trying to work here," he added tersely, emphasizing the word *work.*

"Work? That's what you call this?"

"Yes I do." He returned his attention back to the dancer before she had the chance to move on to her next customer.

Harold stood. "I'm going to have a look around. Meet me over in the other bar after you've finished *working* here."

"Yeah, sure. No problem," he answered, but Harold was not sure whether he actually heard him or not or if he caught Harold's slightly agitated tone.

If Franklin had caught it, he certainly wasn't letting it show. Which only served to frustrate his brother even more.

Choosing the better part of valor, Harold Palmer made a bee line for the small corridor connecting Thunderbirds I to its sister establishment, Thunderbirds II, but at the last second he changed his mind and opted instead to head for the nearest exit and freedom. Or at the least, fresher air. Pushing his way past a throng of partygoers and the like, Harold made his way out of the confines of Thunderbirds and into the parking lot.

The air in the lot was far from perfect, but to Harold it was much sweeter than the swirling mass of pungent odors congealing inside the strip club. He took in a deep breath and let it out, then repeated the maneuver several times. Letting gravity take over, Harold allowed himself a moment of rest and slumped against the far wall of the bar. He listened to the music as it pounded against him through the thickness of the wall. It was incredibly loud in his ears.

People were inside having the time of their lives and here sat Harold Palmer, man of action, slumped against the outer wall. Even in the cool evening air, he felt clammy. He wiped away the sweat from his face and silently cursed himself for not being able to handle this situation better.

"Damn it," he spit out the words.

Rubbing his temple to massage the pounding in his brain away, Harold knew that he had to go back in there. He did not want to.

He had to.

The fear had been eating away at him for many years. Although he could not remember when this fear of being in large crowds started, he could only assume that the cave in he and Ray had gotten trapped in as kids somehow factored into it. The rocks had piled around him, smothering him and that was how it felt to be inside Thunderbirds, smothered by all of those people and those smells.

It was simply too much for his system to handle.

Suddenly, Harold's eyes lifted upward. His hand reaching toward his holster as his heart began to race faster and faster. His eyes darted back and forth across the expanse of the Thunderbird's parking lot. There were people milling about and walking to and from the bar, but none of them seemed particularly interested in him.

Someone is watching me, Harold thought to himself. He could *feel* a pair of eyes boring through him as if he were nothing. Someone was out there. Somewhere. Watching. *But from where?* That he did not know.

Forcing himself back to his feet, Harold Palmer moved back into the lighted area of the parking lot, letting his intuition and experience guide him. Nothing seemed out of the ordinary here, but there was a killer on the loose in this town, even though most of the inhabitants of Sommersville had not been informed as they should have been. There was someone in the town that was a killer, not for revenge or anything like that. No, this person killed for a far more sinister reason. This person killed for fun.

Harold had been helping his brother, who had been helping the local sheriff track down the killer to stop the killing spree before a panic could grip the city of Sommersville. However, the killer would have no way of knowing who Harold Palmer was, much less why he was at an establishment like Thunderbirds at that particular time. How could someone know that much? They had kept Harold's FBI status a secret from everyone in town except for Franklin's receptionist, the sheriff, and a few of his men. Harold was in town in an unofficial capacity after all. He was only there to visit with his younger brother, the local newspaper reporter, not to mention the paper's owner. Harold's involvement in the case was purely coincidental, but his instincts told him, screamed at him, that something, some person, was out there just beyond his scope. And that person was watching him.

"So, who knows who I am?" Harold muttered as he moved back toward the entrance to the bar, verbalizing his thoughts to help arrange them into something more organized than the jumble inside his head. There was something there, just out of his reach of understanding. No one here knew who he was.

"Unless..."

He did not even finish that thought as he forced his way once more inside the mass of people and smells, only this time he was in the bar and lounge area. The smells slammed into him at full force once back inside, but Harold Palmer pushed his way through the fear and the panic. The combined noises slammed against him like a fist, but he pressed forward nonetheless.

I have to find Ray, was the only thought Harold could muster as he pushed his way through the serried masses all around him. This was important. As remarkable as it seemed, Harold knew in his gut that the killer was there at that moment.

At Thunderbirds.

He, or she, was close by. Harold was sure of it. And his years with the Bureau had convinced him to implicitly trust what his gut was telling him. Something was wrong there.

Terribly wrong.

24.

"And there it is."

Thunderbirds was just as Billy Connelly had remembered. He and the other guys had sneaked out to this place many times after graduating from high school. They had liked the place as a hang out and a small slice of freedom from the hum drum life that small communities like Sommersville offered them. It had felt rebellious to run off to a place like Thunderbirds, which made it all the more appealing.

That was part of the reason for them to come here before the reunion.

A party to kick things off in grand style. They would kick back a few cold ones, dance a little, maybe even get up and sing like they used to do back when they had their own little rock 'n roll band. Having a superstar singer like Jake Page as one of their little group couldn't hurt their chances either. Besides, it could not hurt Jake's album sales any to get up and show the old home town that he was still the same old loveable young man he had always been. His feet were still firmly planted as far as Billy could tell from their few phone conversations over the past couple of years.

Billy Connelly had it all planned out, as usual. He was always the ringleader, ever since they had been kids, and the others followed blindly anywhere that he led them.

"Ah," he said with a smile, rubbing his hands together as if they were cold. "It is so good to be home."

"Amen, brother," Charles Phillips agreed as they stood before the entrance, staring up at the large neon sign that sported Thunderbird's massive logo. That was different from the last time these two guys had been here.

"I guess some things must change though," Billy said.

"I guess so," Charles agreed in that annoying habit he had of always agreeing with anything that Billy Connelly said. It almost seemed at times as if Charles could not come up with an original thought unless he ran it past Billy first. The years apart had not seemed to shake him of that habit.

"It works better if you actually go inside. I think you're more than old enough now. No need for the fake ID's."

The voice had come from behind them, but both men instantly knew who it was that had spoken.

"Jake."

"In the flesh," Jake Page answered as his two old friends turned around to face him. Billy enthusiastically grasped the man's outstretched hand and shook it firmly, them he pulled the man in close for an emotional bear hug. "Damn, Billy, it is so good to see you," Jake said as the two pulled apart. He turned toward his other friend. "Charlie."

"Hiya, pal," Charles spit out as they also share a brief hug. "Welcome back."

"Place hasn't changed much has it?"

"No. No it hasn't. We were just talking about that," Charles admitted.

"Billy, did you manage to get in touch with everyone?"

"Yeah I did, Jake. Everyone will be here tonight except Ted. Chris might show. I couldn't get hold of him, but I did leave a message. Funny, he lives here and was the hardest to track down. The girls are on their way. They should be here any time now."

"Good," Jake said. "I'm looking forward to seeing everyone in a happy place."

"Yeah," Charles agreed again. "The last time we were all together wasn't exactly a time for a party."

"I'm just sorry that I couldn't be there," Billy added, quietly. "But, that is all the more reason for us to make tonight as big of a party as we can. Not only for ourselves, but as a tribute to our friend. Nobody could throw a party like Wilson could. Nobody."

"You got that right," Charles agreed yet again.

"Well," Jake began, quickly changing the subject. "What say we get inside and get this party started? Personally, I hear a beer calling my name."

"That's what that sound was?"

"Let's go, guys. I have us a table booked. Let's get to it. They'll let the others know where to find us."

"Cool. So, what are we waiting for? Let's party."

"Sounds like a good plan to me."

"Me too."

The three friends strolled casually across the parking lot and up the small set of steps to the front door of Thunderbirds II where they were quickly ushered in, after Billy told them who they were and that they had reserved a space. The large gentleman at the door grudgingly let them in, then sheepishly asked for an autograph from Jake.

"That must get real old," Charles asked the singer.

Jake replied with a shake of his head. "Not really. I mean, if not for guys like him buying my CD, then I'd be out of business and working at Burger King again."

"We wouldn't want that, now would we?"

"No we wouldn't, Billy." Jake intoned. "No we wouldn't."

Billy introduced himself to a woman who ushered them off to a booth just out of the way enough for the reunion members to have a semi private conversation while still allowing them to be close enough to the action to be a part of the party.

Taking in everything, Billy spotted a familiar face across the room. "Well, I'll be damned," he whispered.

"What's wrong?" Charles asked, clearly concerned.

"Look over there."

"Where?"

"At the bar. There's Chris."

"Well I'll be. I guess he got your message after all, Billy."

"Then why isn't he sitting here waiting for us, Jake? You two get the table. I'll be back in a minute."

"No problem."

Billy worked his way through the growing throng of people, pushing and trying to be as gentle as possible. It seemed to be getting harder and harder to move around in the bar.

Within a minute, he pulled himself up to the bar, sitting next to Chris Jackson. For his part, Chris had not even noticed that Billy had sit down.

When Chris finally acknowledge his arrival, Billy reached out a hand and placed in on his friend's slumped shoulder. "Earth to Chris," he said, annoyed at being ignored.

Chris Jackson flinched under Billy's touch, as if he had been awakened abruptly from a deep sleep. He turned and looked directly at Billy Connelly. Although, at first it did not seem that Chris recognized his old high school friend, but then it all came flooding back to him.

"My God," he said after staring at Billy for what felt like an eternity. "Billy? Billy Connelly!? You son of a gun you," he nearly yelled as he enthusiastically embraced his friend. "How are you man?"

Billy looked hard at his friend. "I was about to ask you that very same thing," he says.

Chris *harumphed* and tossed a fake smile at his friend. "It's nothing." Obviously, the faux smile did not work on Billy, who arched a disbelieving eyebrow at Chris. "Really. I'm okay. I've just had a rough couple of days," Chris said unconvincingly.

Billy nodded, not really believing Chris' word that everything is A-Okay. "I understand," he said to the man. "We've all been there."

"I'm glad you think so."

Dr. William Connelly leaned in close to Deputy Christopher Jackson. In a low, almost nonexistent voice he whispered a few words of encouragement to his friend of nearly twenty years. "I know far more than you think I do. I've been hurt in my day. Hell, you were there for some of them." A crinkle of a smile found its way across the corners of Chris Jackson's mouth. "We all have our bad times. This little group of ours has seen out share of heartbreaks together and apart. No matter what you're going through, always remember that we are here for you." A pause. "No matter how far away we may seem."

"Do you always talk this much?"

"I have my moments."

"Tell me about it." Chris swiveled around on the barstool. He saw Jake and Charles and they each raised a hand in a wave when the noticed him looking their way. "What? Are all of my old friends dropping by tonight just to cheer me up?"

Billy smiled. "It's our lot in life."

"Do tell."

"Well," Billy said as the two men pushed themselves away from the bar and move off toward their waiting friends. "It's a dirty job..."

"But somebody's got to do it," they said in unison, a hint of laughter creeping onto Chris' face.

"By the way, Billy. Thanks. I mean it. You don't know how much your being here means to me." He clapped his comrade on the shoulder.

"It is my pleasure pal. Besides, what kind of party would it be without Chris Jackson?" Billy laughed and Chris followed suit.

"Good point."

"I have a million of them," he said as Chris met and greeted Jake and Charles. "You would be surprised," Billy Connelly mumbled to himself, unable to be heard over the din.

"Hey," Jake yelled. "Here come the girls."

"The gang's all here," Charles bellowed as Lisa and Barbara ran up to their old friends. "Well, almost all here." They commence to hug.

Each and every one of them. This was what their weekend was all about.

Friendship.

Fellowship.

Family.

Together again.

"Together again," Jake said as the stage band started to play behind them.

"My friends, I propose a toast," Billy said as he stood, drink in hand. "To memories of all of our yesterdays and the hopes for all of our tomorrow's. May each and every one of us never forget where we came from or where we are going. We must also never forget why we are all here. And never to forget absent friends. Never forget. And also, that we remember all of our glory days. May those memories never grow dim and may history never forget us or this place we called home."

And with that, as corny as it may have sounded, the six old friends each raised their glasses in unison and with trembling voices echoed Billy's sentiments. "Absent friends," they each said before taking their first drink.

"With the sappy part finished, what say we have a good time?"

Barbara Fram leaned across the table toward Billy. "Glory days?" she whispered.

He shrugged. "What can I say, I was having a moment."

As the friends laugh and start their weekend of celebration, somewhere close by, far closer than any of them dared to realize, the eyes of a killer were upon them. The owner of those eyes watched as they reveled in this place. With their drink and their music and their partying.

It will all end soon enough.

Soon. Very soon.

25.

"The band is very good."

"Yes they are."

The band had been playing for the past fifteen minutes, and they seemed to be playing just a little bit harder than most. Perhaps they wanted to impress the local superstar, Jake Page.

Perhaps.

The song ended with a burst of applause from the ever-growing crowd. The band's front man, a disheveled young man of about twenty or so, thanked everyone for coming out and then he turned to face where Jake and his friends were sitting. The bandleader made a special welcome for "one of his favorite recording artists out there today."

Jake tried to play it off like he did not want the attention.

Sitting across the room, Harold Palmer laughed to himself. How often did you find a celebrity that wasn't interested in attention? *Hardly ever,* Harold guessed, but that hardly explained why the *superstar recording artist* seemed to be blushing. Surely he must get that kind of attention all the time.

Giving up on the search for his brother in the moving mass of flesh packed into Thunderbirds I, Harold Palmer had managed to find a small out of the way table away from the throngs of people and the dance floor in Thunderbirds II. This way he could keep an eye out for anything going on that might seem a little fishy. Although he felt a little better than he had earlier, Harold still felt his gut telling him that the danger was far from gone.

It is here. Somewhere. I can feel it.

After a good bit of urging from the band, the crowd, and his friends, Jake Page reluctantly made his way to the stage. Once there, he threw off a casual wave to the assembled masses of Sommersville and her neighboring counties.

The crowd went wild.

Jake stepped over and shook the bandleader's hand. "Oh, man, it's good to be home," he said, which drove the crowd wild as they clapped and shouted their approval. Jake announced that he thought the band had played a great set. Finally, at the urging of the crowd, he was reluctantly convinced to accept the microphone.

Summoning his courage, Jake faced the thundering crowd. He looked out at them all, not really seeing anything more than bodies. He knew the place was crowded, but from his new vantage point he wondered how anyone had the room to move around. Much less dance.

"Hello Thunderbirds," he announced, his amplified voice resounding in the enclosed area. Again, the crowd cheered wildly. Jake smiled sheepishly while waiting for them to calm down, or a t least to get as quiet as they were going to.

He tried again. "I just want to thank everyone for coming out and supporting Thunderbirds. This place was always something special to me and my friends. We played our first gig here about twelve or thirteen years ago."

Another roar of applause from the crowd.

Smiling despite himself, Harold Palmer found himself truly wanting to like this guy. He had a charisma that reached out to the people around him. Jake Page may not have been the greatest singer around as the bandleader had said, but he was loved by the masses. A man could do worse.

The crowd roared again when the bandleader asked, more like begged, Jake if he'd like to do a song or two. Jake Page blushed again. It was a comical sight, but after several seconds of cheers from his adoring public and a few "go for it's" from his group of friends, Jake Page agreed. "Well, it doesn't look like these guys are going to let me go unless I sing something so…"

The crowd was ecstatic.

"This should be good," Harold mumbled.

Jake turned away from the crowd and conferred with the band. *Probably trying to find out what songs the band knows,* Harold surmised.

After a few seconds, Jake was once again facing the crowd, a large smile plastered across his face. Invariably, someone in the large crowd shouted, "*Freebird*!"

The crowd laughed.

To his credit, the young singer shrugged it off with a slight flex of the shoulders. "The band tells me they haven't learned the music to my latest single, but we'll forgive them anyway." The crowd roared to life at Jake's somewhat lame attempt at humor. "However," he continued over the din. "However, we have picked a few songs that you all probably know."

The band began to play and the crowd burst into cheers of praise as they recognized the music. Jake stepped up to the microphone. "This one is for my best friends in the world," he pointed toward the table where his school friends were sitting. They bowed as if to a king. "A friend of mine said a little earlier that we should never forget our glory days. This one's for you, Billy."

For the next four minutes, Jake Page and the band did a rendition of Bruce Springsteen's *Glory Days* that would have made even *The Boss* proud. Harold watched and listened to this young superstar in the making. "Not bad," he whispered. "Not too bad at all."

Losing himself in the music and revelry all around him, Harold relaxed, possibly for the first time this trip. He listened as the band finished their first song. Again, the gathered crowd thundered their approval. "No way they are only going to let him get out of here with only one song," Harold laughed as he drank his soda. He looked back to the crowd as they cheered the rocker on. "Not a chance in hell," Harold said.

Finally, Jake Page gave in and agreed to do another song or two before getting back to his friends. From Harold's vantage point it looked like Mr. Page's friends were having nearly as much fun as the crowd. For that matter, the singer also seemed to be enjoying himself. Once again he conferred with the band before they began. This time they covered Santana's *Evil Ways,* which they followed immediately with *Tryin' to live my life without you,* an old Seger cover of an even older Memphis tune.

"He should sing like that on his own albums," Harold remarked to the couple sitting at the next table. "That boy has soul he hasn't reached into yet. What a shame." Harold savored the moment, tapping his feet along with the music.

When the last note sounded, the crowd cheered loudly and applause filled the modest sized bar. Harold clapped as loudly as anyone. It was a great show and everyone had a blast, but Jake Page ended it by thanking the audience and telling them that he really came here to spend some time with his friends for their reunion so he bid everyone a fond farewell and a goodnight.

The crowd roared as he waved to them and the sound lingered for a good long while after he left the stage. Wiping away the sweat from his brow, Jake dropped into a chair next to Billy Connelly and Barbara Fram. He downed his drink in two gulps before calling for another. The singing took a lot out of the young man.

Billy, smiling, loomed in close to his friend, not giving him a chance to catch his breath. "Glory Days?" he asked, both amused and curious.

Jake shrugged. "What can I say, you inspired me."

The circle of friends let out a sharp laugh. Billy, chagrined, blushed slightly.

"What can I say," Barbara said, deadpan. "He was in the moment."

They laughed. This time Billy joined in on the revelry.

And they laughed.

And laughed.

Their laughter echoing into the night.

26.

"There you are."

Harold Palmer turned at the sound of his brother's voice. "I was wondering where you got off to," Franklin Palmer said sarcastically. Only a small hint of concern seeped into the younger man's voice.

"I've been right here."

"Oh," Franklin grimaced. "Not having a good time."

It was not a question. Franklin pulled out a chair and slid across the table from his brother. "I miss anything interesting?"

"A little," Harold answered. "That singer you were talking about, Jake Page, is here. He's in town for the reunion. He got up and did a set with the band."

"Cool. Sorry I missed it."

"It was very good. The crowd seemed to like it." He pointed toward the small circle of friends sitting at a nearby table. Jake Page was sitting there with five people that Franklin did not recognize and one that he did.

"Chris."

"Yeah," Harold agreed. "He seems to be close with those guys."

"I didn't know that Jake Page went to school here. I mean, I know he attended college at the University of Georgia, but I didn't know he was from Sommersville. I just heard that he had friends here." Franklin shrugged. "I thought that he might have been from somewhere around here; I just didn't know where."

Harold choked back a fake cough. "Some reporter," he mumbled.

Franklin smiled and ,with his best Curly Joe impression, turned to his brother. "Well, nuyk, nyuk, Harry." Franklin waved for the nearest waitress. She held up a finger as she finished waiting on another table. Then she moved over to the table where the brothers were sitting.

"Yes, sir. Can I get you something?"

"Yes. Yes you can."

As Franklin placed his order Harold glanced around the crowded room. He could still feel the weight of eyes boring into him. He didn't know from where or how, but he knew that it was real. That feeling in the pit of his gut had proven to be accurate on any number of occasions during his tenure with the FBI. He learned to trust that feeling a long time ago, and at that moment it was screaming at him. The volume was high and superseded even the noise of the crowds around him.

Franklin touched his arm, breaking Harold's concentration. "Hey. You want something to drink?" Franklin asked.

"Uh, yes. I'll have another soda?"

With a smile and a nod, the waitress vanished into the seething crowd.

Franklin focused on his older brother. "What's wrong?"

Harold would not answer. Or he did not hear. Franklin wasn't sure which. "Harry?" He asked again. "Harry? Say something, dammit."

"Sorry."

Franklin Palmer sighed. He continued to stare. "I was hoping for something a little more substantial than that." He forced a smile at Harold.

Harold, for the most part, hardly seemed to notice. "He's here," Harry said softly.

"He?" Franklin questioned. "He who? What *He?*" He looked at his brother, as if for clarification. None was forthcoming. "What the hell are you talking about, Harry? What..."

His voice trailed off as a startling realization hit him and his reporter's instincts kicked in. He leaned in closer to his brother. "The killer?" he asked.

Harold nodded.

"Where?"

Harold did not answer.

"Where, Harry?"

"I--I don't know. Not really."

"Then how...?"

"A hunch. I can almost feel a presence."

"A presence?"

"Since when did you become superstitious, Harry?"

"I'm not."

"Could've fooled me."

"Look, Ray. It's hard to explain. It just feels..."

"Feels like what, Harry?"

"Evil, Ray. It feels like evil."

"Evil?"

"Yeah, evil. And it's coming."

27.

Tom Myers walked easily to the entrance of Thunderbirds.

Ben Dooley was only a couple of steps behind him. The doorman recognized the sheriff and his deputy and allowed them to move inside ahead of the line. Tom nodded as he passed and Ben clapped the man on the shoulder. Apparently the two had met before.

"Friend of yours?" Tom asked.

Dooley shrugged. "I helped him out a while back. Kept his son from going to jail for doing something stupid. I'd rather not talk about it here. I'll tell you about it later if you want to know."

Tom waved the subject away. "No need. I trust your judgment. Let's see if we can find the owner and get what we are looking for."

"What are we looking for, Boss?"

"Information, Ben. Information. Let's go."

The two men entered the crowded bar. There were people everywhere. More than usual, Tom suspected. Many of them were people that Tom Myers knew. Many he knew only from face recognition and some by reputation only. Still others were people that he knew personally. Truly, Thunderbirds was the only place to be on a Friday night in Sommersville.

Out of all of the gathered people, three familiar faces stood out like beacons in the night. Franklin Palmer was sitting at a small table with his brother, the FBI agent. They looked to be deep in discussion. Tom wasn't really all that surprised to see these two men here. Franklin Palmer had a well-earned reputation for being thorough and smart as a whip. Those qualities helped make him the top-notch reporter that he was. The surprise to Tom was the presence of his deputy, Chris Jackson, at a booth across the room.

Chris was seated with a small group that Tom could only assume were friends of his that were in town for the reunion. His first thought was that maybe he should go over and introduce himself, but he thought twice about it. This was not the time or the place to get Chris Jackson riled up about the murder case that Tom would not let him investigate. Those conversations were best suited for the office. Besides, Chris had actually listened to Tom's advice and was spending time with his friends. From the look of things, he was having a good time as well. Good. The farther Chris Jackson was from this mess; the better off Tom Myers felt.

Still, he was somewhat surprised, and relieved, that his deputy had decided to take the advice offered by the sheriff to heart. *This is just what Chris needs,* he told himself as he moved toward the manager's office on the other side of the bar.

Climbing the steps one at a time, Tom and Ben arrived at the door to the manager/owner's office. He knocked twice. When there was no answer he knocked again. This time there was a garbled reply that sounded like, "Wait a minute."

Twenty seconds later, the door opened and the two officers were escorted inside.

"Sheriff!"

The owner of Thunderbirds stood as the two officers entered the extravagant office. It had hardwood floors and walls with photos of celebrities that had performed at Thunderbirds over the years and of people the owners had met during their travels. Also on display were several rare albums from well-known, as well as obscure artists, from as early as the late forties. It was a very impressive and, Tom guessed, rather expensive collection.

Jimmy Wilkes welcomed the two men with a broad smile and boisterous demeanor. Mr. Wilkes was one of the co-owners of Thunderbirds. He was dressed immaculately simple. He was wearing designer jeans that looked to have been worn only once before. He sported polished snakeskin boots, a black T-shirt, and topped it all off with a white sports coat. A blazing cigar completed the look of the tycoon that Jimmy Wilkes had worked very hard to perfect. The only thing missing was a white ten-gallon cowboy hat.

"Have a seat," Jimmy said around the cigar implanted between his teeth although it in no way disrupted the man's thick southern accent. Tom and Ben nodded as they moved over to two of the four empty chairs that sat opposite the big man's desk. Taking the offered seat, Tom noticed the revelry in the two versions of the bar. A large window along the wall allowed Jimmy to have full view of Thunderbirds I and Thunderbird's II.

"Nice view," Tom said, deadpan. "Beats fighting with the crowds."

Jimmy smiled a toothy smile and took his seat behind the large oak desk. "Yes it is," he agreed; the broad smile still firmly plastered on his face.

"I'll bet it's good to be the boss, huh?" Ben asked, obviously distracted by the young woman on the dance floor as she swayed to music that they could not hear from inside the office.

"It is at that," Jimmy Wilkes agreed. Then, the big man leaned forward on his desk, propping his elbows there and resting his sculpted chin on the backs of his hands. "Now I know you boys didn't come all this way just to sneak in for a free show, now did you?" Jimmy never dropped the smile and his thick southern accent dripped as the tycoon put on the charm that helped him become the businessman he had become. People seemed to have a hard time saying no to the man. Tom understood why.

Tom Myers had only been out to Thunderbirds once since he took office as sheriff. He had stopped by in his official capacity to introduce himself to the owners and let them know that if there was ever any trouble that the Sommersville Sheriff's Department would respond quickly. Jimmy and his partner, Thomas Allen, had said then that they could not foresee any type of problems that the sheriff would need to concern himself about.

And Jimmy Wilkes had been right. Aside from having the bouncers toss out the occasional drunk, there had been no need for Tom or any of his men to visit Thunderbirds in an official fashion, although several of his officers, Chris Jackson, prominent among them, spent a considerable amount of their free time there. That was their right of course and Tom knew that it was none of his concern. He had spent a good amount of time in places similar to this before he met Mildred and settled his wild ways.

"So," Jimmy said between puffs of smoke. "What can I help you gentlemen with? I assure that everything here is on the up and up."

"Of that I have no doubt," Tom said as he reached into his inside jacket pocket. He pulled out a photo, looked at it then handed it across the desk to Jimmy. Jimmy took the offered photo and looked at it intently. "Pretty girl," he said in a voice like a whistle. "She looks familiar. Someone I should know?"

"Yes," Tom said, mildly disappointed by the man's inability to place the photo of the girl Chris had called Rebecca. "We have it on good authority that this girl works for you. She is a dancer."

"A dancer? Hmm." Jimmy seemed to think it over. He rolled a memory around in his mind. "Like I said, the photo looks familiar, but I can't be sure. If you have a name I can pull her employee file and see what's what." Jimmy reached down and opened a desk drawer. He pulled out a file about three inches thick. A label on the folder read: DANCERS.

Tom let out a sharp whistle at the thickness of the file.

Jimmy nodded. "As you can see we've had many dancers here over the years and all of them are in this file. To protect myself and my establishment, I carefully document every employee and every dancer. It's a tough business and people are always trying to pull something on us."

Tom's brow creased. "Like what?" he asked.

Mr. Wilkes handed the photo back to Sheriff Myers.

"Scams mostly. Sometimes we will get girls in here that have, shall we say, less than pure intentions. We have had some dancers that come to work once and file sexual harassment charges as soon as their first dance is over."

"Really?"

"Sure thing, Deputy," Jimmy said as he handed the file over to the sheriff. "A lot of folks think that just because we are a popular establishment that we are rich and, therefore, easy targets for lawsuits of all kinds. Given the type of entertainment we provide, many folks feel that we would rather pay them off than go to court and expose our, quote/unquote *scandalous ways* to the world." Jimmy exaggerated a shrug. "I mean, I'm not ashamed of the type of business I run. We are one hundred percent legit and we run this place according to the law. What more can we do than that?"

"Nothing I suppose," the sheriff said. "I'm not here because of the nature of your business. I'm here because this young lady," he held up the photo so Jimmy could see her face again. "This young lady is dead," he continued.

"Dead?"

"Yes, Mr. Wilkes. Dead."

"How?"

"Murdered, I'm afraid, but we can't run around announcing that to the world right now. We don't want to cause a panic and lose our lead on the person that did this."

"I understand," Jimmy said. It was a lie. "Not really," he finally added. "I may not have known her personally, but if she worked here, then that makes this very personal for me. What do you need from me, Sheriff Myers?"

"Well," Tom said. "We think her name might have been Rebecca.

That could be a real name or a stage name, but that's all we have to go on. It is our belief that she was a college student working to pay off her schools bills. We're checking out the college now and we hope to turn up something there. But if you can give us a name, an address, anything at all, it would help us very much."

"No problem. I have a back up of all of these files on my computer. I can give you a copy on a DVD if that would help."

"That would help. Thanks."

Jimmy stopped. "One thing though. I have to have your assurance that this list will not be seen by anyone outside of the two of you. Some of the people that are on this list haven't worked here in years and some of them probably don't want to admit that they did this for a living."

Ben coughed. "I thought you weren't ashamed of it?"

"I'm not. Some of the people that danced here in their early college days might have moved on and gotten married or something like that and might not want their significant other to find out about this little detail of their past. I just want to protect the privacy of these people on this list."

"I understand," Tom said. It was a lie. In truth he wondered if he might have misjudged Jimmy Wilkes. Tom had always suspected that people that ran places like Thunderbirds were truly unconscionable people, real scum of the earth. Jimmy Wilkes was starting to change Tom's mind. He seemed like a nice, normal businessman that looked out for the people working for him. That was rare enough in today's society where employers looked at the people that work for them as a faceless name or number.

Tom found that he had a fledgling respect for this man named Jimmy Wilkes.

28.

The remainder of the special evening had gone much the way Billy Connelly had planned. The gang had a large supper and danced the night away, taking time out to tell embarrassing stories that some of the others would have preferred be forgotten and never spoken of again.

During the main course of their meal Billy's cell phone rang. On the other end was their absent friend, Ted Hollis, calling from Atlanta. He was just checking in, to let them all know that he would be arriving first thing in the morning. It seemed that his deposition had taken longer than he had hoped.

Everyone joined together to wish the final member of their entourage a safe journey in a group yell into the tiny cell phone. A feat that only attracted a few extra stares toward them. It felt like half of the place had been staring at them since Jake executed his impromptu performance.

Ah, the price of fame.

But, alas, all good things must inevitably come to an end. And this evening was no exception. At approximately two a.m. the management of Thunderbirds had sounded last call and the place quickly cleared out as the patrons went to their respective homes or to wherever it was that they were planning to crash that night. Billy, Jake, Chris, Lisa, Barbara, and Charles were among the last to leave and they stood in the parking lot for a good fifteen minutes saying their good-byes. It all seemed a little strange, as the group would be meeting again the next day for lunch.

Lisa and Barbara waited with Jake for a cab to take him home. Lisa had, of course, offered to give him a ride, but he had declined. "It would be too far out of your way," he had told her.

So, not to leave him stranded, the two women agreed to wait with him. Barbara eventually sent Lisa on her way home to be with her family. "I'll wait here and Jake can drop me off. Besides, we haven't really had a chance to talk since we got here and this will be the perfect chance to catch up." Reluctantly, Lisa surrendered and headed toward home. Leaving behind two of her oldest friends.

EVIL WAYS

"I thought she'd never leave," Jake remarked when Lisa's taillights finally faded from sight.

"I know what you mean," Barbara agreed as she stood upon her tiptoes and kissed Jake. "I have really missed you," she said as the two of them fell into each other's warm embrace.

Twenty short minutes passed before the taxi pulled to a stop in front of Thunderbirds. Jake opened the door for Barbara then followed her inside the cab. Jake gave the driver a destination, but it was not his parent's home. The driver acknowledged with a mischievous smile and the cab bounced off down the old country road to an out of the way little hotel that Jake had reserved for just this moment.

"By the way," Jake said to Barbara as he looked deep into her sparkling blue eyes. "It's good to see you again."

"You too," she cooed. "You too."

29.

Lisa Woodall had enjoyed herself far more than she had thought possible.

The night had gone off without a hitch. Most of that had been thanks to Billy Connelly's unusual knack for making things happen. The only thing he had not been able to make happen in his life was Barbara Fram.

Billy had been terribly in love, or maybe it was lust, with Barbara since they were young kids. They eventually got together and dated for a few years during high school. Everyone thought that those two were perfect together and that they would eventually get married, have a house with a two car garage, three point two kids, a dog, and live happily ever after, *yada, yada, yada*.

Unfortunately, life has this habit of throwing curve balls at you when you least expect them. Barbara ended things rather abruptly with Billy and he didn't take it well. He was very jealous and just a tad bit possessive. He probably still felt that Barbara was his. Lisa had noticed that Billy acted as if things had not changed over the years. He had been doing it ever since she and Barbara had arrived at Thunderbirds.

Barbara, to her credit, managed to play it off and deal with it. Basically, she ignored him and, surprisingly, Billy hadn't done anything stupid.

He could be that way on occasion, as Lisa well knew. Billy had gotten severely wasted after Barbara had dumped him. He went on a tear and nearly destroyed himself, not to mention her as well. Luckily, Jake and Wilson had been around to help calm Billy down. Billy later apologized for his actions, put the past behind him, and moved on with his life. Which meant moving off to another state entirely. Lisa forgave him. Barbara and the others did the same and moved on with their lives as well. End of story.

A stray thought struck Lisa. Did Billy ever find out why Barbara had decided to call it quits back then? Did he know? Could he know?

Doubtless, she figured. But Billy Connelly was a resourceful man and he usually figured things out. If he did know, he had kept the secret well, which told Lisa that he probably had no idea to this day what had happened all those years ago.

And if he did not know, she sure as hell wasn't planning on telling him.

No sir, not her.

She turned at a stoplight onto the old back road that would lead her home without having to go through town and all of the lights there. Actually, the view on that route was very nice, at least during the daylight hours. The road ran along the backside of the Fort Greene State Park and past the old fort area. Besides, the back road would shave a good fifteen minutes off of her return trip home. Those fifteen minutes would be like heaven since this was the first time in a long while that she and Joe didn't have the kids. They were at their grandparent's place for the weekend. Lisa and Joe needed the quality time alone. Desperately. Plus, she suspected Fram would be out with Jake for a while.

Her headlights flashed across the street sign that pointed her direction.

She had taken this route many times.

Tonight it was the wrong choice.

Since Lisa knew the route home well, she allowed her mind drift far away, only vaguely concentrating on the road. Her mind drifted to thoughts of another time, another place. So lost in her reminiscences she barely noticed the stalled car across the center of the narrow road in time to slam on her brakes. She was scarcely able to stop her car before smashing into the car. Letting out a deep breath, Lisa peered out her driver's side window, looking for the owner of the vehicle. She could not see anyone, but she noticed that the car's hood was propped open. Shouldn't the driver have heard her as she pulled up? Surely the sound of her screeching brakes would have been sufficient to alert someone to her presence. Without another thought, her senses went on alert. *Where is...? Maybe someone has been hurt,* she thought. *Or worse.*

Erring on the side of caution, Lisa elected to remain inside her vehicle. She slowly rolled down her window and a gust of the cool night breeze washed over her. "Hello?" she called out into the night. "Is anyone there? Do you need any help?"

No answer.

"Hello?"

Still nothing.

Lisa could not help but think the worst when no answer to her call seemed forthcoming. She imagined someone hurt and needing her help.

She wondered what to do. Certainly it was not always safe to stop and lend a hand to strangers, but Lisa felt conflicted. If this had been her or her husband, she would hope that a Good Samaritan might stop and offer aid. Her mind made up, Lisa eased open her driver's side door, unhooked her seatbelt, and stepped slowly out into the brisk night air. A shiver ran up her spine.

"Hello?" she asked again in the darkness while she mentally chided herself for not having a flashlight in the car. Joe had told her several times that she needed to be better prepared, but did she ever listen? No. She would have to let him know how right he had been after she got home. And leaving her cell at home no longer seemed like a good idea.

As she approached the car, Lisa could not see anyone inside. Upon closer inspection, peeking in the rolled up window, she discovered that the vehicle was empty. Perhaps the owner had started walking toward town. Or back the other way? She traced her memory back across the past few miles and she knew that she had not seen anyone walking down the small back road from the direction she had traveled. *Where has the driver gone?* she wondered.

Moving to the front of the car, Lisa ran her hand along the front fender to the grill and across the radiator cap. It was warm to the touch. Whoever had been driving the car could not have been gone long. Especially on foot.

And if that person was injured...

The wind blew cold against her neck and Lisa shivered twice before deciding to move on. *There's not much I can do here,* she told herself as she started back toward her car.

As she reached for the door handle a small sound filtered across the night sky on the wind. A cough. There was someone there. Someone probably injured.

Quickly, Lisa turned toward the sound. "Hello? Where are y..."

Her voice quickly died out in her throat as she turned to see a man standing just beyond her arm's reach. He was a tall man, roughly six feet or so with broad shoulders and large arms. Not that she could see much of his arms from beneath the robe that he wore. It fluttered about him in the breeze, but he made no effort to move. A feeling of power radiated off of the man, almost as if he controlled the very wind around them both.

Lisa took a step back and bumped against her car. "Who are you?" She managed to get the words out of her mouth without stuttering. The man simply stared at her from beneath his hooded robe. She could not see his eyes clearly, but they burned through her nonetheless. "What do you want?" Lisa asked again while slowly opening the car door from behind her back. The man simply watched, unmoving. All she could see was the rictus of his wide toothy smile. In the darkness, it was a scary sight.

With speed that she never thought she could possess, Lisa jerked open the door and leapt inside in one fluid motion, then she slammed the door closed behind her. Out of instinct, she pulled on her seatbelt, never thinking about the three seconds it cost her. She snatched the gear shifter and threw the car into reverse. Stomping on the gas, her car swiveled around on the asphalt. Unfortunately, the small black top road was very narrow and Lisa drove off into the ditch backwards. She was stuck.

Panic started to set in as the mysterious man started moving toward her slowly. He was methodical. Deliberate.

Lisa feverishly tried to remove her seatbelt, but her fingers were trembling so hard that she could not make them do her will. She screamed a curse at the seatbelt before she was finally able to tear herself free from its clinging grasp.

The robed man reached inside his tunic, pulling out a small box. A micro cassette tape recorder she noticed. He pressed the play button and a voice echoed around Lisa.

Her own voice.

"*Hello? Is anyone there? Do you need any help?*"

"Oh God," Lisa moaned. This was some sort of trap. *But why? Why me? Why here?* Who knew she would take this route? Or was she simply in the wrong place at the wrong time? Unfortunately, Lisa had no time to ponder those questions. The only question that she had to answer at that moment was how to get away from there.

The man continued toward her. Slowly. Methodically. He depressed the rewind button, which squealed as her recorded voice was reversed.

"*Do you need any help?*" the cassette recorder said again.

Frantically, Lisa pushed open the passenger door and dove out of her car into the ditch, landing rather less than gracefully in the moist mud and grass. She was on her feet almost immediately, breaking into a run. In the distance behind her, Lisa could faintly hear her own voice giving chase. "*Hello? Is anyone there?*" It was unnerving, to say the least.

The robed man watched her as he quickened his pace behind her. "The chase is on," he whispered. Then, he started to run after his prey.

"*Do you need any help?*"

Lisa screamed as pent up fear exploded from her. If she were anywhere else, anywhere close to homes or buildings of any kind, then maybe someone might have heard her cry and responded. Maybe someone might rush to her rescue like a proverbial white knight. However, Lisa Woodall was on a deserted stretch of pavement three miles north of nowhere. On one side of the small country road stretched a flat, desolate cow pasture. Several cows were grazing in the field, all but oblivious to the horror unfolding around them. On the other side of the blacktop sat the dense woods of Fort Greene State Park. And behind her was certain death.

And he was bearing down on her fast.

Tossing all reason to the wind, Lisa changed her course in a split second and made a beeline for the woods just off of the road. A small incline lead upwards to the woods and she hurriedly half-ran, half-crawled the acclivity, slipping and sliding in the wet grass and mud.

Her tormentor stopped at the bottom of the incline and watched her struggle with slight amusement. She did not stop to look at him, but Lisa knew he was there. She could feel his eyes boring through her to her very soul. A shudder ran along her spine, but Lisa refused to let that stop her. She seized the fear, twisting it, turning it, used it to her advantage. Used it to strengthen her. Reaching relatively flat ground, Lisa made an all out run for the tree line as fast as she was able.

She had a passing familiarity of the woods around Lake Greene. She had grown up there, had played in those very same woods for hours on end in her youth. She prayed that nothing much had changed since those days.

She allowed a split second to glance behind her. The man was not there. But he was not gone either. She almost sensed his presence. Fueled by a determination to make it to safety, Lisa pushed forward as fast as she was able. For a brief moment, an all too brief moment, she felt as if she might make it out alive.

Then she heard the man's laughter echoing through the night.

It was a sound unlike any she had ever heard before in all her days. It was a sound that she would never forget as long as she lived. However long that would be.

Distracted as she was by the echoing laughter, Lisa neglected to notice a small hole in the path before her. It was probably a borough for a small woodland creature. Now, it was a tool of evil. Lisa's foot hit the hole and seconds later she found herself face down in the mud and the muck around her. She lay there, pressed flat against the wet ground, hoping that he might not see her there. Maybe he would give up the chase if she hid and did not run. A thousand maybes pressed against her brain, flooding her thoughts with *what ifs* and *why for's*.

It was not helpful.

All of those thoughts rushed through Lisa Woodall's brain like a river cascading over rapids. She craned her neck to look back the way she had come. Her tormentor was nowhere to be seen. She let out a short sigh of relief.

Her relief however, was quickly replaced by fear anew as light washed over the area, casting shadows all around her while simultaneously eliminating her hiding place. She pulled herself back up to one knee as she rubbed at her sore ankle.

Where's the light coming from? she wondered. *Of course. The car's headlights.* He had gotten back in the car. Maybe he had given up and decided to exercise the better part of valor and run.

Wishful thinking.

A shadow divided the bright light from the supposedly stalled car, cleaving up from the ground and blotting out part of the brightness. No. Not a shadow. A silhouette. The robed man was walking up the incline with the car lighting his way from behind. *But how had he been able to get to the car, move it and get back that quickly?* She wondered. She had no time to ponder the thought.

Any second now he would reach the top of the incline and his quarry would be easily seen. Lisa watched, paralyzed with fear, as the man in the muddy, wet robe came to a stop at the top of the rise. He saw her and she in turn could see him. Their eyes locked and a moment passed between them. In that moment, Lisa Woodall knew that she was not going to get out of this easily. With a thought for her husband and her children, she inhaled a deep breath of the cold night air, then, tensing her muscles, she sprinted toward the trees that were only a few feet away.

She ran and ran and ran. Faster than she had ever had to run in her entire life. The pressure built within her until she could feel her own heartbeat throbbing in her ears. Her heart threatened to burst: t o leap right from her chest. Still she ran as if her life depended on it.

In truth, it did.

30.

Harold Palmer was tired.

He and Franklin had only just returned home after several long hours at Thunderbirds. Franklin had genuinely seemed to enjoy himself. Harold a little less so. His problem wasn't with the style or the content of the entertainment that Thunderbird's provided, although he was a little unsettled by it. Harold had never thought of himself as a prude or anything; he just had a problem with crowds. That many people in one concentrated area created in him an overwhelming urge to run. Not that he was afraid of people or afraid of going out and having a good time, but Harold was just shy to a point. As a child, Franklin had often teased his older brother about this urge to shy away from crowds that he seemed to get every time they left the house.

Franklin, to his eternal delight, did not share his brother's feelings in regards to crowds. He loved them. To Franklin, the more the merrier was a way of life. Strange that he would end up in a town with a population as small as Sommersville.

Harold swayed gently in the wooden rocking chair on the deck jutting off of the backside of his brother's house. It was a relatively spacious deck, Harold had said as much when he first stepped out onto it. He found himself a nice seat while his brother went inside to change clothes and then find some refreshments for the two of them.

Harold peered out into the darkness around him and he listened to the natural sounds of the forest. Listening as if for the first time in his life. Closing his eyes, Harold allowed his other senses to take in all of the grandness surrounding him in the darkness, with the full moon providing the only illumination. Serenity fell upon him like a shroud.

The sounds he heard were nearly alien to him. Things he had not experienced since he had been a little boy. He could hear all of the sounds of nature as the woods of the state park that sat just off the far end of Franklin Ray Palmer's property crackled to life as if to perform a private concerto for Harold Palmer. Franklin's backyard was relatively small, all things concerned, but his large front lawn more than made up for that discrepancy.

EVIL WAYS

At the edge of the deck sat a Jacuzzi that looked like it had not been cleaned or used since the Carter Administration. The wooden steps from the deck led down to the grassy yard below which sloped rather steeply downhill about twenty feet toward a small creek at the yard's base. The creek was essentially the property line where Franklin's land ended and the State Park began.

It was a beautiful night.

He had made his nightly call home to tell Beverly and Lucy good night and asked about their day. As he closed the flap on his cell, he heard the door behind him slide open on its track, announcing his brother's return. Franklin moved to his brother and handed him a bottled water, then he silently took the other rocking chair nearby. The two men sat in silence for a moment as nature sang a symphony for them.

Harold finally broke the chorus as he twisted off the cap on his water. Franklin did the same with his beer. "Cheers," he said as he held the bottle up in a salute.

"To your health."

The silence returned briefly as both men allowed a moment to reflect on the events of the day. It had been a rather busy day.

"So," Harold said at last. "Nice place. I like this view. I think I could sit out here forever."

"Sweet isn't it?"

"Um-hmm."

"Sometimes I like to come out here late at night and let the critters out there serenade me to sleep. I've discovered that it is a good way to wind down after a stressful day at the office. Besides, it beats counseling and it is a hell of a lot cheaper than Tom's antique poster collection."

"I should say so. I bet he paid a pretty penny for some of those. Who would've figured that a small town sheriff could make that good of a living?"

"He doesn't really," Franklin added as he took another sip of his beer. "Tom and Mildred, that's his wife, are having a few monetary problems."

"Sorry to hear that."

"Yeah. Me too. Word has it that she wants to sell their land and buy a smaller place in town, but Tom's against selling off his ancestral home. It was about the only thing his father left him when he died. Tom doesn't want to give that up and I can understand how he feels."

"So can I. And since when did you become one to keep up with the gossip on your neighbors, Ray?"

"I'm a reporter. I hear things."

"Uh, huh."

"Really. All you have to do is listen. Didn't they teach you that in FBI school?"

"Must've been absent that day."

"Yeah, well. I can sympathize with Tom and Mildred though. I mean, I remember how much trouble we had when we sold the folk's house after Dad passed away. Mom had already moved off to live with Aunt Rita. She just couldn't stand being cramped up in that big house all alone. I didn't think we would ever get that place sold. I almost expected that we'd eventually just give up and one of us would move in."

"Not likely. It was a beautiful house, but I'm perfectly happy that it's gone. Best to get on with our lives. No sense living in the past, is there?"

"I suppose not, Harry. Still, I miss the old place. There are quite a few memories there."

"Yeah," mutters Harold. "Most of them embarrassing."

"Har, har."

"So," Harold changed the subject. "Where does Myers live anyway? Didn't you say that he lived near here?"

Franklin Palmer pointed off to the right. "Just on the other side of those trees. He has quite a large chunk of land. Twenty-two acres as I recall. There's even a lake on it. Good fishing.
"We may have to drop in before I head home."

"We can probably arrange that."

"Cool. So, did we *learn* anything at Thunderbird's tonight? Or was this your idea of showing me *the sights*?"

"Oh, very funny. I found a few of the dancers that seemed to know our victim. I got that she was a student over in Athens at the University Of Georgia and she was working as a dancer to pay off her student loan. She hasn't been around in the past few days. I guess we know why." A pause as he downed another gulp of his beer. "And what's wrong with the sights?"

"Uh... Nothing. Nothing at all."

"Don't spit on my town, brother dear."

"Yeah. Ok. Anything else?"

"Actually, yes. It seems that Rebecca had recently found herself a boyfriend. She was really happy about it and she was telling her friends that she thought she could really get serious about this one. One of the girl's I talked to said that she had never seen her as happy as she had been the past few weeks before she died."

"Boyfriend, huh?" Harold finished off his bottled water. "Interesting. Got a name?"

The younger Palmer brother let out a bark of laughter. "Oh you are going to *love* this. Her boyfriend was a cop."

"Local cop?"

"Oh yes. But wait, I haven't gotten to the best part yet. She was dating... drum roll please... Deputy Christopher Jackson, Sommersville P. D."

"Jackson?" Harold searched his memory. Franklin watched as his brother put the pieces together in his mind. He could almost see the light bulb flash above Harold's head. "Wasn't Jackson the officer that found the girl's body? I don't recall anyone saying anything about him knowing the girl. Do you?"

"Nope."

"Have you told Myers yet?"

Franklin shook his head. "No. I'll stop by there in the morning after I check in at the paper. But first I think I'm going to get some sleep. I'm beat."

Harold pulled himself out of his comfortable rocker. "Sounds like a good idea. I'm a little tired myself. It's been a few years since I've gone bar hopping."

"Now Harry, going to one bar is not exactly considered bar hopping. If you want to try it tomorrow night I'm game. We can head on over to Athens. Now that's a happening town. Think you can keep up with me?"

"Doubtful," Harold grunted. "Must be getting old."

"Just remember that you said that, not me."

"I'm sure you won't let me forget."

"I'm sure I won't either. Good night."

"Good night, Ray. Sleep well."

"You too, Harry. You too."

The two brothers moved their conversation indoors. Franklin escorted his brother to the spare room where they said their good nights once again.

Harold was asleep ten seconds after his head hit the pillow.

Franklin, however, spent a large portion of the night pondering the situation. Every thought in his brain rushed to the forefront as he lay in bed. He stared at the ceiling while his brain began working to piece together all of the assorted scraps of information he had gathered over the past day or two. It was a good two hours before sleep finally claimed him.

Overhead, the sky rolled and thunder began to peal across the gray clouds with lightning not far behind.

The rain would be returning soon.

31.

Lisa had thought that the trees would protect her.

In her mind she was certain that she could find a hiding place. But her attacker seemed to know these woods as well as she did. Perhaps better.

Panicking, Lisa tried to collect her thoughts and formulate a plan. She failed. Her heart was pounding, threatening to burst. Her head throbbed. *I need help,* she told herself. *But from who? Where?* Then it hit her. Memories of her surroundings came flooding back to her in crystal clarity. These woods were only a mile or so deep. On the other side were houses. One of them even belonged to the sheriff. If she could get to Sheriff Myers he would be able to help her. He would save her.

Good plan.

So she ran again, dodging around trees and bushes, ducking to avoid low hanging branches and sidestepping obstacles that threatened to send her sprawling to the ground again. She was making good time, or would have been were it not someone chasing her, someone who could not possibly have any good intentions as far as she was concerned. She afforded another glance over her shoulder.

The man was not there.

Where her heart rejoiced and begged for her to stop, her brain yelled for her to keep running. This man, whoever he was, was obviously familiar with the terrain. He knew where he was going and could probably guess where she was planning to go. This man was not stupid by any means, as his action to this point had clearly indicated. He would not give up after going to all of this trouble. *No way.* Then Lisa abruptly stopped. "Oh no," she whispered as the realization that she had made a wrong turn hit her. A natural obstacle obstructed her flight path.

Potter's Ravine.

The end of the line. There was no way for her to circumvent the ravine before her tormentor found her. He had been leading her toward this spot. It was all part of the plan. That meant....

He's here!!! the voice in her head screamed. She lurched around, ready to face her attacker. No more running. But to Lisa Woodall's amazement the robed man was not there. Her anger slowly seeped away, only to be replaced by the numbing fear once again. She brought her hands up to her face and the tears flowed uncontrollably. Then, as her body defied all reason and logic, Lisa dropped to her knees and cried out loudly.

It was over and she knew it. There was no hope.

None whatsoever.

Then she felt his presence. It was as if he had just appeared there as if from thin air. Regaining her composure as best as she was able, Lisa forced her eyes to lift to look at the man who was about to kill her. She peered into deep-set eyes that were shadowed by the hood of the dark, mud-encrusted robe. She stared past his eyes and into his soul. She did not like what she saw there. She saw madness and cruelty accompanied by a healthy dose of insanity and glee. This man was getting off on what he did. But there was something else there that struck Lisa Woodall to her very core.

Familiarity.

She knew this man.

"Oh my God," she muttered as he reached for her. "Don't! We can..."

The sounds of the forest around them fell silent as an audible **SNAP!** filled the night, blotting out the sounds of nature. The forest fell silent as the animals mourned the passing of Lisa Woodall. Her last breath, her last split second on this earth, was spent trying to give voice to the words that filled her mind. Thoughts of her husband and her children. Thoughts of her friends. She knew that she was but the first. They would all die and there wasn't a damned thing she could do to help them.

Her friends.

Images of her twenty-eight years swiftly passed before her eyes in the time it took her to blink. Her whole life reduced to a sliver of memory. A single microsecond in the grand scheme of things.

Then she was gone.

The killer looked down at the limp body of Lisa Woodall. She was so still and unmoving. He knelt down and ran a gloved finger across her leg, remembering the fantasy of her and her friend pleasuring him. He followed the curves of her body until he reached her fractured neck. He wove a path around the neck to her chin and then to her mouth. He leaned over and kissed the deceased woman gently on the lips.

"Sleep well, princess," he whispered to the corpse. "You'll have plenty of company soon. My lord will see to it that we send all of your brood to you in short order. Don't worry. Your fear will sustain us. Make us strong."

The killer wrapped his arms around her body and pulled her close as he stood. As silence permeated the air around them, the robed man trudged off with his prize leaving behind only the sound of his footfalls

EVIL WAYS
on the wet, muddy ground and the sound of his crazed laughter.
Your fear will sustain us.

32.

"Hold on!"

From inside the hotel room a voice shouted. Either unhearing or uncaring, the sheriff knocked again. "Yeah. Coming," called the voice from inside room 312.

The door opened, but it was not who Tom Myers had expected to see. "Who are you?" Tom asked the man on the other side of the door.

"What?"

Clearly Tom had interrupted his sleep. With an impatient grunt, Tom pulled out his badge and held it up so the man could see it plainly. "Tom Myers. **Sheriff** Tom Myers." Tom purposefully exaggerated his title for the right effect. "And you are?"

"Hollis. Uh, Ted... Ted Hollis," the sleep shrouded man said quietly. "I just got into town at about three this morning. Billy let me crash on the couch here instead of going through the hassle of getting a room that early in the morning."

Tom scrutinized the man. He was probably another of the folks in town for the reunion. "I'm looking for Dr. Billy Connelly," Tom said impatiently. "It's important."

"He's still asleep."

"Wake him."

"Sure." The man who said his name was Ted sleepily motioned Tom inside. "C'mon in. I'll go wake him."

"That'd be nice."

Tom stepped inside the room. From the look of the couch, Tom guessed that Ted Hollis' story was probably accurate. The hotel was fairly classy, especially for as small a town as Sommersville. Dr. Connelly's suite had two rooms, a bedroom and living room area with a fold out couch. The bathroom sat between the two rooms in a small hallway. Ted disappeared down the short hallway toward the bedroom.

While waiting, Tom impatiently began to pace back and forth across the living room area. There was a knock at the door so Tom stepped over and opened it. Out in the corridor stood Chris Jackson, one of Tom's deputies.

"Tom?" Chris seemed surprised to see the sheriff in his friend's hotel room. "What's the matter? Has something happened to Billy? Tom?"

"Come on in," Tom said as he motioned his deputy inside, closing the door behind him. "Have a seat, Chris."

"Tom..."

Before Chris Jackson could utter another word, Billy Connelly and Ted Hollis emerged from the bedroom area. Clearly, Ted had been forced to wake Billy. The man looked sleepy, his hair disheveled and his eyes were open as slits.

The Doctor scratched at the stubble on his chin. "Can I help you, officer?"

"It's Sheriff, actually. I'm sorry to wake you, but I have a few questions for you."

"Ted!" Chris Jackson barked when he saw his old friend from high school. "When did you get here?"

"Couple hours ago. Work was keeping me a little bit busy."

"What kind of work do you do, Mr. Hollis?" Tom asked.

Ted turned to face the sheriff as if for the first time. "Oh, I'm a cop. Police investigator in Atlanta. Been on the force for... going on eight years now."

"I see," Tom said. "Well, I won't hold you gentlemen up long. I received a phone call this morning from Joe Woodall."

"Joe?"

"Yes. It seems that his wife never made it home last night after going out with you guys to Thunderbirds for a little reunion celebration. Have either of you seen her?"

"No. Not since last night," Billy said, more alert now.

"I just got in this morning," Ted said. "Around four a.m."

Tom favored his Deputy. "Chris?"

"She was still at Thunderbirds when I left. She was with Jake and Fram... uh, Barbara. Barbara was staying with her. Maybe the two of them went off somewhere?"

"Where?"

"I don't know. I'm just guessing. Tom?" Chris addressed his erstwhile boss. "I think we should go out looking for them. Start a search at Thunderbirds and work our way back toward her house."

Tom nodded. "I already have Ben getting the troops together for a search. As her friends, I thought you might want to lend a hand. Maybe you'd have an insight on her way of thinking that might be helpful."

"Of course, Sheriff Myers," Ted Hollis agreed. Just give me a minute to get dressed and we can head out."

"Yes," Billy said. "Just a moment."

"Okay. Chris? I'm going to head on out there. Bring these guys out toward Thunderbirds and find me or Dooley and we'll get started."

"Do you think this is another..." the words catch in his throat. "Is she another one like Rebecca?"

"I hope not, Chris. God, I hope not."

"Me too. Don't worry, Tom. I'll get these guys out there and see if I can find the others. We'll do whatever we can."

Tom eyed his deputy with a newfound respect as he headed out the door. Just yesterday, Chris Jackson was determined to drink himself into a stupor. Today, it seemed, he decided to face his demons head on. Tom couldn't be any more proud of his young deputy. Tom understood how tough facing one's personal demons could be. He wished he could have faced his own that well when they had threatened to overwhelm him years ago. Tom had crawled into a bottle back then as an escape from his problems only to find a whole new set of them on the inside. Only through the grace of God and the love of his wife, Mildred, had Tom Myers managed to pull himself back up to face his problems.

Moving down the corridor to the elevator, Tom reflected. He was happy to see that Chris had done so as well without having to worry about the dangers of withdrawal that had threatened to eat Tom alive when he had tried to stop drinking. Tom hoped that Chris possessed more strength than he ever had. It looked as though he did, he pulled himself together on his own, but Tom was also aware of how easy it was to fall off that horse when the going got tough. The bottle usually seized a very deadly hold on a person. Tom had been there more than once. He knew that temptation would probably come his way again one day. He only hoped that he would be strong enough to fight off those demons when that time came.

As Tom stepped into the elevator, he depressed the button marked **L** for lobby. The doors closed and the elevator descended downward through the shaft toward the floor from the third floor. Tom stepped out into the lobby after the doors parted. He moved through the crush of people, most of which were in town for the reunion, toward the door. He opened the door to his police vehicle, an old and battered brown pick-up truck and he pulled out into the oncoming traffic on his way toward the city limits and Thunderbird's Bar.

All the while, a nagging feeling tugged at the back of his mind.

Chris Jackson's words echoed inside his brain. *"Is she another one like Rebecca?"*

"God I hope not," Tom swore as he turned onto the main highway that led out of town.

"I hope not."

Twenty minutes had passed since Tom Myers left the hotel.

He called Dooley over the police band and told him about his suspicions that Lisa Woodall might be another victim of the same person who killed the girl in the park. Somewhere out there was a psycho preying on young women and it was his job to find that person and stop him. Or her.

Dooley had the other deputies start their search at Thunderbirds and work their way back toward town in the hope that they might find something. Tom told Dooley that he was going to check out some of the back roads that ran along the outer perimeter of the park. They had found Rebecca's body near Lake Greene. If this was the work of the same person as they suspected, then maybe Lisa Woodall would be found near the same place. That was, of course, provided she was dead. Tom had a hard time convincing himself that there was any possibility that Mrs. Woodall was alive.

He had learned to trust his gut feelings.

Tom turned his brown truck onto Winding Creek Road, just off to the far side of the Fort Greene State Park and Lake Greene. He knew that this was one of at least five back roads that could be taken to travel between Thunderbird's Bar and the home owned by Mr. and Mrs. Joe Woodall.

The road was desolate. Empty. Off to Tom's left sat the park. It was nothing short of gorgeous, but Tom had no time for seeing the sights that morning. The park was filled with trees, but the opposite side of Winding Creek road was flat lands consisting of mainly cow pastures and gardens. Tom searched for any sign that Lisa Woodall might have come through there.

He found nothing.

Tom coasted down the less than wide black top of the small country road. He hoped to see any sign that a person might have stopped along the road at some point during the night. However, his search was proving unsuccessful.

Then he noticed something: a small thing that he might have

overlooked had he not been staring out the driver's side window at it directly. He stopped the truck, threw it in reverse, and backed up. He pulled off of the road onto the muddy shoulder. Tom clutched his portable radio from the dashboard and slid out of his truck.

"Dooley?" he called into the hand held walkie talkie.

A split second later, Deputy Benjamin Dooley's voice answered. "I'm here, Boss. Did you find anything?"

"I'm not sure, Ben. I'm on Winding Creek Road. Just to the far end of the park. I've found signs of what looks like someone trying to climb the embankment up into the park. Why don't you grab some of the boys and head on over this way. You'll see my truck where I pulled over."

"Uh, where will you be, Sheriff?" Ben Dooley asked. There was confusion in his question.

Tom smiled, knowing the Ben Dooley was probably scowling at what he knew Tom's next words would be. "I'm going in to take a look," Tom answered.

"I was afraid of that," Ben's voice crackled. "We're on our way now."

"Good. I'll see you when you get here."

"And Sheriff?"

"Yeah, Ben."

"Try to be careful. Don't do anything foolish."

"You know me," Tom quipped as he checked the cartridge on his pistol before sliding back into his shoulder holster. "You know how cautious I am."

"Right."

"Just hurry up and get out here, willya?" Tom said as he pulled a shotgun from behind the seat of his truck. "There's safety in numbers, if you know what I mean."

"Yes sir, Sheriff. I think I do. Dooley out."

Tom quietly tucked the walkie talkie into the clip on the side of his belt. He loaded the shotgun quickly and efficiently then put a few extra shells in his jacket pocket in case he should need them. "Always a good idea to be prepared," he whispered before setting off up the incline in search of Lisa Woodall, her corpse, and/or the person that killed her.

Luckily though, Tom Myers had grown up playing in these woods. He knew them far better than most. Occasionally, he and Mildred went out for a long afternoon walk across their property and into the woods that framed the outermost sections of Fort Greene State Park. They would have the most pleasant conversations out there. They could leave their day-to-day world behind them and lose themselves out in the beauty that Mother Nature afforded them.

After the events of the past few days, Tom Myers doubted he would ever look at these woods the same way again. Maybe it was a good idea for him and Mildred to sell off their land and move into a place closer to town. He would have to think hard about that, but not now. It was hardly the time or place for anyone to let their mind wander. Out there, on the hunt as it were, losing your string of concentration could get you killed.

Or lost.

Tom Myers had no desire to do either.

He pressed onward.

34.

Deputy Ben Dooley pulled to a stop behind Tom Myer's truck.

It had only been about six minutes after the sheriff had radioed in his position. Dooley had gathered as many of his fellow officers as he was able and told them to concentrate their search near the park, possibly near Lake Greene where the other girl had been found. As Ben stepped out of his squad car he noticed a familiar car pull up and park just behind him. Ben immediately recognized Chris Jackson.

"Jackson," Ben said as Chris jumped out of his car and jogged over to his fellow officer.

"Hiya, Ben. Where's the chief?"

"He called in that he had seen some marks that looked like a person struggling to get up the incline." He pointed to a spot that matched that description. "I assume that's what he found. He's already gone in. I'd say at least ten minutes."

"Good," Chris said. "We're going in with you. This is our friend."

"Now wait just a minute, Chris. Did the Sheriff authorize this?"

"Yes. He saw us this morning. We just want to help find our friend. I can't sit by and do nothing. I let that happen before. I won't let it happen again."

Ben noticed that two of Chris' three friends passed a worried look to one another. Chris pointed to the three men and made the appropriate introductions in turn. "Been Dooley, this is Billy Connelly, Charles Phillips, and Ted Hollis. Ted is a cop down in Atlanta. They can handle themselves. Besides, we grew up playing in these woods. Who knows them better than we do? Come on, Ben," Chris pleaded. "Time is wasting."

"Alright Chris, but you better keep these guys in line. I can't afford to lose anyone else in these damned woods."

Chris nodded quickly, before Ben could change his mind. "Understood. I'll need a gun."

"Pardon?"

"Let me borrow a gun, Ben. Mine's still at the station." He lifted an eyebrow at his fellow officer. Ben understood. "I'm supposed to be on vacation. Remember?" Chris said to Ben, who rubbed his unshaven chin.

Exasperated, Ben Dooley let out a puff of air. "Alright." He reached into his squad car and pulled out his extra gun and two clips. He passed them to Chris without preamble or mention of Chris' recent suspension. He figured that the sheriff could use all the help he could get. "Here. And I'll want that back when this is over," he said.

"Gotcha, Ben," Chris said. He turned back to his former classmates. "Come on. Follow me."

Ben let out a whistle at Chris, who turned back to face him. "Here," Ben yelled as he tossed a walkie talkie at the erstwhile deputy. "You might need this."

Chris clipped the walkie talkie to his belt. "Thanks. I'll be in touch."

"Be careful. I'll be in as soon as the others get here." Ben Dooley stood with his hands on his hips and watched the three men as the climbed up the slight embankment. At the top, they broke into a run across the fairly flat ground until they disappeared from view inside the woods.

Chris Jackson led his friends through the fairly thick brush at the edge of the Fort Greene State Park. The going was slow and the ground less than steady but they were on a mission and nothing would stop them from finding their friend. Billy looked around with eyes that had not seen the inside of a forest in many a year. He let out a soft whistle.

"This place sure has changed a lot since we used to play around out here when we were kids." If the circumstances had been different, they might have enjoyed this little jaunt through the woods. They looked for anything, a familiar area that might let them know where they were. After a few minutes hike Billy found it.

A very tall and very old tree stood watch over the younger trees of the woods and all those that trespassed upon the area. All four of the men immediately recognized the tree and the spot. It had been a favorite hiding place for them when they had been younger and looking for an escape, even if it was only for a few minutes.

Slowly, Billy walked up to the large tree. Tentatively, he ran a hand along the trunk, feeling the bark on his palm as his he brushed against all of the history stored in that spot. This had been a favorite spot for him. This was the place where he first kissed Barbara Fram while they were in middle school. This was where he and Charles and Wilson had told each other their deepest, darkest secrets one afternoon when they ditched school. This was where they all camped out during the summer. This was where they had their graduation party. This was the place where

Billy Connelly took his first drink. A few hours later he woke up there with his first hangover.

A lot of memories.

Too many memories to go through now. They had a job to do and each of them knew it. They pressed on. Billy took a second to stare at the large tree for another second before following. He let his index finger trace the carved lines across the side of the tree. The letters *BC & BF 4 EVER* still marked the spot where Billy and Barbara first kissed. Billy exhaled loudly before moving on to rejoin his friends in their search.

"Let's see," Charles said as he tried to determine which direction to take. "Billy lived over that way. I think..." he pointed off to his left at a house that they could not see through the trees.

"No. No. No." Ted stepped to the front of the group. "We just passed the tree. Off to the left is Potter's Ravine. Remember? We built that small bridge so we could get across the ravine instead of walking the mile around it."

"You think the bridge is still there?" Charles asked with an excited little boy voice.

Ted mumbled something, but Charles did not quite hear him as Ted's back was to the group. "Pardon?" Charles asked.

Ted turned back to face them. "Oh. Sorry." He smiled. "I said, I highly doubt that flimsy little contraption we called a bridge could have survived this long. Super builders we were not," he joked.

"It could be," Billy argued. "It has been a long time since any of us has been out here. Right?"

Ted nodded his agreement. "Yeah. I just don't think we built it that well is all. That's all."

"Right. Right. I remember it," Chris agreed. "If it didn't fall apart then the forestry commission might have removed it when they started a clean up project on this place a couple of years ago."

Billy put his hands to his hips. "Well, where to now?" he asked as he scouted out the woods around them. "You're the boss here, Chris."

Chris let out a hoarse cough. "I think we should probably head out toward the ravine then," he said as he started in that direction. "This way."

"Now what makes you think that?" Billy asked after his friend.

"Well, can you think of a better place to start looking?"

"Well, yes, actually. There are several houses to our right and a whole mess of woods around us. What makes you think we should pass all of this by to go to old Potter's Ravine? It just doesn't make since to me. Unless it's a cop thing?"

"Right," Chris suppressed a chuckle. "It's a cop thing." He motioned with his hands. "Just trust me on this," he said, exasperated. "Okay?"

"Chris, what aren't you telling us?" Ted asked as he stepped in closer to the deputy. "I have that '*cop thing*' too, remember?"

Chris' expression deepened, then dropped. "I... There have been some... incidents in the area of late. We have reason to believe that a crime was committed at or near Potter's Ravine two nights ago. I figure that would be a logical place to start our search. I'm pretty sure that's where the sheriff would go."

Billy stepped up to stand beside Ted. "What kind of crime?" His tone was harsher than he had intended.

Chris Jackson looked troubled. The words did not come easily for him. To the three men surrounding him it looked like his heart was ready to leap out of his chest onto the moist ground.

"Chris?" Billy asked forcefully.

"Chris? Talk to us," Charles added as he placed a reassuring hand on Chris Jackson's shoulder.

To his credit, Chris does not flinch as contact was made. Ever since he found Rebecca's broken body, Chris Jackson had been on edge. His nerves were frayed and his skin crawled at the slightest touch. He saw her every time he closed his eyes. Lifeless, she stared at him as he drew closer to her dead body. As he knelt over her to say his final farewell, Rebecca's bruised and blackened eyes snapped open and she peered into his soul only to find a void there. A void left by her departure.

"I lost a...," he covered his mouth as another cough came to him. "...lost a friend here the other night. I think I loved this woman. She was so different from any of the other women that I have ever been with. And someone took that all away from me. Took her away from me."

Charles tightened his firm hand on his friend's heaving shoulder. "I'm so sorry," Charles said just barely above a whisper. "So terribly sorry."

"Yeah man. I had no idea," Billy offered.

"Oh man," admitted a stunned looking Ted. "My condolences, pal. I didn't know."

The Sommersville deputy rubbed the tears from his eyes. "Thanks," he tried to say coherently. "If Lisa or Barbara ran afoul of this... this... monster, then there will be hell to pay. I swear to you on that." Anger replaced Chris' feelings of loss over Rebecca. "I already lost one person that I cared deeply for. I'll be damned if I let that happen again."

Ted let out a deep breath as he patted his friend on the shoulder opposite the one Charles had a grip on. "If that's the case then," Ted said. "Perhaps we should be on our way before we miss out on anything. If you say it's Potter's ravine, then it is Potter's Ravine."

"Thanks guys. I hope I'm wrong."

"So do we," Charles said. "Let's get moving."

"Yeah," Billy agreed. "Yeah."

The four men moved off toward Potter's Ravine and a memory that gnawed at the very heart of Christopher Jackson. The rest of the trip was spent in silence as each of the men reflected on what he had learned that day. Most disturbing was the fact that the place that each of them had called home at one point or anther was not the picture perfect place they all remembered from their youth.

Their memories had been tainted. No matter what else, the place that had been a magic place for all of them in their youth would forever more have a sting of evil and death to it. No more would all of the memories of this place be happy ones. It was amazing how a single and despicable act could ruin the memories and the ideals of a group of individuals in a split second. Things would never be the same for them again. Only for the briefest of moments did these men entertain the wish that they had not come back here to this place.

It is said that you can never go home again and perhaps that is true, no matter who you are. For Billy Connelly, Ted Hollis, Charles Phillips, and Chris Jackson home was no longer *home sweet home*. Things would never be the same again.

And, perhaps, that was the biggest crime of all.

35.

Tom Myers heard them approach.

Although the four men were trying to be as quiet as possible, they made enough noise that the sheriff had picked them up long ago. Had he not found what he was looking for, Tom would not have waited on the others. Unfortunately, he had found the object of his search.

Lisa Woodall.

Or more appropriately, Lisa Woodall's body.

Tom stood at the edge of Potter's Ravine and looked down into the muddy stream that ran along the length of this once magical place. He stared, although he would much rather look at anything else, and noticed all of the pertinent details. He even noted the less than important details. He noticed the position of the body. Lying on her back, her face pointing toward the hidden sun, Lisa Woodall almost looked at peace. Except for the fact that her neck had been broken.

Her body was laid across the length of the small stream and the icy cold waters cascaded around her forming new pathways. Tom watched as the waters instantly changed their course to follow the new paths made by the intruder. Nature simply adapted to Lisa Woodall's presence as if it were nothing more than a mild annoyance. Already the thick mud had started to claim her body as she slowly began to submerge ever so slightly into the muddy waters at the base of Potter's Ravine. The water was part of a continuous flow that traveled from a river not far away. The water flowed through the ravine before making its way to Lake Greene where it pooled.

Two of this town's historical, not to mention beautiful, landmarks had their memories tarnished in as many days. *What's next?* Tom Myers wondered. There were still a few historical sights near the park, a few even located within the state park itself. Tom simply had no answers nor did he have nearly enough manpower to guard every single possible location for this lunatic's next killing.

Tom's stomach knotted at those thoughts and threatened to rip from his body. He heard the others, Chris and his companions. They were closer now. Very close. They would be there in mere minutes. Tom turned his gaze away from Potter's Ravine and faced the direction of the men moving in his general direction. Tom called out to them. "Chris!" Tom shouted.

His deputy shouted a reply. "Where are you, Sheriff?"

"The ravine."

"The...." Chris Jackson did not finish his last thought. There was no need. Tom would not have stopped searching unless he had found something. Since he had not heard his friend Lisa's voice, then he could only assume the worst. He looked at the suddenly bloodless faces of his three old friends and realized that they, too, had understood what happened.

Then, the four high school friends broke out into a full run toward Potter's Ravine and a waiting Tom Myers. Chris arrived first, only three steps ahead of Ted Hollis. Tom held out his hands to keep the two men back. "You don't need to see this," he told them, all the while knowing how futile it was to try and stop them.

"Move." Chris' tone informed Tom that his deputy had already made up his mind. Deputy Chris Jackson and his friend Ted moved over to the edge as Charles Phillips and Billy Connelly finally caught up to them.

"Oh God. No."

Cautiously, Dr. Billy Connelly eased toward the edge of Potter's Ravine. He leaned out to look, guessing what he would find, but hoping beyond hope that it would not be true. His hopes were in vain as the empty face of his friend stared back at him from the abyss.

Billy lunged toward the ravine, intent on helping her. The two officers, Chris and Ted, grabbed him and held the young doctor fast, halting him from his foolhardy gesture. Billy, to say the least, was less than gratified by the gesture they made for him. "Let me go, you bastards! Let go! That's Lisa down there for God's sake."

But the two men held fast, halting their rash friend's urge to fling himself into a dangerous situation. Still, Billy struggled against them. He turned to face Chris Jackson and with a fire in his eyes that could only be caused by a great flaming hatred shouted, **"Let! Me! Go!"**

"No. I can't Billy. I can't lose you too."

Ted loosened his grip on his friend as all of the fight and hatred drained away from Billy Connelly. The young doctor fell to his knees and cried as his friends reached out to comfort him. To comfort one another.

Tom watched as he walked away from them. Unclipping his walkie talkie from his belt, the sheriff toggled the switch and called for the attention of another of his deputies, Benjamin Dooley. Before long, Ben's deep voice crackled across the old communication's equipment. Tom Myers quickly filled Ben in on the events of the past few minutes and he instructed his deputy to call in an ambulance and get the morgue ready for a new arrival.

"And get Franklin Palmer on the phone," Tom said in conclusion. "Tell him that I really need to talk to him."

"Got it, Boss," Dooley added before signing off and rushing to complete the tasks laid out for him.

As Tom reattached the walkie talkie to his belt clip, he noticed that Chris Jackson was no longer huddled with his grieving friends. No, his deputy was walking toward him.

"Tom," Chris said at just above a whisper. "You know that this is the same. Don't you?" His eyes were swollen and threatened to burst and unleash a wellspring of emotion that had long been buried deep within Christopher Jackson.

Tom reached out a hand to his deputy, his friend. Chris backed away a step. "I want this ended here and now, Tom," Chris said a little louder. "I want the person who did this -who did Rebecca- I want him found and I want him..."

The dam burst and the tears came. His knees began to quiver and the world started spinning wildly out of focus as Chris Jackson realized for the first time that his life was coming unraveled at the seams. He lost balance and tumbled forward, but Tom managed to move in front of his friend. Catching the young deputy, Tom held him tightly as Chris let it all flow out of him. He let loose the pain he had been trying to suppress since he had discovered the broken body of his lover just the day before. And now this.

It was simply more than one man could bear.

Tom whispered to his deputy, "And we'll get him. Don't you worry. If it's the last thing I do, I'll draw and quarter this bastard myself."

Reassuring words, but Chris Jackson did not -could not- hear them over the sound of his own sobs echoing those of three of his oldest and dearest friend not three feet away.

In respect to the memory of Lisa Woodall the animals of the forest seemed to fall silent and all that could be heard in Lake Greene State Park were the sounds of men as they mourned the passing of a friend. As they did so, they posed the one question that all survivors seek an answer to.

Why?

36.

Charles Phillips had expected great things to happen during this special weekend.

He had wanted so very much for things to be perfect. His friend, Billy Connelly had taken great pains to make certain that everything was planned out to the letter. This should have been one of the happiest moments of his life.

Too bad it hadn't turned out that way.

The Sommersville Police Department was not overly large as the relatively small brick and concrete building that housed it could readily attest. The lounge/waiting area was scarcely larger than the smallest of hotel rooms that Charles had ever had the pleasure of staying in. And he had spent time in more than a few hotels; ranging from the very nice to the worst of the fleabag motels. His job as a claims representative for a well known insurance corporation kept him on the move and traveling constantly from one disaster to another, whether they be natural or caused by the foolishness of man.

At that moment he felt like a sardine, as he had been crammed into the all too small area of the Sommersville P.D.'s waiting area. He was not alone either. All around him were the friends whom he had come to town to see.

Jake Page and Barbara Fram were sitting on a small couch near the door. It turned out that the two of them had left Thunderbirds together. Apparently they had been intimately involved for quite some time, but they both felt a need to keep it a secret from the others. Charles did not know why. He could think of no logical reason why they should feel a need to hide something like that, but they had nevertheless. He knew that Billy still harbored feelings toward Barbara, as they were each other's first loves and all. Still, that was over with a long, long time ago. Billy should not have had any objections about Jake and Fram's personal lives.

And if he did, so what? They were all adults. High school was such a long way away from them. More so now, it seemed, than ever before.

Chris Jackson was busy talking with one of the deputies on duty.

Charles tried to recall the gentleman's name, but it escaped him. It might have been *Dooles* or *Dooly*. Something like that. Ted was also huddled along side them near the deputy's desk. As a cop himself, Ted probably spoke the same language as Chris and his coworker. They were probably discussing the particulars of the case even now.

Charles figured that as police officers, Chris, Ted, the deputy, even the sheriff had all been trained to deal with situations such as they faced at that moment. That image vanished earlier today when Charles saw Chris collapse in a fit of emotion over their friend's death. Her murder. If the normally stoic Christopher Jackson could not deal with a situation like that, then what hope did an emotionally driven man like Charles Phillips have.

None, he figured. *None whatsoever.*

Joe Woodall, Lisa's husband had been in earlier to talk with the sheriff, but a deputy had driven the grief stricken man home a short time earlier, which was probably for the best. The last thing he needed was to be surrounded by his wife's friends. They would only serve to add to his discomfort and pain. And no one wanted to add any more misery to the man than he already had. They each voiced their condolences in turn before Joe left. After that the silence returned stronger than before.

Billy had not been able to stay in one spot for very long since they had arrived at the police station. He paced around the cramped room for a few minutes. Then, after a short while, he made his way outside and smoked a cigarette. He had told Charles once before that he had given the smokes up, but Charles supposed that the circumstances warranted it, so he had opted to keep quite about it and not nag his friend about the dangers of smoking. As a doctor, Billy undoubtedly knew all of the speeches. He had probably given it a time or two himself. It seemed a simple case of *physician heal thyself,* but that was a conversation that Charles and Billy would have at a later date.

Charles, for his part had been sitting in a hardback chair over in a corner. He had already flipped through the five or six outdated magazines that were haphazardly scattered across the small table that ran along one wall of the waiting area. He had even tried to start conversations with some of the others, but no one seemed very much like talking.

Charles couldn't blame them. He didn't feel very chatty himself, but the utter silence between these old chums was starting to grate on his already frayed nerves. Someone had to break the tension. It might as well be him.

Although his motive had been noble, his plan met with utter failure. No one wanted to take the high road and talk. That made it hard for Charles Phillips to play his usual role of the peacemaker as he had done so many times in the past. No matter how hard he tried he couldn't get anyone to open up about how they were feeling. They were all sad and withdrawn. Of course that was to be expected. One of their own had died and the police had no clues and no suspects.

Stifling a yawn, Charles stood and moved slowly around the much too small room in a desperate attempt to keep himself awake. The place, much like a doctor's office, was causing him to feel sleepy. The sheriff had asked them all to wait while he compiled the information that he had. After that he planned to talk to all of them in turn to see if any of them knew anyone that might have wanted to harm Lisa. Or anything strange that might have happened while they were partying the previous evening at Thunderbirds. So many questions to be asked of them.

So many questions that each of them would be asking themselves as they desperately searched for some clue, some rhyme or reason why this happened. Especially why this had to happen to her. Lisa Woodall had never harmed, or thought of harming, anyone in her entire life. For this to happen to her was utterly unthinkable. Yet it had happened and nothing that anyone could say would ever change that.

So they said nothing.

Before Charles could ask yet again how much longer it would be before they got some answers, the outer door swung open and two men entered the police station. They made a beeline for the sheriff's office door. They made no effort to stop, or to even pay any attention to Charles, Billy, or any of the others.

The two men had a familiar look to Charles and he could tell that Billy had recognized them as well because he walked into the room scant seconds behind the two new arrivals. He watched them as they crossed the room, never taking his eyes from them. Something had happened that they were not aware of.

Something's going on. But what?

One of the two men knocked on the door. The sheriff's muffled voice responded and the door opened. Both men disappeared inside. Over by the deputy station, Charles noticed that Chris Jackson was watching them as well. The only difference was that he knew who they were.

His expression gave that much away.

37.

"We have a problem, Gentlemen."

Sitting in the office of Tom Myers, Sommersville's county sheriff, Franklin Ray Palmer seemed convinced that Tom's statement was more than mere hyperbole. Sitting in the chair next to him was his brother, Harold. For his part, Harold would agree with his younger brother's assessment of their current situation.

Franklin, ever the newspaper man, leaned forward with notepad and pencil in hand. Harold simply leaned back in his chair, listening carefully. Franklin quickly jumped into the conversation without preamble. And head first. "You've had another one." It was not a question.

Electricity passed between them for what seemed an eternity. When Tom spoke, it was a low, almost guttural sound. "Yes."

Simple. Straightforward. Direct and to the point.

Franklin felt his heart freeze. He had hoped -prayed- that the young girl they had discovered two days earlier had been an isolated incident. Even as he allowed himself to believe in that possibility he knew, as did his brother and the sheriff, that there would be more.

"God I hate it when I'm right," Franklin Palmer whispered. Harold frowned at his sibling's ill-timed attempt at humor. Ignoring the glare from Harold, Franklin continued. "Local..." he stopped. "Man or woman?"

"Woman."

"Local woman?"

Tom sat there, staring. His answer did not come quickly. He nodded his head affirmative, then added, "Yes." It almost seemed an afterthought.

"Name of deceased?"

"Lisa Woodall."

"Lisa Wood..." Franklin stopped. He lifted his eyes to make contact with those of the sheriff. "Joe's wife?"

"I'm afraid so, Palmer."

"Oh damn."

Harold spoke up at last. "Who are these people?"

"Oh. Well, Harry," Franklin started. "Joe and Lisa are some folks that I know. They are very respected in the community and they've lived here forever. Lisa is not the sort of person that goes out partying as a rule, but this was a special occasion and, well..."

Tom slid a photo of the deceased gingerly across the table to Harold. He lifted it by the corner and looked closely at the face staring back at him. He recognized her.

"She was at Thunderbirds," Harold insisted. "I saw her there with Jake Page and his friends."

"Yeah. I saw them too," Franklin agreed. "They all used to hang out together when they were in high school. Or something like that. The others were in town for their ten year reunion as far as my information goes."

"Some reunion," Harold shrugged.

"Tell me about it," Tom said as Harold passed the photograph back to him. "My problem is this, gentlemen. We have had two dead bodies in two days. Lisa was apparently killed last night while she was driving home from Thunderbirds. We assume that time of death is somewhere near three O'clock or somewhere around there. I'll know more when pathology reports come back."

"Tom, I have got to report this in Sunday's edition. I held back before and said that I could bury the story on Rebecca's death until Wednesday, but I don't know if I can do that now. People are going to find out about this one and if we try to cover up Lisa's death..."

"Murder," Tom corrected.

"Fine," Palmer held up his hands as to avoid arguing the point. "People are not going to think too highly of us if we start covering up vital information. Besides, we have a psycho out there killing people in the park. We have to warn people. Give them a leg up on this situation. We can maybe cut off this guys supply of victims."

"He's right Sheriff Myers," Harold agreed. "You can't continue to keep these people in the dark about this. The people need to be aware of what is going on around here."

Tom nodded in reluctant agreement. "I know. I only wanted to look out for the town. This could destroy all of our chances for convincing the businesses coming in for this weekend's festival. The festival opens up this evening and runs through Sunday night. That's two days where the town gets to be the center of attention."

"At what cost, Tom?" Franklin Palmer asked.

EVIL WAYS

Tom had no answer. He did not know how far he would be willing to go to protect his town and its image.

Harold spoke up. "We need to corral this killer. That is your job, Tom. Let the city council members deal with the clean up. They get paid to worry about the city's image. Your first priority as sheriff is to protect and serve. It says so on your truck."

"Mr. Palmer, I appreciate all that you are trying to do, but you don't live here. You haven't watched as this place has struggled to stay afloat over the past years. You don't really know what these businesses coming into our county will mean. As a citizen of this town, how can I not try to protect her and help her to grow?"

"Tom, we have to let these people know. They have that right. Your job is to catch the bad guys. Mine is to tell everyone about it and maybe -just maybe- help make your job a little easier."

"I know, Franklin. I know." Tom sighed. "Write it up. I'll tag on extra security for the festival. I already have a call in to the Athens P.D. They are going to loan us some of their officers to help out. Maybe it will be enough."

"You don't expect this person to try something at the festival do you?" Franklin Palmer asked. "Unless you know something I don't."

"I do."

Silence filled the small room. The Palmer brothers were all ears.

"Well?" Franklin said after a second.

Tom seemed to slump gradually. He settled back into his large chair. "I think I may have found a connection between the two victims."

"Really?" Harold exclaimed. "What?"

"Spill it, Tom."

"Okay," Tom cautiously answered in a voice just above a whisper. "The girl we found on Thursday morning was dating one of my deputies."

"Chris Jackson?" Franklin asked. He was sure he knew the answer to that one already.

"Yes." Tom had correctly assumed that the reporter had already learned that information. "Chris and the first victim, Rebecca, were dating. Well, sort of. Anyway, that ties Chris to victim number one. Lisa Woodall was killed on her way back from a get together with her high school friends out there." He pointed toward the waiting area as if they could see the reunion goers through the wall.

"So what is the connection?" Franklin Palmer asked, but even as the question passed his lips the answer became apparent. "My God."

Harold's eyes went wide as he happened upon the connection a scant second later. "The second victim is a member of graduating class that is having their reunion this weekend just like the boyfriend of the first victim."

"Chris is the connection?" Franklin Palmer said, somewhat skeptical. "Is someone after him, Tom. Or do you suspect him?"

"I don't suspect Chris Jackson at this point, but I can't officially rule him out either. There are just too many unanswered questions. And I want all those answers before I'll destroy that man's life and career. Understood, Palmer?"

"I hear you, Tom. I got it."

"Uh, excuse me," Harold Palmer interrupted. "I may have another angle that you might have overlooked."

"And that being?"

"Well, sheriff, while the connection to your deputy seems the most plausible and obvious, I think we could also look at the group of Mrs. Woodall's friends as a whole."

"I'm not sure I follow, Bro," Franklin said.

"Well, Ray, I read Deputy Jackson's statement in the sheriff's report about how he discovered the body of his girl friend in such an out of the way locale. He claims that he received a phone call from someone that wouldn't leave a name, but instructed him to meet his girlfriend out near Lake Greene. Deputy Jackson did so and came across the body."

"That's right," Tom concurred.

"As statements go, that one falls on the flimsy side."

"Indeed it does," Myers agreed.

"Do you believe him?"

"Chris told me that he was a little suspicious of the call, but he couldn't just ignore it. Granted, he should have called for back up. Or just called me, but he didn't. We can't change that, but yeah, I believe him."

"Then I'm willing to give him the benefit of the doubt," Harold said with a nod.

"We've had no luck with the phone call he received," Myers continued. "There just wasn't enough evidence there to go on to even start a search for the caller."

"My point exactly." Harold leaned forward and gestured toward the sheriff as he tried to explain his train of thought. "Now follow me on this. Whoever called your deputy had to know enough about him to know that he had been dating this girl. Right?"

"Makes sense so far," Harold's brother agreed. Tom simply nodded.

"Okay. Now it is possible that someone could have been keeping an eye on your deputy. This is a rather small town and gossip trails probably let everyone in on what everyone is doing. That sort of thing happens no matter where you are. Anyway, even if the killer went after Deputy Jackson's girlfriend, why? And why call the deputy to get him out to the lake? In the age of caller ID and technology that allows people to trace almost any call, why would the killer go to all that trouble? Unless..."

"Unless he knew that Chris didn't have a caller ID box."

"Right, sheriff. Whoever called your deputy to get him out to that lake and the body of his girlfriend had to know him. At least had to know a little bit about him. That could mean anything from acquaintance to stalker. Neither of which helps narrow down a suspect list."

"Does that apply to Lisa's case as well?" Franklin asked.

"Maybe," Tom answered, intrigued by the FBI agent's string of deductions. "We haven't found her car yet and there seems to be no sign of struggle on the road. The only signs visible were where someone scampered up that embankment toward the woods. We just assumed those tracks were made by Lisa. Maybe the killer made them."

"Maybe."

"Or both of them?" Tom asked.

"Maybe the killer chased her?" Harold offered. "Or vice versa."

"Why not cover those tracks up then?" Franklin scribbled something onto his notepad even as he asked the question. "If the killer was careful enough to take the car, why leave indications as obvious as those?"

Harold answered before the sheriff had the chance. "He wanted someone to find the body. The car would have been too easy. This way the sheriff and his people would have to spend time and manpower on a search."

"And there is a lot of wooded land out there in the park," Tom added.

"Right. But why go to all that trouble unless the killer wanted you out of the way for some other reason."

"Like what?" the sheriff asked.

"I don't know." Harold sighed, rubbing at the bridge of his nose with his left hand. "All I know is what I've dealt with before. Some killers have used anguish and torment to their advantage. If you want to hurt someone you don't kill that person straight out. That's too easy. Over too quickly. No, you go after someone that person cares about and you destroy it. That causes more hurt to pile up on the true victim, thereby making the kill that much sweeter. Making an enemy suffer can be more satisfying to the killer or killers than killing their victim straight out."

Tom scratched the nape of his neck. "You think someone is after the group of folks waiting out there in my lounge?"

"I can't say for certain, Tom. If someone isn't after all of them, then maybe they are only after one of them, but wants to hurt the target by killing off his or her friends and loved ones." Tom knew what that last suggested. He only hoped it was wrong. Harold continued. "Now this is all just a theory of mine, but I would suggest that you keep an eye on them just the same. If I'm wrong in my assumptions, then no problem. However, if I'm right then we just might save their lives."

Tom considered it for a moment. "Alright," he said, getting to his feet. "I'm going to talk to each of them. See if they have any enemies that might just want one or all of them dead. Maybe we'll get lucky and learn something from one of them, but I highly doubt it. In any event, I just want to thank you for your help, Mr. Palmer. You've made my job just a little easier."

Harold waved off the compliment. "No problem, Tom. I'm sure we'll see you at the festival tonight. I've always wondered what a country hoe down would be like. Now I'll have my chance. Might even be fun." Harold actually forced a smile as he made his bad joke.

"At least it won't be dull," Franklin added as he extended a hand to the sheriff. "Thanks for your time, Tom."

Tom Myers shook the offered hand and then motioned the two men toward the door. They accepted and moved off. Harold took a short second to once again glance over the sheriff's movie poster collection.

"And Palmer," Tom said as the reporter stepped out the door. "Call me if you find out anything."

"But of course," Franklin said as he bowed toward the sheriff. Tom shook his head as he watched the two men leave through the small waiting area. The people out there watched as the two men left. Then they looked toward Tom in search for answers.

Tom Myers just wished he had some to give them. *"Let's get this over with,"* he thought. "Ladies and gentlemen, I appreciate your indulgence and your patience. I will see each of you in turn. We can get this over with and let you folks get back to your lives. We'll start with..." Tom checked a list on a clipboard he had carried from the office. "...Mr. Charles Phillips, please."

"That's me," Charles answered, raising his hand.

"Come on in," Tom said as he stepped back into his office.

The others watched as their classmate walked into the sheriff's office and closed the door, probably at the insistence of the sheriff. Now the wondering began again for each of them.

Inside, Charles Phillips took the seat offered to him by Sheriff Myers. The sheriff chose not to sit, but leaned against the large desk set against his office window. The sheriff looked at the man for a few heartbeats before pulling a folder from his desk and opening it up. He flipped through the file for a few more seconds before regarding Charles again.

"Now, Mr. Phillips. I have just a few questions."

"Okay."

"Don't worry, Mr. Phillips, this will all be over before you know it."

The Sommersville Autumn Festival happened once a year like clockwork.

The town set aside one week every year where the citizens could get together to beautify their town and prepare for the huge celebration on the weekend following. The whole community turned out for this one event. The only other events to rival it were the big Christmas Cantata and Armed Forces Day parade that ran the length of Sommersville every year as well.

The Autumn Festival allowed everyone a chance to participate whether they were young or old, black or white, rich or poor, healthy, wealthy, wise, or not. It made no difference. For the span of one week a spirit of kinship descended on the people of the small North Georgia community. Old wounds and prejudices were temporarily forgotten, set aside in favor of strengthening the community. Friends got together to talk over old times and several of the local churches made plans to hold their homecoming services on that weekend as well.

The Autumn Festival was meant to be a time of togetherness. So when the high school decided to plan the year's class reunion it was not a hard verdict to make in terms of the date. The festival would have one more thing to celebrate and some of the town's 'lost lambs,' as a recent newspaper article had referred to the returning graduates, would be returning to the town that they all loved so much.

At least that had been the plan. No one had expected for a murderer to be on the loose. Least of all Franklin Ray Palmer. He had been so excited to be involved with the festival. When he had first moved into town two years before, he did not have the time or the resources to do his part. Since that time, he had learned to appreciate what it meant to the town. His town. He found himself looking forward to that time of year with a zeal that he once thought lost to him forever.

Unfortunately, he also knew that the Sunday Edition of his newspaper, the Sommersville Gazette, could very well spell doom for the entire town. It could ruin the good feeling that everyone embraced around that time, and it would put a dark spot on the memory of the

Autumn Festival that could never be removed. Quite possibly, his article (Not to mention the fact that it was *his* paper) could cause the businesses that the city council had been wooing to turn their attention elsewhere after they read the headlines in the Sunday paper.

The thought of it made his stomach knot up and his heart ache because he understood that it would be his fault. If he was lucky, he figured, he might only be run out of town. As his nervous mind raced through many different equations, he automatically embraced the worst-case scenario. It was simple human nature and Franklin Ray Palmer was most definitely human.

At least on most days. On this day he felt a little less so than usual. *How can I do this to these people?* He wondered. These were his people now. Deep inside, Franklin knew that he was not responsible for the events of the past few days. In no way, shape, or form could anyone honestly blame him. But try as he might, he could not force that thought from his brain. How could he do something this terrible to them?

Because it was his job. And no matter how much he wished it to be different, that sad truth was the sole reason that the article will run as planned. He just hoped that the people of Sommersville would one day find it in their hearts to forgive him. Or that he might one day forgive himself. If such a thing were at all possible.

The morning sunlight shone through the glass door at the office of the Sommersville Gazette and Franklin let the blessed warmth flow over him. Anyone who had not been around for the past few days might think that it was always beautiful and sunny there, never knowing that it was the first break in a record number of storm systems that descended on this small community for weeks.

The tiny town of Sommersville had been beset by many fierce thunderstorms, flooding, lightning storms, and even one tornado in the last year. The storms seemed to go on forever, buffeting against the tiny dot on the map.

Franklin Palmer cared about none of that at the moment. He could feel the awesome power of the internal storms that were brewing around the town that he had come to call home. People were afraid, at least those privy to certain details. By Sunday afternoon everyone would know. The truth would be revealed at last. Why, then, did Franklin feel that he had let everyone down?

He felt the warmth from the sunlight as it was amplified by the door's glass. He felt the gentle probing fingers of the sun's rays as they played across his face and his hair. It strengthened him, made him feel alive. He opened his eyes and chanced a glance at the world outside his door. All around him he witnessed volunteers making their last minute preparations for the start of the festival that night. Yesterday he would have happily been out there with the others, enjoying the beautiful weather and the fellowship of those around him.

Now he just felt dirty and saddened.

He had not known Joe and Lisa overly well, but they were on a first name basis with one another. They always spoke when they saw him in that friendly southern manner most folks seemed to possess around the community. Those two had always been very friendly toward him and that was something that Franklin Palmer would always remember. They were a nice couple. She was a nice lady and she didn't deserve to die like she did.

Not like an animal.

Behind him, seated at his receptionist's desk, he heard his brother's even-tempered voice as he talked to his wife and daughter back home in Washington DC. He would undoubtedly tell Beverly about the events that had been going on around here, but Franklin also knew that Harold would try to protect his wife from the terrifying details as best he was able. That was just the kind of man that Harold Palmer was.

Rebecca was busily typing up copy for the advertisements for the coming deadline. She was one hell of a typist and Franklin would be lost without her. As much as he would like to get someone else in here to help out, it just wasn't something that Franklin could squeeze out of his already over inflated budget. The money just was not there.

So many problems.

So many worries.

So many mysteries.

And all of them seemed to be lodged on the shoulder of Franklin Ray Palmer.

He would be the first to admit that he was the last person in the world to want those kinds of problems, but they were there nonetheless. And his responsibility, whether he liked it or not. He sighed, knowing that he had done all he could. Still he wished that he could do more.

He heard his brother as he wished his daughter a happy weekend and then as he told his wife how much he loved her and how much he missed her. And for a moment, the briefest of moments, Franklin envied his older brother. Although, he would never admit that to another living soul. Ever.

He could hear the love and longing in his brother's whispered tones.

"Bye, Beverly. I'll be home some time next week. Yes, I'll call before I head out. Yes, honey I'll be careful. Talk to you soon. Ray sends his love. Bye." Then Harold Palmer hung up the phone and turned his attention once again to his brother and the solemn mood that had befallen the man since the early morning meeting with the sheriff.

"You alright?" Harold asked as he took up a position just behind his younger brother at the door. He noticed that Franklin seemed a little older today than he had when Harold blew into town. "You did the right thing you know," he added.

"Did I?"

"From where I stand, yes you did. Your story will probably save a few lives."

"It could also scare off the killer and Tom will never be able catch him."

Harold placed a reassuring hand on Franklin's left shoulder. The younger man was tense. "That's always a possibility," Harold agreed with the assessment of the situation. "On the other hand, the killer could be scared into making a mistake and then Sheriff Myers could be there to catch this sick-o when he does."

Franklin said nothing.

Harold tried to press his point. "Makes a weird kind of sense, does it not?"

Franklin stood there in silence, hating that his brother was making a valid point. Yet he could not stop himself from staring out the glass door at the world beyond. The shadow of the words **SOMMERSVILLE GAZETTE** fell across his shirt to leave a negative image of the name of the town and of the newspaper that Ray loved so much. Possibly more than anything else in the world.

"Ray?" Harold said, his tone a bit more stern than it had been before. "Dammit, Ray, say something. Anything."

"Come on." And Franklin opened the door and stepped out into the sunlight, leaving a dumbfounded Harold to glare after him.

Of all the things that could have possibly been uttered from Franklin's lips, that was probably one of the few things that Harold had not expected him to say. He was taken aback for a moment with an expression on his face that screamed volumes. *"Duh-ohh!"*

Unsure, Harold followed his wayward brother outside. When he finally found his voice he asked, confusedly, "Where exactly are we going?"

"To a party."

"Great," Harold dead panned. "And me without my dancing shoes."

# # #

"This is the place."

Two blocks east of the building that housed the Sommersville Gazette sat the Sommersville courthouse and a slightly weather beaten historical site with an old train depot dating back roughly a hundred years.

A large parking lot sat between the two sites. This parking lot was cordoned off to make room for the festival. Tomorrow morning the rest of the streets through the center of town would be similarly closed off and booths set up along the main street and some of the side streets. Arts, crafts, foods of all sizes, shapes, and smells, not to mention diverse forms of entertainment provided by locals will adorn the entire town.

A good time to be had by all. The festivities should spill over into every corner of Sommersville.

At least that was the plan.

Franklin pointed all of these details out to Harold as they took a leisurely stroll down the sidewalk toward the spot where later that night a street dance and party to honor the ten-year class reunion of Sommersville high school would take place. A stage had been erected along the side of the large antique train that was stilled forever, housed in the historic rail station.

Plans had been made for several bands to come in and play a few sets. A DJ was scheduled to be on hand to spin some tunes for the folks to dance to, every thing from country to rock to reggae. All the bases had been covered in the hope that there would be something for everyone.

"Nice," Harold said.

"They will probably try to get Jake Page to do a set I'm sure," Franklin shrugged.

"I don't know, Ray," Harold said with sympathy for the pop star. "He may not exactly be up for it. This has been a rather emotional day for him and the rest of his friends. They may not be in the mood to party."

"Can you really blame them, Harry? I mean, look what they've been through."

"I understand all too well."

"I know. Look, let's just check the place out and we'll get that steel trap FBI issue brain of your working on this particular problem. Maybe you can come up with a detail or two that Tom Myers and his boys might have missed."

"Like what, Ray?"

Franklin Palmer simply shrugged at the question. "I'm sure we'll know it when you find it."

"Great," Harold exhaled. "Your faith in me is astounding."

His brother simply smiled a devilish grin.

39.

Enough is enough!
Billy Connelly had finally reached his limit.
He'd had enough.

He could not stand to be cooped up in his hotel room any longer. The mood of his friends had been somber ever since they had left the police department. He understood what they were going through. Lisa had been his friend too. He had cared for her nearly as much as the others, a nd he would miss her terribly.

But he also knew that she was gone and they each had to concentrate on the living. *It is what she would want for us*, he told himself. So, after much soul searching, Billy Connelly had at long last come to a major decision: he just had to get out and he told Ted and Charles as much. Ted knew that Billy needed a little time alone; so, he told his friend that he would be there when he got back, but Charles could not be swayed. Or Charles was simply too addle brained to understand his friend's need. Maybe he understood all too well. He told Billy in so many words that he was coming along for the ride whether the young doctor liked it or not.

Finally, Billy surrendered and he, with Charles in tow, pulled away from the hotel, then Billy turned his car onto Main Street and headed south, past the park and out to the place where he had grown up.

For fifteen minutes, the two men rode in silence as each of them wrestled with their own thoughts and fears. The weekend was not turning into the festive vacation that Charles had expected. He had expected a few minor problems, most notably between Billy and Barbara, but to his surprise that was the only problem that they had not been forced to face. At least not yet.

"Where are we headed, anyway?" Charles finally asked in an effort to break the monotonous silence.

Billy simply laughed. "It *has* been a long time hasn't it? We're headed out to my mom's place. I've finally decided that the time is right to get rid of the old place. I just wanted to get out here and see it one last time. You know, sentimental reasons."

"It's about time," Charles joked.

"Yes. Yes it is."

"I was beginning to think you were never going to get rid of that place."

"Me too."

Five more minutes passed in silence until they arrived at last. The house was not as large as Charles remembered it, but then again everything looked so much bigger when you were a kid. Unfortunately, the house had not fared well over the years. Time and the elements had joined forces to beat the dear old abode into submission. The house put up a struggle but Mother Nature seemed to be winning the battle.

For a long time Billy just sat in the car, simply staring at the house. So many memories were buried in that old place. So many memories and so many dreams. So much of his life, all of their lives, was tied up in that one place.

Eventually, though, Billy gathered up his nerve and got out of the car and slowly approached the house. He found that the closer he got to the old edifice, the more the years stripped away until he felt like a small boy no older than ten or eleven. And the memories and sensations that he associated with the place assailed his senses.

He smelt the sweet smell of the flowers that his mother had planted and cared for nearly every day of her life. Even now they still grew, unaware that she was no longer there to enjoy their fragrance. Unless there was still a lingering trace of her spirit still attached to the old place. The front steps were worn from years of rain and termites had taken up residence in at least one of the steps. Careful to avoid any loose boards, the two old friends made their way toward the large porch and the front door just beyond it.

The porch moaned beneath them as their combined weight pressed down on the aged boards. It sounded as if there had been no visitors on them in ages, which would be about right. Billy felt the tug at his heartstrings. A few years ago, this place would have sold for big bucks. The only thing at that moment of monetary value was the land. The time had come, Billy finally realized, to sell the place and move on with his life.

"Time to let go of the past. I'm never coming back here."

"I beg your pardon?"

Billy hadn't been aware that he had spoken aloud. He waved away his friend's question. He noticed several windows had been shattered. Probably rocks thrown by some of the neighborhood kids. He should be angry, but Billy was a kid once himself. Most days he still felt like one.

"Do you have a key to this place?" Charles asked. He seemed eager to see the inside again. In truth, Billy was kind of curious himself. "It has been awhile."

Digging in his pocket he produced a very old key. "As a matter of fact, I do." Taking the key to the door, Billy Connelly unlocked the large oak door and with a little effort managed to push the door open with a loud *creak*.

They stepped inside. The air tasted stale, with a musty scent. Instinctively, both men put their hands to their noses as the less than fragrant odors assaulted them all at once. They moved easily through the large living room. This was where Billy and his friends would lay when they were kids, watching their favorite television programs or playing one of the dozen board games that Billy's mother would keep in the hallway closet until the whole gang would come over. She would dig them out for all of them to play while she made cookies and Kool-Aid for them. *She loved to bake*, they remembered. "Cookies and Kool-Aid. Mom was a wonderful woman," Billy said, fighting off the emotions welling up inside of him. He truly missed his parents.

"Yes she was," Charles readily agreed. "She was the best."

"I've got to get out of here," Billy said as he suddenly sprinted toward the open door. Once there he inhaled several large gulps of fresh air. Charles ran up behind him, concerned.

"You okay?"

Billy coughed once, then twice. "I'll live. I think. I just couldn't take it in there. It's too much to handle all at once."

"I know. You did good, though. I think you made a good decision."

"Me too," Billy said after his breathing returned to normal. The two men took a seat on the top step of the porch. "I always did like it here. If for nothing else but the view. It's amazing. Too bad I'll never see it again."

"You could always live here again. Maybe not in the same house, but the land is..."

Billy interrupted him. "I--I don't think so," he said. "I just don't think so. No matter how beautiful it is."

Charles had to agree with that assessment though, especially now, as he took in the surroundings. There was not another house within eyeshot of that spot. He could see a lot of trees. So many trees that it was easy to forget just how close civilization really was. He listened carefully as the birds sang their genial tunes. He could smell the fresh water from nearby

Lake Greene. He could also see the path that... lead... to...

He let the memory drop in mid thought. He could see the small path that led through the woods from Billy's house to Potter's Ravine. When they had been younger, Charles, Billy, Jake, and the others had built a small bridge across the ravine and they had gone down that trail to get there. They had spent many a day at the ravine and on that trail. Although the bridge was long since gone, the trail still remained. Undoubtedly, there was probably a whole new generation of kids that transformed Potter's Ravine into their personal playground as Charles and his friends had done so many years ago.

Funny that he had not remembered the small footpath until that moment. With that flash of memory came questions. Questions that Charles knew would need an answer before long. They had all assumed that the person responsible for Lisa's death had gone back to the road to remove her car. That had made sense at the time, but now Charles wondered where the killer, or killers, if indeed there were more than one, had gone after disposing of her car.

Curious that the thought had not occurred to him before now.

They had been in constant motion since the news of Lisa's disappearance had reached them in the form of Tom Myers asking them for any information they might have had on her whereabouts. Since then, they had all been moving so fast that they have had no time to ponder all of the little details that might be nagging in each of their minds.

Charles wondered what thoughts were going through Billy's head at that particular moment in time. He did not ask his friend that however. They sat there in relative silence for the next twenty-two minutes before Billy decided to leave and return to the hotel. He tried his best to check out the house and make sure it was secured before they departed. Not long after, the two men sped away in Billy's car. Soon after, they would be back in town and they could start to get on with their lives.

At least that was Charles Phillips fondest wish.

He just hoped that wish would come true.

For all of their sakes.

40.

"Welcome everyone!"

A hail of welcomes from people he had never laid eyes on before in his life bombarded Harold Palmer as he stepped inside the parking lot next to the old train depot where he had stood the night before.

The party seemed to have started a little earlier than advertised.

The Autumn Festival generally began in earnest around sunset, but the people had started to arrive by three thirty in the afternoon to set up and prepare for the events of the evening. Guests and partygoers started drifting in shortly thereafter. More continued to pour in by the moment. Surprisingly, Harold found himself sufficiently impressed by all of it. Never before had he been fortunate to be a part of anything remotely similar to it. And he probably never would again.

Music was blaring out across the open area and small groups had already started dancing, a few were even trying to sing along, but most were just talking and laughing as if they didn't have a care in the world. Some of them did not. He thanked the Lord that the music was not as loud -or confined- as it had been at Thunderbirds on Friday night.

Pushing through the throng of revelers, Harold moved toward a rather secluded area away from the train, hoping for a bit of relief from the obstinately cheerful townsfolk when he spotted a familiar face. Someone else who decided to evade the growing crowd as long as possible. A face that looked as uncomfortable here as Harold himself was.

"Sheriff Myers." Harold called as he approached the older man, his hand outstretched. "Enjoying the festivities?"

Tom gave him a look that said, *Don't ask.*

"Mr. Palm--- uh, Harry. How are things?" Tom shook the offered hand firmly.

"The usual. I hate these types of things," Harold answered, motioning toward the festivities all around them. "Mostly I just hate the crowds." He neglected to mention how much he also hated being called *Harry.*

"Crowds don't usually bother me," Tom declared with his southern accent intact. "Except for this one."

"Yeah. I know what you mean."

"One of these people could be a killer," Tom said, sighing. "It could be any one of them. Look at them. How am I supposed to know? They don't teach things like this in cop class. This is beyond anything I've ever had to deal with."

"I'm afraid I can't help you there. The Bureau doesn't usually teach us that sort of thing during our short stay at Langley either." Harold shrugged. "Sorry. I'm afraid we have to rely on evidence and good old fashioned gut work." He let the comment hang there for a second. "At least most of the time," he chuckled.

"I tend to trust my gut's instincts," Tom assured Harold. "My wife says that's probably why I'm still alive and in one piece."

"So do I. Those gut reactions have saved my bacon a time or two in the past."

"I'll bet," Tom agreed.

"Oh," Harold sneered. "I could tell you stories."

# # #

Three hours passed. Three long, agonizingly uplifting hours and Harold was just about ready to explode. *On the upside,* Harold realized, *nobody has died yet.*

Harold and Sheriff Myers had been keeping a close eye on Chris Jackson and his friends. Harold was also aware that there were several deputies roaming around the festival. Some were in street clothes, but most were in uniform.

The small circle of friends spent most of their time together, away from the dancing throng. Harold understood. They were probably not all that interested in a party with everything that had happened. Still, they had made it out as planned. They were moving on with their lives.

Harold made several observations and he shared a few of them with Tom Myers.

He noticed that Charles Philips seemed a little bit distracted. He spent a majority of his time circling the perimeter of the party. Almost as if he were afraid to enter. Every so often he would see a familiar face and greet an old classmate, but then Charles would retreat back to the edge of the excitement. Charles had a tendency not to distance himself from the group, especially Billy. The man followed the young doctor around much like Franklin had followed Harold around when they were kids. Perhaps Billy was like an older sibling to Charles? The FBI agent had no idea. It was just a hunch. *Perhaps he has a dislike of crowds like I do,* Harold wondered silently.

Jake Page and Barbara Fram spent all of their time together. Harold had heard rumors from his brother that Jake and Ms. Fram were something of an item. Seeing them together, Harold could believe it. They weren't overtly cuddly or anything of the sort, but there was a sparkle between them that Harold noticed early on. And she wasn't the jealous type either from the looks of things. Jake had more than his fair share of admirers in the crowd. He happily signed autographs, shook hands, and made pleasant little chitchat. These two were used to putting on a happy face for the public. Even when they felt less than happy. He as the rock star flavor of the month and her as an up and coming actress, Harold thought they were handling things very well.

Dr. Billy Connelly spent the majority of his time watching Barbara and Jake. "Old boyfriend?" Harold guessed. Tom confirmed that was the case. "Looks like he hasn't quite gotten over her yet," Harold added.

Tom only nodded his agreement.

Chris Jackson was on guard. The eternal officer, ever vigilant and protective of his friends. Tom told Harold a great deal about Chris and he knew how close Tom and his deputy were. They shared a bond that went way beyond working professionals. It made Harold think of Carter.

Chris looked to Harold as though he had not slept in days, since the ordeal began. Understandably, the man had been under a tremendous amount of pressure and it was starting to take its toll on him. He looked much older than he had when Harold had first met him at the crime scene on the edge of Lake Greene. That seems so long ago that it was hard to believe it was only a couple of days before.

Ted Hollis was the newest arrival and Harold didn't know much about him other than that he, like Chris Jackson, was a police officer. He was fairly energetic and actually made it to the dance floor a few times during the evening, but he always strayed back toward his friends after a while. He seemed to stick closest to Charles, but that in and of itself was not unusual. They were childhood friends. Why wouldn't they stick together and watch out for one another?

The party continued.

Although it would not seem possible, more and more people arrived every hour. The train depot was already full to capacity and the crowd had moved out onto Main Street. Luckily the sheriff had his deputies close of the road to through traffic earlier as a precaution.

EVIL WAYS

The sun had long since vanished only to be replaced by a deep black sky, spotted with brilliant stars. It was a beautiful night, not that any of the partygoers had noticed. Or cared. When the natural light faded the large electric powered lights set up by the city were turned on and the train depot and courthouse parking lots were as bright as if it were still day time. Maybe more so.

Harold was starting to feel very tired. Tired of the whole thing. He and Tom Myers had spent about and two and a half hours swapping stories about various adventures and minute details of their lives. After those discussions, Harold felt that he knew the sheriff a little better and his faith in the man had begun to grow. Besides, it was nice to have the company. Harold hadn't seen much of Ray since the festival started. On occasion Harold would catch a glimpse of his brother as he moved in and out of the growing crowd, but that was the extent of it. Harold had considered trying to find Ray out in the mess of people, but thought better of it.

Eventually, Tom Myers had wandered off as well. He had decided it was well past time to check in with his deputies and he wanted to do it in person. Without using the walkie talkies, Myers and his men could keep a constant watch on the crowds without alerting too much attention to why they were watching. As an added precaution, the sheriff wanted his Deputies keeping close watch on Chris Jackson and his circle of friends. One or more of them might be the next target.

Worse yet, one of them might be the killer. They had no evidence to support such a theory, but Harold could not get the nagging feeling out of his mind that one of them was behind this. He just wasn't sure which one, although he had his suspicions.

Even with all of the extra precautions he had implemented, Tom Myers still wanted to avoid upsetting the populace of Sommersville and beyond. Harold had to admit that the sheriff's loyalty and compassion for his town were sincere.

He looked around at the growing crowd. There was no telling where some of these people were from. The festival was such a widely known event that people came from all over to join in the celebration. Some from as far as one hundred miles away.

Harold still didn't know what it was specifically that they were celebrating, but in truth he really didn't care. He just hoped that everyone could survive the night so they could celebrate a little more tomorrow.

Harold gripped the bridge of his nose as the pain there began to mount. Another headache threatened. He had had more than his fair share of headaches since arriving in this town. Tonight was proving to be no exception.

Deciding that the music --the overly loud music-- was partly, mostly, to blame, Harold decided it was time for him to take a little stroll away from the music and the crowds. The fresh air would do him a world of good.

Passing by Sheriff Myers and Deputy Benjamin Dooley, talking near one of the small roped off areas, Harold threw them a wave, signaling Tom that he would be back soon. Tom acknowledged with a nod, and Harold stepped out onto the sidewalk and started to walk away from the party.

"Not a big partyer, huh?" Ben Dooley asked after the departing FBI agent.

Tom shook his head. "Naah. He told me that he didn't care too much for crowds. I guess he just needs a little air. Maybe just some peace and quiet."

"I know how he feels," Ben agreed. "My head is pounding."

"Speaking of headaches," Tom laughed. "Have you seen the other Palmer brother around here anywhere?"

Deputy Dooley scratched the nape of his sun burnt neck. "You know, as a matter of fact I haven't. Not in about an hour at least."

"Me neither."

"Something wrong, Sheriff?"

"I don't know." Tom waved it off and shifted questions. "How are our pigeons?"

Ben smiled at the reference. He pointed to a small group of people standing off to the far end of the stage near the old train site. Tom followed the finger to see that Chris Jackson and his high school friends had all gathered together in one corner, away from everyone else. "They've been hanging out right there for about two hours now. I'm surprised they made it out."

Tom shrugged. "This *is* why they came back here, you know. It would be a shame to miss it." Tom stopped. "Of course, it doesn't look like they're really involved in the celebration as it is. Oh well. I guess this makes keeping an eye on them easier."

"Yeah. I just don't know how I could deal with this," Ben said. "I wouldn't feel much like being at a party with a couple thousand people around."

"I don't blame you one bit."

"Hey Sheriff. They're breaking apart. Splitting up."

"Alright," Tom said while silently cursing himself for jinxing things. "Keep an eye on them. I'm going to go over and check on Chris. See how he's coping." Tom started to walk away from his deputy. "I'll check in a little later," he told Dooley.

"Sure thing, boss."

Tom forced his way through the throng of people. He tried his best to nod and say hello to those in the crowd that he recognized, but as there were so many people crammed into the small space. It was rather hard to move around without bumping into someone. And in a small town such as this one, nearly everybody knew everyone else.

"Chris!"

Upon hearing the sheriff call out his name, Chris Jackson turned then stopped as he noticed Tom Myers approaching. He waved a hand to the older man. Tom threw his hand up as well as he continued to forcefully navigating his way through the crowd that separated them.

Finally, Tom clapped his friend on the shoulder. "How you holding up, Chris?" Tom asked, trying to catch his breath. Getting through all those people was a workout in itself.

"I think I'll live," Chris said.

"I'm really sorry about Lisa," Tom said compassionately. "I know that you two were fairly close."

Chris let his head drop. No need to hold pretense before Tom Myers. They had known each other too long. "It's hard, Tom. But I'll manage. I'll cope." Chris took in a deep lung full of air. "Just like I've been doing." He sighed deeply as the weight of the world pressed down against his broad shoulders.

"I know you will, Chris," Tom said. "You've been through hell the past few days. I just wanted to see if there is anything more that I can do."

Chris leaned in closer to the sheriff so no one could overhear them. "Just one thing," Chris whispered. "Find out who did this, who killed my... my friends. I want you to find this bastard *and kill him*." A shudder of rage pulsed through Christopher Jackson. "You do understand, don't you?"

"Yeah, I understand."

All too well.

"Just stay close to your friends tonight, Chris. We're starting to think that one of you might be a target." Chris did not flinch at the suggestion that either one of his friends or he himself might be a target for murder. Chris had probably already made that same determination. He was a very clever man and a damned good cop as far as Tom was concerned. Chris nodded in response to the sheriff's suggestion.

Tom continued, "Our thought is that maybe one of you has an enemy, and that perhaps that person or persons has decided to hurt the target instead of killing him or her right out. That make any sense to you?"

"Yeah," Chris huffed. "But, what makes you think that? There's nothing to connect Rebecca to Lisa." Chris stopped as a thought struck him. Pain stabbed at his eyes, ready to unleash a torrent of emotion. "Except..."

Tom looked Chris right in the eye. "Except...?" he repeated, already guessing what the answer would be.

"Me."

Tom nodded.

It all seemed so clear to Chris Jackson at that point. Could someone have killed one of his oldest friends and killed his lover, just to get back at him for something and if so, then for what? What had Chris Jackson done that would make someone angry enough to kill for it? Then the question became a little tricky. "Who?"

"I wish I knew, Chris. That would make my job so much easier."

"Let me think," Chris mused. He scratched at his chin.

Tom tossed out a suggestion to get Chris on the right track. "Perhaps someone that you've busted? Someone that you arrested? Gotten into a fight with? An argument? Anything like that?"

"Oh come on, Tom," Chris nearly laughed at the thought. "In this town?"

"Stranger things have been known to happen, Chris."

"Not here. Hell, Tom, the biggest crime we've had here in the past few months was when the Macavey's were fighting. Mr. Macavey hit his wife and she decided to fight back. Dooley and me arrested them for domestic disturbance. Put them in lock up until they calmed down. Fairly simple." A second ticked off. "Other than that I can't think of anything at all."

"Maybe it was someone that had a personal connection with Rebecca. She did see a lot of people in her line of work."

"How does that connect her to Lisa? I just can't see a connection. Aside from the obvious one."

"Well, I suppose it's a stretch, but I don't want to rule out anything. I just want to find this..." A tense pause. "...this person before anyone else gets hurt."

"What do you need from me?" Chris asked, desperate to help out in any way he could. He was involved in it already. Not being actively involved in the case was hard.

Tom pursed his lips then eyed his erstwhile deputy as if seeing him in a new light. "Keep an eye on your friends for me. I need to make sure they're safe. Can you do that for me? I need to know that they'll be safe before I can investigate."

"Yeah. Yeah I can."

"Good," Tom said. "Glad to have you back son."

41.

Harold Palmer breathed a sigh of relief.

Outside of the confines of the party to kick off the Autumn Festival, he found his head clearing and his thoughts becoming more and more clear. The farther away from the party he got the more he realized how empty the town of Sommersville was after dark. The old joke of closing up a town now had a new meaning for the FBI agent. However, he found a small bit of comfort in the peace and quiet surrounding him.

He drew in a deep cleansing breath and held it for a brief second before exhaling. The air had a taste to it that reminded Harold of the smell of rain. With all of the storms that had hit the area in the past few days it was a good bet that more rain would be on the way before morning.

Everyone was hoping that the rain would hold off until the festival was behind them.

Wishful thinking as far as Harold was concerned. *No one can truly predict the rain,* he thought with a chuckle. *Not even me.*

He stopped, wondering how long he had been away from the festivities. *It can't have been too long,* he guessed, but a quick check of his watch told him that his little breath of fresh air had escalated into a fifteen-minute walk. "I'd better get back," he said to the empty street.

Slowly he did an about face and started slowly back toward the lights from the historic train depot in the not too far off distance. "Maybe Ray's missed me or something," he harrumphed.

#

Tom Myers felt his anger begin to boil. He and his deputies had been keeping a discrete eye on Chris Jackson's friends, yet they had all but successfully disappeared into the large crowd of revelers in the parking lot between the train depot and the courthouse.

"Dammit," he cursed wishing that he could scream it from his lips to the far corners of Sommersville. However, self-control won out and he simply gritted his teeth, straining to contain his mounting fury.

He whirled around in a futile effort, hoping that he would see those he was searching for. Occasionally he would spot one of his targets, or someone who could be one of them. It was hard to be certain with all of these people around.

"I give up," he exclaimed as he pushed his way free of the crowd toward his deputy, Benjamin Dooley. "I give up, Dooley" he repeated. "Maybe we'll be alright as long as they stay at the party."

"Maybe," Ben agreed.

"Yeah."

"But," Ben started, even as Tom tensed, "When was the last time that a suspect or a witness did what we expected?"

"I see your point," Tom said, resigned to head back toward the pulsating crowd of dancers. "But walking through that is a bitch," Tom motioned to the people around them.

"We could dance our way through," Ben said jokingly.

"Not in this lifetime," Tom said in his best matter of fact tone.

Ben clutched at his heart. "You wound me, dear sir."

Tom started to respond when a loud noise broke the sound of the music. Many of the festival patrons stopped top look around them, searching for the origin of the loud booming sound. Another loud boom cut through the night and one of the big spotlights surrounding the dance area went dark. Seconds later the sound of falling glass hit Tom Myers' ear.

"Gunshots!" Tom and Ben Dooley said in unison.

The two men moved as one in the direction the shot probably came from. Of course, to hit the light, one would have to be on the other side of the parking lot from where they were standing. The wall at the far end of the parking lot to be precise. It was the same place he had been talking with Harold Palmer earlier in the evening. A perfect place for a sniper.

Tall brush above and behind the wall could possibly camouflage a person long enough for he or she to get off a couple of shots. At least that was Tom Myers' observation as he and Ben pushed their way through the surprised and confused crowd, many of whom were not sure of what had just happened.

Tom reached the wall two steps ahead of Ben Dooley and three steps ahead of Chris Jackson. Tom quickly pulled his service revolver before he lunged to one side of the wall for a quick look behind it. There was no one there, not that Tom had expected the sniper to wait around after popping off two shots.

"Anything?" Ben asked.

Tom said, "No," before giving Dooley his marching orders. "Get on the horn to the guys. Find out if anyone was hit. Where are they, Chris?"

"I don't know where everyone is. I ran past Jake and Barbara after I heard the gunshot. They're fine. I sent them inside the depot for protection."

"Damn," Tom said between gritted teeth.

"What happened?" Franklin Palmer screamed as he ran up to Tom and Chris. "Tell me you got him?"

Tom simply shook his drooped head.

"Damn."

# # #

Harold Palmer was still far enough away from the celebration that the noise the DJ called music wasn't so loud that he thought his brain was going to explode. He could still hear the music and the sound of a few hundred people, each trying to talk above the other.

Part of him, granted it was a small part, wanted to stop right where he was. Maybe call it a night and head back to Ray's place. This was supposed to be his vacation after all. Shouldn't he be relaxed on his birthday? Of course he should. The true question remained. Would he have that chance?

Probably not. After the first thunderclap, Harold looked skyward into the ever-darkening night sky. His initial reaction was that a fireworks display was taking place, but he was sure that Ray would have mentioned it if they were planning fireworks. No. This was something else entirely. So lost in this line of thought was Harold that he had not yet noticed the decline in the noise from the parking lot where the dancing was taking place.

The second thunderclap physically jarred him and a sudden realization gripped at Harold's heart like a vise. Instinctively, he reached inside his jacket for his gun as his training took over. Then a single thought struck him. "Ray?" he whispered, hoping that his brother had the smarts to stay out of whatever was happening. Of course, he knew better than that.

With a renewed vigor, the elder Palmer brother ran toward the train depot as fast as his feet could carry him.

Leo Brand was the chairman of the reunion committee. When things went wrong, he was expected to take control and solve whatever problem arose. He felt the responsibility of calming the crowd was his so he ran to the stage and tapped on the microphone to get everyone's attention.

"Ladies and gentlemen!" he shouted. "If I could have your attention please! If everyone will remain calm we will have this situation under control! Please! Everyone continue dancing!" He turned to the hired disc jockey. "Maestro, if you please..."

The twenty something DJ looked dull eyed at the chairman of the reunion committee as if he were speaking a foreign language.

"Play something, you twit," the chairman spit out. "Now!"

And the music started up once again.

"What's the word, Tom?" Franklin Palmer asked.

"Not now, Palmer."

The two men were out of sight of the reunion's parking lot location and were on the other side of the wall and behind the bushes. This was where the sniper had fired. When Tom Myers went over the wall less than a minute before to search for any signs of the person that fired those two shots, Franklin decided it would be a good idea to follow him. After all, Tom might need some help.

Well, it seemed like a good idea at the time.

"Tom?"

Silence answered.

"Tom. If this is a joke I'm not finding it very amusing."

There was a rustling nearby.

Damn, Franklin thought. *I really need to get myself a gun.*

"Palmer."

The reporter flinched in spite of himself. He put his left hand against his heart just to make sure that it was still where it belonged. Fortunately, it was.

"What the hell are doing? Gave me a fucking heart attack!"

Franklin's nervousness had converted to anger and he was directing that anger toward Tom Myers.

Tom held up a finger to silence the younger man. When Franklin had calmed down, the sheriff crooked the finger, motioning for him to follow. Palmer did so in silence until he saw what Myers had found lying on the pavement in an expanding pool of blood.

"Oh God. Is that...?"

"Yeah."

"Damn."

42.

Harold was nearly out of breath.

He topped the hill just in front of the Sommersville county courthouse at a full run. He paused briefly to catch his breath when he saw something he had not expected to see. Someone was running toward him.

No. Not toward him. Just in his general direction.

Harold's first thought was that this guy just needed to get away from whatever was happening at the train depot. At least that was what Harold assumed until a small shaft of light from a nearby lamppost reflected off of something shiny in this person's hand.

A gun.

Harold tried to get a good look at this person, but he or she was wearing a jacket with a hood. A good enough way to disguise yourself at night, but the way the figure was moving suggested to the FBI agent that this person was undoubtedly a man. Harold raised his own weapon, pointing it at the approaching figure. From the looks of things the person with the gun had not seen Harold at that point. Well, Harold would just have to do something about that wouldn't he?

"Hold it right there! Federal Agent! Drop the gun and take two steps backward! Now!"

The man in the hooded jacket stopped abruptly, the light plays across the gun in his hand. The shadows lay across his face in such a way that Harold could not make out who it was. Of course, Harold only knew a small handful of people in this little town as it was. So he doubted very seriously that he would know the person before him even without the hood. Unless his hypothesis about their list of would-be suspects was true, this man could be anyone.

"Drop the gun," Harold said again. "I don't ask more than twice."

The man let go of the barrel of the gun and let it swing freely on one gloved finger. Harold silently breathed an inner sigh of relief.

The gun slipped from the finger to the ground with a slight clunk.

Without lowering his guard, Harold carefully made his way toward the suspect.

EVIL WAYS

He stopped just out of arm's length of the man in the hooded jacket. A tingle of something *not right* touched the base of his skull. His gut screamed to him that something was wrong with the situation. Very wrong.

Moving faster than Harold could counter, the man reached out with his left foot and caught the agent completely unaware. Harold doubled over in pain, clutching at his stomach, and his gun clambered to the ground. Harold turned to look up at the man in time to see a booted foot speed toward his face. Then all he could see was a wash of red as a mind numbing pain exploded through his brain.

Reflexively, the trained FBI agent rolled away from his attacker. He rubbed at his face as if to wipe away the thousand flashbulbs going off inside his brain all at once. Luckily, Harold had managed to roll near where he had dropped his gun. Planning, actually, as luck had very little to do with it aside from the fact that Harold was still conscious.

The blur that was his attacker feinted to the left and Harold snatched the fallen gun up in his right hand, pivoting on his heal, and firing off two shots at the figure that he could barely see. He heard the two bullets ping off of a nearby brick wall and knew that he missed. It didn't matter really. The sound of the gunshots should bring the sheriff. Unless he was otherwise engaged, which would not be good for Harold.

Harold closed his eyes tightly as another bright flash played across his vision then it miraculously faded as quickly as it had began. He could see again, although everything had a slightly fuzzy edge to it. And what he saw scared him.

The man in the hooded jacket advanced on Harold with a lead pipe or a baseball bat. Whichever it was, Harold could not be certain. He raised the gun again, but the attacker moved faster, and with one swing disarmed the FBI agent. Harold let out a groan as the feeling went out of his right hand. Harold lunged backward to narrowly avoid the attacker's next swing.

All Harold needed was a moment to catch his breath and get his bearings. Too bad that his opponent was not about to grant him that moment.

Then another miracle happened.

Something slammed into the attacker with astonishing speed, knocking the man in the hooded jacket to the ground. Not something. *Someone?* The lead pipe rolled away after two loud bounces.

This small distraction bought Harold the three seconds he needed to get his act together. His benefactor, to his surprise -and the last person he would have suspected- was Dr. Billy Connelly.

43.

"Charles Phillips."

Franklin Palmer managed to croak out the words. One of the two fired into the crowd had taken the life of Charles Phillips, a man they were there to protect.

"But why kill him here of all places?" Palmer asked. "With all of those witnesses so close by. Someone could have seen. Or heard."

Tom Myers had no answers for the younger man. Only questions. And every minute only served to bring about even more. Never any answers. Tom could, in all probability, rule out witnesses. No one had been paying close attention to anything outside the dance floor. Not even Tom's deputies. He doubted he'd get much help in that regard.

"We'd better..."

Myers never got a chance to finish that thought as two more gunshot's cut through the night. These shots came from a distance. To the two men, separated from the others as they were and unobstructed by the loud noise of the DJ the sound was clear. Unmistakable. The large wall served to muffle the noise only slightly. Probably why the killer decided to kill Charles there. *But why shoot out the one spotlight? Did the killer want or need an audience?*

Instinctively, Tom and Franklin turned to face one another, startled looks playing across their faces as they each reached the same conclusion simultaneously.

"The courthouse," Tom said.

And, as if reading one another's mind, both men said in unison, "Harold."

# # #

The timely intervention of Billy Connelly bought just enough time for Harold to get his bearings.

His world was still spinning, but at least he could see. And what he was seeing was not good. The man with the hooded jacket easily tossed Billy against a nearby brick wall. Probably the same wall Harold had heard the bullets hit scant seconds before.

Billy let out a grunt as the air was forcefully exhaled from his lungs on impact. Then the man in the jacket tossed the young doctor aside as if he were no longer worthy of his attention. Harold made his move and closed in on the attacker.

The man who had put this incredible pain in Harold Palmer's life turned his attention back to the approaching FBI agent. Harold swore he saw a smile play across the man's lips, but it was probably his imagination.

Harold steeled himself for an attack; doubtful that he could survive another pounding like he had received before.

The attack did not come.

Instead, the man coolly turned away, sprinting off down the alleyway, jumping over the stunned Billy Connelly. Harold wondered what could have scared him off. It certainly wasn't the battered FBI agent. He would consider himself lucky if he could move in the morning. Then he heard the sound of the cavalry approaching in the form of Sheriff Myers and his younger brother.

Oh God he'll never let me live this down, Harold mused as the two men reach him. "That way," he croaked out, pointing toward the small alleyway. Without a second thought, Tom Myers leaped over the stunned Billy as Harold's attacker had and headed down the alleyway after the elusive killer. Billy stirred as the older man moved deeper into the darkened alleyway.

Harold leaned on his brother's shoulder and the younger of the two Palmer boys helped him to a bench only a few feet away.

"Myers?" Harold asked. "Need's help." The last words barely came out coherent.

"He's got it under control. Just relax." Franklin noticed the young doctor get to his feet. "You alright over there, Doc?"

Billy Connelly silently waved off the question. He peered down the alleyway, seeing nothing. So a decision was made. Billy ran off down the alleyway after the town's sheriff. Franklin called out his name, but the young doctor refused to stop or even respond.

Franklin started after him, but his brother grabbed him by the arm, stopping him cold. "Help me up," Harold ordered.

# # #

Tom knew the alley fairly well. He had patrolled the streets of this town for more years than he'd ever cared to admit. In that amount of time he learned the highways and byways fairly well.

And Harold Palmer's attacker, who quite probably was the same person who killed Charles Phillips, couldn't have picked a better place to plan his escape.

That made the sheriff think a bit. Could the killer be a local?

The thought was almost as hard to believe as it had been to conceive. But he could not simply dismiss the notion out of hand. It was quite obvious that the person he was after knew his way around Sommersville.

And that thought scared him.

But he did not have time for that now. He had to find the killer, attacker, suspect, whatever he was being called at the moment.

And he had to find him quickly so they could put this madness behind them once and for all.

No sooner had Tom stepped from the alleyway onto a side street than he became the hunted instead of hunter. The hooded man swung at him from out of the shadows. Tom barely had time to get his arm up to block the attack.

Tom screamed as the knife he had not seen before ripped through his forearm.

A back kick to the gut put Tom down for the fight.

By the time Billy Connelly exited the alley, Tom's attacker was gone.

# # #

Harold Palmer was a stubborn man and his brother took some small measure of delight in pointing that fact out to him. But, once Harold had it in his mind to do something it a person would be hard pressed to dissuade him. Unless that person was his wife, a woman against whom even the overgrown Boy Scout was defenseless.

Reluctantly, he was forced to admit that he could not do it alone. That he needed help. He needed Franklin.

Allowing his older brother to lean on him for support, Franklin moved into the alleyway. Cautiously, they followed the narrow path to its inevitable end.

They did not have to walk far.

The alley opened onto a side street. There was only one streetlight working on the street and Harold could just barely make out a street sign. East Lively Street. *Ironic name for a street,* Harold thought.

The two men scanned the area for any sign of those they sought.

"There, Harry."

"I see them. Come on."

Together, they cautiously moved across the empty street to where Billy Connelly was sitting in a slump against a storefront window. Sheriff Myers sat just to his side. Harold immediately noticed that Sheriff Myers was holding his left arm. He had been injured.

There was no sign of the man they chased.

He got away.

44.

Charles Phillips was dead.

Tom Myers added the name to the list of victims that had been discovered in the short span of a few days. Less than a week.

Two other bodies had been discovered a few weeks back. One was a John Doe. Approximate age: twenty-eight or twenty-nine. The second victim was Janice Deane. Mrs. Deane was a rural route delivery person for the Postal Service. A veteran of twenty years, Mrs. Deane was well respected by her peers. She had a lot of friends, a loving family.

There were no clues to indicate any enemies the woman may have had. She was discovered missing when she did not return from her daily route one Monday afternoon. Her car was found later that evening off of the side of Manning Creek Road, just outside of the city limits.

Manning Creek was a tiny little road that headed away from Sommersville North. There was nothing out there but cow pastures and farmer's fields. A perfect place to get ambushed. But the official word was that those incidents were unrelated and isolated. Now, Tom Myers wasn't so sure.

Tom and his officers found no other clues so the investigation stalled. Truth of the matter was, the Sommersville Sheriff's Department was ill equipped to deal with situations like the ones they'd had to handle in the recent past.

They had thought it was over when no third victim turned up.

They should have known better.

Chris Jackson's girlfriend, Rebecca (there was not a last name on file for her in the official record) was the first victim this week.

Lisa Woodall's body was found earlier that morning in the wooded area at the far end of Fort Greene State Park. Not far, in fact, from where Rebecca had been found. Tom wondered if there was a connection there. If so, he had not any luck piecing it together.

Lastly, Charles Phillips, who had been shot less than one hundred feet from the sheriff and his men. Murdered in plain sight. In front of a couple hundred witnesses no less.

Tom Myers was not having a good night.

# # #

Deputy Sheriff Benjamin Dooley strolled into the office from a side door. He had gone home to freshen up and get a bite to eat before things could get too busy. Plus, he wanted to let his wife know what had happened and to tell her to be extra cautious.

Ben dropped his hat onto his cluttered desk against the back wall and walked over to the officer manning the main desk. The deputies took rotating shifts at the front desk. A job none of them cared overly much for, but a necessary part of the job nonetheless. Tonight's lucky contestant was Theodore Janetti.

Janetti was going through the file on Charles Philips' murder. As usual, Janetti had a lit cigarette clenched in his teeth. Even though he knew he was not supposed to smoke inside the station. Myers had scolded him about the breach of county statute, but Janetti knew Tom wouldn't press the matter unless he had to.

Benjamin cleared his throat, alerting the deputy to his presence. "What have you got, Janetti?" Deputy Dooley asked the investigating officer.

"Not much, Ben," Janetti said between puffs of his cigarette, totally ignoring Ben's throaty cough. "One bullet to the head. Poor bastard was dead before his body hit the ground." Officer Theodore Janetti made a gun with his fingers and pointed toward his forehead as a dramatization.

Deputy Dooley could have lived without the demonstration and the attitude. "Let's show just a bit of respect for the dead, please," Ben said as his men wrapped the body, preparing it for transport to the coroner's office. "And put out that damned cigarette. You know you aren't allowed to smoke in here."

Janetti extinguished the offensive cigarette in a nearby ashtray. That had not been Janetti's first smoke of the night by the looks of the ashtray.

"What's the matter with you, anyway?" Ben asked.

Officer Janetti backed down respectfully. "Sorry."

Ben nodded apologetically. "Forget it," he said.

Janetti changed the subject. "So, if this guy, Philips, was killed up close with one shot, why'd the killer fire twice?"

"He took out the light with the first shot." Ben surmised. He shrugged. That had been his best guess on that, but he had no answer to what he knew would be Janetti's next question.

EVIL WAYS

"Why?" Janetti asked. "Why get that close and then draw attention to yourself? As close as this guy had been to Mr. Phillips he could've knifed him and no one would have known."

"There's a cheery thought," Ben added.

Janetti shrugged. "I got a million of them."

"I'll bet. *heh.* I'm thinking our guy wanted the attention. The light could have been to cover his escape, but it wouldn't have made that much of a difference." He looked around the nearly deserted party area. The dancers had all been sent home after the Sheriff's run in with the killer.

The bell above the door chimed as Franklin Palmer walked into the building. "Hi guys," he said. "Ben, I need to see the Sheriff. He still in there?"

"Yeah, but I don't think he's in the mood for company right now," Janetti said. Palmer ignored him and looked to Ben Dooley.

Dooley nodded and Franklin Palmer quickly crossed the reception area to the Sheriff's office door. He knocked. There was no answer. After a moments silence, Franklin knocked again. A muffled voice filtered through the door. The reporter opened it and stepped inside.

Once the reporter had vanished from sight, the two officers continued their speculation. "If he killed Philips and no one witnessed it, why did he run? Why not blend in with the rest of the panicked crowd?" Janetti asked.

"I'm not sure. Palmer ran into this guy at the courthouse. So, how did our guy get from here to there? Did he go over the wall or walk right through the crowds here as you suggest? With the light blown and everyone looking around in confusion, this guy could have easily walked right past us. It's almost as if he wanted the crowd to panic. Maybe he got off on it."

"I suppose that's possible," Janetti agreed, albeit reluctantly.

"Could our shooter have circled back and rejoined the party so no one would miss him?" Ben asked. "If so, he could witness the terror he caused up close and personal." He shrugged.

"Like when an arsonist returns with the crowds to watch it burn?"

"Something like that. Could be his reward for a job well done, I guess."

It all fit the scenario. At least now Dooley had a plausible scenario to present Sheriff Myers.

"Could be, Ben. After all, things were very hectic here after Tom discovered the body and ran off after the killer. Pretty brave of the man.

Who would have thought he had it in him?"

"Yeah," Deputy Dooley answered. "Who would have thought."

# # #

Tom Myers sat in his office.

The lights were out and only a small shaft of moonlight filtered through the blinds covering the large window behind his desk.

Another body. Another fatality. Another murder. One that he should have prevented. He was the Sheriff. It fell to him to protect the innocent after all.

He failed.

Tom and failure had become close friends of late. Nothing seemed to be going right these days.

He heard a knock at the door, but decided to ignore it. Unfortunately, the person on the other side pushed the door open anyway and stepped inside.

"Tom?"

"What do you want, Palmer?"

"Just wanted to make sure you were okay. The Doc's just finishing up with Harold, so I'll take him back home. I'd like to get there before it starts raining again. I just wanted to see if you were okay before I left. That's all."

Silence answered him from inside the office.

"Oh-kay," Franklin Palmer said as he turned to leave the Sheriff alone with his misery and self-pity.

"Thank you, Palmer," Tom Myers said before the door closed. "I'll be fine. Just need some time to think."

"I understand."

"I'm glad your brother wasn't hurt too badly."

"Yeah. So am I. I'll talk to you in the morning, Tom. Try to get some rest, okay?"

"Sure."

As Franklin Palmer closed the door behind him again, he was suddenly elated by the fact that he did not have to do Tom Myers' job.

Very happy indeed.

He wondered if he could handle the responsibility. He wondered if he could even try. *I've got enough responsibility as it is,* he thought. *Just the way I like it.*

Tom Myers watched as the door to his office closed behind the reporter. Once again, he was alone with his thoughts. They were harsh thoughts, too. Tom could not help but blame himself for what had happened. He took the full measure of responsibility for the death of Charles Philips. They were there, Tom and his men. They should have been able to do something.

Anything at all.

But they didn't. They could not do anything to save Charles Philips.

And they almost lost Harold Palmer as well. If not for the timely arrival of Billy Connelly. Tom knew he should have been there instead.

He should have been there.

That thought would replay itself over and over again in his mind for the rest of the night and well into the morning.

Outside, the thunder began to roll.

Once again Mother Nature threatened Sommersville with rain.

Jake Page had decided not to return to his parent's home.

After leaving the hospital and then the police station, he just wanted some space. The death of his friend, Charles was tough. They had known one another for years. Charles had even shown up in line at one of Jake's autograph sessions at a music store in Washington DC. Charles had been in town on business so he decided to surprise his friend.

Jake knew his parents would be there for him, would console him, but he also knew they wouldn't understand. *How can they when I don't even understand it myself?* There was no rhyme or reason for what had happened.

First Lisa, then Charles.

Why? he wondered. There was no reason for it. No reason he could think of.

Maybe that was the point. Could it all just be so senseless?

At the Sheriff's insistence, Jake had rented a room at a hotel just two blocks away from where his friend had died only hours before. His other friends were staying there as well. The cops felt it would be easier to keep watch over them if they were all in one place. Jake tried to sleep, but there was no way to shut out the images that bulldozed their way into his dreams. No way to silence the terror gnawing at him from the inside.

A brilliant flash of lightning flooded the room with a blue tint, dissolving the shadows. A deep roar of thunder echoed through the building a second later.

Rolling over as he had done at least two dozen times already Jake looked at the electronic clock. Red numerals blazed at him. 2:45 a.m.

"Damn," he murmured as he rolled over once again, trying to get comfortable, but failing terribly. "I give up," he said as he rolled out of the bed. The carpet was cool beneath his feet, but he hardly noticed. He began to pace around the room, much as he did whenever he was worried about something. It was his way of coping.

He was jolted back to awareness by a soft knock at the door.

Now who could that...

Suddenly very concerned, Jake Page crept toward the door. He grabbed a pair of shorts from the top of the dresser and slid them on quietly. Once at the door, he looked through the peephole into the hallway.

He exhaled loudly when he recognized the visitor at his door. "Barbara?"

He unlatched the door and opened it a crack to see if she was alone. She was. Jake opened the door and motioned her inside. She entered without a word, just a sad expression on her otherwise remarkable face.

Jake took one quick look around the hallway before closing the door. He made double sure that it was securely locked. He found it odd that a single door lock could put him at ease so readily. He tried not to think about how easily someone could kick open that door. At least he tried not to think about it.

"Barbara?" he asked in a voice just above a whisper once they were alone. "You alright, sweetheart?"

Barbara Fram sat on the edge of the bed. She had been crying, and from the looks of things she was not quite finished. Jake's heart sank at the sight of the sadness in her eyes. Lisa had been her best friend. Charles was also important to her.

Jake sat beside her. He placed his hands on her shoulders in silence. Although they had kept it quiet, these two had been together for a couple of years off and on. No words needed to be spoken for them to understand one another.

Barbara laid her head on Jake's bare shoulder. He hugged her gently, but with enough firmness for her to know that he would let nothing harm her. Once she felt safe, there in his arms, she allowed the tears to fall.

Jake simply held her close. She needed him to be strong, but he had tears of his own to shed. Together, they comforted one another for as long as the other needed a shoulder to cry on.

Outside the rain began to fall.

# # #

Billy Connelly stood outside in the pouring rain.

He barely noticed the deluge around him. His thoughts were elsewhere. He mumbled something under his breath as he walked aimlessly toward the street.

"Hey!"

Billy could not hear the shout that was aimed at him. He was entranced by his private thoughts. So engrossed was he that he was vaguely conscious of the fact that he was walking. Much less where he was walking.

"Billy!"

Again, he did not hear.

"Hey! I'm talking to you!"

A hand clamped down on Billy Connelly's shoulder. A firm, tight grip that stopped him short and spun him around.

"Billy!"

The young doctor was physically jerked around to face the owner of the voice. It was Ted Hollis, his friend.

T... Ted?" Billy asked. "What's...? How the hell'd I get out here?"

Ted motioned toward the hotel and Billy seemed to remember as if he were coming out of a deep sleep. "You okay, pal?" Ted asked.

"I... uh.... yeah. I'm fine. Just lost in thought. I guess I was a little too lost, huh?"

Ted forced a cheeky grin. "I'd say. Come on. We need to get you inside before you catch a cold or something. Then I'd have to find a doctor. And you know how they are." And he laughed.

Without argument or comment, Billy Connelly allowed himself to be led back to his room. His thoughts were on his surroundings. It had been years since he had walked in his sleep.

"Maybe returning home after all these years wasn't such a good idea," he told his friend.

"Maybe you're right," Ted said softly.

Franklin Palmer pulled his Chevy Blazer onto Main Street.

The Sheriff's Department receded from sight in the rearview mirror. This had been a day that the young reporter would never forget. He had held back on a story and it had gotten someone killed. Whether anyone else saw it that way or not, Franklin Palmer was guilty in his heart. He made a silent vow to never cover up the truth again.

No matter the consequences.

In the passenger seat next to him was his brother. Harold was unusually quiet. Neither had said a word since Franklin's visit with Sheriff Myers. Harold was obviously hurting, but the doctor had told him that his injuries were minor. The ringer in his head would stop soon if he allowed himself time to rest and heal. The doctor had offered to keep him overnight, just in case. Of course, Harold refused.

He could be very stubborn at times. Franklin assumed he took that after their mother, but he did not say that out loud.

"What's on your mind, Bubba?" he asked Harold.

"Hmm?"

"You awake over there?"

"Just thinking, Ray."

"About what?"

Harold turned to look at his brother, a look that told the reporter how stupid the question had been.

"I meant specifically," Franklin said by way of clarification.

"Oh," Harold said. "I don't know what it is, Ray."

"What *what* is?"

"I just keep going over it in my mind. It doesn't make sense."

"There's a whole lot about this that doesn't make sense. Would you care to elaborate?"

"The guy I fought. He was good. Really good."

"So? Come on, Harry. There are people all over that take martial arts classes, boxing at the Y, or any number of places that he could have trained. He could have been a fighter at one time for all we know."

"True," Harold agreed. "But there was something familiar about this guys moves. Almost like the training we put special operations officers through at the Bureau."

Franklin almost laughed. "You think the killer is a fed?"

Harold shook his head then regretted it as a flash of pain stabbed at him between the eyes. "No I don't think that. All I know is what I saw. The man was trained. And trained well."

"Okay," Franklin said as he pulled the Blazer over toward the curb outside of his office building. "We can look through some of the old files and see if anything jumps out at you. Think that will help?"

"Can't hurt, I suppose. Of course, we could be barking up the wrong tree."

"Well, Harry, it's not like we had anything else to do, now did we?"

Harold Palmer sighed. "I guess not," he answered as he slowly got out and walked toward his brother's office through the steady downpour of rain. He had a hunch it was going to be a long night.

Harold had guessed right. It was turning out to be a long night.

He and Franklin had spent two hours going over the town's records, old newspaper stories, and a fairly thorough Internet search. They had not found too many people in Sommersville who had the kind of training that Harold thought the man had demonstrated. There were a few folks that had joined the Army, and one guy joined the Marines. He was from the class of '02 also, the same year Chris, Jake, Billy, and the others graduated from Sommersville High. They thought that was a coincidence and an intensive search confirmed it, marking him off the list of suspects. He was on assignment in Baghdad at the time. That ruled him out as a possible killer. So they kept digging.

"Look, Harry, I know that you think we're going to find something in all this mess," Franklin motioned toward the piles of file folders strewn across his office floor. "But let's face it this guy could be an out of towner with no records of any kind in Sommersville."

"I know, Ray. I know, but I just can't shake this hunch."

The FBI agent's brother let out a deep breath. "Okay. I guess we keep digging then."

Harold rubbed his tired eyes. "Look, we need to find someone with military or federal training. A little more than the usual kickboxing stuff. That guy had some moves. He knew what he was doing. Believe me."

"Well, we've exhausted everyone from the reunion that is in the military, Harry."

Harold looked up from the file he was reading. "What about former military?"

"That's a longer list. We have a lot of World War Two vets living around here. Mr. Pierce, who owns the deli down the street, was in Korea. He worked as an army doctor at a MASH unit. Mr. Nudell who lives down the road from my house was a truck driver in Vietnam. Delivered rations and equipment if I remember correctly."

"I don't know," Harold said, "The age isn't right. The guy that clobbered me was younger. Probably younger than me."

"Okay, old man" Franklin said as he typed in a new parameter in his Internet search. "Let's see here. Okay, that narrows the list considerably." Franklin read off the names in mumbles. Harold could not understand half of what he said, but he was only half listening. Instead, he intently studied a copy of the Sheriff's report on Rebecca Doe [no last name on file], Lisa Woodall, and Charles Phillips.

"There's something about the victims that seems wrong," Harold repeated. "The last two vics were part of a small group of friends in town for the reunion. The first vic was a dancer at Thunderbirds, but she was also involved with Chris Jackson, another of the same friends. That's too much of a coincidence."

"The friends are the targets. That much seems certain," Franklin said while he read off the computer screen.

"What we don't know is why and by whom."

Both were questions they desperately needed answers to.

Barbara Fram couldn't sleep.

She looked over at Jake, lying beside her. He had finally dozed off about twenty minutes earlier. But Barbara could not make herself fall asleep. As tired as she was, sleep would not come. As soon as her head hit the pillow, all of the thoughts in her brain clicked into overdrive. She thought about the friends she had lost; Wilson, Lisa, and Charles. They were a part of her life. She could not let their deaths go. It was a traumatic time for her, for all of them.

Jake had been helpful. He listened to her when she had shown up at his door without warning. He had comforted her. They talked, they tried to laugh, they made love, and now she was staring at the ceiling hoping for peaceful sleep to come.

But the sandman wasn't making house calls this night.

It made her feel weak. No longer in control of herself. And that scared her.

Lightning flashed, washing the room in a bluish white then quickly fading to darkness again. She had left the curtains pulled open in the hopes that the rain and lightning flashes would help her fall asleep.

So far it hadn't helped.

Jake moaned softly as he rolled over onto his back. Barbara stared at him for a long moment. She had come to love the man sleeping beside her. It seemed so hard to remember how she wouldn't even give him the time of day back in high school. *How much things change,* she smiled. It felt good to smile. Even in the midst of the tragedy surrounding them it made her heart lift ever so slightly. Barbara had not had many reasons to smile of late. Jake was the exception to that. When it came to him, she was always smiling.

Suddenly, Barbara sat up.

She thought she heard something. A sound, perhaps coming from the hallway. She realized that she was holding her breath. "I'm starting to let this get to me," she whispered, "Now I'm jumping at shadows. This is a hotel. It's not unusual to hear someone walk down the hallway. Ooh, I need a vacation." She relaxed a bit, feeling her shoulders slump.

What she really needed was sleep.

The knock at the door nearly scared her out of her wits.

It took all of her might not to scream. She turned toward Jake. He was still asleep. Not that she was surprised. She had joked that Jake could sleep even if a train ran through his bedroom. Barbara was still getting used to it. She was a light sleeper and heard every sound, every creak.

There was another knock at the door.

"Damn," she whispered. She wondered if she should wake Jake, but thought better of it. He needed his rest. *Besides,* she thought. *I'm only going to go see who it is. I'm not stupid enough to open the door.*

Throwing off the covers, Barbara searched the chair next to the bed for something to put on. She found one of Jake's shirts. It was a light blue button up shirt that was long enough to fit her. It came down just past her knees.

Walking slowly, on her tiptoes, Barbara crossed the single room toward the door. The bathroom sat off to one side near the door, leaving a short hallway to the door. Cautiously she approached the door, careful not to make a sound.

There was another knock, louder this time.

"Who's there?" she asked instinctively. She regretted the question as soon as she said it. She cursed herself inwardly.

"Me." The person on the other end of the door seemed surprised to hear her voice. The visitor probably expected Jake to answer the door.

"Me?" Barbara asked. She looked through the tiny peephole. A friendly face peered back at her.

She let out a breath.

"Hold on a second," she said as she started unlatching the door.

# # #

"Uh, Harry?"

"Yeah. You find something, Ray?"

"Oh I'd say so," the reporter said.

"What is it?"

"You'd better come look at this."

"Okay," Harold said as he moved across to the computer table where his brother was surfing the net for information. "What have you got?"

Franklin turned the computer screen so his older brother could easily see it. "You're not going to believe this."

"Why? What did you..." Harold's voice trailed off when he saw the file on the monitor. A familiar face stared back at him. "Oh God," Harold muttered.

Harold was moving before Franklin could process that he was no longer beside him. Halfway to the door, Harold grabbed his coat. "Come on, Ray. Call Myers and tell him to meet us over there. We've got to go. Throw me your keys. I'm driving."

Franklin tossed his car keys to his brother while grabbing his own coat and cell phone. He hoped he wasn't making a mistake letting his brother drive. Harold's luck leaned toward the bad when it came to automobile accidents. And Franklin had just bought the Blazer a few months earlier.

And it was pouring down rain.

Not a good combination.

Barbara Fram unlatched the single lock on the door and slowly opened it.

The man on the other side pushed forcefully, knocking the startled Barbara against the wall. "You little slut," the man yelled.

Barbara got to her feet and called for Jake, hoping he would hear her and wake up. Not hearing anything, she screamed again. "Jake!"

The man stepped up close and backhanded Barbara. She hit the floor hard. Barbara could taste the blood in her mouth. Probably bit her lip or tongue.

"Jake!"

The man she thought she knew walked past her toward the bedroom. It was only a few feet to the end of the hallway. Jake bolted around the corner and came face to face with the *friend* who had just knocked his girlfriend to the floor.

"What's... Y-You?!" Jake stammered. "What are...?"

Jake hesitated. The attacker did not. A punch to the face sent Jake reeling. He fell over the chair, knocking his and Barbara's clothes to the floor with him. Jake rubbed the blood coming from his nose. It felt broken.

Jake got back to his feet, his world spinning. Everything was disoriented. He made a move toward the attacker.

"I wouldn't," the man said, pulling a gun. Jake thought it was a .45 Magnum, but he couldn't be certain. All he knew was the gun was pointed at his head. There was no way Jake could dodge the bullet at that range.

Barbara was lying against the wall behind the man they thought of as a friend. He was smiling, enjoying himself. He seemed to be taking some kind of sick pleasure in the slaughter of those closest to him.

"Why?" Jake asked.

"Oh please! Don't act so surprised. I don't need your pity now, *friend*. It's simply your time to die. I am the messenger that will deliver the message of death upon you."

"You're insane," Jake admitted.

"Probably. Then again, I killed the last person that called me crazy. If I kill everyone that thinks I'm crazy, then I'll be sane, right?"

Jake was at a loss. He did not know what to say to the man before him.

Barbara made her move. She grabbed the lamp off of the dresser and swung hard at her attacker with it. It struck home with a resounding *thud*. Barbara thought that would be the end of it. She was wrong.

The man did not fall. He was shaken, but still conscious. He turned on Barbara and knocked her against the wall one more time. She slumped to the floor as stars and flashbulbs went off behind her eyes. For a moment she thought of the paparazzi she hated so much. Taking advantage of the interruption, Jake lunged at the man who had attacked his girlfriend.

He was not quick enough.

The gun instantly focused on Jake again. The man pulled the trigger and Jake Page screamed as a puff of air launched fiery death at him. Another shot pushed the singer into the far wall. Jake fell hard on the bed before bouncing off it onto the floor.

His blood covered the wall.

Barbara tried to scream, but couldn't form the sound.

She was helpless.

The man responsible for everything that had happened to her over the past few days calmly walked toward Jake's unmoving body. He pointed the gun at the singer, smiled, and pulled the trigger once again. "Just to be on the safe side," he said.

Barbara's heart sank for she knew she was next.

That was Barbara Fram's last thought on the subject as peaceful unconsciousness claimed her.

# # #

Harold Palmer sped away from the newspaper office.

The hotel was only a few miles away. His brother, Franklin screamed out directions when it looked like Harold would miss them. Harold didn't know the town very well.

"Left!" Franklin screamed as they neared the hotel's entrance. Harold jerked hard on the steering wheel, whipping the Blazer into the parking lot sideways. Franklin closed his eyes preparing for the worst.

"Let's go," Harold said as he threw the vehicle into park and killed the engine. Harold was already half way across the parking lot by the time Franklin got out of the Blazer.

Franklin cursed loudly and ran off after his brother. By the time he reached the lobby of the hotel, he could see no sign of that FBI agent brother of his. Wiping the rainwater from his hair and face, Franklin Palmer made a beeline for the elevators. He tapped the call button for *up* and waited for the next available car.

Don't do anything stupid, Harry, he thought while he waited impatiently.

The elevator chimed, announcing an arriving car. It opened far too slowly for Franklin's taste. Finally open, the young reporter leaped inside and pressed the button.

"Hold the elevator, Palmer!"

Franklin looked between the closing doors as Sheriff Tom Myers ran across the lobby toward him with Ben Dooley and Theodore Janetti in tow. Franklin held open the elevator doors as the three men stepped inside.

"Thanks," Tom said. "Are you sure about this, Palmer?"

Franklin nodded. "Pretty sure."

Tom noticed Janetti looking around the elevator. "Hey, Palmer. Where's your brother?"

Tom and Ben noticed as well that the elder Palmer brother was not in the car with them. They both turned to look at Franklin in askance.

"Well, where is he?"

"Where do you think?" Franklin said, pointing toward the ceiling, indicating up.

"Great," Tom said. "I hope he doesn't do anything stupid."

"That makes two of us," Franklin said under his breath.

49.

Harold Palmer burst through the stairwell door onto the third floor.

From his conversations with Sheriff Myers, Harold knew that Ted Hollis, Billy Connelly, Jake Page, and Barbara Fram were all staying on the third floor of this hotel. *Why isn't there a guard posted?* he wondered.

"Now what was the room number?" he asked aloud, searching his memory. "312. That's it." Harold turned and ran toward the room he was looking for. *Three eleven. Three twelve. Here we go.* Harold slipped his right hand under his jacket on the left side. He felt the gun holstered there and that reassured him. Carefully, he unclipped the strap holding the gun in its place.

Back against the wall, Harold pulled his weapon and held it in a ready position, aimed toward the floor in front of him. Quietly he inched his way to the door. It was open just a bit. He could hear a faint sound from inside. Hard to make out, but it was someone talking.

Switching the gun to his left hand, Harold pushed open the door to room 312 with his right. The stench of alcohol hit him square in the face. Instinctively he threw his hand over his nose. "Jesus," he yelled.

He took in three or four deep cleansing breaths then made his way inside the room. It was in disarray. Clothes and food wrappers from the fast food restaurant across the street littered the floor. "Must've been one hell of a party," he whispered.

The first room was empty. Harold couldn't see anyone. There was a smaller room off of the backside of the main room. Harold eased through the clutter toward the door. Easing it open, Harold inched his way in gun first.

"Anyone in here?" he called.

A gurgled answer was the only reply.

Harold turned at the sound, gun pointing the way, but the person making the noise posed no threat to anyone, save himself. Harold lowered his weapon and walked across the room to where Billy Connelly lay against the unmade bed. He was swaying to music that only he could hear. In his left hand was a half-empty bottle of Jack Daniels whiskey.

Small driblets of the alcohol were steadily falling on the light gray carpet. Two other bottles lay at the young doctor's feet. They were quite empty.

Billy looked up and noticed Harold for the first time. "Hey!" Billy tried to say, but the sounds melted together into a unique word all its own.

"Damn," Harold said as he got to his feet. The young doctor reeked of alcohol. *This must be his way of coping,* Harold decided. *Not the smartest way, mind you, but to each his own.*

Harold started back toward the other room when a coherent word escaped the doctor's lips. "Jake..."

"What?" Harold asked as he turned around. "What did you say?"

Unfortunately the moment of clarity was gone. Harold swore. "Jake is staying here also," Harold whispered as he made his way toward the door. "Jake is here too. What room?"

No answer.

Harold broke out into a full run toward the door. Turning to the right once he reached the hallway, the FBI agent headed down the long corridor, checking each corner, each doorway as he reached it.

The elevator opened as Harold ran past. His brother's voice caught his attention. "Harry! Hey! What is it? Where is he?"

Harold turned. "Where's Jake Page staying?" he asked the sheriff.

"Last room on the right," Myers answered. "Why?"

"He's next," Harold yelled as he took off toward the last room on the right. "Connelly's in three twelve."

"Dooley," Tom said, motioning for his deputy to follow Harold Palmer.

"Right, Chief," Dooley said as he pulled his service weapon and fell in step behind the FBI agent. "Wait for me, Palmer."

As Ben Dooley and Harold Palmer raced to the room rented by Jake Page, Tom Myers, Theodore Janetti, and Franklin Palmer looked in on Billy Connelly. They found him babbling incoherently, just as Harold had only moments before.

Three words caught Tom's attention, n or were they lost on either of the other two men. "Ted..." "Potter..." "Jake..."

Those were the only words that made sense.

"What the hell does that mean?" Janetti asked.

Tom and Franklin turned to face one another. They were afraid they knew the answer to that question. Tom looked over at Janetti. "Why don't you go check on Ms. Fram. She's in three oh eight down the hall."

Janetti moved toward the door. "Got it," he said as he turned into the main corridor, moving in the opposite direction of Harold Palmer and his fellow deputy.

Harold reached Jake Page's door two steps ahead of Deputy Benjamin Dooley. They approached cautiously, weapons drawn and ready. They immediately noticed the door was ajar.

"What do you think?" Dooley asked.

"You won't like what I think."

"Oh..."

They moved into the room carefully, slowly. For every move one made, the other was there to cover him. The room was in shambles.

"This doesn't look good," Dooley noted.

"Must be the maid's day off," Harold quipped, trying to hide his own apprehension. "Over there," he pointed. "Look."

The two men moved toward the unmoving body of Jake Page. At first glance, Harold noticed three distinct bullet holes. "He was shot at close range from the looks of it," he told Deputy Dooley.

The deputy agreed.

"Silencer?"

"Probably. Otherwise, it would have woken someone."

Harold bent down and touched Jake Page's neck, searching for a pulse. By some miracle he found one.

"Oh God," Harold said. "He's still alive. Get an ambulance." He looked up at Dooley. "And tell them to hurry!"

Deputy Dooley pulled his police radio from his belt and called for an immediate emergency response team to the hotel. The emergency services department at the local hospital responded. They would arrive within five minutes.

"Just hang on there, buddy," Harold told Jake.

Jake moaned softly. Having never been shot himself, Harold assumed the man was in intense pain. He was more right than he could ever know.

Harold took a quick inventory of the room. "Someone's missing," he said.

"I beg your pardon?" Dooley asked.

"Someone else was in this room."

"You mean besides the asshole that shot him?"

"Yeah. Jake here was entertaining a guest."

"How do you know that?"

"Look," Harold said. He pointed toward the clothes scattered about.

"You see that? Men and women's clothes. There was a woman here."

"Probably Barbara Fram. We found out they were having a secret little romance going on. They tried to keep it hush hush, but it came out when their friend was killed."

"Which friend?" Harold asked.

Dooley flinched. "Oh, that's right. Uh, Lisa Woodall. Ms. Fram was supposed to be with her, but snuck away with Mr. Page for another kind of reunion. If you know what I mean."

"Yeah. So, where's the girl?"

Ben Dooley looked around the room. "Now that's a damned good question."

"Yes it is."

50.

The rain started to lessen.

Not that it made a difference to Chris Jackson. He walked into the atrium of the hotel where his friends were staying wiping away at the water that covered his body. He wanted -no needed- someone to talk to. Things were falling apart all around them and he desperately wanted to do something -anything- to make things better.

He just didn't know what that could be before he got there. When he saw Sheriff Myers' truck, Ben Dooley's patrol car, and Franklin Palmer's Blazer parked out front, he could only speculate the worst-case scenario. Another of his friends was dead.

He entered the hotel lobby at a full run. Bypassing the elevators all together, he took the stairs two at a time until he reached the third floor. Before opening the door, the deputy pulled his personal pistol from his belt and checked the clip. Clicking off the safety he eased open the door, careful to conceal his weapon in case there was no immediate trouble.

He stuck his head out the door carefully.

There was nothing there. No one was in the hallway, but that didn't keep Chris' mind from running wildly through possible scenarios.

Stepping cautiously into the deserted corridor, Chris moved toward his friend's room. 312. The door was open and he could hear voices inside. He chanced a glance around the corner. From the door he could not see into the far room. That was where the other voices originated. Steeling himself, Chris Jackson stepped into Billy Connelly's hotel room.

"Hold it!" he yelled.

His boss turned to stare him down. "Jesus, Jackson. What are you trying to do, give me a coronary?" Tom was trying to catch his breath. Chris noticed that Tom Myers' right hand rested on top of his pistol. At that moment, Chris discovered that he could have been shot if his boss had not noticed him as quickly as he had.

Saying nothing for a change, Franklin Palmer was shaking his head, but he did not keep his silence long. "What the hell's the matter with you? Cops. Sheesh."

"That's enough, Palmer," Tom said, clearly irritated with the reporter's glib attempt at humor.

Clicking on the safety, Chris tucked his gun back in its place in his belt. "What I want to know is what's going on here?" he asked.

"We're still trying to figure that one out ourselves," Franklin muttered.

Tom walked over to Chris, who asked again if something was wrong. This time more forcibly. "Look, Chris," Tom said, his voice barely above a whisper. "We're looking for Ted Hollis. Have you seen him tonight?"

"Ted? What are you looking for Ted for?"

"Let's just say I'm curious about his whereabouts. You seen him?"

Chris shuffled uncomfortably. "Not since after the dance. I escorted Ted, Billy, Jake, and Barbara here to the hotel. I wanted to make sure they got here safely before I went home."

"Okay. Stay here while I go check on the other Palmer."

"S--sure," Chris said. Clearly, he wasn't sure what was happening.

Tom headed down the hallway toward the room rented for Jake Page. Before he could get there Harold Palmer came barreling into the hallway from said room. "We need an ambulance here now!" he shouted to the sheriff. "He's been shot."

"Is he alive?"

"Barely," Harold said between gasps for air. Obviously the FBI agent was still sluggish from the pounding he had taken earlier in the evening. "Did you find the girl?"

"Ms. Fram?" Tom asked.

Harold replied by shaking his head.

Tom cooked his thumb over his shoulder. "Janetti's checking on her now."

"She won't be there," Harold predicted.

Tom was confused. "And how do you know that, Agent Palmer?"

Harold took in a deep breath. "Her clothes are in Page's room. She was with him. Remember, they were rumored to be an item."

"Damn. You're right. I'd forgotten about that."

"Somebody remembered."

"But who? Hollis?"

Harold shrugged.

"So..." Tom speculated.

Harold nodded. "So whoever shot Jake Page has Barbara Fram."

"First murder, now kidnapping."

"Or she's in on it."

Before Tom could answer, Theodore Janetti came running up the hallway toward them. "Tom!" he yelled. "The Fram woman's not in her room."

As one, Tom and Harold, rushed toward Billy Connelly's hotel room. They needed answers. "God, I hate it when I'm right," Harold whispered.

Nearby the elevator *pinged*, announcing the arrival of a new car. Instinctively, the law officers each drew their weapons and pointed them. Too much had already happened tonight to take any chances.

They were relieved to see the paramedics inside when the doors parted. The paramedics were not as happy to see them however. They stood stock still as four guns were pointed directly at them.

"Sorry, guys," Harold said as he lowered his gun. The others lowered their weapons as well. Chris noticed the disapproving look Tom Myers gave him upon seeing the gun in his possession again. Chris was surprised when the sheriff said nothing, but he was certain they would speak on it later.

The paramedics pushed back their fear. They had a job to do first. Tom pointed toward Jake Page's room. "Down there, fellas. Last room on the right. Multiple gunshot wounds. One of my officers is in there with the vic. He'll get you whatever you need."

"Right. We're on it." The paramedics ran down the corridor and disappeared into the specified room.

Tom followed Harold into the room rented to Dr. Billy Connelly. Franklin was still kneeling beside the young doctor. He was babbling continuously, albeit incoherently. Harold tapped his brother gently on the shoulder. The younger Palmer brother moved to the side so Harold could get closer to Billy.

Harold knelt beside Billy. He tried to ignore the intrusive alcohol smell from his brain. The scent made it hard for him to concentrate. Harold had little tolerance for people that felt a need to drink themselves into a stupor. *It's probably his way of dealing with the trauma.* Harold had met other medical professionals who behaved similarly.

"Billy! Where is Ted Hollis?"

Billy smiled. Harold wasn't sure if the young doctor even knew Harold was speaking, much less understood him.

Grabbing Billy Connelly by the collar, Harold brought the man to his eye level. "Billy!" he shouted. It worked. The doctor's eyes fixated on Harold's face. "Where. Did. Ted. Go." Harold accented every word sharply. He wanted to make sure the man understood every single word.

"Ted..." Billy mumbled.

"Yes. Ted!"

"Hewentothhrevin."

"What?" Franklin demanded from the far end of the room.

Harold cast a harsh look at his brother's outburst before turning his full attention back to Billy Connelly. "Billy! Concentrate! Where is Ted now?"

"Potter's."

"Potter's?" Harold repeated. "Now where have I heard that name before?" Harold asked.

"We were there earlier. It's close to where I first met you, Mr. Palmer," Tom said.

"The ravine where Jackson found the body?"

Tom nodded.

Harold shook the doctor for more answers, but Billy Connelly had passed out. "Dammit! Tom, how fast can we get to this ravine?"

Tom shrugged. "Ten, fifteen minutes."

Harold followed the sheriff toward the door. "Ray, you stay here," he told the reporter.

"Like hell I will," his brother prompted. Suffice it to say Franklin did not much care for his brother's plan.

Harold tried not to let his dissatisfaction show, but he knew better than to argue with his stubborn brother. He simply said, "Whatever."

"I'm coming too," Chris Jackson said.

Tom stopped at the doorway. Someone had to stay behind and keep an eye on Dr. Connelly. In case he woke up, or worse. They had no way of knowing if Ted Hollis would be returning to the hotel to finish what had been started.

"Janetti," Tom said. "You stay here until you can get enough guys over here to seal this place up. Then, you and Dooley get out to Potter's Ravine as fast as you can. Got it?"

Janetti looked at the man slumped on the floor. "Yeah, boss. I don't think he's going to give me much trouble."

Tom turned to the others. "Let's go!"

Minutes later, Franklin Palmer's Blazer screeched out of the parking lot behind the Sheriff's pick up truck with Harold Palmer behind the wheel and Franklin Palmer holding on for dear life.

51.

Lightning crashed all around.

The rain had slowed to a drizzle. Perhaps the trees were merely blocking the worst of it. Either way, Ted Hollis found the woods of Fort Greene State Park calm and tranquil.

Not at all like his life.

No, his life was in constant turmoil. There were so many things that he had to do. So many wrongs to right. So many things to do for... for... the thoughts escaped him. There was no way for him to concentrate for any long periods on one subject. A voice that only he could hear spurred him onward. He focused on it and was reassured everything was going to be all right.

He listened to the voice.

The voice was his master.

His master had told him to bring Barbara Fram to the Ravine. She moaned softly in his arms as he carried her across the wet grass and mud, careful to avoid the places where roots jutted freely from the ground, hoping to trip any passers by caught unawares. He had studied this place so many times. He knew it well enough to navigate without light.

Others had not been as careful when trudging through the thick underbrush. His mind flashed back to the girl with the chocolate skin. She had been careless. The roots had grabbed her and pulled her to the ground. As they would him if he had not planned for every contingency.

Ted Hollis had learned to be careful a long time ago.

And a very painful lesson that was too.

Lightning flashed again overhead, casting a sharp spike of brilliance over the surrounding area. Ted laughed. The master was lighting the way for his faithful servant. It could only be a sign. Even as Ted Hollis thought this, he knew that things were far from over.

There was still much to do.

Much to prepare.

# # #

EVIL WAYS

Theodore Janetti stood at the door of Billy Connelly's hotel room. The paramedics were wheeling their patient past him in a hurry to get him to the hospital. They had to work quickly. Even though Jake Page was still alive he wouldn't last much longer without emergency surgery. Seeing them approach, Janetti tapped the elevator call button for them and held the doors open until they arrived. Dooley walked behind them.

"How is he?" Janetti asked his fellow deputy.

Dooley shook his head. "It doesn't look good," he said. He was shot three times at point blank range. Frankly, it's a freakin' miracle he's lasted this long."

The paramedics tapped the button for the lobby and the doors closed behind them. The soft hum of the descending elevator filled the nearly deserted hallway.

Janetti motioned toward the room rented to Billy Connelly. "I'm watching over sleeping beauty here until our replacements arrive," he told Dooley.

"Good," Dooley told him. "I'm going to help the paramedics get out of here then I'm going after Tom. Where'd they say they were headed?"

"Potter's Ravine," Janetti replied.

"Okay. I'm off. You be careful, Janetti."

"You bet. Watch yourself, Dooley."

Theodore Janetti walked back into the room and closed the door behind him. With the doctor still out cold, Janetti sat down on the couch and began flipping through a magazine he found lying on the floor.

"I hate this," the deputy mumbled, "I really, really do."

#

Benjamin Dooley was in great physical condition so he didn't wait for the elevator to come back up for him. He sprinted to the stairwell and ran down the three flights of stairs to the lobby. As he arrived the paramedics were just exiting the main doors at the other end of the room.

Dooley ran across to help them. "You guys need an escort?" he asked.

"No. We've got it. You've got enough to do. Go. We'll be alright."

"Thanks." Benjamin Dooley ran toward his car. He opened the door and climbed inside. Seconds later he was streaking down Main Street in search of his comrades.

And a killer.

# # #

Thunder peeled through the night, rattling windows in the hotel.

A few minutes later a flash of lightning light up the night sky and cast a light blue shade across everything in its sight. Another rumble of thunder followed quickly behind the lightning flash. The scenario repeated itself several more time before the rain began to beat down far harder than it had at any point over the past week. Sommersville had received far more than its fair share of bad weather for one season.

Upstairs, Janetti waited impatiently.

Although he was inside and away from the harsh weather outside, he was anxious for something -anything- to happen. He hated guard duty, especially when the one being guarded was out cold.

But more than that, Theodore Janetti craved a smoke. It had been a full twenty minutes since his last one and he was dying to have a cigarette. He had already read all of the interesting articles in the sports magazine he had discovered lying on the floor next to the bed. It hadn't help take his mind off of his cravings. The frequent cigarette ads placed sporadically (every three or four pages it seemed) in the magazine weren't helping either.

Cursing inwardly, the deputy gave in. He could probably sneak a few puffs before his backup arrived. He could do it, but not in the room. The room was officially a crime scene. His cigarette smoke could possibly contaminate some evidence. He even regretted moving the magazine from the floor.

He stepped out into the hallway and eased the door shut behind him. Inside, Billy Connelly was oblivious to the world around him. He wouldn't cause any problems for the deputy in the next few minutes. Janetti fired up the cigarette. It felt so good as he puffed that first whiff of smoke. "Ahh," he sighed. "That's better."

He closed his eyes and savored the moment as he paced back and forth up and down the hallway. The tension sliding off of him with each puff of smoke he exhaled.

He felt the person standing behind him immediately.

At first he thought it was his imagination, but then a shadow fell across the floor in front of him. Janetti gasped, dropping the cigarette even as he reached for his gun.

The deputy spun around quickly, but it was too late. The thick glass whiskey bottle crashed across Janetti's face. The bottle did not shatter on impact, but it was successful in its purpose. The deputy went down. Janetti felt the gun fall from his grasp of its own volition and bounce quietly on the hallway's carpet. He reached for it, but could not take his eyes off the man standing before him. "No! Wait!" he started, but it was too late.

The bottle crashed down again and again on Theodore Janetti faster than the deputy could react. His blood splattered, covering the bottle as it was battered again and again against him. Blood streamed across the hotel walls with each upward arc. The bottle swung down hard against the unmoving deputy until it finally shattered against his skull.

And Theodore Janetti died.

52.

Lightning flashed.

The road lit up like a beacon had been turned on, marking the way.

Tom jerked hard on the wheel of his old pick up truck and swerved sideways onto the highway leading to Lake Greene. Franklin Palmer's Blazer successfully copied the maneuver with the elder Palmer behind the wheel. Franklin had one hand on the dashboard and another held firmly to the handhold above the door. Harold remembered how their Dad had called them *OhmiGod's* because that was what you screamed when you grabbed them.

Their Dad had a wonderful sense of humor.

Unfortunately for Franklin, he didn't share his father's particular type of humor.

Harold on the other hand...

# # #

Lightning flashed again.

The ground came alive in washes of blue and white. The shadows temporarily retreated to the trees above only to return after the lightning subsided. None of this bothered Ted Hollis in the least. He knew there would be another flash, even as he knew his destination was close at hand. Without being able to see it, he could feel the deep darkness of the ravine ahead of him. He was almost there.

The voice sang out to him from all around. Ted felt a wave of euphoria wash over him as the masterful voice commanded him. Ted would not fail in his mission. He could not fail in his mission.

Failure was simply not an option.

Another flash of lightning pinpointed his destination. It would all end at the ravine where it started all those many long years ago. Ted Hollis smiled as he gently laid Barbara Fram's unmoving body on the wet ground near the edge of the ravine. A soft moan escaped her lips as her body made contact with the cold forest floor. Moans of pain were the only sounds she had made since they left the hotel. Ironically, the sounds of pain echoed the sounds of pleasure Ted had fantasized about over and over again since his fascination with the opposite sex began as a teenager.

Ted grimaced. He hoped that she would wake up soon. She had to be awake. The plan depended on it. She had to wake up.

Or all would be lost.

Plus, he wanted to see her beautiful eyes one last time.

# # #

Tom Myers navigated the rain slicked back roads of Sommersville like a pro.

Not surprising since he had lived in the town his entire life, save the four years he was in the Navy. He quickly turned from the highway onto the mud path that ran along the length of Lake Greene. Chris Jackson sat silently in the passenger seat. His thoughts were already ahead of them, wondering after the friends he left behind and the friend he was hoping to save. Or maybe his thoughts were on the friend he would have to kill? It was hard to say.

Tom noticed the Blazer still behind him in the rearview mirror.

Without missing a beat, Harold Palmer swerved his brother's Blazer into the mud behind the pick up. Harold immediately noticed that Tom Myers had stopped.

As the sheriff unhooked the chain that was stretched taut over the muddy half road, Harold chanced a glance toward his brother. "How you holding up over there, Ray?"

"Peachy."

"Hey. It won't be that bad. Just stay behind me and Tom. We'll take care of this." Harold was trying to reassure Franklin, but having no luck.

"You know, Harry," Franklin began. "We could just let Tom and his boys handle this. You don't have to go in there."

"Oh hell yes I do, Ray."

"Why, Harry? Macho pride? Protecting the FBI's honor? What makes this your business?"

Harold sighed. His brother just didn't seem to get it. "Let's just say that I take it personal when a psychopathic killer beats the shit out of me and calmly strolls away like I was nothing. I take it you understand that?"

Franklin nodded. Obviously, the reporter had more to say, but Tom's truck started moving again. Harold did not know the roads of

Sommersville well, at all actually, so he had to follow Tom's trail closely and carefully. Their discussion about doing the right thing would have to wait until Ted was in custody.

Then they could talk to their hearts content.

Ted Hollis was prepared. Earlier that day he had hidden a bag of things he knew he would need near the ravine. Everything was proceeding at its pace.

The master would be pleased.

He quickly set about preparing for the ceremony.

The time was almost nigh.

He could feel them approaching.

Soon.

Soon.

"Hold on!"

Harold's warning came a second too late as the Blazer hit a deep, muddy hole. The tires lost their tenuous hold on the road and the vehicle slid uncontrollably off the road and directly into a ditch.

Franklin let out a breath of relief.

Harold let out a simultaneous curse. He pressed the gas to get them started again, but it was a useless endeavor with the right rear wheel not making contact with the ground. The Blazer was completely immobile in the ditch. There was absolutely no way they could get any traction on the wet, muddy surface.

Tom Myers kept driving. The Palmer brothers were on their own.

Under normal circumstances he would have stopped to help, but circumstances were far from ordinary. He had to reach Ted Hollis before anything happened to Barbara Fram. That was the most important thing at the moment.

The Palmer brothers would just have to fend for themselves.

"Harold hit the steering wheel in anger and frustration. "Dammit!" he yelled. "How much farther to the ravine?" he asked Franklin.

Franklin pointed toward a spot in the distance. Harold could just see Tom Myers' taillights as they rounded the corner. "Not far. On foot we can cut through the woods. We should get there right behind Myers."

EVIL WAYS

"Good," Harold said as he opened the door. "I'm going after Tom and Chris. You coming with me or staying here?"

Franklin slid out the driver's side door behind his brother. He forced a less than convincing smile. "What, stay here and let you have all the fun?"

"This isn't a game, Ray," Harold told him. "This is dead serious."

"I know."

"So long as you do."

"Look, Harry. We can sit here and argue if you want, but I'm coming along. I have an obligation to tell the story as it happened. I can't know the truth if I'm not there, now can I?"

"I guess not."

"You guess not."

"Let's go then," Harold said as he pulled a small flashlight from the door pocket.

Franklin fell into step behind his older brother. "Right behind you," he said, "Right behind you."

53.

Tom Myers drove quickly.

At least as quick as he was able over the wet, uneven mud slicked path that laughably passed for the road leading to Potter's Ravine. Several times his old pick up truck swerved sharply, pulled against him. Even as he fought for control he was acutely aware of how easy it would be for him to end up in the middle of Lake Greene.

And Lake Greene was fairly deep as he recalled.

He trudged forward as best as he was able. Just ahead of him was a dip in the road. It was actually closer to a hole and it was filled with a mixture of mud and rainwater. Tom swerved to miss it, but there was not enough room for his truck on either side. Setting himself he stomped on the gas pedal, pushing it to the floor. The old battered pick up bolted toward the hole. Chris grabbed the dashboard for support as the truck's speed increased. Tom hoped he had enough speed to barrel through to the other side without getting stuck.

He should have known better.

The truck bottomed out in the muddy water. The sheriff heard the crunch of metal hitting the ground and he winced. His deputy swore a muffled curse from the passenger seat. He heard sounds like that before and knew it was not good news. But he couldn't give up. A woman's life was at stake.

He pressed down on the gas one more time, pushing against the truck's floorboard, and the back tires of the truck spun wildly, sending a spray of mud, water, and grass behind it. It was no use. The truck was stuck. If he had enough time he could probably wedge it free, but time was something that he did not possess in abundance.

Nor did Barbara Fram.

The Sheriff slammed his fist against the steering wheel in anger. "Dammit!" he yelled as he grabbed his yellow rain slicker with the word *POLICE* emblazoned across the back. He grabbed his waterproofed hat and flashlight. Once more he checked the clip in his gun. He was fully loaded, even though he hoped it wouldn't come to that.

Although with the killer's track record Tom was afraid he would have to use it before the night was through.

The last item Tom Myers grabbed was his walkie talkie. He turned the volume down as low as he could. The last thing he wanted to do was announce his presence before he had a chance to stop Ted Hollis. He wished at that moment that he had given the Palmer brothers a walkie of their own. Tom had no idea where they were at the moment. The last he had seen of them was when Franklin Palmer's Blazer had slid off the road into a ditch a short ways back.

He had no idea what had happened to them after that. Tom just hoped they could take care of themselves.

And that they didn't get lost.

# # #

"Which way, Ray?" Harold Palmer asked, a tinge of bitterness in his voice.

"Off to the left. The Ravine should just be on the right. The road will lead to the right side so Myers will have that covered." Franklin wiped away the rain from his face as he pointed out the directions to his brother.

Harold nodded. He tossed the flashlight to Franklin. "Take this," he told his younger brother. "And stay behind me."

Franklin looked at him skeptically. "If you're in front won't you need the light?"

"Not really," Harold said as he clicked off the safety on his gun. "I'll sort of have my hands full."

"Oh. I see."

"Ready, Ray?"

He shrugged. "Do I have a choice?"

Harold huffed. He did not really want to get into any arguments or debates with his brother at the moment. He had far too many other things on his mind. Not the least of which was keeping himself alive. Not to mention keeping Ray, Myers, and Ms. Fram in one piece as well.

"That's what I thought," Franklin said as he pointed toward an incline. "That way, I think."

"You think?"

"Hey, it looks different out here at night."

"That's reassuring."

"Just trust me okay."

Harold really had no other choice. He motioned toward the direction his brother had pointed out. "Lead on McDuff," he offered.

The two brothers began to climb. The incline was steep, but not so steep they couldn't walk it. Several times they would slip or slide on the wet leaves, but both managed to reach the top in relatively good time.

Franklin knelt next to a tree, trying to catch his breath. "The ravine should be right over that next hill," he pointed out.

"Okay," Harold said. "Just remember to keep out of sight and be careful. This guy is dangerous."

"I can take care of myself, *Mom*," he said sarcastically, even though he was glad his brother was feeling protective. "You watch yourself too, bro," he added.

Harold nodded and started his way down to the next small hill. This hill did not rise as sharply as the one before had and neither of them had any trouble reaching the top. Once there, Harold could make out movement in the distance. He had to assume that was Hollis and Fram. Of course, it could have been pigs, or dogs, or cows for all he knew. But Harold had a hunch. He always followed his hunches.

Franklin slid into position behind his brother. He too could see the movement in the darkness. And like Harold, he couldn't tell what was moving. Just that it was moving. "What is that?" he asked, his voice just above a whisper.

Harold grunted, "I haven't a clue."

Then a spark erupted in the middle of the darkness.

Franklin gasped as it startled him. Harold quickly clamped a hand across his brother's mouth before he accidentally gave them away. Harold held a finger over his own mouth to signal Franklin to stay quiet and calm. Franklin nodded that he was okay and in control again before Harold removed his hand.

"Thanks," Franklin Palmer whispered.

Harold's response was a nod. He said nothing.

They watched as the spark of a lighter igniting repeated itself again. And again.

And again.

"What's he doing?" Franklin asked, his voice barely above a whisper.

"Lighting candles," Harold replied simply.

"Why?"

"Haven't a clue, Ray, but it looks to me like a ceremony of some kind. See how the candles are placed?"

Franklin peered into the semi darkness. He had to strain to see with any clarity through the rain, but he could see Harold had nailed it. Sure enough, Harold was right. With each candle Ted Hollis lit, a pattern began to emerge. Several candles were prearranged in a circle. Why he was placing lit candles around, Harold could not be certain. Luckily, it was taking time for Ted to prepare for whatever he had in mind for Barbara Fram.

That bought Harold and Franklin time.

Not much time, but a few minutes at best. Harold would have to put them to the best use he could. He had a few thoughts and theories on what Ted was doing, but kept those to himself.

The *why* could wait until later. The first priority was to stop the killer from carrying out his plan. Whatever it might be.

"Where's the Fram woman?" Franklin asked.

Harold pointed over to the side of the area where Ted Hollis had cleared space to do his work. "There," he said.

Franklin followed the line from Harold's finger to a tree. "I don't see her," he admitted. "Where is she?"

Harold whispered, "See that tree there?"

"Yeah."

"She's tied to it."

"How do you know that, Harry?"

"There are ropes tied around it. Plus, I can just barely make out one of her arms as she moves. I think she's out cold. Or drugged."

"Is that good or bad?" Franklin asked.

"I don't know, Ray," Harold said, wishing he had a better answer to give.

The only other concern Harold had besides Barbara Fram's current condition was the whereabouts of Tom Myers. The Sheriff's pick up had continued on after the Blazer had slid off the road. Myers should have reached the ravine already. *Something must have happened to him,* Harold thought. He hoped the sheriff was unharmed. He had become quite fond of the man after their conversation on the night a few hours before Charles Philips had been killed.

"So what's the plan, boss?" Franklin asked.

Harold didn't answer.

Franklin leaned in closer to his brother. His mouth was poised just beside Harold's left ear. "You do have some sort of foolproof FBI master plan to deal with situations like this," he asked. "Don't you?"

Harold slowly turned to look at Franklin. The look on his face was enough to tell Franklin everything. *Great,* he thought. *Harry's playing it*

BOBBY NASH

by ear.

"Great," he whispered so Harold could hear him.
"Just great."

54.

Ted Hollis began lighting the last of the candles.

Careful to do things in the exact pattern as the master had instructed him in his dreams. There were a certain number of candles needed and they had a certain position to be placed in. Everything had to be perfect in order for the ritual to work. Truthfully, Ted knew little of the *whys* and *wherefores* of his mission. He only knew that the voice that spoke to him decreed that this be done.

So he did it.

Unquestioning.

Unwavering.

Loyal to the end.

And loyalty will be rewarded.

He heard those words echo through his brain over and over again in rapid succession. They rattled off at the most opportune times, almost as if someone had drilled through his brain and placed them there.

Loyalty will be rewarded.

Ted Hollis eagerly awaited his reward.

Whatever it may be.

# # #

Tom Myers and Chris Jackson had one advantage over Harold and Franklin Palmer.

The officers both knew the woods around Lake Greene, knew them very well in fact. As a kid, Tom and his friends had spent many a day at play in the area in and around the lake and the ravine. Most parents, Tom's included, had vehemently forbid their children to play in the ravine. Of course, that meant there was no better place to play than there. Perhaps the fact that it was *off limits* made it more enticing. Perhaps, but that was a debate for another day.

He was sure that Chris had spent many a day here as a child as well. It seemed that every child in Sommersville found his or her way to Potter's Ravine at one time or another.

Tom made his way through the thick rain at an even pace. He was moving fast, but took great pains to be careful. He had no intention of announcing his presence so that Hollis would be waiting for him. Tom was smarter than that.

If only Dooley would hurry up and get here, Tom thought. Back up would be a wonderful thing for him to have at the moment.

At this point he would have even been happy if Janetti would show up. But Tom did not regret his decision to leave Janetti behind to keep watch over Billy Connelly. If, on the slim chance Hollis was not working alone, then the young doctor would need someone there to protect him.

Tom's thoughts were interrupted by a flash of light from the edge of the ravine. The other edge. He slowed his pace and took up position behind a large oak tree. He watched as Ted Hollis was lighting candles in the area around the edge of the ravine. The other side of the ravine.

Dammit!

That thought had never occurred to him. He never thought about covering both sides of the ravine. He just assumed that Hollis would be on the side that the road led to. It made since. The only other way in was to hike through the woods as they had in their search for Lisa Woodall. Or to come across the footbridge from the old Connelly place.

Tom's eyes went wide. "My God," he whispered.

"How could I have been so stupid."

# # #

Harold told Franklin to stay put.

He was going to make his way down the hill to get in closer to Ted Hollis before he finished his preparations for... well, for whatever he had planned for Barbara Fram.

Time was running out.

Franklin kept a close watch on the kidnapper as he continued lighting candles in a circle near the edge of Potter's Ravine. Franklin still couldn't be sure why the candles were important. Obviously they could burn in the rain, which was a plus. The trees had managed to provide cover, blocking out some of the rain, but only a small portion. The candles also poured light into the clearing. All the leaves were raked away, Franklin noticed. Obviously Ted had, had a very busy day. It looked like he was prepared for everything.

Franklin hoped the one thing he wouldn't be prepared for was his brother's plan, whatever it might be. Suddenly, he felt very vulnerable and alone. For the first time in his life, Franklin Palmer wished he owned a gun.

The reporter watched as Harold inched himself closer and closer to the clearing. Franklin actually lost sight of his brother several times in the cloying darkness. He hoped that meant that Ted Hollis wouldn't be able to see him either.

Franklin lost sight of Harold again in the dark. He scanned the immediate area near where he had last seen him, but couldn't make out any signs of movement. The reporter fought down the urge to panic and launch himself to his brother's rescue. He knew that the big Boy Scout could take care of himself. He was trained for this sort of thing. All Franklin could do was watch and wait.

Then, Franklin Palmer did something he had not done in years.

He said a prayer.

# # #

Tom Myers eased into position at the edge of Potter's Ravine.

He could clearly see Ted Hollis and the preparations he was making. The Sheriff had no idea what the significance of the candles was, but that wasn't a priority at the moment. What he needed to know was Barbara Fram's condition.

Slowly, he crept toward a large oak tree. Silently motioning for Chris Jackson to take up a position off to the other side of the dirt road. With a nod of understanding, the Deputy did as instructed. He found a hiding spot and got out of sight. If Ted were to see them before they wanted him to then Barbara would be killed instantly.

Unless she were already dead.

Myers looked over the clearing from his hiding place behind a large pine tree. The sap clung to his fingers and jacket every time he touched the old tree. It took him only a couple of seconds to locate the woman. She was tied to a tree on the far side of the clearing. Tom swore under his breath. He had no idea how he was going to get Barbara Fram to safety. It was certain that neither he nor Chris could jump across the ravine.

It was hard to get a good target with all the trees and bushes around.

From a short distance away, Chris perked up. Something across the ravine caught his eye and he nearly gasped. Tom had not seen anything so he quickly scanned the area again. Tom thought he could see something, but wasn't sure at first.

Then he saw movement behind Barbara Fram's body.

# # #

Ted Hollis was quickly running out of candles.

As instructed, he had placed forty candles in a large, assigned circular pattern that was designed in perfect detail. The details were important to Ted. He thrived on them. The number of candles and their placement had to be exact. There was no margin for error in the plan.

Ted smiled. He did so enjoy his work.

The master would arrive soon.

Very soon.

# # #

Harold Palmer slowly pulled a pocketknife from his front left front pocket.

Quietly, he clicked it open and began cutting at the thick ropes tying Barbara Fram to the tree. He was acutely aware of the closeness of Ted Hollis. It wouldn't take much for the killer to see him and come running. Harold barely came out of their last confrontation intact and he wasn't eager for a rematch. All Ted had to do was glance toward the tree and he would know that the FBI agent was there and what he was attempting to do.

Harold quickened his pace, but the ropes would only cut so fast.

All he needed were a few seconds longer.

Unconsciously, his mind began to focus as he had trained it to so very long ago. He had memorized something that helped him in tough situation.

A Scout is Trustworthy, Loyal, Helpful...

# # #

Tom Myers watched as Harold Palmer cut the ropes tying Barbara Fram to the tree.

At least that was what it looked like he was doing. In the darkness and partially hidden by the tree, Tom could only surmise the FBI agent's plan.

Of course, Tom realized that if he could see Palmer, then all Ted Hollis had to do was look in the direction of his victim to see Harold

Palmer. Tom knew he had to do something to keep that from happening.

Motioning for his deputy to hold back, Myers stepped from his position behind the tree and out into the open. A very vulnerable position. He walked to the edge of the ravine and pulled his flashlight from his pocket. With the light in one hand and his gun in the other, Tom Myers flipped on the light and pointed it toward Ted Hollis.

Chris watched in silence as his boss stepped out from behind his cover. He was out in the open and vulnerable. It fell to Chris to watch Tom's back.

"Hold it right there, Hollis!" Tom shouted across the void. His voice was unwavering, confident. Nothing at all like he actually felt.

Ted stopped, frozen in place.

He turned his gaze slowly toward the light from Myers' flashlight. He saw the sheriff standing there with a gun pointed at him. Light from the flashlight obscured his vision. Ted's mind filled with rage, not so much because he had been found out, but because the plan was being disrupted.

The master must be testing me, Ted thought.

"Hollis! Put your hands on your head and drop to your knees!" Myers shouted.

Testing my resolve.

"I'm warning you, Hollis. On the ground. Now!"

He will find me worthy. Loyal.

"Hollis..."

And loyalty will be rewarded.

Ted Hollis stood to his full height.

"Ted," Tom Myers started. "Don't make me shoot you, son."

And my reward is long overdue.

Ted raised his hands next to his side at chest level. His movements were slow, meticulous. Tom watched carefully. He hoped Harold would pick up on his plan and move in behind Ted.

"Get."

"Down."

"On."

"Your."

"Knees."

Ted Hollis stood his ground. He even managed a smile at Tom Myers across the gulf that separated them.

It was a smile that sent a shiver through Tom Myers' heart.

He knew Hollis was not going to go easily.

55.

Harold Palmer nearly leapt out of his skin when Tom Myers shouted.

He glanced around the tree to see Tom square off against Ted Hollis. Both men were out in the open. Neither of them had cover. Harold wondered if the Sheriff knew he was there, trying to free the prisoner from the tree. Not that it mattered.

The only advantage Ted had was that he was clearly insane.

And he had a hostage.

Although not for long on that second part.

Where was Chris Jackson?

The rope snapped and Harold Palmer eased Barbara Fram's unconscious body into the darkness behind him. Careful not to alert Ted to his actions, Harold moved slowly. His top priority was to get the hostage to safety. Tom could hold out that long on his own.

He would have to.

Harold found a nice tree to lean his charge against a respectable distance from the clearing. He deposited her carefully before motioning for Franklin to come take care of her.

Franklin got the message and began sliding down the incline toward Barbara Fram's position. Harold started his return path to the clearing before Franklin reached his destination. The younger Palmer brother dropped to a crouch next to Barbara. He wiped the matted hair from her face. She was a very striking young woman, but he had known that before meeting her in person. He had seen her in a television movie of the week that aired a few months earlier. He thought she showed a lot of promise. She had a future in the movie business as far as he was concerned.

Harold reached the tree where Barbara had been tied. He carefully made his way off to the left so he could get a closer, better view of Ted Hollis. Ted and Tom were still locked in their standoff. Ted's hands were raised, but not very high. Harold was afraid that something was about to happen.

Something bad.

EVIL WAYS

Harold stepped out into the edge of the clearing just out of Ted Hollis's view. The man would have to turn around to know that Harold was there, but Myers would be able to see the FBI agent coming. Harold assumed that would give him less chances of getting shot. Getting shot was a bad idea and didn't fit Harold's plan.

Carefully, he pulled his gun and clicked off the safety. The sound, while nearly inaudible with all the other sounds of nature, rang very loud to Harold's ear. He was sure Ted would hear. But the killer did not turn to look.

Harold slowly walked toward his target; gun in hand and ready for anything.

Tom Myers watched as Harold moved closer. He had to stall Ted, keeping his attention focused until the FBI agent was close enough to strike. "Hollis?" he asked. "You want to tell me why you're doing this?"

Ted smiled. "Not really," he said.

"Oh, come on, Ted. I can see it in your eyes. You want to tell someone. So why not tell me what this is all about. Tell me how you could kill your friends in cold blood like that. Tell me what made you do something like that to people that care about you."

"Friends..." Ted Hollis laughed. "My friends..."

"Yes," Myers prodded. "Your friends. You went to high school with them, didn't you? I believe someone told me you guys still get together every few years or so. So, what happened, they forget to send you a Christmas card last year?"

"They..." he faltered slightly, but quickly regained his composure. "They were my friends once, but now they are something else. Something more."

"More?" Tom asked, watching Harold advance. "What's more than dead?"

"You have no idea," Ted answered. It was all he could do not to laugh again.

"Then tell me."

"She's the last," Ted screamed as he turned to point at Barbara Fram. Only Barbara Fram was no longer tied to the tree where he had left her. What Ted Hollis saw instead was Harold Palmer. His happy, in control features softened slightly only to be replaced by surprise.

Then anger.

"You..." Ted began.

"Damn," Harold swore, then launched himself at Ted Hollis.

Harold Palmer slammed against Ted Hollis hard.

The two men fell to the ground and slid awkwardly through the mud. Harold planted a fist in his enemy's face, hoping to end the fight quickly. He still held the gun in his left hand and refused to relinquish it.

Ted fought back like a man possessed, arms spinning madly, h is fists whirling around searching for something to connect with. Though it took some effort, and a lot of luck, he managed to wrench the gun from Harold's left hand. Harold let out a scream of pain as his hand became useless. The gun splashed as it landed in the mud not far away.

Harold tried to press an advantage against the man, but Ted Hollis' training was superior to the FBI agent's. Maybe Tom would just shoot the man and get it over with.

Nah, that'd be too easy.

Harold grappled for all he was worth, but it was not quite enough. Ted used his legs to toss the FBI agent away from him. Harold landed awkwardly and lost his balance. Ted was on his feet first and he made a move toward Harold.

"Not so fast, Ted!" Chris Jackson shouted from across the ravine.

Harold could see that both Sheriff Myers and Deputy Jackson were armed and had their weapons leveled at Ted Hollis. Unfortunately they were on the wrong side of the ravine. And he doubted their aim would be perfect over the distance, with trees, limbs, and other assorted natural barriers between them. And he assumed that neither man would be able to jump from one side to the other to help. Harold was going to have to subdue him on his own.

He was beginning to wonder if he could.

"Listen to them," Harold said to the man standing above him as he struggled to his knees, in a crouch. He never took his eyes off the crazed suspect.

"You have no options left, Ted," Tom Myers shouted.

Ted held the two men in his gaze, waiting for them to make the next move.

Harold slowly stood to his full height and walked next to Ted. He seemed not to notice Harold's presence any longer.

Slowly, Harold carefully reached out for Ted's wrist with his one good hand.

With lightning fast reflexes, far more than he expected from the man, Ted lashed out at him. Harold barely saw the fist before it connected with his face.

He hit the ground again.

Blood dribbled across his lip.

Ted Hollis grinned.

"NO!" Tom and Chris shouted simultaneously. The helplessness of their situation was painfully obvious, even to a deranged psycho like Ted.

Ted turned toward them again, still grinning like a child on Christmas morning after seeing all the gifts under the tree with his name on them.

Tom started toward the edge of the ravine telling Chris that he was going across and to keep the suspect covered. Chris reluctantly agreed and watched uneasily as Tom moved toward the edge.

Tom didn't get far before headlights cut through the night. His first instinct told him that it was his other deputy.

Ben Dooley had arrived with back up. That would be a good thing.

He thumbed up the volume on his walkie and clicked the talk button.

"Dooley? That you?"

Static was the only answer.

"Ben?"

# # #

Lightning flashed, illuminating the circle of candles around Ted Hollis and Harold Palmer. Reflexively, Ted shielded his eyes by turning away from the brightness. As his vision readjusted he noticed Barbara Fram's absence for the first time. He couldn't have gotten her out himself, Ted knew. That meant that the FBI man was a diversion.

He had help.

An accomplice.

A partner.

Careful not to alert the person hiding in the woods with Barbara Fram, Ted scanned the area. He had memorized every inch of the woods in the area. He was prepared. To make sure that he was ready he had studied the area. And he remembered things from his past, growing up near the park.

Yes, he remembered.

There was not one stick of wood in the area around him that he was not aware of. There was nowhere to hide.

Not from him.

Ted was master of these woods.

# # #

The headlights remained on, the truck's engine idling in park.

A figure walked forward from the truck. Tom immediately recognized Benjamin Dooley's pick up. Ben had come over on the side that Ted and Harold were on. Ben would finish things quickly.

"Ben! Boy am I glad to see you," Tom called.

His deputy did not answer.

Chris walked over toward Tom, never once lowering his weapon from Ted Hollis. "I don't like this," he whispered to his superior.

"I'm starting to not like it, too."

"Ben?" Tom called again.

The man stepped out of the glaring light from the pick up trucks bright headlights. As Tom was already beginning to suspect, it was not Benjamin Dooley.

"What the f...?" Chris started, surprised by the new arrival.

Harold Palmer wasn't as surprised by the man's appearance. In fact, he was a little disappointed it took the man this long to arrive. "What kept you?" he asked the new arrival he knew he would be coming.

Ted was also not surprised by the newcomer.

Billy Connelly stepped into the clearing.

He was soaked to the skin from the rain that had only stopped a few minutes earlier. And blood was splattered across his clothes. He had a gun in his hand, but not just any gun.

Police issue. Tom recognized it even from a distance.

"Where's Dooley?" he yelled to the young doctor.

Billy didn't answer. He acted as if the officers were not even there as he approached Ted and Harold. His face, impassive, Harold wasn't sure what to expect next.

Ted seemed to brighten at his friend's approach.

Billy walked up to Ted and spoke to him calmly, trying to soothe him. Calm him. Tom could not make out the soft words he spoke, but they were having an effect. The rage gone, Ted seemed to sag as he relaxed.

He fell into Billy Connelly's arms, sobbing heavily. The doctor folded himself around his friend in a comforting embrace.

From the looks of things, the crisis was drawing to a close. Tom wasn't sure if things had just gotten better or worse.

After a minute, Ted stood up and backed away from Billy. He thanked his friend for helping him.

"No problem, Ted," Billy said as he raised the gun and pointed it toward the suspected killer. "Your loyalty will be rewarded," Billy said with a smile.

Ted watched intently, returning the doctor's smile, all the while staring at the barrel with awe, yet made no effort move or even try to get out of the way.

He did not run.

Or beg.

Or plead for his life.

Harold started forward.

He was too late.

Billy pulled the trigger and the gunshot echoed through the forest surrounding them. Blood splattered everywhere as Harold dove for the ground to avoid being shot himself, m ore out of an instinct for survival than anything else.

Ted Hollis fell.

He was dead before he hit the ground.

Harold got to his feet quickly. He wasn't sure what was going to happen next. The last time he had seen Billy Connelly, the man had been drunk out of his mind. Perhaps he wasn't even aware of what he was doing even now.

Harold wasn't sure what to do next. Although he had an idea about Billy's earlier drunken binge, he still had not put together all of the pieces of this puzzle. He had his suspicions that were confirmed when he arrived to find Barbara Fram still alive.

Tom and Chris were still out of range to help unless they planned to shot Billy. Harold didn't want it to come to that. He tried to talk to Billy much in the same way the young doctor had spoken to Ted in the moments before he killed him.

"Why don't we just talk this out nice and easy, Billy?" he asked, reaching out a non-threatening hand. "Just hand me the gun, Billy."

Billy looked at the gun as though he had never seen one before. Did he even know it was in his hand? Harold, on his feet now, took a step closer, talking calmly. "That's it, Billy. We can work this out. I promise."

Then Billy shot Harold Palmer.

57.

"No!"

Tom Myers screamed out the word a second time as he watched Harold Palmer fall to the ground, a spray of blood fountaining from his wound. He was still alive. The bullet tore through his shoulder and Harold appeared to be in extreme pain, but he was alive.

Tom saw no recourse but to shoot the suspect.

He pointed his gun and shot at Billy Connelly.

Unfortunately, he missed.

Billy turned on the sheriff and fired two bullets in his direction.

The first bullet missed, exploding against a nearby tree, spraying bark and timber chips across Tom's face. Instinctively, Tom lifted a hand to protect his face, throwing his weight off balance.

The second bullet clipped Tom in the arm.

Tom fell to the ground, bleeding. He would live, but his arm was all but useless.

# # #

Chris Jackson saw his boss, his friend, fall to the ground. Shot at the hands of another friend. It was almost too much to bear. Chris leveled his gun at Billy, but could not bring himself to pull the trigger, no matter how much he wanted to at this point.

He had known this man too long. They had been through too much together to end this way. But Billy had killed Ted.

And Ted had killed Lisa and Charles.

And Rebecca!

Never forget what he had done to Rebecca, Chris told himself.

Suddenly the pieces fell into place.

He didn't know why, but Rebecca was murdered to hurt him. Lisa died to keep them all off balance. Jake was because…

Suddenly, the pieces fell into place. Chris saw a pattern to the killings. Why hadn't he seen it before?

Chris could not understand it. There was no reason for either of his friends to have anything against him. No grudges lingered between them. Chris had never lied to Billy. Except the one time.

He knew, but would not tell Billy that he knew about Barbara and Jake's love affair.

But surely that wasn't reason enough to do all this.

Was it?

He would find out soon enough.

Billy walked to the edge of the ravine and stared across the gulf at his childhood friend. No words were spoken for a long moment. Chris still had his gun pointed at Billy, but the doctor had lowered his stolen gun to his side.

"Why?" Chris asked shakily.

Billy chuckled.

Chris did not like the sound of that. It was a scary sound that shook him to his core. How could someone he knew this well, someone he loved like a brother, be this completely evil?

"You really want to know why, Chris?" Billy asked.

"Yes."

Billy smiled at him across the expanse.

"Yes. I really do."

"Are you sure you really want to know? The answers might surprise you."

"I'll take that chance."

Billy contemplated a moment.

"Why, Billy? Why the fuck did you do this?" Chris screamed.

Billy seemed to ponder this briefly then the smile returned.

"Why not?" he said.

# # #

Barabara Fram awoke with a start.

A loud sound, like a firecracker exploding next to her ear, had startled her from her unconscious state. As the darkness moved away, she was uncertain where she was or how she had gotten there. An unnerving sensation.

Her first impulse was to scream. Or call out to Jake. She opened her mouth, but before any sounds could be uttered a hand clamped tightly around her mouth.

Barbara's eyes went wide with fear as she remembered how she came to be in her current predicament. She struggled.

EVIL WAYS

Franklin Palmer tried to calm Barbara, but his efforts were less than extraordinary. She was struggling in his grip, but he could not allow her to scream, cry, or make any noise.

The killer would hear and then he would come for them.

Franklin had watched in horror as Ted Hollis had attacked his brother. He watched as Billy Connelly arrived to talk Ted down. Franklin had allowed himself a small amount of pleasure that the trouble was over at last.

Then, Billy shot Harold.

And he shot the sheriff as well.

Franklin doubted very seriously that he would have no compunction against shooting a reporter and a former girlfriend.

"Shhh..."

Barbara realized that it was not her abductor at her back, but someone new. She turned slowly to look at the owner of the voice. Recognition filled her face and the terror ebbed slightly from her. He had been at the police department when they were there after Lisa's body had been found. Barbara remembered seeing him and the other, taller man there.

Franklin lowered his hand from her mouth.

"You have to keep very still and very quiet," he whispered softly in her ear.

She nodded in understanding.

"We have to get you out of here," he said.

"No," she blurted, louder than she had meant. "I can't. I have to stop Ted from..."

The man stopped her. "Ted is dead."

"Then the danger's past, right?"

He shook his head.

"Then, what are we..."

But she could see for herself as another flash of lightning illuminated the clearing where she had been held prisoner.

"Billy...?"

She nearly choked on the name. Barbara just could not believe this was happening to her. How could it be happening to her? Could it get any worse?

YES.

As the lightning allowed her to see her former lover, so too did it allow him to see her as he was no longer looking at Chris Jackson. He must have heard her. Their eyes locked for a moment and time stood still.

A deep grin creased Billy's handsome face.

And Barbara Fram's blood ran cold.

Harold had been shot before.

It hurt like hell then. It hurt about the same this time.

He felt his life was over. The shadow of death moving over him, just waiting for the time to strike. There was no way that he could take care of Billy Connelly in his present condition. He was shot in the shoulder and his left hand was almost useless where Ted had hit it.

What the injured FBI agent couldn't understand was why Billy hadn't finished him off yet.

Despite the increasing pain, he forced himself up. He needed to know what was going on. He couldn't do anything while lying on the ground. Besides, the rest of his body worked, even though it felt like someone had been tap dancing across his entire body for the past week.

He watched as Billy stared into the woods.

During the last lightning strike he had been able to see Barbara and Franklin. They were no longer safe. If he could see them so could Billy.

Harold had to do something since it was obvious the deputy couldn't bring himself to shoot the suspect. He got to his feet, trembling as spasms of pain ricocheted throughout his frame. The pain was intense, but he dared not cry out. Surprise had to be his or he was doomed.

He could not, would not, let anything happen to his baby brother.

"HEY!"

Billy Connelly whipped around to face Harold, gun pointed directly at him.

Harold was already on the move.

Using the same tactic (such as it was) that he had used when he first engaged Ted, Harold Palmer's body slammed into Billy, knocking him to the ground.

Harold landed on top of him.

Billy recovered far more quickly than Harold, but the injured agent managed to get a foot out and trip Billy. The young doctor fell to his face in the mud. Harold thought he heard the man's teeth slam together and felt a small twinge of satisfaction.

Harold got up on one knee as fast as he was able.

Not fast enough.

Billy was on his feet again, the gun pointed at him, held steady.

"You just don't get it, do you?" he snarled. "You are nothing. You were never part of this equation. I don't need to kill you like I did them. You don't need to know the fear. I only have to kill you. No presets like the others."

He smiled, an evil grimace like something out of a B grade horror flick.

"I can have fun with you," he said.

"That's funny," Harold choked out. "I thought Ted was doing all the work."

Billy barked out a sharp laugh. "Ted has his job. I have mine. He was the fear bringer. Where as I..."

"What, you bring the dip and chips?" He hurt every time he spoke, but he had to keep the killer occupied a while longer. Buy Franklin more time to get away.

"I bring death, Mr. Palmer. Particularly yours in this case."

"I'm touched that I rate your personal touch."

"You should be." The gun hand wavered slightly, but the gun was still pointed directly at Harold's head. "You see, my friend, there is an order to things. Hitler, Mussolini, Genghis Khan, and those like them, they understood."

"Understood what?" Harold balked. "They were all nut jobs. Insane. They were killers!"

"They *were* killers," Billy agreed. "Best of the breed to be exact, but there was more to them than that. They carried death to the next level. Made an art form out of it. History remembers them as so much more than simple killers. To them it was more about the fear that preceded death. They tortured and maimed before delivering the final blow. Waited for the precise moment when to end a life."

"You can't be serious?"

"From the fear comes the power, Agent Palmer"

"You're insane," Harold murmured, never taking his eyes from the gun pointed at his head.

"Maybe. But I think I also see a little of the fear in you. It's rather intoxicating."

"Go fuck yourself, Doc!"

"Oh, you can tell me, Mr. Palmer. You do feel the fear, don't you?"

Harold said nothing.

"Yes, I think you do. You can feel it clutching your chest in a vice grip. Admit it, you fear me, don't you?"

Harold felt his jaw tighten, but kept his tongue, holding in the remark that wanted to surface. Uttering it would only bring a swift death. At best he could let Billy ramble on until something else came along. Maybe someone would come to his rescue. It was a slim hope, but it was all he had left. At least Ray and Barbara would make it out.

"And now, Mr. Palmer," Billy said as he pulled back the hammer on the pistol. "It's time for you to go bye-bye."

He closed his eyes and allowed a mental image of his wife and daughter, Beverly and Lucy, to pass before him as he awaited his execution. He could make out every detail of his life. Could mentally trace every curve of his wife's body, feeling her silky smooth skin quiver beneath his touch. Could smell her shampoo on the breeze. Could feel the soft kisses his daughter would plant on his cheek when he would come home from work. In an instant, he relived every happy moment of his life.

If this was to be his last moment on Earth, he could think of no better memories to carry with him.

He flinched when he heard the gunshot.

But felt nothing.

Surely Billy couldn't have missed from that close range.

He opened his eyes and saw that Billy was lying on the ground. He was bleeding and had lost the gun.

Chris Jackson had shot his friend.

But he hadn't shot to kill. Harold doubted the deputy would be able to kill his old friend any more than Harold could one of his.

Harold pressed the advantage.

He slammed into Billy again, struggling to pin the man like a pro wrestler. But the killer struggled mightily. Harold, in his impaired state, was no match for the younger, less injured man. He never stood a chance.

Billy tossed him aside like he was less than a rag doll.

Harold was spent. He had nothing left to throw at the man.

If only Chris would just shoot again.

But he didn't.

He couldn't.

Deputy Jackson fell to his knees, staring helpless across the void that was Potter's Ravine. Harold knew better than to expect any more help from the man.

As the blackness moved in to claim his conscious thoughts, Harold was relieved that he had given his brother time to escape with Barbara.

"*Ray?*"

It wasn't really a question. He knew who Ray was. Why did he think that? His brain had been turned to mush and thoughts were jumbled.

Harold's eyes snapped open, fighting off the darkness that clouded his brain.

"*Ray!*"

Franklin Palmer came out of nowhere. As his brother had before, the younger Palmer tackled Billy. The two men fell to the ground and slid across the clearing in the slippery mud.

Candles tipped over and rolled every which way. Luckily the ground was far too saturated from the weeks worth of rain to catch fire. With a small sizzle, one by one, the overturned candles extinguished.

Franklin pressed his advantage, pummeling Billy with blow after blow. Unfortunately, the madman was laughing off the punches as if they were nothing.

Harold had to help his brother, but he also knew there was no way he could reach him. And he was in no shape for another fight.

Then he saw Billy Connelly's stolen revolver lying on the ground just a few feet away.

Just out of reach

#

Franklin Palmer had never been much of a fighter.

When he was a kid, and all the way through college, he had used his off beat sense of humor to get him out of tough situations. But there was no way in hell he could just sit around and watch his brother be beaten to death.

So he did what he expected Harold would do. He attacked.

Franklin was doing his best. He grabbed the man by the scruff of the shirt to hold him down, but Billy was thrashing around wildly. Franklin didn't know if he was hurting him or not.

So he pulled his punches.

Billy didn't.

With a surprise left, the young doctor caught the reporter on the side of the head. Franklin fell to the side and out of the circle of half overturned candles. As he fell, he released his hold on Billy's shirt.

# # #

Only a few feet away, Harold Palmer crawled through the mud until his fingers brushed against the cool metal of the discarded gun.

With a grunt of effort his fingers found purchase.

Now he had a weapon.

All he needed was the strength to lift it and use it.

He was beginning to wonder if any strength remained within him.

# # #

Billy froze as a bullet from his own stolen gun smacked the ground at his feet.

He watched as Harold Palmer tried to lift and aim the gun.

He laughed. The man had no strength left.

Billy Connelly had nothing to fear from Special Agent Harold Palmer and he knew it.

Franklin found himself outside of the clearing. Clumps of mud and leaves were piled haphazardly around the area. Probably a result of the work Ted had put into his preparations.

His hand fell upon a tree limb and he hefted it in both hands as if it were a club.

One weapon was a good as another as far as he was concerned.

Distracted by the futile attempts of the wounded FBI agent, Billy had turned his back on Franklin Palmer.

Franklin took advantage of the moment.

He had to catch his breath.

# # #

Billy began to chant softly, but his voice was steadily growing louder and louder. Harold could hear the words, but they made no sense to him. *Probably more words about the power of fear,* he guessed. Whether that was normal or a result of his injuries or the pounding in his head he could not say.

All Harold Palmer knew was that he hurt from head to toe, even in places he didn't even know he had. He had to get up. He refused to die lying in the mud, but his body refused to cooperate.

Against his wishes, his hand released its hold on the gun, dropping it to the ground with a soft splash.

The pain finally won out and darkness claimed Harold Palmer.

# # #

Billy continued his chant.

# # #

Barbara watched in abject terror from her hiding place in the woods.

# # #

Chris Jackson felt his body shut down as conflicting emotions welled within him.

Try as he might, he could not bring himself to shoot Billy Connelly.

EVIL WAYS

#

Tom Myers moaned softly as he regained consciousness.

#

Franklin Palmer moved in for the kill.

Moving like he was going for a home run in a softball game, he swung the tree limb with all his might, catching Billy across the back of the head.

The man should have dropped under the weight of the attack.

But he didn't.

Franklin swung again, but the element of surprise was gone. The make shift club broke in half with a loud *CRACK* upon contact with Billy's arm, which he'd raised like a shield.

Franklin could not believe that the man could take this much punishment and still be unhurt. Perhaps, whatever he was chanting was responsible. Or the man was whacked out on drugs. Or possibly, he truly was insane. Franklin could not understand the words, which told him that whatever was being chanted couldn't be a good thing.

He attacked again with the small stump of tree limb he had left.

Billy grabbed it in mid swing without even looking toward his attacker.

Franklin gasped, surprised, as Billy turned to face him. There was something behind his eyes, something not quite right. Something not even remotely normal.

If Franklin Palmer truly believed in the flights of fantasy he read about so often, he would have guessed that Billy had been possessed.

Of course, that would be down right impossible.

Wasn't it?

60.

Billy Connelly looked into the eyes of his attacker.

He saw fear in those eyes too.

And rightfully so. *He should be afraid. They should all be afraid.*

"You know, I've had just about enough of you Palmer boys. Everywhere I go, there you are. You live in my town. You eat in my diner. You poke your nose into my business."

"It's a gift," Franklin said, joking out of habit.

"This is my town, Palmer. You don't belong here!"

"Tell that to my mortgage company."

"You're funny, Palmer. I like that. Under different circumstances, you and I might have even become friends. But I don't need friends anymore. I have all the friends I need. They look out for me. They protect me. Before long everyone will come to know and fear me and give me the fucking respect I'm due."

Billy reveled in the fear of others. It washed over him like a warm spring. He had worked so very hard to reach this point in his life. He had made a pact. Today, he paid back that which he owed.

"It's payday!" he told Franklin Palmer as much.

"Are you insane?" was the reporter's response.

"No, Mr. Palmer, I am not. In fact, I don't think I have ever thought more clearly than at this moment."

"You don't say?"

Billy raised an eyebrow. Took a step forward. "You know what, why don't I give you the exclusive on this one. I bet you could sell millions of copies with this story. I see books, maybe even a movie of the week. What do you say?"

"What did you have in mind?"

"Of course, that would mean I'd have to let you live, wouldn't it?"

"I have no problem with that arrangement," Franklin said, trying to remain calm. For every step Billy took, the reporter retreated one of his own.

"I'd rather take you to hell with me," Billy countered.

"Hmm?" Franklin huffed. "I always assumed I'd be going in the other direction."

Billy smiled at that. His smile was scary.

"Well," he said. "You know what they say happens when you assume."

"Yeah, my old man loved to tell me that one when I was a kid. So, why do you want to go to hell anyway, Mr. Connelly?" Franklin acted calmly, professional, as if this were a normal interview. Although nothing about his present situation was even remotely close to it. As long as the homicidal maniac was talking to him, he was another minute he was alive.

Franklin kept talking, hoping to buy the extra time he needed. Time for what he didn't know, but stalling nonetheless. If he could only keep the lunatic talking...

"I'm going to rule it," the maniac continued. "How nice is that?"

"I think the guy with the horns and the long red tail might have a thing or two to say about that, don't you?"

"Touché, Mr. Palmer," Billy said, smiling. "I've made a deal that will allow me to act as..." he paused and seemed to think on his answer, "shall we say second in command."

"A lofty position."

"Only the best will do, Mr. Palmer."

"And what qualifications do you have that makes you right for the job?"

"Have you not been paying attention? I tricked one friend into murdering four people. Would have been five already if you hadn't gotten in the way."

"What, you too good to do the deed yourself?" Franklin hoped that didn't go too far.

"Just think of me as the power behind the man, if you will." He shrugged. "Besides, ol' Teddy had a gift. It would have been wrong of me not to exploit it."

Franklin looked at the killer with clear amusement on his face. "You know, you are seriously nuts."

Billy pushed the reporter to the ground. Franklin shuffled for hold as his left foot slipped over the edge of the ravine. He staggered, his balance tenuous at best, but managed to stay on solid ground. He had not even realized they had gotten so close to the edge.

Franklin wondered if his opponent had noticed.

"Watch that first step, Palmer. It's a long way down."

Guess that answered that question.

Billy's eyes narrowed as he stared hard at Franklin, holding him tightly by the shirt. He seethed anger. Anger at the world. Anger at those around him. Anger toward his mother for dying. And finally, anger at Franklin Palmer for daring to question his sanity.

"I!"

"AM!"

"NOT!"

"INSANE!"

Franklin moved slowly, cautiously. He began moving away from the edge of the ravine. "You sure about that, Billy boy?"

"You just signed your death warrant, Mr. Palmer. I'll see you in hell."

"You first," the reporter quipped.

Without warning Franklin lashed out with his legs, using a variation on a scissors hold his father had taught him as a child while playing around in the back yard. Billy's balance was gone and he stumbled, falling forward.

Franklin jerked his legs and added momentum to his enemy's fall.

Billy tumbled over the edge of the ravine, fingers clawing at the rain-slicked mud, but somehow he managed to grab hold with his right hand, finding purchase in the sticky red Georgia clay. He started pulling himself back up hand over hand. His fingers deeply embedded in the mud and clay, but slipping fast as the ground dissolved away beneath each grip.

Luckily, Franklin got there first.

He punched Billy across the nose, breaking it, and splattering blood across his face. Blood flowed freely down Billy's mouth and chin, but the man's eerie smile remained in place only now his perfect teeth were stained red with his own blood. Pulling himself up the remainder of the way, he stood at the edge of the cliff.

"I need one more sacrifice before I go, Palmer," he said. "I had wanted so much for it to be Barbara, you know, for old times sake, but I guess you've ruined that for me."

He turned to look over his shoulder at the ravine behind him where he had almost fallen only seconds before. He felt his heart beat in his chest, exhilarated at the prospect of almost dying. He had never felt so alive. It was a long way down and, in the dark; he could not see the bottom.

"Since you robbed me of my Barbara, I guess I'll have to take you instead."

"Thanks," Franklin said. "A lovely offer. I'll have to pass."

Billy grabbed Franklin by the shoulders much the same way he had the ledge when he fell. He held fast, refusing to let go.

The two men grappled along the precipice and either, or both, of them could go over at any moment. All it would take was a misstep, a slip in the mud.

Or one man to get very lucky.

But neither would concede to the other.

#

Tom Myers got painfully to his feet; careful not to touch his throbbing, blood soaked arm.

A lot had happened during the time he was out of it. Franklin Palmer was tussling with Billy Connelly now. It did not look good for the reporter.

Tom had to do something.

One shot could end it, but Tom knew he could never hit the suspect in his current state. He picked up his fallen weapon in shaking hands and pointed it skyward.

He pulled the trigger.

# # #

The sound was enough to grab the attention of both combatants.

Instinctively, Franklin pulled back and luckily managed to tear himself free from Billy's grip. Billy lost his balance.   Then he went over the edge.

A mixed look of pleasure and terror crossed his face as the realization sat in that he was leaving this world without his sacrifice. That scared him so he struggled to catch himself. Miraculously, he found purchase.

His "*master*" might not take kindly to his new acolyte showing up empty handed.

And the devil wasn't known for keeping promises.

But no matter how truly evil the man was, Franklin Palmer could not let him simply die. That would be too easy. He lunged for the man, trying to grab him. Trying to save him.

He was a scant second too late.

Billy fell over the edge and plummeted into the darkness.

A wet, muffled *thud* announced his departure from the world of the living as his body hit bottom.

Franklin lay there in the mud, on the edge where he had landed, his arm dangling over into the darkness. He waited for a sign that the killer was going to spring back up at him, like they so often did in the movies. After a few seconds, Franklin knew it was over. He felt the irony of the situation as it buzzed around inside his brain. Billy left the world in the same manner as he had dispatched his victims. Only a wet, muffled sound marked his passing instead of the blaze of glory he had intended.

"Give my regards to Hitler, you son of a bitch," Franklin whispered into the darkness of the ravine. Deep inside, he hoped that Billy Connelly could hear him as he roasted in hell.

Overhead, lightning crashed.

And the rain began to fall again.

62.

The sun finally came out over Sommersville.

Harold Palmer stood on the small concrete steps at the offices of the Sommersville gazette. He smiled as the warm, welcome rays flowed over his body.

"If I'd known your leaving town would have made the sun come out I'd have sent you packing days ago."

Without looking, Harold smiled. "Hello, Tom," he said. "How are you feeling?"

"I'll live," the Sheriff said as he motioned toward the cast on his arm. "And you?"

"Well, I've been shot before. I don't recommend it, but you learn to live with it. I won't get to ride the bike home though. Franklin's going to drive me to the airport and I'll catch a flight home."

"Well, I just wanted to thank you for your help. I don't think we could have done it without you."

"Well, I don't know about that," Harold said modestly. "You seemed to have a handle on the situation. More or less."

"If you say so," Tom laughed. "I've never seen anything quite like it."

"And you think I have?" Harold asked. "This would be my first devil worship, psycho killing high school reunion. I doubt I'll ever see anything else like it again. At least I hope not."

"Well, it's a big, strange world."

"That it is. It's been a pleasure to meet you, Tom."

"And you, Harold. Enjoy your flight."

"Thanks. I will."

Harold watched Tom Myers walk away. The older man crossed Main Street and strode the one block over toward his office. Tom felt fortunate to be alive.

A feeling Harold knew well at the moment.

Harold had checked on Chris Jackson earlier in the morning. With the shock of everything that had happened to him, Chris' body had simply shut down, but he was slowly coming out of it. The doctors at the community medical center thought he would make a full recovery, but he needed rest and a good bit of therapy.

Harold wondered if he would recover himself. Perhaps Chris wasn't the only one in need of a shrink. *Naah, what would I need a shrink for?* he wondered.

Ben Dooley was also on medical leave. He had been found on the side of the road where Billy Connelly had dumped him after beating him senseless. If the killer had not been in a hurry, he would have probably killed Deputy Dooley. Luckily that didn't happen. Harold had started to like the deputy and would have hated to see anything bad happen to him.

Jake Page was also alive. He was in much worse shape that the others, but he was expected to live with major amounts of physical therapy. He would have to cancel several upcoming shows and concerts, but he was alive and would be back singing sooner or later.

Barbara Fram was at his side, ever vigilant.

There had been no sign of the devil in all of this. Not that Harold had really expected to see him. Or it. Whichever. He truly believed Billy Connelly had been completely and utterly insane. No other option mattered. He was insane. Case closed.

Well, not quite. There were still a lot of unanswered questions. Who else's strings had Billy been pulling? Were there others involved? Harold had made a call to the FBI and passed along everything he had to them. They would check out young Doctor Connelly's associates in Florida. Maybe they would find a lead. Maybe not.

Harold had done his part, although he promised Franklin to call with an update on the investigation. Sort of an epilogue to this little adventure for the follow up story Franklin was writing for his paper.

It was over.

At long last it was over.

"Ready to go?"

Harold did not turn at the sound of his brother's voice. "Yeah. I think I've had about all the vacation I can stand."

The two men walked to where Franklin had parked his newly battered Teal Green Blazer. He opened the door and held it as Harold eased himself inside. The arm was still next to useless and he was under strict doctor's orders to take it easy.

He probably wouldn't listen, stubborn as he was, but those were the orders.

And his little brother was going to send him home to his wife and child to recover. Of course, Franklin promised to come out and visit soon.

Maybe this time it would happen, but Harold wasn't planning to hold his breath waiting.

"So, Harry," Franklin asked as he pulled out onto Main Street. "What do you think of our sleepy little town?"

Harold laughed at the innocent, if not leading question.

"Well, Ray," Harold said with a smirk. "I don't know."

"Oh?"

"Yeah. It's too quiet for me."

The end.

ACKNOWLEDGEMENTS

Oh, it's good to be back!

The novel you hold in your hand has traveled a rough and rocky road. From the earlier version published by a publisher who shall not be named, to tolling in an out-of-print obscurity that made me sad, until finally finding new life in the version you've hopefully just finished reading. If not, why did you skip to the end and read the acknowledgements first? Go read the novel then come back. It's okay. I'll wait.

Oh good. You're back. I've missed you.

Now, where was I? Oh, yeah. This is the one that started it all.

Evil Ways was my first novel sale in 2004 and the book has certainly opened some doors for me in terms of getting to write some interesting books. Putting this new edition of Evil Ways together was equal parts a fun jaunt down memory lane and sheer terror. I'd like to think my writing skills have improved in the intervening years since Evil Ways originally saw the light of day way back in August 2005. When I started toying with the idea of re-releasing the novel I knew there were a few things that had slipped through the cracks in the editing stage the first time around so I wanted to fix those. The real problem was knowing when to stop. I was sorely tempted on multiple occasions to do some big rewrites, but ultimately decided not to do so.

Why?

Good question.

I decided to leave the story more or less as originally written and focus on Harold Palmer's next thriller, Evil Intent (coming soon, I promise. Don't believe me? Check out the preview at the end of this very book). Plus, I didn't want those who purchased the novel the first time around to feel lost when Evil Intent comes out. (Not a very good business idea, huh?). The biggest change to Evil Ways is the date. In the original release, it was the class of 1995. Now, it's the class of 2002 so the story is current. Other than that and a few minor grammatical fixes, typos, and assorted pieces of dialogue that particularly bugged me, the story remains the same.

Although generally written by a lone shackled to a computer, no novel is truly an island. There are so many folks who offered advice or listened when the writer whined about one of his characters not doing what he wanted them to do or one of the dozens of things we writers like to fret over. To all of you, you have my everlasting appreciation. There's not enough space here to mention everyone individually, but there are a few folks I would like to single out.

Firstly, thanks to R.O. and Margaret Nash, the greatest parents in the world (just ask them) for offering not only support, but also encouraging me to keep pushing toward my goals. You can't ask for better cheerleaders to get out there and spread the word about my books.

Thanks to brother, Wesley, who, even though he has never read Evil Ways (nor do I suspect he ever will), listens to me go on and on about my abusive relationship with my characters and the grief they sometimes put me through. Oh, yeah. He also provided the template (voice and mannerisms) for Franklin Palmer in this novel. Harold and Franklin's conversations could easily be ours.

Evil Ways was born way back when in Harriette Austin's creative writing class. It flourished in the writer's conferences that carries her name. For that, she will always have my deepest gratitude. In Harriette's honor, no animals were harmed or killed in the writing of this novel. Inside joke. Nothing to see here, folks. Move along.

I also wanted to thank Jeff Allen for sparking the original idea that kicked off Evil Ways. He and I had talked about producing a movie. I started writing a loose plot that eventually became the basis of Evil Ways. It would still be fun to get a movie made one of these days.

Of course, big Thank You Very Muches to some folks who offered moral support, listened to me complain and whine about my characters not cooperating, (remember that abusive relationship I mentioned earlier?), and generally kept me on track. Big thanks to Michael Gordon, Sean Taylor, Jeff Austin, Frank Fradella, Andrea Judy, and 2011 Rondo Artist of the Year (I love saying that) Mark Maddox. You guys rock!

Special thanks to FBI Special Agent Stephen Emmett. Although I didn't know him when I wrote Evil Ways, he gave me some wonderful advice that will come into play in Harold Palmer's next thriller, Evil Intent, although a few of those tidbits made it into this revised edition.

And finally, thank you, dear reader, for taking a chance on this novel. Kick back, get comfortable, and enjoy. Hopefully, we can get together like this again soon.

Bobby
Bethlehem, GA
www.bobbynash.com

Harold Palmer will return in Evil Intent.

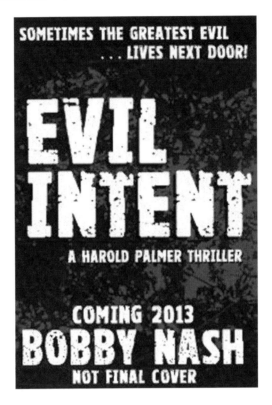

Look for an exclusive preview of
EVIL INTENT
at the back of this book.

**BEN-BOOKS.BLOGSPOT.COM
WWW.BOBBYNASH.COM**

Sheriff Tom Myers returns in Deadly Games!

**NOW AVAILABLE
WHERE YOUR FAVORITE BOOKS ARE SOLD**

**COMING 2013
DEADLY GAMES! 2 (tentative title)**

**BEN-BOOKS.BLOGSPOT.COM
WWW.BOBBYNASH.COM**

A SNEAK PEEK AT EVIL INTENT

It has been a couple of months since the climactic showdown with Billy Connelly in Sommersville and FBI Special Agent Harold Palmer returns to work after recovering from injuries suffered in Evil Ways. A backlog of casework awaits him, but easing back into things isn't an option as the Joint Terrorism Task Force tracks one of America's most wanted domestic terrorists, unaware that he has targeted them with EVIL INTENT.

"We interrupt this program for an important announcement."

"Good evening ladies and gentlemen," the man on the television screen said with a voice of perfect pitch. "I'm Herbert Rothfield for CMN. Earlier this evening we received word that recent peace initiatives instigated by the President of the United States in the Middle East have failed. The White House has confirmed reported rumors that tensions have indeed been rising in the region in and around Afghanistan."

The screen shifted to show footage of United States military personnel on the ground in the war torn region. Much of it was reused stock footage from the archives. It had been almost a week since the Army had begun evacuating journalists, despite the protests of many that they be allowed to remain.

National news anchor Herbert Rothfield oozed confidence from his perch behind the artificial oak desk at the *Cable Media Network* offices in Washington, DC as he read the text off the telex. He was not part of the writing staff on this story and he had not even seen it until seconds before the broadcast. His job was simply to read the story and make it seem as if he knew what he was talking about. Knowledge equaled power, especially in the halls of the political news media, but sometimes the only requirement was the appearance of knowledge. Case in point: Herbert Rothfield.

"According to White House sources," Rothfield continued as the screen shifted back to him sitting behind his polished desk. "President William Montgomerey has ordered ships from the Fifth Fleet into the area in an effort to maintain the peace. Washington DC insiders who did not wish to appear on camera told us that the situation was dire and that we should expect a rise in the national threat level by morning."

Rothfield looked directly into the camera, directly into the living room of the American family. "CMN will continue to cover this breaking news story and will return right after this commercial break."

CMN, the Cable Media News satellite channel kept its eyes and ears open to news. They had been dubbed third in the country, following behind the more widely popular CNN and the even more sensational FOX News. Still, the struggling third place all-news-channel had finally secured itself a foothold in the public consciousness.

In other words: People were beginning to trust them.

Herbert Rothfield was a thirty-year veteran anchorman who had jumped ship from CNN in Atlanta to lead the anchor team at the fledging CMN. He had seen it all. Whether reporting from Baghdad during the height of the Gulf War or a story at home, he earned his reputation by being a Johnny-on-the-spot reporter.

Of course, the whole thing was an act.

Rothfield was little more than an actor filling a role. He read his script and delivered the lines he was fed with enough believability that people thought him very knowledgeable on a wide variety of topics.

A recent poll conducted by The Washington Post declared the CMN lead anchor as one of the top ten most knowledgeable, most trustworthy newscasters. But get him alone and start a conversation and one would be quickly dissuaded from the man's public persona. The extent of his personal knowledge involved college football, drinking, and women. Not necessarily in that order.

He sat behind the news desk wearing a black suit with a nice striped tie. There was not a wrinkle to be seen on him. As usual, he looked exquisite for the camera. His perfect hair was, well, perfect, with each hair in its place and just the appropriate hint of gray at the temples to sell the lead anchor position. The color was right. It all worked. He wore just the right amount of pancake to hide any imperfections in his skin.

He looked like a million bucks.

All part of the image.

All part of the act.

The producer snapped her fingers to get everyone's attention. "And we're back in four, three..." she silently ticked off the two count with her fingers then pointed at the anchor.

"In a statement released only moments ago, the White House announced that all United States involvement in the growing crisis is strictly as a safeguard," Rothfield read aloud. "At this time we are being told that no new U.S. troops will enter the conflict. The fifth fleet will remain on high alert and will stay in the area to provide support and to keep the fighting from spreading to outlying areas outside the current conflict zone, but they will not enter the fray unless they are first fired upon. Containment is the first order of business."

"This is the latest in a long history of violence in the region. Despite the failure of previous peacekeeping initiatives in the region, a spokesperson for the White House stated unequivocally today that an American presence was crucial to ensuring peace in the Middle East."

"Just a moment, please," Rothfield said as he touched his ear piece as if he were receiving the most important news of his career. His face went impassive and slowly moved toward pensive as he listened to the report being fed through.

Also part of the act.

He turned to read from the monitor once again.

"I have just received word that the President has scheduled an emergency press conference for this evening at eight o'clock to discuss the crisis and the United States plans to deal with the situation. Of course, we will carry the press conference live here on CMN with commentary from our usual roundtable of experts. We hope you'll join us."

"And now, in other news..."

# # #

Jimmy Fletcher sat in the small bar and downed the last of his beer.

His sixth or seventh of the evening. He tried to recall exactly how many he had, but couldn't quite remember. Motioning to the bartender, he tapped the once polished surface twice with his index finger, the universal signal for *I'll have another*. The bartender nodded and dropped a freshly opened bottle on the bar in front of him.

"Here you go," the man said as he paid for the beer.

The bartender took the cash without a word then he moved over to help another customer, a very attractive woman wearing a very revealing low cut blouse and tight jeans at the end of the bar. The bartender had been paying serious attention to her ever since she came in a little over twenty minutes before happy hour ended a couple hours earlier. And she was certainly enjoying the bartender's attention.

The bartender was trying to be suave and for the most part he was successful. Jimmy had to admit that the younger man wasn't bad to look at, a fact he obviously knew. Apparently, the bartender fancied himself a ladies man. He knew all the right moves.

And he was using each and every one of them on her.

The woman was not quite drunk enough yet to fall for all of the lines completely, but at the rate they were going she would probably wake up next to him in the morning.

Not that the man that watched the scene unfold at the opposite end of the bar really cared one way or the other about the sexual escapades of two drunks in a bar. Jimmy was just there to suck down a few beers before heading home for the night.

Jimmy Fletcher was one of those guys that most people barely noticed. He did nothing to draw attention to himself and did not stand out at all, which was the point. The fact that he looked a lot like most of the bar's patrons was a carefully orchestrated act. Jimmy Fletcher was an Average Joe, a working man who had come in after a hard day's labor, and it did not matter what kind of work. He was tired, dirty, and in need of a shower, a shave, and a haircut. And he was thirsty. That's all that anyone noticed. He wasn't interested in striking up conversation and shied away from any of the other patrons who did so he was left alone for the most part.

He was not exactly a regular, just a guy who came in for a few beers every couple of weeks. If anyone were to ask about him, Jimmy doubted most of the drunks that surrounded him would even remember what he looked like.

Unlike most of the men he worked alongside, Jimmy never visited any diner or watering hole with any sort of pattern. And never on the same day and at the same time.

He did nothing to suggest anything out of the ordinary.

It was not his habit to frequent any one particular establishment for any length of time, but for some reason he liked this place so he made an exception. It was out of the way enough for him to get lost in the rustic charm the place offered. Wanted as he was, he could ill afford to get attached to any one particular place, but he had found nothing out of the ordinary about this bar from previous visits. He felt safe there. Perhaps even to the point of dropping his guard just a bit.

Well, maybe he lowered his guard at least.

Never drop your guard, a small familiar voice from the past echoed in his mind.

Never.

Dropping your guard, even for an instant, leads to disaster, that

EVIL WAYS

selfsame voice shouted at him in that way that only a drill sergeant could.

You should know that better than anyone, shouldn't you, soldier?
Yes, sir. I should.

Once upon a time he'd had a family of his own. He had loved his wife and kid. Perhaps he still did on some level, he supposed. He had even been happy with his life, despite all that he now realized was wrong with it. If his eyes had not been opened it was likely he would have remained, kept living the lie that had been spoon-fed to him.

So he left.

He had entertained the notion of taking his family with him, but quickly ruled that out. His wife could never handle the road he was destined to travel. And the kid would quickly become a liability at best, a hindrance at worst.

No, leaving them to fend for themselves was the best course of action at the time.

He had believed it was the right decision then and time had proven him right. They never would have made it this far.

Leaving as he did, when he did, was the greatest act of compassion he had ever shown his family although he doubted they saw it that way. He had never regretted the decision. Despite that, however, every so often the urge to call would tug at him, but he fought it. He dare not attempt a call as the lines were undoubtedly monitored. Of that much he was certain.

Until he was killed or captured - he had no plans on being taken alive, by the way - Lori and little Wila would remain under constant surveillance. The part of him that still cared wondered if that made them safer or not. Regardless of the answer, there was nothing he could do about it. He had made his decision.

If he had to do it over again, he would do it the same way.

Jimmy noticed the special bulletin alert flash on the television screen behind the bar. One of the customers, a loudmouthed redneck with an uneven beard and a beer gut had been watching the sporting report on CMN and shouting at the screen until he sauntered off to parts unknown. Instead of turning the set off, the bartender had simply turned down the volume.

The recognizable features of the anchor were the first clue that this was a *big* story. Herbert Rothfield did not report on stories that were not considered big news. That was his thing. He was not Cronkite, but like the legendary newsman had been for CBS for decades, Rothfield was his network's big gun.

Behind the reporter was a graphic that read: CRISIS IN THE MIDDLE EAST. The words flowed over computer generated flags of the countries involved in the seemingly never-ending conflict.

Great. Just what America needs, Fletcher thought. *More trouble As if we don't have enough to deal with over here.*

"Hey! Can you turn that up?" he asked the bartender as he pointed toward the mounted television set behind the bar.

Acting like it was an inconvenience, the suave bartender moved slowly to manually change the channel on the flat panel TV mounted above the bar. He seemed to have forgotten about the remote control he had stuffed into his shirt pocket after turning the tube on for the sports nut earlier.

Moron.

The sound came up and the man listened carefully as he took another drink of his beer. CMN was reporting about a new incident in the Middle East.

No shock there, he thought. *When wasn't there some kind of trouble brewing over there?*

Rothfield and his panel of so-called experts were commenting on the President's unwillingness to send the troops in to quickly and cleanly solve the problem.

No shock there either. This was an all too common thread that the media liked to tug at in recent days. On the one hand, they claimed that the President wasn't doing enough to solve the problem, but yet the moment he takes any action they jump all over him for being a warmonger. Jimmy Fletcher was no fan of William Montgomerey, but even he was growing tired of the flip-flopping of the American people. He remembered a time when Americans made a decision and stuck with it. He missed that time.

He heard Rothfield utter the phrase "*retain the peace*" a couple more times. It was his phrase for the day. Fletcher knew the truth. He knew what it meant.

Nothing.

That was what they were going to do.

Absolutely nothing.

Typical of the United States thinking these days, Jimmy thought. *Montgomerey's not a warrior. As a peacetime President he's adequate at best. But during a war? He's out of his element.*

None of this he could say aloud, of course. Not that he expected much in the way of a lively political discussion in this podunk little town bar.

He could not stand to listen to any more of mouthpiece Rothfield's BS so he turned his attention back to drinking his beer. He finished it off quickly and motioned for one more.

One for the road.

The bartender dropped the beer on the bar and removed the empty bottle. He sat the bottle carefully under the bar. The drinking man probably did not even notice that he had not thrown it away as he had every other bottle he had collected.

As he stood from the uncomfortable bar stool, he downed the last swig of the cold beer. He was ready to go.

Time to call it a night.

It had been a long and busy day at his day job and Jimmy Fletcher was tired. There was still work to be done before he could sleep, however, and he knew he had best get to it.

No rest for the weary, he thought as he dropped a couple crumpled bills on the bar.

Walking away from the barstool he noticed a new image plastered on the television screen behind the anchorman that stopped him in his tracks. Rothfield's voice was barely audible with the set's volume turned down, but the meaning of the story was clear.

They were still searching.

The search for militant leader Donald James Lemann had been ongoing for a little over twelve years, twelve very long years with no apparent end in sight.

Taking a moment, Fletcher stopped to look at the screen and couldn't completely disguise the joy etched on his face. He imagined what the CMN mouthpiece might be saying. Not that it mattered. They all said more or less the same thing. Rothman had reported the same facts about his case so many times that he probably knew them by heart. And since there was nothing new to report, they could have simply re-aired the same segment over and over for all he knew.

What held his attention was the photo of Donnie Lehmann on the screen. Blonde, with full, wavy hair, and a clean shave, Lehmann looked like an All-American boy next door.

Just like Captain fucking America, baby!

He smiled at the irony.

It's been so long since I looked like that that I almost didn't recognize myself.

He ran a callused hand over the full beard he now sported and wanted to laugh, but held it in. If he could not recognize himself in the mirror these days, he wondered if anyone else could. Still, he decided. It was not wise to tempt fate on the off chance one of the drunks took a really good look at the photo and put two and two together.

Jimmy Fletcher was one in a long line of alias Lehmann had used over the years. Jimmy Fletcher was one of his favorites though. It had been his name for the past three years. He hoped he could keep it for awhile.

Everything was perfect.

There was no way anyone was going to find them unless of course they wanted to be found. And they certainly did not want to be found, did they? No. Of course they didn't. And they would not be found. Donnie was too good to make any kind of blunder that would tip the Feds to his location, despite how tired he was.

Even after twelve years the network dusted off his story a couple times a year, usually whenever anything bad happened and the obligatory compare and contrast between the latest incident and his *crimes* equaled sure-fire ratings gold. This new crisis heating up in the Middle East was just the type of story they loved hitching the domestic terrorist train to. It made for good TV and kept the sheep tucked away in their homes with their heads under the covers, afraid that the big bad bogeyman would come and get them.

Rothman had one thing right. They should be afraid.

They should be very afraid.

There was a bogeyman out there, but it wasn't him. It was a big faceless enemy and they did not see him coming. The men in power, the true enemies of the country that Donnie Lehmann and his brothers in arms had fought for, were selling off pieces of the United States of America to countries that would like nothing better than to see this once great nation ground under their boot heels. Those men in power, the true enemies of freedom and democracy had sold out their country. The brave men and women Donnie Lehmann had fought shoulder to shoulder with in the hot desert sands of countries that he wished he couldn't find on a map had died for freedom and liberty and here they were just handing it away to evil men with evil agendas. Donnie Lehmann saw all of it happening and wanted to help. He loved his country and wanted to keep it safe.

There was a quote he had learned once. "All that is necessary for the triumph of evil is that good men do nothing." He couldn't remember who had said it, but the words rang true.

Donnie Lehmann saw the evil happening to the country he loved.

And he would do something about it.

Just like he'd been doing for years.

Best not to tempt fate, he decided.

Stretching away the kinks from a hard days work, Donnie Lehmann made his way on fairly steady legs toward the small, battered pick up truck he owned. Or rather that Jimmy Fletcher owned.

While waiting for the truck's engine to warm up in the cold winter evening, Donnie watched as a few others exited the bar after him. Three regulars walked out, more like staggered he decided, to their cars. With luck they would make it home in one piece. He was almost concerned enough to say something to them, but he dared not risk it. It was against the rules.

He had to protect himself from any scrutiny.

The other patron leaving the bar was a stranger. With good reason, Donnie was distrustful of strangers, even more so now than ever before.

He sat in the truck and watched the stranger all the way to his car. The man climbed into a fairly beat up Mazda Miada and turned the ignition. It took three tries before the engine caught and the car purred to life. Donnie watched it all from the warmth of his own vehicle parked away from the lights that highlighted the parking near the bar's entrance.

The stranger had not looked in his direction.

Not even once.

Nothing to worry about.

The Mazda bounded off down the dirt road that served as the last mile from the main highway to the bar out in the middle of nowhere. A perfect place to get away from it all.

Shaking away the suspicions that often plagued him, Donnie dropped his truck into gear and followed the Mazda toward the main highway.

If he had listened to those suspicious notions that nibbled at the edge of his consciousness he may have noticed the blue Chevy Tahoe that pulled out onto the road behind him.

Or he might have noticed that the bartender and a few of the patrons inside the bar, including the bartender's potential conquest and the loudmouthed sports nut were huddled around the bar, deep in discussion.

Or he might have noticed that the bartender had carefully placed the beer bottle with his fingerprints on it in a plastic evidence bag instead of the garbage. If only he had listened to that suspicious voice in the back of his mind his life might have gone a little easier.

But only a little bit easier.

The night still had some life left to it.

Anything could happen before morning.

Harold Palmer faces a domestic terrorist out for revenge on the FBI in EVIL INTENT! Coming soon!

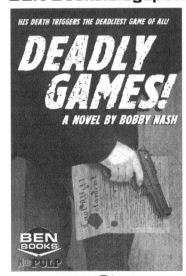

BEN BOOKS
WHERE FICTION LIVES

BEN-Books.blogspot.com / bobbynash.com

Deep space.

The science ship Aquarius, under the command of Captain Jeremiah Rains has finally reached the end of its exploratory mission to the depths of uncharted space and is returning home to Earth.

Captain Rains and his skeleton military crew are tired and bored from the lack of adventure they expected to find out in the great beyond. The scientists, however, are extremely happy with their many discoveries.

When the ship comes upon the wreckage of a destroyed space vessel, the crew is surprised to find one survivor; a woman, quite possibly the most beautiful woman any of them have ever seen. Her name is Lari and all she wants is someone, some Good Samaritan, to take her home.

The catch is that her planet is located at the center of a black hole.

SAMARITAN

A NOVELLA BY BOBBY NASH

AT THE EDGE OF KNOWN SPACE...

LIES THE ULTIMATE TERROR!

HUMANITY HAS GONE TO THE STARS.

Earth, once barren and decimated by war and the depletion of natural resources has been reborn.

Scavengers prey on small mining colonies. The United Planetary Alliance Marshal's Service seems unable to stop these raids. They are outmanned and outgunned, but is the only law on most worlds.

In Earth orbit, the Space Lab facility becomes the first Target in a plot to reclaim Earth.

In deep space, an officer uncovers a plot against the Alliance. They have targeted the UPA city-ship Ulysis.

Meanwhile, in the deepest regions of space an enemy has returned. An enemy seeking vengeance.

SAMARITAN

EARTHSTRIKE AGENDA

Earth. Take One Last Look.

A NOVEL BY BOBBY NASH

EARTHSTRIKE AGENDA

BEN-Books.blogspot.com / bobbynash.com

BOBBY NASH

ABOUT THE AUTHOR

From his hidden base just outside of Atlanta, Georgia, Bobby Nash writes.

With an interest in multiple genres, Bobby writes a little bit of everything including novels (Evil Ways; Deadly Games!; Earthstrike Agenda, Samaritan), comic books (Fuzzy Bunnies From Hell; Demonslayer; Domino Lady vs. The Mummy; Lance Star: Sky Ranger "One Shot"), short prose (A Fistful of Legends; Tales of The Rook; Zombies vs. Robots), novellas (The Ruby Files; Lance Star: Sky Ranger; Blackthorn: Thunder on Mars; The New Adventures of The Eagle), graphic novels (Yin Yang; I Am Googol: The Great Invasion; Bloody Olde Englund), screenplays (Zenoids: "Animal Crackers", Starship Farragut: "Conspiracy of Innocence"), media tie-ins (Yours Truly, Johnny Dollar; Green Hornet Case Files; Green Hornet Still at Large; Nightbeat; Box 13), and even a little pulp fiction (Domino Lady; Secret Agent X; The Avenger; The Spider) just for good measure. Somewhere in there he manages to eat, sleep, read, and watch too much TV.

Between deadlines, Bobby is a part-time extra in movies and television productions. He also co-hosts the Earth Station One and Earth Station Who podcasts (www.esopodcast.com), and writes for the All Pulp news site (http://allpulp.blogspot.com). Bobby is a proud member of the International Association of Media Tie-in Writers.

Evil Ways was Bobby's first published novel.
This edition is a re-edited re-released version.

Bobby is currently hard at work on Harold Palmers next adventure.

Please visit Bobby at
www.bobbynash.com
www.facebook.com/AuthorBobbyNash
www.twitter.com/bobbynash
www.lance-star.com
http://BEN-Books.blogspot.com

BOBBY NASH

Made in the USA
Columbia, SC
29 April 2023

15697774R00176